THE NOWHERE HOUSE

SAMUEL THOMAS FRASER

First Amazon edition published in 2021.
First paperback edition published in 2021.

Cover design by Shaun Stevens
Cover typeset in Rumble Brave (Alit Suarnegara) and Grenze (Omnibus-Type)

ISBN: 978-1-7771190-2-7

To learn more about the author, visit:

https://samuelthomasfraser.com/
https://www.facebook.com/STFupperlip
https://twitter.com/STFupperlip
https://www.instagram.com/samuelthomasfraser/

A NOTE FROM THE AUTHOR

In the modern world of digital publishing, word-of-mouth and person-to-person buzz can make or break an indie title. If you enjoy this work, please consider leaving a review on Amazon or recommending it to your friends in person or on social media. Happy reading!

BOOK ONE:

THE STRANGE HIGH HOUSE

IN OUR MIDST

CHAPTER 1

DOUBLE-DOG DARE

HE DID it because of a dare.

It made sense to him at the time, but before long Will Brady would come to regret going through with it. So reckless. So dangerous. So very, very stupid.

He had no choice, he'd tell himself. Not after the other boys ganged up on him. Not after they called him a chicken and a queer and a little pussy. Those words hurt Will more than he could ignore. Those were the kinds of words Papa always used when things were bad.

Right now, in Will's head, he could almost hear Papa behind him. He could feel Papa's hand on his shoulder, squeezing just a little too hard and shaking him a little too roughly. *You ready for this, boy? Ready to show these little pukes a thing or two?*

I'm ready, Papa, Will thought to himself.

Then quit acting like a girl. Show some sack.

Will took one last look down the dusty hill and watched the moon shining on the lake. Then he did a one-eighty where he stood, and stared up at the rotting hulk of the Harcourt House in front of him.

The Harcourt House was one of those places that naturally attracts ghost stories. Big, old, and empty for most of a century, most of the adults in town liked to pretend the Harcourt House just wasn't there. But the kids had always treated it like a game. Step right up, step right up, folks, try your luck in the haunted house. See a real ghost and win the big prize. As Will understood it, that was the whole reason for the big chain-link fence around the property. Somebody's cousin's brother or something had walked into the House once and they hadn't walked back out, or so the story went. For Will's money, he always thought of the place like a fat, ugly insect. A botfly cooling its heels on the forehead of the town, waiting for the right moment to seed its eggs beneath Delapore's skin.

Faded khaki walls met under the black wedge-shaped roof. Broken windows and crooked, splintered shutters dotted the façade. Half the black paint had peeled off the front door and the big brass knocker was lopsided. The doorjamb had rotted away from the door back in the '70s, and the rust on the hinges was the only thing keeping the door from swinging freely. A crumbling chimney leaned against one wall, looking like it would collapse any day now. As Will climbed the creaky front steps, he noticed the nails poking out of the banister, and the dark patches of rot and mold around the doorway, and he thought maybe he'd had it wrong. Maybe the House wasn't a fly. Maybe it was a spider. Maybe *he* was the fly.

From behind him, someone called out, "Whassamatter, Brady? You chicken or something?"

Will looked back. There was Mark Petrie sitting cross-legged on the gnarled tree stump just this side of the fence, with four other boys clustered around him like Viking shield bearers. Mark was one of those guys who, as Papa would have said, thought his crap smelled sweeter than most. It was Mark who'd issued the dare, just because he could.

"Hey! I said 'you chicken,' Brady?"

Will tried to smile, even though his heart was going like a hummingbird. "I'm just giving you one last look at my butt, Petrie! 'Cause pretty soon you're going to be kissing it!"

The other boys 'oohed' dramatically. Mark jumped off the tree stump and moved into Will's personal space. That was one of his go-to moves. "You remember the deal?"

"Half an hour inside. And I gotta check all the rooms I can, so I'm really *inside* the House. Easy money."

"You think so? I bet after fifteen minutes in there you won't feel like such hot shit."

Will refused to have the hotness of his shit called into question. He stood on the bottom step and pushed back into Mark's personal space. "I could go fifteen *hours* and it wouldn't make a difference, crud-for-brains."

More 'oohs.' Mark narrowed his eyes and snarled. "We'll see… You got a timer?"

Will flashed his wrist to show off the digital watch his mom had given him for his birthday, and set the timer with a dramatic flourish. "Half an hour, and we'll just *see* what's what."

"I guess we will," Mark replied.

Will turned back toward the door as Papa started whispering in his ear. *Little a-hole's scared, Will. It's there in his eyes. You make it in there, he won't be able to say spit against you. And you are going to make it, right? I didn't raise no queer.*

Will pushed the door open with both hands. The hinge groaned like it was just waking up from a long nap and the House belched out a gust of cold, sour air. As the smell lingered in the back of Will's throat, he turned back to the other boys for one last look. Mark Petrie smiled like he was expecting Will to turn back, so Will just gave him a nod and walked into the House.

When he was alone inside, Will closed his eyes. Counted to ten. Took a deep breath and gagged at the smell. There was Papa in his head again. *You're not going soft on me, are you, William? You said you were up for this.*

Will shook his head and tried to forget that voice. Papa wasn't here. Papa wasn't ever going to be here.

A man stands by his word, Papa advised. *I did raise me a man, didn't I?*

Will braced himself against the smell of the House and took a breath so deep that he thought his lungs would pop. He opened his eyes and fumbled in the pocket of his hoodie until he found the little silver penlight. Technically, it belonged to his mother, but she only ever used it during traffic stops on the weekend, to shine in the faces of what she called dee-you-eyes. She'd hardly miss it tonight.

He went into the den first. It was big enough for a couch and two large armchairs, set up to face the fireplace. Every surface in the room was fuzzy and grey with dust, and it reminded Will of the lint trap in the dryer at home. He could see the dead, silky white strands of old cobwebs that threaded from the backs and cushions of the seats to the floor. Little grey motes danced in the beam of the dee-you-eye light, making his eyes water and his nose twitch. Beneath the broken front window, there was an overturned spinning wheel with a sheen of fuzzy green moss on it, and a sliver of moonlight peeked through the crumbling chimney.

The back wall of the den opened into a larger living room. Will didn't even want to go in there. The floor was dotted with holes and deep scratches, and two cracked ceiling beams sagged dangerously in the middle. Dozens of exposed nails shone in the beam of Will's light, like the teeth of a hungry predator.

He shuddered and covered the light with his hand. At least in the dark he could pretend all the claw marks and spider webs weren't there. As he left the den and climbed the stairs to the second floor, he saw more claw marks on the walls and the banister, and he started to think of the Rat King.

The Rat King was a bogeyman that Papa had invented. Will understood that now, but when he'd been four years old, it had scared him to death. According to Papa, the Rat King was nine feet tall and wore a raggedy green cloak to cover the scabby hump on his back. His legs were like tree trunks and his knees bent backward so he could jump from the street up onto the roof of a house. He had a thick pelt of greasy salt-and-pepper hair over his whole body and a long pink tail that hung from his backside like a big slippery worm. His face was long and pinched, with little black marbles for eyes and lots of sharp yellow teeth that smelled like bad meat. Over one shoulder, he carried a big sack that he used to scoop up naughty little boys, so he could carve them up with his sharp black claws and eat them for supper.

The House groaned as it settled, and Will had a terrible vision of the Rat King waiting for him at the top of the stairs. He'd been sharpening his claws on the walls of the den and the living room, and he'd kicked all those holes in the floor because he was getting impatient, waiting for someone to sneak into the House. Sneaking into someone else's house was, of course, a very naughty thing to do. Even if that house was empty.

Will reached the second floor and reminded himself that he was *not* scared of the Harcourt House. He was scared of the Rat King, who might be in the Harcourt House, but he was not scared of the Harcourt House.

He shone the penlight on dark doors and empty rooms. He laughed at himself for being such an idiot, and he laughed at the House for being so ordinary. But he stopped laughing when he reached the last door in the hall.

As soon as he put his hand on the knob, his stomach lurched. A foul, toxic smell drifted out of the room as the door opened, and Will's eyes began to water. It was a cloying stench of rotting meat that stung his nostrils and sat on the back of his tongue. It was the smell Will had always suspected the Rat King might give off.

Will realized that if something had come up this way to die, then it definitely wasn't safe to be here. Chances were he'd already walked through a cloud of bacteria, and when he got home, he'd start feeling sick, and he'd be in bed with a fever of 104 until Labour Day.

And if Mom's going to get on my case for trespassing, he thought to himself, *what'll she say if she finds out I'm messing around with dead animals?*

Will held his breath and kept going all the same. He wasn't a chicken, or a girl, or a queer, no matter what Mark Petrie or Papa said. Feeling a nervous sweat run down his back, Will pushed through the door into a small bathroom. There was a clawfoot bathtub against the far wall, a sink underneath a cracked mirror, and an old-fashioned toilet with a pull chain. The toilet tank had long since fallen from the wall and smashed bang-smack onto the bowl, leaving several inches of exposed lead piping.

Will's lungs started to burn and his heart thumped in his chest. He couldn't hold his breath much longer. But he needed to. He couldn't bear to smell the Rat King again. His foot struck something on the floor and it skittered toward the tub. Will exhaled sharply. On the inhale, the smell hit him again, and he could feel sweat tickling between his shoulders.

The thing he'd kicked had hit one of the tub's claw feet and fallen open. Will saw cramped black writing on brittle yellow pages, with a few weird sketches done in red. From this distance, the writing didn't look like any language that Will recognized. It was more like a code or a space alien's alphabet. Curiosity won out over paranoia, so he went in for a closer look. As soon as Will picked up the book, the dead smell rankled in his nostrils again, and his penlight went looking for the source.

Three animals lay heaped together in the clawfoot tub, under a rusty ring of dried blood. At the bottom was a sleek-coated German Shephard with a blue collar. A ginger-haired cat lay flopped over the Shephard's belly, its head resting against the head of a little white bunny rabbit with a bright pink nose.

The German Shephard's back had been broken and twisted around so it would fit in the tub. Its dark eyes pointed to the ceiling and its jaw hung open, lips curled to show off its teeth. Something sharp had ripped into its belly, spilling its guts at the bottom of the tub. The cat's limbs dangled like those of a ragdoll, equally broken. Its tail had been severed close to its anus and narrow open wounds festered on its back. The rabbit's neck had been snapped, and its white fur was mottled with clumps of dried blood and feces. It had the same collection of open wounds, but here it was easier to see the pale green tinge of the skin around the cuts.

Will dropped the book and bit down hard on his knuckles to hold back the scream he felt bubbling up inside. It wasn't the Rat King who had done this. These wounds were too deliberate to be the work of a larger predator. This was calculated torture. This was experimentation.

This was practice.

Will turned and bolted out of the Dead Room. Something vile and twisted *was* lurking in the Harcourt House and, human or supernatural, Will was in no rush to meet it. In the hallway, he saw a flutter of green fabric in the corner of his eye and heard a deep, hungry growl. Will's heart beat a tattoo against his ribcage as he turned and came face-to-face with the Rat King.

The Rat King's eyes weren't like Will had imagined. Papa had always said they were black like buttons on a raincoat. But the creature standing here had bright, pale red eyes. They reminded Will of the old Hammer Horror movies his Cousin Walt liked, with Peter Cushing and Christopher Lee in fancy Victorian costumes and whole buckets of cheesy, bright red blood.

The Rat King shrieked and raked his claws along the floor. Will scrambled down the stairs and the Rat King skittered after him on all fours, holding his burlap sack in his mouth. At the bottom of the stairs, something snagged on the back of

Will's sweatshirt. A quick glance behind him showed the Rat King, teeth bared, with Will's hood in one clawed fist.

Will screamed and pushed through the front door. His sweatshirt ripped in the Rat King's hand and he saw Mark Petrie looking at him with cocksure *I told you so* pride. Mark was just about to make some smartass remark when Will ran down the front steps and shouted, "GO! EVERYBODY GO! GET THE HELL OUTTA HERE!"

Mark faltered for a second, and that was long enough for the Rat King to appear. He seemed to melt rather than squeeze through the open door, and he screeched as he rose to his full height.

Will was the first over the fence, and was already zipping down the hill on his bike as the other boys met the Rat King's Hammer Horror glare. They flailed and fell over each other amid a cacophony of screams and curses, trying to scramble up the chain-link and get to their bikes as the Rat King opened his sack.

Racing down the hill, two of the boys were crying like toddlers, and Mark Petrie's bladder trembled nervously. His front wheel went over a rock, and Mark bucked in his banana seat. When he landed, a stream of something warm and yellow ran down his left leg.

On the hilltop, the Rat King slung his bag over his shoulder and lumbered back inside the House, to wait for the next dare.

CHAPTER 2

A MIDSUMMER NIGHT'S DREAM

SOMETHING WAS coming.

Something *had* to be coming, otherwise why would she be here?

This was the fourth night now that Abby Henderson had had the same dream, about the derelict mansion on the dusty hill. The *what* of the dream was so familiar to her now that she knew the house's rotting façade like she knew her own face, and she had a pretty good idea of the *where*—the moonlight off Okanagan Lake was a dead giveaway. But the *why* still mystified her.

That was the problem with prophetic visions. They never came with annotations.

At a glance, Abby looked like a lot of other twenty-somethings in the Pacific Northwest. Short hair, which she dyed in a rotating variety of hues. Tattoos over most of her upper body. Enough piercings to make a metal detector sweat.

But Abby was also a Gospel: a magically-augmented human born with a suite of psychic abilities including telepathy, clairvoyance, and astral projection. Abby saw a whole world of ghosts, demons, and spirits that most people could never perceive, as well as corporeal creatures like zombies, vampires, and faeries which most people chose not to perceive. The Gospels' ability of precognition usually acted as an early-warning system to keep them from getting themselves killed in the magical world, and Abby knew this dream was a red alert. Something bad was brewing in this house, and with her luck she was about to stumble bass-ackwards into the middle of it.

A lethargic creak carried across the hilltop as the front door of the old house swung open. Abby looked up as two cicadas buzzed out the door, flitting lazily around the front porch and darting in and out of the house. More cicadas followed them, and then the noise of a whole swarm hit Abby like a tidal wave, filling her ears and making her eyeballs vibrate in their sockets.

The buzzing swelled to a crescendo and then suddenly stopped altogether. In fact, *all* sound stopped, from the wind to the groan of the door to Abby's own heartbeat. She stood for a moment in literally absolute silence, watching the impassive house.

Two points of orange candlelight glowed in the doorway and the front window, and Abby took her first muted steps up to the front porch. A rotten board creaked under her foot, and all the sound returned to the world in an instant. She heard a hoarse voice in her head, whispering a fervent mantra. *"Cutting and cutting and cutting and cutting. Feeding, feeding, feeding. Blood. Blood. Blood. Life. Life. Blood. Life. The blood. The life."*

Passing through the door, Abby emerged in a long dark hallway. A hardwood floor creaked beneath her, and a long dark red carpet was laid down the middle of the path. It stretched perhaps a hundred feet into the distance, like something from a Hollywood premiere. At the far end, Abby saw the outline of a red door illuminated by two candles fixed into sconces on the wall. Behind the door, the chanting continued. *"Cut. Cut. Cut. Cut. Feed. Cut. Feed. Feed. Blood. Blood."* The whispering grew louder, more urgent, and the buzzing of the insect colony picked up again.

A hundred feet turned out to be a very conservative estimate. Abby ran faster and faster, but got no closer to the door. She might have run for ninety seconds or nine hours, she didn't really know. The door was always the same distance away. But the noises sounded as if they were getting much closer. Abby reached a hand out in front of her, vainly grasping for the red wood, and the floor beneath her shifted. In a heartbeat, something yanked her down the hall and she cleared the impassable hundred feet before she could blink, slamming into the door with a force that knocked all the air out of her body.

The door opened, and she stumbled through into a large featureless room with the same hardwood flooring. On the floor was drawn a circle of red chalk wide enough for several people to stand in, with a large red sigil at its centre. High above, a young woman hung in mid-air, her back to the ceiling and her limbs locked in a spread-eagle position. Four candles floating around her illuminated the expression of sheer terror on her face. The buzz of the insect colony filled the room, and the woman's throat split from ear to ear. Abby shut her eyes and bit back a scream as blood splattered onto the chalked-out sigil and soaked into the floorboards.

A short, strangled croak came from across the room. Abby looked past the gory display and saw a young boy standing alone on the other side of the red pool. He held his hands over his eyes, and his shoulders heaved like he wanted to vomit. He was about ten years old, with messy hair the colour of copper wire and a long, sharp nose that his mom probably told him he would grow into.

"What?" Abby said to herself. She looked to the ceiling, demanding the dream give her an explanation. *"What?"*

This was a new one on her. In the four nights she had dreamed of this house, there had always been something different behind the red door. But whatever it was, Abby had always discovered it alone. If you didn't count the girl on the ceiling, then this boy was the first company she'd had in the dream.

Abby circled around the bloody pool toward the boy. He was still covering his eyes and shaking with fright and nausea. "Hey!" she shouted at the boy. "Hey!" Once again, it took about five times as long to reach him as it should have, based on visual estimates. "Hey, kid!"

*****

Will Brady screamed and backed away as a human shape came running at him out of the darkness. Minutes ago, he'd been in bed asleep, and then suddenly he'd found himself being carried to the Harcourt House as if by some invisible hand. He was just trying to find his way out when he stumbled on this gruesome spectacle. God, he just wanted to go home.

When the skinny woman with the blue-green hair and the gappy front teeth appeared from nowhere, Will's first instinct was to run. But a loose floorboard had other ideas, and he ended up falling on his butt. The skinny woman was on top of him in a second, her hands gripping his shoulders. He screamed and wriggled away. "Don't come near me! Please! Go!"

The woman raised her hands in surrender and dropped her voice. "It's okay," she promised. "It's okay. I'm not going to hurt you."

One look in her eyes, and Will knew she was telling the truth. Whoever this woman was, she was as surprised to see him as he was to see her. But that didn't explain what she was doing in his dream.

"W-what is this?" he stammered. "Who are you?"

*****

Abby missed the question entirely. "This doesn't make any sense," she murmured. "You're not a part of this... You're..."

The word she was looking for was 'real.' While the boy was looking Abby in the eye, her gaze was fixated on the space around him. All living beings radiated unique auras of mystical energy, which the Gospels could read like books. And right now, Abby read the boy as human. He was asleep in his bed somewhere at this very moment, and by a billion-to-one shot he was having the exact same dream as her.

By a trillion-to-one shot, he was also having the same thought she was. "You're real?" he gasped. "Oh my God, you're real! Y-you're not one of them!"

"One of who?" Abby asked.

Will pointed over Abby's shoulder, and she turned to look at the pool of blood. A stream of bubbles broke on the surface, and something groaned deep below. Abby rose and shook her head. "Oh, that can't be good..."

A human hand shot out of the pool and dug its nails into the hardwood. As Abby moved in front of Will, another hand followed the first.

"When I tell you to run..." Abby whispered. A man was pulling himself out of the pool of blood. His features — red hair, a thin moustache, and a sharp, roguish jawline — were blurred and misty, like images projected by a dirty lens, and his aura was an ethereal shimmer. Not at all, Abby decided, like the aura of a living person.

"Go!" he screamed at them. "Get out, now! Get out!" The blood frothed as something tried to pull the man back under. "Please! You have to run while there's still time! You're doing exactly what he wants! You mustn't let him —"

The blood foamed and roiled. Something roared deep beneath the pool, and then it dragged the man below the surface. He screamed as he disappeared, and Abby grabbed Will's hand with a command of "Run!" She dragged him away from the pool at full sprint, toward a green candlelit door behind them.

"Oh God!" Will gasped. "Ohgodohgod! Why is this happening?"

"That is an excellent question!" Abby replied as they made the ceaseless journey to the green door.

"What is any of this?" Will pleaded. "Who are you?"

"Abby! Abby Normal! I don't know how, but you ended up in my dream!"

"Abby? I'm Will Brady. And this was my dream until you showed up!"

"Six of one, kid!" Abby shouted. Suddenly they were at the green door. She pulled Will through, slammed the door shut again, and froze. Maybe this was his dream.

They'd come out in a room Abby had never seen before. But from the look on Will's face, he knew exactly where they were.

*****

Will stared at the clawfoot tub while the woman called Abby braced herself against the green door. They were in the Dead Room, and that familiar hateful, toxic smell filled his lungs. But it wasn't coming from the tub.

Every surface of the Dead Room—the sink, the walls, the toilet, the tub—was covered in a thick, syrupy, blackish-green substance that bubbled and oozed like lava. Sticky patches of the same foul gunk covered the floor, and long, gooey tendrils of it hung from the ceiling, like saliva from the jaws of a very large dog. Will jumped from foot to foot, trying to dodge the stuff as it slopped onto the floor and recoiling whenever it puddled near him.

The walls shook as though the house itself was laughing at them. Following the laugh was a thin, hoarse voice with the faintest trace of a middle-class English accent. *"Ahh, you've come at last, have you? But... you've picked up a spare..."*

Abby looked up at the ceiling. "Listen to me, whoever you are! You don't have to hurt the boy!"

"Why should I hurt the boy?" asked the voice. *"It is the boy I want. You... are none of my concern, woman."*

Tentacles of the black ooze exploded out of the wall and coiled around Abby's arms, dragging her back toward the slopping mess. She screamed and thrashed and dug in her heels to slow the goo down, but it just pulled harder.

"Let her go!" Will screamed at the ceiling. "You let us out of here right now, you... you... *house!*"

The ceiling rattled with the voice's laughter. *"Oh, no, no, no. You do not give the orders here, child. I am The Master of this place."*

The clawfoot tub jerked and scraped across the hardwood. Something inside it squelched as it lurched toward Will with a vengeance. He reached for Abby's hand, found it wasn't there, and then the lip of the tub slammed into his midsection. He saw more blood pooled at the bottom of the tub, and sitting in that blood, a full human skeleton, with its head cocked back lazily and its teeth stretched into a wide rictus. The bones were gray and brown, with musty dirt and clay packed between joints and gaps, and a light coat of moss running down one side of the skull.

Two points of light appeared in the eye sockets. They were the same blazing, Hammer Horror red of the Rat King's eyes. The skull tilted toward Will, and the Master's voice trickled out from between the yellow teeth. *"I know I am not much to look at now... but soon... I shall have all the power in the world..."* One of the arms jerked up, and three of the fingers curled back, leaving the index extended toward Will. *"And you are going to help me... William..."*

Behind him, there was a manic scream as Abby dropped her center of gravity and took a huge bite out of one of her gooey ropes. The rope shrieked and loosened its grip, and after she was done dry-heaving, she was able to pull one hand free and take a step forward. She repeated the process with the rope around the other hand, spat on the floor, and growled, "I have *had it* with this shit!" Then she grabbed Will's hand and yanked him back out the green door.

As they booked it down the hall, the oozing walls bubbled and vibrated with the sound of swarming cicadas. Then the wall in front of them exploded in a spray of black slime and buzzing insects. Abby stopped dead, and Will ran into her.

"Leaving so soon?" said somebody behind them.

The pair turned back toward the green door. A human figure, with blazing Hammer-Horror-red eyes, was rising out of the black muck.

"Not you!" they both exclaimed at the same moment. "You're dead!"

*****

Abby heard a crackle and a hiss, as of an old gramophone, and then a tinny male choir began to sing. Her hands started shaking despite her best efforts, so she pressed them over her ears and shut her eyes. It wasn't real, she told herself. He couldn't be here. Not him. Not after all this time.

Give me that old-time religion!
Give me that old-time religion!
Give me that old-time religion!
It's good enough for me!

A hickory walking stick bounced off the hardwood floor, keeping time with the beat, and a man in a white three-piece suit sauntered toward Abby. "There you go again, Abigail." His voice was calm and mellifluous, with a Tennessee drawl. "Always thinking with your feet."

Dr. John Leland pressed a hand to Abby's head and tilted her face up to meet his. "When are you going to stop running and face your problems like an adult?"

Leland pointed his stick toward the ceiling. Invisible force grabbed Abby around the middle and yanked her off the ground. Another twitch of the walking stick, and she pinwheeled through the air toward the wall of cicadas. She felt the bugs splatter and crunch against her skin, and the buzzing rose to a fever pitch as another swarm erupted from the woodwork, to fill the gap she had made.

Abby couldn't move. The bugs were crawling all over her, making her itchy, blotting out what little light remained, and curiously exploring every body cavity they could find. Abby hacked and spat as a raiding party of bugs made it past her lips and plumbed the depths of her esophagus. She tried to stick a finger down her throat, to vomit the disgusting vermin back up, but all that did was shuffle more of the things toward her mouth. She was losing consciousness. The bugs were shooting into her airways, filling her lungs and suffocating her. When the usual points of entry got too clogged, they made camp on her skin and chewed their way in past muscles, tendons, fat. She could feel them inside her, digging deep into her organs and feasting on her from the inside out.

Abby had never considered herself particularly claustrophobic. Nor was she afraid of being buried alive. But a tomb made of eight billion writhing insects can make anyone change their mind in a nanosecond. She closed her eyes and screamed herself hoarse.

*****

Will was vaguely aware of Abby dropping to her knees beside him, covering her ears to block out some unpleasant noise. But whatever she was hearing, it was lost on him. No, he was more concerned about the smell. The sweet, maple-y tang of Crown Royal mixed with the sour stink of Craven A cigarettes. As the big man in the Old Navy jeans—the man who had climbed out of the slime on the floor—drew nearer, the smell got stronger, choking the breath right out of Will's little lungs.

"Fifteen minutes," said the big man. The Habs jersey he wore covered the solid frame of a once-great high school athlete, now going to seed. The rusty red hair on his head was starting to go grey and beating a hasty retreat away from his forehead. His nose—broken several times over—was red and blotchy from years of boozing. "You couldn't last but fifteen minutes in here. So much for half an hour, huh?"

The big man's open palm smacked lightly against his thigh, like he was itching to hit something. "Is this what you are without me? Is this the kind of man you're mother's raising? Huh? Goddamn queer is what you're turning into! You promised those boys a half-hour, William. You broke your word to them."

Abby raised her head and looked toward the ceiling. She didn't even see Will now. All the better, Will thought, as he bit his bottom lip and ran the back of his hand across his nose. Crying in front of a girl was what Papa would call "real faggy behaviour," and if there was one thing Papa hated, it was faggy behaviour.

"You're not here!" Will shouted. "You're dead! You're dead, and I'm dreaming!"

Papa sneered. "Tell yourself that. Tell yourself whatever you need to hear. It's not going to change what's coming."

"Stay away from me!" Will commanded. "Stay away!"

Papa did not stay away. With two big steps, he closed the gap between himself and his son and clamped one meaty paw around Will's forearm. Will screamed and thrashed, and his arm nearly came out of its socket.

He heard Abby shriek and watched in horror as she sailed through the air and disappeared into the swarm, screaming her head off. He hadn't even seen what grabbed her.

"Bring her back!" he hollered. "You bring her back right now!"

"This was supposed to be between you and me, William. Keeping it in the family, a man and his boy. That stupid dyke wasn't supposed to see any of this."

"Shut up!" Will screamed, beating his fist against Papa's chest. "You can't say things like that!"

Papa froze, his red eyes nearly bugging out of his skull. "The hell did you just say to me?"

Seeing the wrath boiling over on his father's face, Will hunched his shoulders and flinched away. Now he had screwed up. "I'm sorry, Papa, I'm sorry, I didn't mean it."

"You mouthy little shit." Papa raised his hand to the sky and struck Will once across the face.

Will's cheek exploded with pain and little stars danced in the corner of his left eye. He tasted copper and realized he'd bitten his tongue. He fell to the ground on the backswing and landed in the black slime. His ears rang as his head bounced off the floor, and Papa took another step forward. The skin on Papa's hand rippled and squirmed. A cicada crawled out of his sleeve and up his forearm.

"Look upon me, William," commanded the Master. *"Look upon your past... your future..."*

Papa opened his mouth and vomited up a cloud of buzzing cicadas. As the swarm rushed into the hall, his body deflated and sank like a balloon with a bad leak, and the Master crowed, *"Soon! Soon!"* Will curled into a tight ball as the swarm descended on him. All he could hear was that terrible buzzing, and the Master's *"Soon! Soon! Soon!"*

*****

At 2:30am on the morning of July 29, Abby Henderson awoke from a nightmare, screaming, in her small Vancouver apartment. Almost 400 km away, in the small town of Delapore, Will Brady did the same thing a mere five seconds later.

CHAPTER 3

WAKEY WAKEY

WILL BRADY kicked his bedsheets onto the floor and smacked himself on the chest, the arms, the legs. He had to get the bugs off him. Had to get them off!

A few seconds of ineffectual slapping yielded no splattered bugs, so Will reached for the reading lamp and turned it on. The sight of his own, safe bedroom allowed him to finally exhale. There was his *The Force Awakens* poster on the far wall. His dusty bookshelf, dotted with all his second-hand Bionicle figures. (A gift from Cousin Walt after he got too old for them.)

Will climbed out of bed and was rearranging his bedsheets—Spider-Man-patterned, to match his pyjamas—when he heard the footsteps coming down the hall. His mom threw the door open, her brown eyes as wide as dinner plates. The colour was high in her clay-coloured face, and her black hair, loosed from its usual bun, hung messily over her forehead like stray bits of yarn. She moved toward him with jerky, hesitant steps, as if she were afraid that the wrong move might start him screaming again.

"My God, Will, are you okay? I heard you screaming clear across the house!"

Will took a deep breath and smoothed out his duvet as his mother sat down and put her arms around him. "I'm fine. I-I just had a bad dream is all."

Will's mom looked at him and asked, "Was it the Harcourt House again?"

"No, Mom, it wasn't anything like that!" Will lied. "It was just—"

"Will," she said softly, "you're not going to get in trouble again, okay? I mean, I can't fault you for having a nightmare. You can talk to me."

Yeah, that was exactly the problem. Will had tried to talk to her. After the Very Stupid Thing, and after she'd finished chewing him out, he'd told her about the Dead Room—about the practice animals in the tub. That had gotten her attention, and she and another officer had gone up to check it out, but...

We searched the whole house. There was nothing there, Will. Just dust and creaky floorboards.

She was convinced he'd been fibbing about the Dead Room, or mistaken. But Will knew he wasn't mistaken. That smell wasn't one you *could* be mistaken about.

"Will. Will, are you listening to me?"

"I'm sorry," Will murmured. "I was... guess I'm a little distracted."

His mom sighed and kneeled on the floor. One hand on Will's shoulder, one on his head, trying to give his hair a playful muss. "What did you see tonight? What was in the Harcourt House?"

A bite of the lower lip. A wet sniff. A sleeve rushing across the face, taking snot and salty tears with it.

Men don't cry, whispered Papa. *Real men don't ever cry. 'Specially not in front of the women.*

Will lowered his head and whispered into his own chest. "Papa."

"What did you say?"

"I saw *him*, Mom. I saw Papa."

Mom went pale and shook her head. She hugged her son tightly and laid a gentle kiss on his forehead. "Oh, William... I just... are you okay? Do you want to talk about it? Do you... want to sleep in my room tonight?"

Will pulled away from his mom and took another deep breath. "I'm fine. It... it freaked me out for a bit, but I'm fine now."

Mom rested her head on Will's and stroked his hair with one hand. He remembered another time she'd done that, after Papa had lost his cool. Her hand had been in a cast that time, and the plaster had made his head itch so bad.

In the other room, Mom's cell phone went off. She ignored it and hugged Will even tighter. The ringing continued, and eventually she let him go with a sigh and returned to her own bedroom to answer the call. If someone was phoning her this late, it probably meant she had to go in to work.

From his spot on the bed, Will caught some fragments of the call leaking through the thin walls. It was a little too obvious that she was trying to stop him from hearing her. Mom imposed a strict separation between her work life and her home life, believing that the realities of police work were too much for her ten-year-old son to handle. And that ticked Will off something awful. She said things like, "You can talk to me," but she could be pretty choosy about what she let him talk about. When it came to cop stuff, "You can talk to me" always seemed to turn into "When you're older."

As quietly as he could, Will tiptoed out of his bedroom toward his mother's closed door. He pressed himself flat against it and cupped one ear to the wood.

"Where did they find her?" his mom whispered. "And the vic was...? Mm-hmm, just like last time... Yeah. Yeah, give me... I don't know, half an hour... Yeah, yeah, I'm going to have to find someone to watch Will... Okay. Thanks for the heads-up, Eckhart."

Will jumped back as the bedroom door opened and his mother walked out with a weary look on her face. "I thought I told you not to eavesdrop, Will."

"I know, I'm sorry. But I wouldn't have to if you talked to me! I can handle it, Mom!"

Mom shook her head. "You don't know that. Even if you can, I'm not sure you'd want to."

"You have to go out, don't you?"

Mona nodded and bent down to hug him. "Yes. I'm sorry, Will. Something happened in the park. I might be a while."

"What happened?"

She mussed his hair and kissed him on the cheek. "You don't have to worry about that. Just try to forget about the Harcourt House, okay? I'm going to call Mrs. Tenenbaum across the street and see if she can look after you while I'm out."

"Okay… what if I have another bad dream?"

"Call me if you do. I probably won't be able to come home, but I'll try and find a couple minutes to talk."

Will squeezed her. "Be safe."

She squeezed him back. "Be good."

Will went back to his own bedroom and shut the door behind him. He did not, however, go to sleep. Instead he went to the window and looked up, at the peak of that beetle-black gabled roof on the hill.

He thought about the woman in his dream. Not the dead woman on the ceiling, but the one with the funky hair and the big gap between her front teeth. "Abby Normal," she had called herself. But who was Abby Normal? She'd talked as if *she* had dreamed the whole thing up. But that was impossible. She didn't look like a local. Will doubted she'd ever seen the Harcourt House even from a distance.

How, then, could she dream the House so accurately, let alone the Dead Room? How could she know about Papa?

Who was dreaming what?

****

"AGH! Jesus!" Abby caught her breath and clutched her forehead with both hands as some damn fool rammed a railroad spike into her brain. "Oooowww, *fuck.*"

The light went on beside her, and a tired voice croaked, "Abby?"

Abby winced. "Oh, shit, did I wake you, Lee? I'm sorry."

Leanne Waller sat up on her side of the bed and opened the glasses case she kept on her nightstand, taking out a pair of black-framed bifocals. With her round figure and short bob haircut, the glasses completed Leanne's "blonde Velma Dinkley" look. She blinked a couple times as the world came into focus, then put one arm around Abby and asked, "Bad dream?"

"Yeah. Same one, too. With the big old house and that weird red door."

"Jeez, *again*? Abby, you have to tell Simon about this pronto. There's clearly something behind it."

Abby sighed and rolled her eyes up toward the ceiling, but there was a trace of a smile on her lips as she did so. Leanne and Abby had been going steady long enough for Leanne to get used to the mystical, occult side of Abby's life. And Leanne was, by her own admission, an overly-protective worrywart. Whenever spooky stuff started happening, Leanne would drop everything to make sure it didn't send Abby over the deep end.

Leanne gave Abby a light smack on the arm. "Hey, don't roll your eyes at me! I'm serious!"

Abby put both arms around Leanne and kissed her on the cheek. "I know. I just hate it when you're right."

There was something stiff and awkward in the hug. Leanne felt it and looked Abby in the eye. "Is something wrong?"

"There might be," Abby replied bluntly. "This vision… it went really off the rails tonight. I saw the house and the red door, like before, but there was more than that this time. A kid, and… and something in the walls. And he was there. Leland."

Leanne gave an involuntary squeak and reached for a golden cross necklace that hung from her reading light. The name of John Leland was taboo in their apartment. The leader of a psychotic cult of demons, Leland had plotted to sacrifice Abby in a blood ritual that would have unleashed an ancient god of darkness upon the Earth. He had killed Abby's mother and crippled her best friend when they stood in his way, and he had left as many scars on Abby's mind as he had on her body.

Putting the cross around her neck, Leanne crossed to a dresser on the other side of the room and yanked open the bottom drawer. "That settles it. I'm calling Simon. Just try and stop me." She pulled a small jewelry box from the drawer, and from this she extracted a black-and-purple crystal with a string looped through one end. A piece of masking tape on the string said "L," differentiating it from the other, identical crystal in the box which was marked with "A."

Leanne held the Vokarion crystal up and spoke into it like a microphone. "Hello? Hello, Simon? Natalie? Is someone there?" As the telepathic amplifier picked up Leanne's brainwaves and sent them off into the aether, it began to glow. When the return message came in a few seconds later, the glow got brighter.

"Leanne? Is that you? What's up?" The responding voice was deep and female, with a pronounced Haitian accent.

"Natalie, hi. Quick question, what are you and Simon up to right now?"

"I'm in the armoury at the Letterbox. I think Simon's asleep. Why, what's the matter? It's pretty late for you, isn't it?"

"Abby was just telling me about a dream she had. It sounded like it might be in your guys' wheelhouse."

"How so?"

Abby got out of bed and hurried to Leanne's side. "I saw Leland, Natalie. Back from the dead."

There was a heavy pause. When Natalie came back, her voice was all business. "Get dressed. Get in your car and come to the Letterbox. Now. We have to talk about this."

That was her last word on the matter. Leanne stood and looped the crystal around her neck next to her cross. Abby opened some more drawers and tossed an outfit together on the bed. "Can you make some tea or something? I think we're in for a long night."

Leanne nodded. "I'm going to have a shower before we go, so if you want to pee or anything, do it now."

"Roger that." She shed her pyjamas and smiled at Leanne. "And thanks for being so patient."

Leanne shrugged. "It's too hot to sleep anyway."

Abby blew her a kiss. It would have been sweet if she weren't hopping around on one foot, fumbling with the leg hole of her *X-Men* panties.

*****

Mona Brady stepped out of her car, and the heat hit her like a blast from a hair dryer. Even at this late hour, it was almost 25 degrees outside. Problem was, it was wildfire season. Delapore had been spared so far, thank God, but there were 100 hectares burning between Penticton and Naramata. Winds from the south were carrying the smoke up this way, trapping the whole town in a dry, hazy greenhouse. The moon over Mona's head looked like a ripe satsuma—had done for nearly two weeks now—and everything in Hudson Park had an eerie, slightly orange tint.

Mona took a left past a cluster of squad cars, ducked under the police tape threaded across the main trail, and marched down to the footbridge, where all the action was. She approached two uniformed constables and called out to them: "Eckhart! Foley! What's the situation?"

The first officer was a jowly, wooly-headed man with wire-frame glasses. Constable Ernest Eckhart held two bottles of Coca-Cola, and he gestured with them as he spoke. "Couple of young lovers, out for a romantic night in the bushes. About an hour ago, one of them spotted a body floating in the creek." He pointed to the edge of the water, where a group of officers were huddled inside a semicircle of yellow construction lights. A large black shape was lying on the shore of the creek, snuggled up against one of the bridge's concrete supports. "We think it came down from the lake. The major crime team is on its way and we've been ordered to hold the scene as is until we hear from Inspector Pembroke."

Mona nodded as a camera flash illuminated the black lump. "Have we taken statements?"

The second officer raised his hand. He was young and trim, with floppy fair hair and a constellation's worth of freckles. "I spoke to the lovebirds just after Eckhart called you," said Constable Linus Foley. "Guy went to take a leak, decided the creek was the best public convenience available. He was just zipping up when the body floated in. Neither of them saw anyone lurking in the park, and they don't know how long the victim was in the water."

"Mm. Coffee?"

Constable Eckhart held out one of the Coke bottles.

Mona rolled her eyes. "Really?"

Eckhart raised an eyebrow that was as bushy as the rest of his hair. "Come on, Sarge, are you really going to look me in the eye and tell me it's coffee weather?"

"*Touché.*" Mona took the bottle and approached the crowd under the construction lights. As she got closer, she could see the blue bungee cords wrapped around the king-sized black trash bag. A hand poked out of a tear in the plastic. Two of the fingernails were missing, and the fingers themselves looked like black licorice. One officer was kneeling over the body, taking pictures of the victim's face. Mona called out to him. "What do you have, Rickards?"

The officer stood and passed the camera to one of his colleagues. With his square face, sticky-out ears, and flattop haircut, Corporal Benjamin Rickards looked a bit like a young Matt Dillon. "Female victim, Caucasian, early to mid-twenties. Her throat was slashed open, just about ear to ear. Been dead at least a month. She's not in the best shape, so the pathologist will be able to tell you a lot more than I can."

"And where is Dr. Hummel, exactly?"

"Knowing him? Fell asleep watching TV. Ten bucks says it's *Jeopardy* this time."

A tall, Asian constable with spiky hair interjected, "I'll see your *Jeopardy* and raise you *Family Feud*. Doc loves him some Steve Harvey."

Rickards chuckled. "Thank you, Constable Pang. Anyway, the super's trying to get in touch with the doc right now." He jerked his head over to a picnic table twenty yards away, where a big man with a silver flattop and a ruddy face was yelling into a cell phone.

"He looks chipper," muttered Mona.

"I think he's getting pretty sick of the Margot Pembroke Major Crime Variety Hour."

"Well, it's time he got used to it. Different set of rules once a body turns up."

"No offence, Sarge, but you're starting to sound like Pembroke."

Mona frowned. "You watch your language, Corporal."

"Sorry. There's something else, too," Rickards added. "Have a look in the girl's mouth there. Tell me what you see." He bent down and nudged the victim's mouth open with two gloved fingers. Mona squatted beside the dead girl, took out her dee-you-eye light, and shone it on the six-legged body curled up on the victim's tongue. "What the hell? Is that…?"

Rickards nodded. "According to Wikipedia, that there's a specimen of *Magicicada septendicem*. In plain English: a Pharaoh cicada."

*****

Simon Lockhart frowned down at the mug in front of him, pointed one finger at it, then whispered a word and set to stirring his tea with a minor telekinetic effort. "I must say, Abigail, this dream of yours has me rather stymied."

Abby, as yet unlearned in the ways of telekinesis, twirled the spoon in her own mug and nodded. "That's one word for it. I'd have gone with 'petrified.' 'Triggered,' maybe. 'Scared shitless' at a stretch." She gripped the mug tight with both hands and her shoulders curled unconsciously inward. "I think seeing… him again brought back a lot of stuff." Standing behind her, Leanne wrapped both arms around Abby, kissed her on the head, and pressed her cheek against Abby's scalp. She didn't say anything, but the familiar sensation of her body made Abby feel a little better.

"Well, I can certainly understand that," said Simon. "This is the first time you've dreamed about him since May, I think you said?"

"Yeah. What a comeback, huh?" She sipped her tea and gave Leanne's hand a grateful squeeze.

"But tell me more about this boy you saw in the dream. Will, was it?"

"Will Brady. I don't know who he is, but he means something to whatever's in that house."

"And you got no indication of particular psychic ability from him? No hint as to how he might have entered your dream?"

"He was just there."

Simon telekinetically agitated his tea some more. "Hmm… yes, 'stymied' is the word…"

That wasn't the answer Abby had been looking for. Simon Lockhart was the lone survivor of a magical race called the Vanguard, and one of the smartest people Abby or Leanne knew. An accomplished sorcerer and cleric, he had roughly 1500 years of monster-fighting experience and magical knowledge under his belt, and there wasn't much that stymied him on the best of days.

"Can't you give me anything?" Abby pleaded. "You're always the guy with the answers."

From across the vast library in which they were sat, there came a shout of, "Found it!" A pair of heavy boots came stomping across the carpeted floor as Natalie Arnaud—six-and-a-half feet of undead muscle, who never met a fight she couldn't pick—lumbered out from between the high bookshelves jam-packed with tomes of mystic esoterica and slapped a thick manila folder down on the table in front of Simon. "How many times have I told you?" she chided him. "Fix your damn filing system, or I'm fixing it for you."

Simon raised his mug to her in salute. "Thank you, Natalie." Opening the folder, he turned back to Abby and said, "As it happens, I may be able to offer one or two insights. Not on this William Brady or the sudden reappearance of You-Know-Who—I need to do more research there—but some of what you've just told me does dovetail with another puzzle I've been trying to piece together for a little while now." He spread out the contents of the folder and pointed first to a newspaper clipping from about a month ago. "At the start of July, the body of a young woman was found in a dumpster up in the town of Delapore, just west of Kelowna. The victim was badly mutilated and nearly drained of blood." From the newspaper article, Simon's finger traced a line to a photograph of a young woman with curly brown hair and steel-framed glasses. "The victim was later ID'd as one Jennifer Styles, 26. She was a cashier at the local supermarket."

"So, what's this have to do with us?" Leanne asked.

"Well, when they found Ms. Styles, she'd been dead for more than a week. But the trouble is, she had only been officially missing for a couple days. I have a source up in that neck of the woods, and he says that no less than four eyewitnesses were able to place Jennifer Styles at a local Canada Day celebration, as little as three nights before her body was discovered."

"Her already-dead-for-a-week body," Abby clarified.

"Precisely."

Leanne swallowed. "Simon, you said the body was… exsanguinated." She gave a little shiver of revulsion. "Have you given any thought to what might have done that? Could this be a vampire?"

Natalie shook her head. "That was my first guess, but the MO's not right."

"Indeed," Simon said. "According to my source, the victim's throat was slit, and there were multiple wounds on her person which suggested she'd been tortured for some time before she was killed. No bite marks, however."

"Slit?" Abby asked.

"'Ear to ear' were his words." He raised his eyebrows pointedly.

"The woman in my dream was…"

"Exactly. And that has me wishing you'd told me about this sooner."

"But the woman in my dream wasn't Jenny Styles… it was her!" Abby pointed to another photo from the folder, this one of a girl with green eyes and a long dirty blonde ponytail.

Simon nodded. "Sonia Hall. Well, well, the plot thickens."

"Meaning?"

"Since the end of June, there have been four missing-persons reports filed by the Delapore detachment, and the RCMP have sent investigators from their Major Crime Unit into town." Simon tapped each photo as he rattled off the names of the missing. "Sonia Hall, 23. A nursing student at

UBCO. David Prudhomme, 29. Junior auto mechanic at the local garage. Bill Grover, 42. A carpenter with a business in town. Jennifer Styles. We've already met her, of course."

"Shit," Abby exhaled. "This might be a serial killer."

"A serial killer *and* a psychotic talking house," said Leanne. "That dream of yours can't be a coincidence."

"So, when are we going to Delapore?" Abby asked.

Simon tilted his head. "Are you sure you're up for this? If that vision of John Leland was any indication, then the Celestial only knows what kind of psychological terrorism we may be facing up there."

"Whatever we find up there, I'll deal," Abby retorted. "I told you guys: after the Following, after what happened to Kelly and my mom, I'm not sitting on the sidelines anymore. Lee and I have been training our butts off all year just for something like this. I've lost count of all the bruises Natalie's given me during self-defence class."

"I took a St. John's Ambulance course in case some Big Bad tried to start something," Leanne interjected. "That has to count for something. And what are the odds that Abby would have this dream if it wasn't important? God wants her in Delapore ASAP. Or at least somebody on His payroll does."

"I don't know what the hell I saw, but this kid's in the middle of it," Abby concluded. "And if there's a child in danger, then it's going to be my fight. Every single time."

CHAPTER 4

DEAR ABBY

"...AND DR. Hummel has come back with an ID on our second victim: Sonia Hall. Yes. Yes, sir. No, sir, I'm not 'jerking you around'!"

During the summer, Will Brady never got out of bed before 9:00 on Friday morning. His mom knew this, and she would let him sleep in while she got ready for work and welcomed in Mrs. Tenenbaum, Will's regular sitter.

Not this Friday, however. It was just past 8, and Will was out of bed and dressed, with one ear pressed against the dusty vent on his bedroom floor. He could hear his mother downstairs, talking to her boss on the phone.

"Yes, sir, I'm going to chase up Dr. Hummel today and ask about the autopsy report. Yes, I'll talk to our squad, too. Sir, I—Yes—I understa—I realize the dates don't line up, but the rest of the facts do! Either we fished Sonia Hall out of the creek the other night, or this is the most seamless identity theft I've ever seen!"

The noise from downstairs devolved into a lot of furious muttering and incoherent grumbles. Will guessed that his mom had hung up so she could rant about Superintendent Campbell privately.

There was a killer loose in Delapore. His mom could be as secretive as she liked, but Will could see the evidence stacking up. He'd been right about the Dead Room all along, right about the Harcourt House, and now it was coming back to bite the whole town in the butt. But the town just didn't want to stand up and do anything about it. His mom, the police, the other neighbourhood kids. To hear Mark Petrie tell it, the Very Stupid Thing might as well have never happened. Will was getting fed up with it all. And if nobody in town was going to take him seriously, well, he'd just look for help out of town. Fortunately, he already knew where to start looking.

Will stood and brushed the dust off his ear and collar. Tiptoeing across the room, he went to the nightstand and retrieved the cell phone his mom had given him for Christmas. Then he pulled up his web browser and opened a page he had bookmarked.

When the woman with the blue-green hair had appeared in Will's dream, the name she'd given was "Abby Normal." Will didn't think there were too many Abby Normals out there, so he'd run a Google search on the name the next day. He hadn't found much. YouTube clips and movie quotations, chiefly, from Mel Brooks' *Young Frankenstein*. But there was one promising lead. A few pages in, Will had found "The Abby Normal Blog": a webpage with a couple dozen entries — some as short as a few sentences, some as long as his *Percy Jackson* paperbacks — about supernatural phenomena, mostly in the Vancouver area. Hauntings, possessions, creatures right out of a Universal Studios haunted house. If Abby the dream-girl was also Abby Normal the blogger, then it sounded to Will like the Harcourt House would be right up her alley. And if she'd seen what he'd seen, she might be willing to help.

Will scrolled up to the blog's top menu and clicked the link that said "CONTACT." Then he started to type out a message in the big empty text box that came up.

Dear Abby Normal, I had a dream about you the other night. And I think you might have had a dream about me.

My name is Will Brady, and I live in the Okanagan. There's this creepy old house in my neighbourhood that a lot of kids say is haunted, and I believe them. Actually, I think that house is evil. I've tried to warn people about the Harcourt House, about the things that happen up there. They don't listen to me, or else they're too scared to do anything. Something bad is happening in Delapore, and nobody IN Delapore is going to do anything about it. I know this probably sounds crazy, and I don't know if you'll even read this message, but if you do: I need your help, Abby Normal. Please. PLEASE. Help me.
Sincerely,
Will Brady

*****

Abby took off her sunglasses and looked away from the ripe-satsuma sun, blinking the smoke particulates out of her eyes. They'd just passed through the city of Merritt, about an hour and a half west of Delapore, and right on the perimeter of the smoke cover from the southern wildfires. The air out here was thick and heavy as syrup. Every time she inhaled, Abby felt the smoke scratching at the back of her throat, and in order to relieve it she was chugging water like there was no tomorrow.

The four of them were in Natalie's car: a blue '59 Ford Thunderbird, which wore the scars of a few dozen collisions. While Natalie drove, Simon butted in with unnecessary directions, and Abby guzzled water, Leanne was trying to dig up what she could on the house from Abby's dream. When she found what she'd been looking for, she gave Abby a nudge and passed the device to her. "Does that look familiar?"

Abby looked at the image on the screen—a sepia photo downloaded from the website of the Delapore town archive—and the hairs on the back of her neck did an anxious little dance. "That's the place."

Leanne enlarged the image and held up the iPad for all to see. "This," she declared, "is the Harcourt House. Seems like it's a bit of a local legend in Delapore."

As the Thunderbird turned off the Coquihalla Highway, Leanne rattled off an abridged history of the Harcourt House and its original inhabitants, which she had cobbled together from archived newspaper articles, real estate and census documents, history websites and blogs, and a true crime webpage.

"So: Delapore," said Leanne. "First settled in 1889, incorporated twenty years later, named after the French missionary who built the first church there, blah blah blah. In 1912, construction begins on the Harcourt House. Josiah Harcourt is the town's first real bigwig. Most of the oldest buildings in town are courtesy of his architecture firm. He put a ton of money into local causes through most of the 1910s and '20s, and he was the first chairman of the town's chamber of commerce. Widowed in his thirties, but he had three kids before that happened. Isaac and Hector were twins, and Oliva came a few years later."

Abby scratched her head. "Hector Harcourt… why do I know that name?"

"You're the one who likes all those true crime podcasts. You tell me."

Abby blinked. "Wait a minute… holy shit, these are *those* Harcourts? As in, the Harcourt Horror Harcourts?"

Leanne nodded. "The very same."

"I'm afraid you're ahead of me on this," said Simon. "What's 'the Harcourt Horror'?"

Abby took up the story from here. "Okay, it's the fall of 1927. This rich kid from the Okanagan—"

"Hector Harcourt," Leanne provided.

" —Hector Harcourt hasn't spoken to his family in, like, two years or something. Hasn't even been in the same town. On the 3rd of November, he shows up out of nowhere. Comes into town on the last train with a revolver in his pocket and a huge fuck-off axe in his luggage. Walks up the hill to his house at something like 11PM."

"And?" Simon asked.

"And the next morning, the milkman finds Hector hanging from a tree in the front yard. He's still wearing the same clothes from last night, but now they're covered in blood. The milkman follows the trail of blood into the house, and there's the family and their two servants. Absolutely butchered and shot to pieces."

Simon raised his eyebrows. "Blimey. I think that's the answer right there. Proper old-fashioned ghost story, this. A violent act like that is bound to create a few unquiet spirits."

"I think it did," Leanne said. "Because after November 3, things get all kinds of weird. The town really tried to kill the story: they destroyed police records, they buried the Harcourts in unmarked plots, and they voted to demolish the House itself way back in 1933. But they just... never could. Every demolition crew that went up there came back with stories of apparitions, inexplicable bad feelings, and noises in the wall. The most commonly cited is the buzzing of insects and a voice whispering in tongues. Local kids still go up there just because they can, and a lot of them say the same thing. There's even a couple rumours about people disappearing or dying in the house, but I haven't been able to verify any of those yet."

"That sounds like typical ghost behaviour," Natalie said. "But these murders and Abby's dream, that's not normal."

"Something must have upset the spirit in the Harcourt House recently," Simon concluded. "We need to figure out what that something is and stop the presence from doing any more damage."

*****

"And what colour did you say this van was, Mr. Cardinal?"

Jimmy Cardinal screwed up his face and had a scratch at his three-day beard. "Well, it was pretty dark, you have to remember. This was, like, going on midnight or somethin.'"

"If you had to make a guess," Mona prompted.

Cardinal shrugged. "Gun to my head? Kinda yellowish. Maybe a dull orange."

"Was there anything else you noticed?" asked Corporal Rickards. "Did you get a sense of the van's make? The year? Did you happen to notice the licence plates at all?"

Cardinal shrugged again. "I think it was a Ford. A big Ford, and not a new one, either. Probably… mid-oughts, if I had to guess."

"Is there anything else you recall about the van?" asked Mona. "Or about the night of July 12?"

By that, Mona meant the night David Prudhomme disappeared. Jimmy Cardinal had been the last person to see David alive before his disappearance, and he'd called the precinct to make his statement first thing that morning. The discovery of the second body was all the local press could talk about, and the stories on Page 3, 6, and 8 all reprinted the same quote from Inspector Margot Pembroke of the Southeast District Major Crime Unit, urging citizens to call such-and-such number if they had any information that might assist the police in their inquiries.

Jimmy Cardinal had another scratch at his beard. "You know what? There is one thing sticks out. So, like I told you, me and Davey was down at The Gaslights on the 12th. You know, the pub on McNair Street there. I'm coming back from the can, and I see this guy cruisin' past our table, givin' Davey the stink eye. And Davey's staring back at this guy, and he's just white as a sheet. And after we've settled the bill, Davey drags me outside and says, 'His eyes, Jim. Jesus, did you see his eyes?' He kept talking about how red this guy's eyes were.

I told him he was hammered, but he wouldn't let it go. He was really scared."

Mona nodded and made a note. "Did you get a good look at this individual, Mr. Cardinal?"

"He was walking away from me. Never got a look at his face. I think he was on the tall side. Kinda lean. Like a... a runner or a swimmer or something." He pointed at Rickards. "A bit like your sort of build, actually. But I noticed he was wearing a ring. Real flashy gold number on the left pinky. I think it was one of those ones some of the church folks wear, over at St. Catherine's."

"You and David parted ways outside The Gaslights, correct?" Rickards asked. "And that's when you saw this Ford van pull out from the curb on the next block and drive in the same direction he was walking."

Jimmy Cardinal nodded. "That's about the size of it, yeah. I know I shoulda said something before now, but I was pretty trashed that night. They're saying there's a serial killer in town, now. Can you believe that? A serial killer. In fuckin' Delapore. Asscrack of the fuckin' Okanagan, this place, and now we got a serial killer?"

Rickards tucked his notepad into his back pocket. "Thank you for your help, Mr. Cardinal. We'll be in touch if we have more questions."

Mona opened the front door of the double-wide trailer, and as the pair departed, they could hear Jimmy Cardinal muttering to himself. "Never can tell, eh? Sleepy town like this, hidin' a fucking serial killer. Doesn't make a lick of sense, you ask me."

*****

The Little Bear trailer park was as close as Delapore got to a ghetto. A dozen or so trailers dotting a flat expanse of concrete, about two-thirds the size of a football field. The lot had once been the home of Delapore's first drive-through restaurant. Now, it was one of the most frequent stops on the Delapore RCMP's daily patrols. At least for once they weren't being called out over a domestic dispute or a start-up meth lab. As they walked back to the squad car, Mona turned to Rickards and asked, "Do you think his info's good?"

Rickards gave a small shrug. "With Jim Cardinal, it's tough to say. He's sent us on plenty of wild goose chases before, and that's just when he was sober. I remember about this time last year he made a complaint that Rick Mercer was sneaking into the park every night to let the air out of his tires. Man's not exactly a reliable source."

Mona nodded. "But what he said about the ring has me thinking. Jenny Styles and Sonia Hall both wore the same ring. And Reverend Jansen has a mid-2000s Ford van, doesn't he?"

"He does. But so does Bill Grover. So does Arlo Keating, Chuck Hale, Bob Wilkie, and I'm sure a half-dozen other people in town."

"Well then, we should start ruling people out. Put together a list of all the Ford vans in town that match Jim Cardinal's description, and we'll set up interviews with the owners. Then we need to talk to Reverend Jansen: two of his parishioners have been killed in the last month, and a third was seen with David Prudhomme the night he disappeared. We need the names of all the male parishioners at St. C's who wear that ring."

"That's a long list, Sarge. I'm going to be the first name on it."

"You never struck me as the church type, Rickards."

"I'm not so much these days. But I was big into it when I got out of high school. I did some volunteer work for Reverend Jansen back then, and I still wear the ring when I'm off-duty."

"Well, set up an interview with yourself and find out where you were on the 12th."

"Will do."

"I also want you to… to…" Mona trailed off as they neared the cruiser and she saw the dead man in the front seat. Blood and grime streaked down his roguish face and stained his white shirt like a butcher's smock, and he kept both hands on the dashboard so she could see the long-handled axe he was clutching. He stared into her eyes, watching her watch him, and she realized that she recognized him under all the gore. "No… that's impossible… he can't…"

Rickards stopped in his tracks and looked at his sergeant. "Is everything okay? Sarge?"

Mona undid the clasp on her holster and stumbled toward the car with her other hand extended, reaching for the door handle. "No… no, no, no…"

Between laying one hand on the butt of her gun and yanking the car door open, there was a brief moment where Mona blinked and sucked in a quick breath. And in that moment, the man was gone. The car was empty, and Mona had her gun half-drawn before she realized she was drawing it at nothing. She just stood there, breathing hard, as Rickards came up behind her and coaxed her away from the door. "Jesus Christ, Sarge! What's gotten into you?"

"I… I don't… I thought I saw…" Mona stammered.

Rickards gently guided her gun back into its holster for her and slowly shut the car door. "Mona. There's nothing there. Look."

Mona took a breath and shook her head. "You're right. It must have been a trick of the light. A reflection off the window."

"That was probably it. These killings, all the fires: the whole town's on edge. You just have to take a deep breath and relax."

Mona looked up at the hazy sky and smiled. "'Deep breath'?"

Rickards chuckled. "Poor choice of words. Look, you want me to drive?"

Mona nodded and walked around to the passenger's side of the car. "Yeah, thanks. You're right, Rickards. I just need to get my head on straight."

CHAPTER 5

THE WELCOMING COMMITTEE

IT WAS a quarter after two when Natalie's Thunderbird pulled off the Okanagan Highway onto a bumpy, cracked stretch of road that cut straight through the heart of Delapore. A crop of low, bushy shrubs grew along the road's hilly left shoulder, and the glistening waters of Okanagan Lake were visible in the distance on the right. Straight ahead, there was a life-sized wooden carving of a grizzly bear, erect on its hind legs, its front paws resting on a green and yellow sign that read "WELCOME TO DELAPORE." A backpacker with a thick black beard and a bright yellow woolly hat was walking along the shoulder, and as the Thunderbird came near, he stuck out his thumb.

As they passed the hitchhiker, Abby looked at her phone and gave Natalie directions to the local library. She'd received Will's email when Natalie stopped for gas a half-hour ago, and had arranged to meet the kid there so they could put their heads together when they were both awake. Will had chosen the spot because it was quiet, not too far from his house, and some place both his mom and his sitter trusted him to go on his own.

"I hope you'll forgive me if I give this rendezvous a miss," Simon said suddenly, "but I have an appointment of my own that I need to keep. You can let me out at the next corner, Natalie."

"Where are you headed in such a rush?" Abby asked.

"As it happens, I was in touch with my local contact when we stopped for gas. He's acquired copies of the police files on Sonia Hall and the others. I'd like to have a look at them so I know what we're dealing with."

"How did he manage that so fast? We've only known about Sonia for two days."

"I'm afraid I can't answer that. My source values his privacy too much."

"Well, we can manage on our own while you're off being mysterious. Let us know when you're done."

The Pearson Heights housing development rose up on the horizon in front of them, and with it, that hideous black speck of the Harcourt House above. Abby looked up from her phone and fixed her eyes on the place. "There it is."

Leanne shuddered and hugged herself. "Brrr. Even from down here, it's creepy."

Simon swayed in his seat, his eyes fixed on the House. "Is it just me, or does it seem to… follow you? Whichever way you're looking, it's always right in the centre of your eyeline."

Natalie made a similar motion. "Yeah. It's like one of those paintings where the eyes move."

So transfixed were they all by the Harcourt House, that nobody noticed the stop sign coming up until Leanne gasped and shouted, "Pedestrian!"

Natalie slammed on the brakes and brought the Thunderbird to a screeching halt, an arm's length from the white line of a crosswalk. Behind them, an old Volkswagen skidded to a stop, its horn blaring angrily, and in front of them, a pedestrian in the crosswalk raised his middle finger at them.

*****

The Delapore Public Library was a two-storey red-brick building in the Georgian Revival style, with faded white cornerstones and sparkling clean glass doors, which had obviously been added within the last five years. The words "BANK OF MONTREAL" were carved into the molding above the front entrance, and a brass plaque beside the book return slot provided context: the building was the original sight of the town's main bank, designed by none other than Josiah Harcourt in 1921, and had been converted to a library in the mid-1990s.

As she entered the building, Abby guessed that, front doors excepted, the place hadn't changed much since its conversion. A dull tan carpet covered the floor, and from where Abby stood, she could pick out multiple stains of varying hues and size. The check-out desk was badly chipped, and manned by one po-faced librarian who sat, rather redundantly, beside an electronic self-checkout scanner that looked more than a few years out of date.

The first floor of the library was mostly dedicated to the non-fiction and reference sections. Signs on the wall pointed the way to the computer lab, the records room, and stacks of dusty old periodicals. Leanne broke off for the records room and said, "I'm going to see if I can find anything more about the Harcourt House."

Abby and Natalie left her to it and climbed the stairs to the second floor. One half of this level was given over to children's literature and middle grade fiction, as well as a story time area where a rowdy pack of six-year-olds were currently being treated to a reading of *James and the Giant Peach*. The boy from Abby's dream was on the other side of the building, sitting alone at a table between the DVDs and the large-print fiction and watching a YouTube video on his phone. Seeing him in the flesh was more of a shock than Abby expected, and she slowed her pace as she sized him up.

"That's him?" Natalie whispered. "He looks so… normal."

"Yeah. And that's weird enough by itself."

Natalie hung back in Mysteries/Thrillers and pretended to browse while Abby approached Will alone. Keeping her voice low, she gave him a cautious tap on the shoulder. It would be a hell of a time for someone to walk past and yell "Stranger Danger."

"Excuse me?" she whispered. "Will Brady?"

Will looked at Abby and blinked, like he wasn't sure she was really there. "It is you… Abby Normal…" He removed his ear buds and shook his head. "I almost didn't think you'd come. I was starting to worry I made you up."

"I had the same thought once or twice. You mind if I sit?"

Will made a *go ahead* gesture, and Abby took the chair opposite. As she sat, the boy kept his eyes on the stacks, watching for any movement.

"What's up?" she asked.

"Just being careful. If my mom knew I'd been talking to you, she'd be really mad."

"Your mom a bit overprotective?"

"No, she's okay. But she's a cop and she has a thing about me talking to strangers."

Abby smiled in mischievous silence for a few seconds before striking with the punchline. "Well, I should warn you right now, Will. There's not many people stranger than I am."

It took a moment for Will to process the wordplay, and when he did, he jammed a hand in front of his mouth to stifle a laugh. Abby waited till he'd gotten all the giggles out, and then she turned serious. "So, what's the whole story here, Will? What do you know about the Harcourt House? Why the hell were you in my dream?"

Will took a deep breath. "Okay, let me answer one question at a time." He started his story with the Very Stupid Thing, and worked his way forward. In graphic detail, Abby heard about the Rat King, the swarm of cicadas, and Papa. It was the mention of the latter that particularly interested her.

"Wait, back up… this was when we were together in the dream? The figure coming out of that black sludge… that was your father?"

Will looked down and muttered a small, hesitant, "Yeah."

Abby drummed her fingers on the table. "You didn't see anybody else? Maybe a man with white hair and glasses? A Southern accent?"

"I think I'd remember that," Will replied.

Abby made a note of that on the *Weird Shit* list in her head. "So, what happened next?"

Will shrugged. "There's not much more to say. I mean, you know what happened in that dream as well as I do. Then I found your blog, and I got in touch, but nothing major happened between then and now. I gotta say, I didn't think you'd get my message nearly so fast."

"Actually, Will, my friends and I were already on our way up here when you emailed me. We were going to look into these recent, uh, disappearances."

"You can say 'murders,'" Will grumbled. "I used to see Sonia Hall around town; I knew it was her on the ceiling."

"Listen to me, Will. I think all this stuff, from the Rat King to the murders, is connected. My friends and I are going to stick around town for a few days, and we're going to do some digging. We're going to find whatever is messing with this town, and I will personally kick its butt six ways from Sunday, and make sure it never messes with anyone again. That," Abby concluded firmly, "is a 100%, no joke, Abby Normal promise."

Will smiled. "I really hope you can."

Abby smiled back and held up one hand, curled into a fist. "Hey," she said. "Pound it."

Will bumped his fist against Abby's. She opened her hand dramatically and made an explosion noise with her mouth.

Will smiled and whispered, "You know, Abby, you don't talk like most of the grownups from around here."

Abby smiled back, showing off the big gap between her front teeth. "Between you and me, I'm not really a grown-up. I'm a dumb kid in a *very* convincing grown-up disguise."

Will covered his mouth again and snorted through his nose.

*****

When she was sure no one was looking, Abby invited Natalie out of the stacks and made the introductions. She'd been nervous about introducing the kid to Natalie, whose size alone was enough to put most people off her. Not to mention her grey, unblinking eyes and the bloodless, stretched-too-tight look of her skin. But Will was more awed than he was frightened, and told Natalie that she should be in a *James Bond* movie.

"You could *totally* beat up Daniel Craig," he said.

Natalie smiled at this. "Oh, I've thought about it. Little snot-rag still owes me money."

To make sure they were all on the same page, Will told Natalie a shorter version of the same story he'd told Abby. Then, forty minutes after they'd left her to her own devices, the three went down to the records room to meet Leanne. When Abby asked if she'd found anything interesting, Leanne's eyes lit up and she eagerly dragged Abby to a table in the back corner of the room.

"I might actually have something pretty major," said Leanne. "You know those old newspaper articles I found about the Harcourt murders? Turns out the guy who wrote them, Arnold Tremblay, left a whole bunch of his papers to the library when he died."

Abby carefully flipped through the binder. The papers behind the laminate were yellow with age, most of them typed but a few handwritten. Each page started with an underlined header, and Abby guessed these were the original rough copies of Tremblay's articles for *The Delapore Sunday Times.*

Leanne pointed to the shelves behind her. "There's eight or nine more binders like this. Each one covers two years that Tremblay wrote for the paper. This is 1927 and 1928. Check the article for November 13 of '27."

Abby flipped to that page and read the faded black type. One sentence had been crossed out in pen, and a note had been scribbled in the margin of the page. *They were on the <u>floor</u>, Arnold. I've told you once.*

Leanne popped up beside her and said, "Check the article for November 6."

Abby did. It was the first article written after the Harcourt murders, and one sentence had been underlined. It referred to *Joseph Alexander, 45, and Celia Alexander, 19, found hanging from the ceiling with their throats slit.* A note in the margin said, *They were <u>on the floor in the living room</u>. Just like the others.* The handwriting was the same as the last note.

"Explain this to me," she said to Leanne.

Leanne pulled out her iPad and showed it to Abby. "Okay, so these are scans of the printed articles. I found them while I was doing background research on the House earlier. And they say the servants' bodies were on the floor in the living room. But that's not what Arnold Tremblay wrote in his rough drafts."

"How could he make that mistake twice? Floor, ceiling, those are pretty hard to mix up."

"I don't think it was a mistake. Check the back of the album."

Abby flipped to the last pages in the binder. These were personal letters between Tremblay and various associates: his wife, his editor, close friends. One of the last letters was from a Superintendent John Alexander Boyce Campbell.

Mr. Tremblay,

Regarding your letter of last Thursday, I regret to inform you that I cannot release the Harcourt files to your newspaper. They contain sensitive information that may yet prove relevant to one or more open investigations, and we cannot risk a leak of that information.

In answer to your question, it is the <u>official opinion</u> of this department that Joseph and Celia Alexander were killed by Hector Harcourt at the same time as the rest of the family. There is <u>no evidence</u> that suggests another cause of death. You will of course be aware that the same conclusion was reached at the inquest, and we consider the matter to be closed.

Respectfully yours,
J.A.B. CAMPBELL,
Superintendent, Royal Canadian Mounted Police

The letter that followed was Tremblay's response. It was short, direct, and blunt.

Superintendent,

I spoke to the mortuary attendant. The servants were dismembered nearly an <u>hour</u> after they died. He's sure of it.

<u>What aren't you telling me?</u>

Abby read the letters twice and then flipped back to the draft articles. Superintendent Campbell's handwriting was the same as the notes insisting that the servants were on the floor. She checked the date on his letter: December 12, 1928.

Abby looked at Leanne. "You think this was a coverup?"

Leanne nodded. "Arnold Tremblay knew something. Every time he mentions the servants, he says they were hanging from the ceiling. There are letters between him and the town doctor in the binder for 1931 and '32. He congratulates the doctor on his retirement, and then he asks for the truth about Joseph and Celia off the record. Whatever happened in 1927, someone fudged the official details."

"But Arnold Tremblay had a peek at the unofficial ones. He tried to uncover the lie. And the cops lost the Harcourt files, didn't they?"

"In 1933. I found J.A.B. Campbell in the *Minutes and Memoranda of Delapore City Council* for that year. Those are the records of every major town meeting since incorporation. He notifies the city council about a fire in the police archive. Destroyed half their files going back ten years."

"Convenient," Abby grumbled.

"And five pages later, the council passes the motion to demolish the Harcourt House."

"So, something happened to the servants before Hector went all 'Here's Johnny.' Something the High Heid Yins didn't want people knowing about. The cops doctored the files that went into the public record, and when someone came looking for the truth, they had themselves a cookout."

"Seems that way."

There was a sharp knock on the wooden shelves as Natalie approached. "What are you two being so hush-hush about back here?"

Leanne snapped some pictures on her iPad and put the binders away. "I'll tell you outside. Come on."

Will led them out of the library. The burning orange sun smacked Abby in the face and she threw a hand over her eyes. "Holy *crap*, that is bright!"

"You want me to guide you?" Leanne asked with a laugh.

Abby smiled. "I'm not quite ready for the white cane just yet."

Halfway across the parking lot, her ears picked up the rumble of an engine. An accelerator roared, tires screamed, and Abby's heart went *thumpa-thumpa-thump* as the sound got closer. She snapped her head up and blinked once, just in time to see the bright yellow Ford hurtling toward her at 70 km/h. Will grabbed her hand and screamed, "Move! Abby, MOVE!"

Suddenly, one of Natalie's hands was on the back of Abby's neck, and the other was on Will's. She heaved them aside like two bales of hay and planted her feet right in the van's path, gritted her teeth, and opened her arms to embrace four tons of speeding death.

Will screamed as the van hit Natalie head-on. For a second, it seemed like the van had just vaporized her, but then the tires screamed and the engine started to whine. Abby looked under the van's wheelbase and saw Natalie's heavy boots scraping against the pavement. One of her hands was sunk into the hood, crumpling it like tinfoil, and white smoke leaked from between her fingers. The back end wobbled as the driver cranked the steering while, and then the whole thing fishtailed and struck a large pickup truck. Amid a hellish cacophony of breaking glass and shrieking metal, the pickup truck swiveled like the needle of a compass and its back tires left the ground. The pile of timber in the bed went flying out, clattering on the pavement and spearing the windshields of two other cars.

Still holding onto Will, Abby picked herself up and ran toward the Thunderbird, ignoring the raw pain of the fresh road rash on her knees and elbows. Will was hiccupping in short bursts of panic and staring at the van's front end. "What about Natalie? Is she okay?"

"Don't worry," said Abby, looking in the same direction. "She can take it."

Leanne approached them from a hiding spot between two cars. She was breathing hard and had one hand on her chest. "What on *earth* was that?" she coughed.

Abby held her in a life-or-death hug, but Leanne winced and pushed away. "Ow! Ow! Don't do that!" She rubbed her chest and gritted her teeth. "Natalie pushed me out of the way before she got you. I feel like she hit me in the boobs with a baseball bat. *Ow.*"

Abby looked toward the van, where a man was climbing out of the driver's seat. He was tall and thin, with tangled brown hair that hung past his shoulders and a beard flecked with specks of grey. His clothes were filthy and ragged and there were livid dark rings under his eyes. He had a claw hammer clutched tight in one hand, and as his shoulders twitched and spasmed, he swung the tool through the air like he was swatting at flies nobody else could see. When his head snapped around toward Abby, and the hammer swung again, she could guess he wasn't looking to hang a picture.

The man took a few lazy, lumbering steps toward the group, his knuckles whitening around the hammer's grip. He swayed like he was under the influence of a powerful narcotic, and he let slip a low, wet growl from somewhere deep inside him. Suddenly, he squeezed his eyes shut and smacked his forehead with the palm of his free hand. "Get out…" he muttered. "Get out. Get out, GET OUT!"

Metal squeaked as Natalie released her death grip on the front of the van. She lurched around to the driver's side, clearly the worse for wear, and loomed over the man. "Okay, asshole, where's the fire? You could have killed someone!"

The man twitched and looked at Natalie, shaking his head. "No… no kill… no more! Stop! Got to… stop!"

The man's hammer hand twitched again. Leanne seized Will's hand and Abby told them both to get to safety. Will's face was bloodless, and nothing came out when he tried to answer. The two tried to duck out of the parking lot, but the man with the hammer pointed at them and shouted, "DON'T! Don't go with them, Will! They're in on it! All of them! They'll trick you! Take you!" He pointed at Abby and howled, "You think I don't see? I see you all! I see the magic in you! *His* touch! The Master's Mark!"

As Leanne led Will away from the scene, Natalie grabbed the man by both shoulders and lifted him off the ground. She swayed as she did it, and one of her hands shook a little. Definitely not on her A game, Abby realized.

"I'm only going to say this once," Natalie growled, "so you and your Master better listen very carefully. Put the hammer down right now, or we're going to have a problem."

The man lashed back and forth, struggling against Natalie's grip. "Can't... won't... no! Won't stop! You can't see it, can you? You're like me... like I was... The shell moves, it talks, but there's no fire in its furnace!" He kicked Natalie in the chest, and her grip loosened a bit. "Filthy, filthy *slave!*"

Natalie's lip curled in disgust. "Say that to me again. Say that word one more time."

A crowd was forming at the edges of the parking lot, and people were even pressing themselves against the library windows to see what was happening. The madman howled like a panther and kicked Natalie up under the chin. She reeled back and dropped him, and he went in with the hammer.

Natalie had the height advantage, but the madman had speed on his side. As she grabbed for him again, he seized her wrist and obliterated her elbow with an awful *crunch*. While she fought back a scream, he readjusted and swung at her face. *CRACK.*

As Natalie went down, Abby bolted for the doors of the library. The librarian was scrambling to get them locked and draw down the security gate. Abby just cleared the first step before she felt a hand tug at the waistband of her shorts. The madman threw her to the ground, and her skull bounced off the pavement.

Pain exploded in her head. She tried to move, but every muscle felt like it was made of lead. A connection had come loose in her brain, and now her limbs wouldn't respond to her brain's commands. The man with the hammer stepped over Abby, a thin coating of foam now trapped in his beard. "I see you, girl! I know what you are! Abby Normal, the last of the Gospels! The heir of the Elder Prince, the seeker of wisdom and truth! You want answers like he wants them! You and him, flip sides of the coin! All the same! All the same!"

Abby rolled as the man swung his hammer. He missed her by inches and she kicked him in the chest. She tried to run, but she was still woozy from the knock on the head, and the best she could manage was a drunken stumble.

Natalie came to her feet, her bones crackling and popping as they mended themselves from the inside out. She stepped toward Abby, but the big man regained his footing and grabbed Abby's wrist. He threw her to the ground once more, bouncing her head off the pavement a second time. Then he got on top of her and drove his knee into her chest. He'd dropped the hammer, so he reached behind him and pulled a long screwdriver out of his belt.

"BACK!" the man shouted at Natalie. "Get back!" He brushed the screwdriver's head along Abby's neck, and she tried not to move lest he flinch and open a vein. "Why do you protect her?" the man demanded of Natalie. "Who do you think this is? You know what she can do! If *he* can do it, so can she! All the same! I can't… can't let that…" He leaned in close enough that Abby could see the crumbs stuck between his rotting teeth. "I can't let you become him…"

Sirens howled at the edge of the parking lot and a police cruiser hopped up onto the curb. A lanky man with a flattop and a stocky Indigenous woman jumped out and drew their weapons.

"FREEZE!" said the male cop. "Put your weapon down, your hands in the air, and step away from the girl this minute!"

The man with the screwdriver shifted his weight as he turned to look. Abby found the space to move her arm, and she raked her fingernails down his cheek. He screamed and turned back to her, and she noticed his eyes for the first time. His pupils were massively dilated, and his irises were shifting colour, from brown to bright red and back again. Abby could see tiny dots of light darting around in each pupil, like miniscule insects.

The eyes… said a voice in Abby's head. *Yes, for God's sake, go for the eyes!*

The man had shifted his weight again and Abby's other arm came free. She jammed both her thumbnails deep into his eyes, and the man fell off her with a scream. Abby hobbled back to Natalie and collapsed on the curb, trying to regain her coordination. The madman with the screwdriver rose to his knees and shook his head as the cops approached him. "Get out… no… can't… get out!"

The female cop lowered her gun a few inches and spoke softly. "Bill? Bill Grover, is that you? It's me, Mona Brady. I'm here with Corporal Rickards. Do you recognize us?"

Bill Grover shuddered and pulled himself up with jerky, stuttering movements, like a character from a low-rent Rankin/Bass production. As he stood, he shook his head, and for a moment he seemed more lucid. "Mona… I… there was something… something I needed to tell you…"

Mona took a cautious step forward, extending a hand to Bill Grover. "You can tell me any time, Bill. Right now, why don't you put the screwdriver down, okay? Just… put it down… You've been gone a long time, Bill. Your family's been worried about you."

"F-family?" Bill Grover stuttered.

Mona nodded. "Yes! Shirley, Eric, Jessica. They've been worried about you, Bill. We all have. We've been looking for you for weeks!" She stepped forward a few more paces, beckoning Bill Grover toward her. "Let me take you home. We can get Eric and Will together for a play date and go for a walk in the woods. What do you say to that?"

Bill Grover jerked away from Mona, flailing his screwdriver. "No! I can't! I can't… can't go back to them…" He sucked in a breath and clutched his forehead. "He's… he's fighting… trying to get back in… he'll take me… can't let him take me!"

"Who's 'he,' Bill? Where's he going to take you?"

Bill screamed and shook his head. "Who's he? Look around you, Mona! He's standing right beside you!" He pointed at

Abby, then Natalie, then Rickards. "He's inside her! And her! And him! He's in me and you and your son and in this whole town!" He paused, sucked in a quivering breath, and choked back a defeated sob. "He *is* this town."

"Who, Bill?"

"The Master," Bill Grover replied. He twitched again, his eyes flashed red, and he raised the screwdriver once more. "The Master is Good. The Master is Wise. The Master is Kind." He closed his eyes as the tears made tracks down his filthy cheeks, then he wrapped both hands around the tool and pressed it to the side of his neck. "That's what he told me, Mona. That's what he made he think. But what he made me do… What I saw…"

Mona holstered her gun and raised her hands. "Listen to me, Bill, just listen. It doesn't have to be like this. We'll get you some help, okay? We'll take you to the hospital, and you can talk this out with someone who'll listen. They've got good people at Kelowna General. You don't have to do this. You don't have to hurt yourself. You're safe now."

"No, I'm not," Bill cried. "I never am! I feel him, Mona. I still feel him *inside*! He's coming back…"

Mona took another step forward. "Okay, Bill. We can get you protection from him. That's why we're here. I know you must be hurting right now. You've been gone so long, and you're confused right now. But if you just trust me, then I promise you it'll be okay."

Bill opened his eyes and tightened his grip on the screwdriver. "No. It won't."

The crowd screamed as Bill rammed in the screwdriver. He dropped to his knees with both hands still tight around the handle and a smock of blood running down his front. Mona stood frozen as Rickards holstered his gun and rushed to catch the falling man. He pulled the radio from his vest and screamed at dispatch to call an ambulance.

Abby already had her phone out, but she'd hardly dialled 9 and 1 before Bill Grover went slack in Rickards's arms and let go of the screwdriver. Rickards held the tool steady with one hand and applied pressure with the other. "Sarge! First aid kit, trunk of the car! Hurry!"

Mona unfroze and felt her mouth go dry as she approached the fallen man and put a finger to the opposite side of his throat. "Rickards, it's no good."

Rickards finally relented and took a step back from Bill Grover. The screams and chattering from the library patrons softened as Mona called in the incident, and a still hush fell over the whole lot. It was suddenly so quiet, to coin a phrase, that you could hear a pin drop.

And then the pin did drop. The body twitched once on the ground. Twice. His mouth stretched open and a hundred cicadas buzzed and hummed out into the hazy sky. Then the screaming started again.

CHAPTER 6

SINS OF THE FATHER

"HAD YOU ever met the deceased before today?"

"No," Abby replied with a shake of her head.

"Had you had any contact with any member of the deceased's family?"

"Nope."

"And can you think of any reason why the deceased might have wanted to hurt you?"

"Not a one," Abby murmured. She was overthinking every word that came out of her mouth, trying to keep her voice level, and clenching her hands together so they wouldn't shake. "It just… it all came out of nowhere. Full-on 'Do you read Sutter Cane?' kind of thing."

The clock on the wall of the police station said 3:30PM. At this very moment, a team of officers had the library closed off, and were picking over the wreckage of Bill Grover's van. The man himself was in the morgue, in the trusty care of Dr. Bernard Hummel. Mona and Rickards had gone to the dead man's house to break the news to his family. Abby and Natalie were giving statements to the two most junior constables on the payroll.

The constable questioning Abby had introduced herself as Pruitt, and she looked like she was hardly a week out of high school. To keep her mind off memories of the attack, Abby had been concentrating on Pruitt's aura throughout the interview. As a rule, the strength of a person's aura depended on how in sync they were with the mystical forces of the world—what was known as the True Magic. Pruitt's aura was barely worth noticing, a mere haze of greys and lifeless earth tones. It was boring and human and thoroughly non-mystical, but every so often Abby caught a flash of Pruitt's stress. Twinges of resentment for the men looking over her shoulder, waiting for her to screw up.

"Please, Miss Henderson, restrict your answers to 'yes' or 'no,'" Pruitt said. "Is there any reason Bill Grover may have wanted to harm you?"

"Sorry," Abby said. "No, I can't think of a single reason."

Pruitt paused to consult a little spiral notebook on her desk. "Here's the problem I have with that, Miss Henderson. We've obtained a cell phone video of the library incident. A video in which Bill Grover clearly addresses you as 'Abby Normal.' Does that term mean anything to you?"

"Old high school nickname. It's kind of a long story."

"But you see my trouble. How could he know that nickname if you two had never met previously?"

Abby paused. That was actually a very good question. Her blog wasn't exactly well-publicised, and there were no pictures of her on the site or personal information in her posts that could be traced back to her. Unless Bill Grover had been stalking her since the fire at Applegate Asylum, she couldn't think of a way he could come by that name.

Pruitt shifted in her chair and cleared her throat, and Abby realized she hadn't actually answered the question yet. "I honestly don't know," she said suddenly. What she didn't add was, *And I would love to find out.*

Pruitt locked eyes with Abby for a moment, trying to determine if she was lying. Abby held the constable's gaze with stoic grace and saw Pruitt's flickering aura at the edge of her vision.

Pruitt trudged through a few more questions about Abby and her friends' activities before Bill showed up. How long had they been in Delapore? How long were they planning to stay? Was the library their first stop in town? Abby kept Will's name out of it, but was forced to admit to her interest in the Harcourt House. Pruitt said nothing to this, but several dark thoughts flashed in her aura. She fought to suppress them, and Abby had to wonder if Constable Pruitt had once done a Very Stupid Thing herself.

Pruitt flipped back through her notes and sighed. "You can go now, Miss Henderson. I've got no further questions."

Abby left the constable to it and worked her way back to the lobby of the building, pausing only briefly to fix herself a cup of horribly weak tea from the station's small kitchenette. Leanne sprang up from a chair in the reception area and wrapped Abby in a hug. "Thank God you're okay! I've been waiting here for half an hour!"

Abby kissed her. "I'm just a little banged up. I'll live. How's Will?"

Leanne shook her head. "I wish I knew! We got clear of the library just before the cops showed up. I heard screaming in the parking lot and I turned around for two seconds to see what was the matter, and he was just… boom! He was gone! I ran after him for six blocks! I must have looked like a crazy woman! I just—"

Abby put a finger on Leanne's lips and shushed her. "Lee, Lee, it's okay. It's not your fault he ran. I would've done the same thing if I was him."

Leanne sighed and rested her head on Abby's chest. "Sorry. This day just has me a bit frazzled."

Abby looked up. "Talking of frazzled…"

The front doors burst open as Simon rushed into the lobby. He was wide-eyed and sweating like he'd just run all the way from his meeting with his mysterious contact. "Bloody hell, I just heard what happened! Are you alright? Are you hurt?"

Abby broke off from Leanne. "I'm okay. Little bruised, but I've had worse. You get the files you wanted?"

"I did. There's a motel just off 2nd Street. My contact arranged to have them dropped off there. I was just going to book us some rooms when Natalie called me."

Abby exhaled. "God, I would *kill* to stretch out on a real bed right now. Even a crappy motel bed."

"Well, we can head over when they're done with Natalie. We'll regroup and reassess our situation."

Leanne removed her glasses and wiped them on her shirt. "Speaking of, I found something at the library that you'll want to hear."

"Tell me when we get settled and unpacked. I'll need to spend some time reviewing these files anyway."

Abby finished her tea and crushed the cup in her hand. "If you guys have the research thing covered, I'm going to duck out for a bit. I'll catch up with you later."

Leanne put her hand around Abby's waist. "Is everything okay?"

Abby kissed her on the forehead. "I'm fine, Lee, I promise. Or I will be once I've had some time to think. You guys check out this motel. I'm going to take a walk around town and try to clear my head."

"Okay. I'll text you when we're unpacked."

Abby dropped her cup in the nearest trash can. "Cheers," she said, as she gave her friends a two-fingered salute and walked out the door.

*****

From the police station, it was a twenty-five-minute walk to the edge of town, and then a further ten minutes up through Pearson Heights. It was coming up on 4:15 by the time Abby crested the hill. The sun was edging toward the Harcourt House, and the chain-link fence cast a shadowy grid on the

House's façade. Sitting before the fence, legs hugged tight to his chest, was Will Brady.

"Why am I not surprised you're here?" Abby said as she approached the fence.

Will kept looking at the House. "Just leave me alone, Abby. I don't want to talk."

Abby sat down beside the boy and put a hand on his shoulder. "You don't have to talk. But I don't think you should be alone after what happened."

Will kept staring at the House. But slowly, without looking back, he brought one hand up and squeezed hers. "I… don't understand…" he whispered. "Why him? Why Mr. Grover?"

"You knew him, didn't you? I thought I heard your mom say you and his son…"

"Yeah. Eric's in my class. He was with me that night."

"When you saw the Rat King?"

Will nodded. "He was such a nice guy. Mr. Grover, I mean. He never… he wasn't like… *that*."

"How much did you see of what happened?"

"Enough. When he attacked you, he'd never do anything like that to anyone." He looked at Abby for the first time, and she saw tears in his eyes. "I promise. He wasn't like that."

Abby wrapped both arms around him. "It's okay, Will. I don't blame him for what happened. Not at all."

Will sniffed and wiped his nose on his sleeve. Then he glared up at the Harcourt House. "It was this place. It must have gotten into his head somehow. It made him sick."

Abby nodded silently.

"Did you see the cicadas? It was just like the dream." Another sniff, and a few grunts and groans to clear the crying away. "Whatever's in this house, whatever those cicadas are, that made Mr. Grover sick." Suddenly, Will jumped up and shook the fence with both hands. "And it killed him!" he sobbed. "This stupid, evil, no-good house killed him for no reason! He never hurt anyone, and this *place* just… it

MURDERED HIM!" A waterfall of tears poured down the boy's cheeks, and he picked up a rock from the ground. "You hear that, you stupid house! You *fuck*! You murdered Mr. Grover!" He lobbed the rock over the fence, and it shattered one of the House's few intact windows. But that wasn't enough, so he picked up another rock and threw it. Then another. And another. And he kept venting.

"How do you like it, you bastard! You *shit*! How do you *fucking* like it! Where's your Rat King now! Where are your bugs! Come on and get me, if you're not too chicken shit! COME! AND! FUCKING! GET ME!"

The last rock went high and knocked a shingle from the porch canopy. It fell onto the old tree stump and broke into a dozen pieces. Will stood there, exhaling noisily, and then he plopped down where he was and just cried.

"It's okay," Abby said. "Let it out if you have to."

Will sniffed again and wiped his eyes. "You know what my dad used to say to me? 'Men don't cry. Men don't ever cry in front of the women.'"

And then it all clicked for her. She remembered Will's sudden shyness at the library, his reluctance to answer when she'd asked him about his dad. "Will, do you mind if I ask you a personal question?"

"Depends what it is."

"What kind of guy was your dad? Did he ever... um..."

The boy drew his knees up to his chest and mumbled into them.

"Sorry?" said Abby.

"I said, 'a couple of times,'" Will snapped.

"What do you mean by 'a couple of times'?"

A dark shadow fell across Will's face. "I mean half the time he didn't even look at me. When he wanted to hit something, he mostly went straight for my mom."

Abby's nostrils whistled with the effort of a heavy sigh. *Oh, Jesus.*

"Papa," Will said, "he liked… he liked to control things. And when things didn't go his way, he got angry. Like this one time when I was six, I was running around inside and I broke a lamp, and he…" He swung his fist weakly through the air and whispered, "Bam. He gave my mom a black eye, and he did it right in front of me. It was always like that: something went wrong, he blamed my mom, and if she couldn't fix it…"

"Bam?" Abby said.

Will nodded. "Bam." He extended his arms behind him and leaned back, sighing deeply. "And then my mom finally had enough. She left and took me with her, and that's when we came here and I never saw him again. A couple months later, he got really drunk and tried to drive home one night… Instead of going to the funeral, we stayed up late eating pizza and watching *Toy Story* movies. And I'm not sorry we did."

"I don't think you should be. Sounds to me like your dad doesn't deserve it."

"No. I guess he doesn't." Will paused for a minute. "Abby… don't tell my mom I was swearing, okay? She doesn't like it when I swear."

"Your secret's safe."

"Thanks.

Will's cell phone buzzed in his pocket. He had a brand-new text from his mom:

Where r u, Will? Call me ASAP. Please. Something's happened. Need 2 know u r safe.

He put the phone away. "Was she there?" he asked Abby. "Did she see what Mr. Grover… did she see the cicadas?"

Abby bit her lip and said nothing.

He banged his head against his knees and clenched his fists. "I can't… all this stuff is just… why is this happening, Abby? Why is *any* of this happening?"

Abby stood and stretched. "That's what I'm here to find out. Come on: I'll walk you down to your block. Then my friends and I have some work to do."

As they started down the hill, Abby turned her head to sneak one last look at the Harcourt House. From a window on the second floor, a pale face stared back at her: a teenage girl with long red hair and a gaping axe wound in her skull. The girl disappeared when Abby blinked, but the sight of her knocked something loose in Abby's mind. Flashes of the past. Memories belonging to the House itself. A branch. A noose. An axe and a pool of blood. The man with the moustache and the roguish face in a hysterical fit, his hands smeared red, his eyes desperate. And she heard the buzzing of insects — a million cicadas beating their wings like thunder...

"Abby? Abby, are you okay?"

Abby blinked again and the images disappeared. She was sitting on the ground, having fallen on her butt while the vision assaulted her. She realized Will was shaking her knee, trying to get her attention, and she smiled weakly. "Oh, yeah, no, I'm fine."

"Are you sure?" Will asked. "You kinda zoned out there for a minute."

Abby stood and rubbed her sore *derriere*. "I'm okay, really. I just had... kind of a funny turn there. But I'm fine now, I promise."

But as they descended the hill, Abby put a hand on Will's shoulder and he felt the tremors in her muscles. She was nowhere near fine.

*****

Mona dropped her pen on the desk and gave her hand a shake. Jenny, Sonia, David, and now Bill... how many forests would have to die for the sake of her paperwork? Her cell phone buzzed in her pocket, and she discovered a new text from Mrs. Tenenbaum. *Will's come home. I'll keep an eye on him til your here.*

Mona had called home to check in with her son just after she and Rickards delivered the death message to Shirley Grover. Mrs. Tenenbaum had picked up on the third ring. *Will went to the library*, she'd said. *He told me you had OK'd it.*

She definitely hadn't. And she hadn't seen him there the entire time she'd been there, trying to talk Bill Grover off the proverbial edge and then picking up the pieces after he jumped. She didn't know where he'd been for the best part of an afternoon, and that scared the hell out of her. All those dreams he'd been having, the dead animals he said he'd seen in the Harcourts' bathtub... what if he really did know more of the story than even he realized? What if the person behind all this decided that meant trouble?

And speaking of trouble... Mona braced herself and turned her attention back to her computer monitor. Pressed "PLAY" for about the tenth time that afternoon.

The cell phone footage from the library filled her entire screen. It was a badly-framed rush job, starting just after Bill Grover climbed out of his van. On the screen, Bill Grover raised a claw hammer in his left hand, and swung it at a tall black woman in an olive tank top and khaki pants—Natalie Arnaud, according to her eyewitness statement. The camera shook as the woman fell to the ground, and the audio devolved into a cacophony of horrified screaming.

The footage itself wasn't what disturbed Mona. No, the disturbing part was that half a dozen eyewitnesses swore blind that Bill had flattened Arnaud with his van before he went after her with the hammer. Mona could see on the video where she was bleeding from getting her head caved in. But then the video also had her getting back up, totally coherent. When she'd come into the station to make her statement, there wasn't a scratch on her. That wasn't medically possible.

And just where the hell had Bill been all this time? In his last moments, he'd been acting like he'd just come down off another planet. Raving about "the Master." Spitting up cicadas.

Cicadas. Just like in Sonia Hall's mouth.

Jesus, she needed a break. Placing the last of her paperwork in the "OUT" tray, Mona stood, stretched, and walked toward the breakroom. Constable Foley had just put on a fresh pot of coffee, and Mona eagerly poured herself a cup. She savoured the first few sips, and reveled in this single moment of freedom.

Then Superintendent Campbell lumbered out of his office, stuck two fingers in his mouth, and hurled a shrill, teeth-rattling whistle at his officers. "Listen up, people! I just got off the phone with Constable Innes. We got a situation at the library. If you're not actively having a heart attack, drop what you're doing and get down there, pronto!"

Mona set her coffee down. "What's the matter, sir?"

"They found blood in Bill Grover's van. Spots on the rear fender and inside the door handles. Major Crime is already mobilising, and Pembroke wants every available hand on the scene. Forensics, crash analysis, the works. We need to close off the entire block. Nobody touches that van with a fifteen-foot pole. I'm going to see about a search warrant for Bill's house."

"Do we think he's a suspect?"

Campbell nodded. "There was a cell phone under Bill's passenger seat. Had one of those protective cases with a pocket for a card on it. Sonia Hall's student ID was in the pocket."

"Jesus. This is going to kill Shirley."

"You let me handle Shirley Grover, Sergeant. You worry about the van."

"Roger that." Then, turning to face the bullpen, Mona roared, "Let's move, people! You heard the boss!"

CHAPTER 7

SMALL TOWN BRINGDOWN

SATURDAY MORNING came as a literal breath of fresh air. The winds had changed direction to the south, and the smoke from the wildfires was now blowing toward the Kootenays, well to the east of Delapore. Simon and Abby had spent the pre-dawn hours reviewing the police files Simon had procured and decided there were some gaps that needed filling in. The natural place to start was the Safeway where Jenny Styles had worked, and where her body had later been found. Distorting time, according to Simon, was the most complicated and dangerous branch of magic there was. If Jenny had been a victim of time manipulation, there would be signs at the place where her body was discovered. The cops would have missed those signs during their first search of the area, but Simon was confident that they would resonate with Abby even now.

As they crossed the parking lot, Abby took a moment to check her reflection in the window of a shiny new Tesla. The figure that looked back at her had a short frizz of mousy brown hair, no visible piercings or tattoos, and was dressed in the unflattering uniform and bulky vest of an RCMP constable. She looked down at her own body, clad in denim shorts, sneakers, and a t-shirt that read "DESERT BUS FOR HOPE," and then looked back at her reflection. "You sure this is going to work?"

Simon came up beside her, grabbed her right wrist, and fiddled with the strap of the leather bracer on her forearm. "Trust me. Natalie and I have done this a hundred times."

Abby winced. "Ow! Not so tight."

"Sorry. It needs to be secure. Otherwise the illusion won't hold." He lifted his own right arm and tightened an identical bracer.

"Explain to me again how this works?" She had turned around so she could inspect the view from the back. The uniform trousers really didn't do her reflection any favours.

"If we want to get anywhere with this investigation, we need the locals to think we're here in an official capacity. As ourselves, we don't look very official." He tapped his bracer. "These arm-guards project a glamour around us, so whoever looks at us sees what we need them to see. Hey presto, Simon and Abby the paranormal investigators become Sergeant Lockhart and Constable Henderson of the Major Crime Unit. It's an old trick I picked up from the Fair Folk."

"What about badges?"

"Good point." Simon fished two playing cards from his pocket and gave one to Abby. "There you are."

"The three of clubs?"

Simon sighed. "Check the reflection."

Abby held the card up to the glass. The three of clubs in her hand was reflected back as an RCMP badge in a leather holder. When she moved the card, the badge took on an ethereal shine, and the hazy outline of the card became almost discernible underneath. "Probably shouldn't wave this around too much, should I?"

"Fortunately, you're not going to a rave, so that shouldn't be much of a problem. The same rule holds for your attire, by the by. Too many sudden movements, and the illusion will shut down."

"What if someone recognizes me? You know, after the whole Bill Grover thing?"

"As far as I'm aware, Mr. Grover attacked a young woman with garish turquoise hair and several oversized tattoos. Definitely not the sort of person you'd ever see in a police uniform. Now, just follow my lead and act natural."

Abby shrugged and put the playing card in your pocket. "Well, it's worth a shot at least. And what do you mean, my hair is 'garish'?"

They entered the store, took a second to enjoy the technological marvel of air-conditioning, and then approached one of the cashiers. She was a tall Indian girl with her hair in a ponytail, and she smiled them her best customer-service smile when they got near. She asked how she could help them and Simon flashed his playing card. Abby followed his lead.

"Gurinder Dhillon?" he asked gravely.

The cashier dropped the smile. "Yeah?"

"Sergeant Lockhart and Constable Henderson, Royal Canadian Mounted Police. We're looking into the death of one Jennifer Styles."

"We understand you were the one who found Ms. Styles' body," Abby added. "The morning of July 4?" All this information was in the police report, but it was worth their time to double-check if the cops had left out any 'unusual' details.

Gurinder looked down and tightened her arms across her chest with a shudder. "Jesus, don't remind me."

"Would you mind walking us through the events of that morning?" Simon inquired. "We're trying to establish a timeframe of events."

"I already gave my statement to the cops," Gurinder said. "Actually, I think most everyone here did."

"We're here to follow up," Simon replied. "There have been some… new developments in the case."

Gurinder eyed them suspiciously. "I've never seen you around here. And there have been cops all over town for weeks."

"We've just arrived from the city," said Simon. "Someone decided they needed more manpower out here after the second body was found."

"Right. And where'd you transfer from? Baker Street?"

"The kingdom of Wessex, actually."

"It's just… you don't sound much like a cop. At least, not one from around here." She gave Abby the once-over and added, "And you don't look much like one. You're way too young to be working a murder case."

"We're part of a special unit out of Kelowna," said Simon. "It's all very hush-hush. My colleague here works mostly with the youth. Undercover. In the gangs. Would you believe she just turned 40?"

"I definitely wouldn't."

"Which is exactly the point!"

Gurinder must have remembered that she wasn't getting paid enough to listen to this bullshit, because she sighed and asked, "What do you want to know?"

"Just tell us what you saw," Simon said. "As best you can."

Abby suspected the girl was just playing along to get rid of them, but hey, progress was progress. "It was probably between 7 and 7:30 in the morning," said Gurinder. "I was on opening shift that day, and I know I took the garbage out back in that first half hour, and that's… well…"

"That's where Jenny was," Simon prompted.

"Yeah. Took me a few minutes to figure out it was her—hell, it took me a few to figure out it was a *person* in there. She was, like, wrapped up in this big black trash bag. A couple times a year, we'll get people dumping stuff in our trash when they think no one's looking, just 'cause they were too lazy to drive out to the dump or whatever. That's what I thought at first: that somebody had been by early in the morning and pitched some old junk they were clearing out of the garage. But then I noticed the smell. It's not like that end of the parking lot smells like sunflowers and candy canes on a good day, but the smell that morning… it was like bad meat left in the sun too long. You know how some smells are so bad you can taste 'em in the back of your throat? This was like that. And then I open the dumpster, but my hand gets stuck on the lid. 'Cause the whole inside is covered in this weird black goop, and a few seconds after I touch it, my hand gets really hot and starts itching like crazy. And that freaked me out, 'cause what if this shit's some kind of biohazard or something? So I wiped my hands off on my pants best I could, and that's when I noticed the trash bag."

Abby raised an eyebrow at Simon. There'd been nothing about 'black goop' in the official report. Something else for the *Weird Shit* list.

Gurinder was still talking. "So I look at this trash bag, and then I see a hand poking out at the bottom. It was wearing Jenny's ring, and it had the same tattoo she had. 'Corinthians.'"

Simon nodded. Both Jenny's and Sonia's missing persons reports had listed a tattoo on the left wrist as an identifying mark. The word 'Corinthians' written in cursive script. However, the reports had failed to elaborate on any ring, so he asked about that next.

Gurinder shrugged. "I think it was like a church thing. It was this little signet ring with a cross and the letters 'S.C.' on it."

Simon double-checked the notes he'd copied from the police file. "'S.C.' Would this be St. Catherine's Anglican Church? Reverend Matthew Jansen?"

"You got it," said Gurinder. "Jenny went every Sunday. She was a member of this sort of youth group down there. Actually, so was that other girl, Sonia Whatsherface."

Abby jumped in. "What can you tell us about this group?"

"Reverend Jansen has this group he works with on the weekends and during the summer. At-risk teens and young adults, mostly. Lots of kids from out on the reservation. They do all kinds of work in the community, to give them purpose in life. At least, that's what Reverend Jansen's always saying. The signet rings are like a symbol for them. I sometimes saw Jenny around town, doing stuff like bake sales and community car washes and all that. Always wearing that damn ring."

Gurinder had little else to offer that wasn't in the report. After a chat with two other cashiers who had been on the July 4 morning shift, during which they learned nothing new, Abby and Simon headed back outside. They circled around the back of the store to a row of dumpsters beside the delivery entrance. Traces of tattered police tape still clung to the dumpster on the far left, where Jenny Styles' body had been discovered. Abby held her nose, gagging at the odour of sun-baked garbage, and said, "My turn, yeah?"

Simon got down on his hands and knees and started crawling around, peering closely at the ground beneath him. "Indeed. What Ms. Dhillon said about that 'black goop' has me thinking. Didn't you mention something like that in your dream?"

"Yeah, the House was covered in stuff like that, floor to ceiling."

"Clearly, our victims are being taken to the Harcourt House to be killed, and their bodies are being dumped in secondary locations. We need to know how they're being transported and why. You're the best magical radar we have, so I defer to you, young Henderson."

"Okay. I'll give it a shot." Abby turned away from Simon and closed her eyes. Growing up, her Gospel senses hadn't been something she had control over. But ever since she'd been training regularly at the Letterbox, she'd discovered that the perception part of her ESP was often most acute when she wasn't focused on it. If she was already in a heightened emotional state, she was much more receptive to signals from the other world.

Abby sipped in a few short, shallow breaths and tried to remember the sights and sounds of her shared dream with Will. She pictured the face of John Leland, her own personal bogeyman, and tried to squeeze her feet back into the metaphorical shoes of a thirteen-year-old girl standing petrified in front of her bathroom mirror.

The psychic alarm bells started clanging in her head and she opened her eyes. The world came into a sharper, clearer focus than before and her skin tingled with electricity. Her nerve endings worked themselves to the max, magnifying every sensation from the dry southern breeze on her neck to the smoke particles tickling her nostrils. She could hear the beat not only of her own heart, but of Simon's, twelve feet away.

Unfortunately, when every sense was heightened, *every* sense was heightened. The acrid tang of the lingering smoke, combined with the reek of the dumpsters, made Abby weak in the knees. Breathing exclusively through her mouth, she crouched down on her haunches and looked around carefully.

Everything changed when she got low to the ground. There was a sheet of cold drifting around the parking lot at knee height, and as soon as she entered that space, Abby seized up. A thorny, invisible fist wrapped itself around her heart and her guts and squeezed tight. She blinked, and wisps of smoky blackness rose from the ground, bucking and dancing like inky flames. They reminded Abby of a demon she'd once known, but really, they were the residue of a dark curse.

The smoke formed a rough trail that crept toward Jenny's dumpster. Holding her breath, Abby lay flat on her belly and reached underneath, and the fist squeezed tighter around her insides.

The source of the smoke was a thin shaft of wood, not more than five inches in length, with a custom carved handle. It looked like a longer piece had been snapped off it, and it made Abby's hand tingle the longer she held onto it. Gradually, the tingle grew to a slow burn, and Abby threw the shaft away, clutching her hand to her chest. The hyper-aware sensation faded away and her senses returned to their normal capacity.

Simon called over, "Did you find something?"

Abby stood and looked at her hand. Her palm was red and raw, with angry little welts rising in the area where she'd held the wood. "Yeah. Yeah, I found something. But I wouldn't touch it if I were you."

Simon joined Abby by the dumpster. "Are you okay?"

Abby winced as Simon prodded her hand. It itched and prickled with heat all the way from her fingertips to her wrists. "I hope so. I think that stupid thing burned me."

Simon looked toward the shaft of wood, which lay on the ground before them. "What, that?"

"Yeah. The thing's swimming in dark energy. I guess I had a… reaction to it."

"Hmmm…" Simon pulled a white cotton handkerchief from his back pocket and laid it over his hand, before picking up the wooden shaft. He then held it at eye level, and turned it over carefully. "Curious," he announced after a moment. "If I'm not much mistaken—and I rarely am—then this is wood from a tree in the genus *Taxus*." He rolled the shaft around some more before concluding, "My best guess would be *Taxus brevifolia*, the Pacific yew."

Abby blinked, confused. "Yew? I'm pretty sure yew trees aren't native to this part of BC."

Simon nodded. "You're quite right about that. If I'm remembering my botany correctly, the Pacific yew grows mostly near the West Coast."

"So, what the hell is this splinter doing here?"

Simon wrapped the handkerchief tightly around the piece of wood and stuck both in his back pocket. He then began to pace around the lot, a pensive hand on his chin.

Abby looked at him and said, "Um... Simon?"

Simon continued pacing and spoke to Abby without even looking at her. "You know, I might have a theory about this..."

"Any chance you could share it with the class?"

"Well, when I was a lad, many of the human magicians in the area where I grew up cultivated yew trees. The Vanguard of course never had much call for it, but those who used it absolutely swore by its mystical properties, said it even surpassed oak in its ability to store and conduct magical energy."

"Okay. So?"

"So those human magicians often used yew for the construction of their wands."

Abby blinked. "As in... magic wands. As in 'the blank chooses the wizard, Mr. Potter.'"

Simon nodded without a hint of irony. "Precisely, magic wands." He turned to Abby and explained, "You see, what separates the Vanguard from the human race is that we are naturally attuned to the mystical energies of the universe, the unexplained forces that make up True Magic. We can command these forces with minimal effort, and shape reality to our designs. Humans don't have that same affinity, so human magicians compensate by using enchanted objects and devices that attract and manipulate the magical energies for them. Those objects are your wands and charms and the like."

"So, what, wands are like magic prosthetics or something?"

"In a sense. Wands are amplifiers for a magician's own willpower and their emotional connection to the energies of the universe, which is what drives magic in the first place."

"Gotcha," Abby nodded. "So, if this is a piece of a wand or a staff, then we're looking at spell-work. No kind of demon, ghoul, vampire… Our killer is a human sorcerer. But that still doesn't explain how this splinter got out here."

"Despite what the films may tell you, wands often aren't very sturdy. It's perfectly easy to call too much power into a wand, so that it breaks when the spell is released. That's why talismans and staves are much more effective for offensive magic. My bet is our man broke his wand, tossed it in with Jenny's body, and then dumped them both here. When they pulled her from the dumpster, this fragment ended up on the ground and was forgotten."

Abby nodded. "Makes sense to me. So what now, Holmes? You want to talk to that Reverend Jansen and see what he knows?"

"Good guess. I imagine Leanne and Natalie have their hands full with Sonia Hall's family, and it will be a long while before we can begin the next phase of the operation."

Abby looked out to the western horizon and saw the morning light cutting a sharp outline around the Harcourt House's black gables. "Right… now that we've seen the secondary location, you want to check out the primary."

Simon winked. "Top of the class, Henderson."

CHAPTER 8

TIME OF THE PREACHER

ST. CATHERINE'S Anglican Church was a small, white wooden building with a forest green roof and steeple, standing on a lot that dominated most of the narrow cul-de-sac it occupied. A sloping churchyard pockmarked by white and grey grave markers dominated the left side of the street and a large parking lot stood opposite. A one-floor parochial house sat on the last lot by the corner, with a large Ford van—not unlike the one that had almost flattened Abby—parked in the driveway. As she and Simon turned onto the block, they spotted a tall, fair-haired man in his mid-50s struggling out the front door of the house with a bucket of soapy water in one hand and a washcloth in the other.

Abby cleared her throat and called to the man. "Excuse me? Are you Reverend Jansen?"

The man set down the bucket next to the van and looked up. He was built like a runner and dressed in ragged jeans and an old t-shirt covered in paint stains. "That is the rumour," he said with a smile. "You'll have to forgive the attire, but I was just about to give this old monster a wash." He patted the side of the van. "To what do I owe the pleasure, Constable...?"

On cue, Abby and Simon flashed their playing cards. "Henderson. Constable Abigail Henderson and Sergeant

Simon Lockhart. We've been seconded from Kelowna to assist on the Styles and Hall inquiries."

Reverend Jansen's smile dropped. "I see. I've already spoken with Sergeant Brady about this."

"Just being thorough. We won't keep you long."

The reverend sighed. "Oh, alright. Do you mind if we do this in the house?"

Abby smiled and made a gesture with her hand. "Lead the way, Reverend."

The reverend's house was neat and conservative. A stainless white couch sat under the front window, facing the TV and an IKEA coffee table. The walls and the carpet were the same shade of white. There was an end table next to one arm of the couch. A St. Catherine's signet ring sat on the table next to a framed photo of the reverend with two women — one was dark-haired and middle-aged, with large glasses and a plump maternal figure, and the other was young and fair-haired with a line of freckles across her nose.

The wall above the TV was covered with photos. In every one of them, the reverend was standing outside the church with a dozen or more teenagers and young adults. The portraits acted like a timeline, showing the different incarnations of Reverend Jansen's youth group over the past decade. Abby recognized several faces in the pictures as some of the same ones she'd seen around Delapore since they'd arrived. Here was the chubby girl with the nose piercing who'd been stocking shelves at the Safeway. There was the ginger-haired kid from the front desk at the motel, whom she'd caught staring at her boobs when she checked in. And there was Not-Yet-a-Constable Pruitt, wearing the exact same haircut she'd had at the police station.

"Lovely little spot you've picked out," said Simon. "Must be nice having such a short commute."

The reverend smiled. "I like to tell people I'm available day or night. It wouldn't do much good if someone needed spiritual guidance at three in the morning, and I had to drive from halfway across town. Plus, it's much more convenient for Grace if home and work are so close."

"Grace?"

"My daughter. I never like to be too far from her."

As Abby and Simon sat on the couch, Reverend Jansen brought a chair out from the kitchen and set it opposite. "What do you want to know?" he asked.

Abby took the lead this time. It had taken her some time to find her feet when she and Simon were at the Safeway, but now the investigator role was coming more and more easily to her. Thank God for all those crime novels she'd read in university… "We understand that Jenny Styles and Sonia Hall were both members of your youth group," she began. "Let's start there. How long had you known them?"

"Hmm… well, the Halls have been attending St. Catherine's since before Sonia was born. I think Sonia herself joined the group about seven or eight years ago, and a year after that, Jenny started coming with her."

"And how were Jenny and Sonia with the rest of the group? Was there anyone there they didn't get along with?"

"Good Lord, no. Jenny and Sonia were two of the most gracious people I've ever known. Incredibly hard workers. Everyone in the group adored them, and they were fully committed to the church. All the work we do in the community is on a purely volunteer basis, and every member of the group is free to attend as often or as little as they wish. The same goes for our group meetings on Saturday evenings. I don't think Jenny or Sonia missed a meeting or an event in all the time I knew them."

Abby shot Simon a furtive glance, and he shot it right back. Jenny and Sonia were starting to sound like the poster girls for 'too good to be true.'

"Do you know if either of them had any trouble at home?" asked Simon. "Would anyone in town have reason to hurt them?"

"Sonia didn't have any trouble that I was aware of. Her relationship with her parents was stable. She didn't have a serious boyfriend. I believe she was mostly focused on her schooling. She was planning to graduate at the end of the year," he added sadly.

"What about a non-serious boyfriend?" asked Abby. "Did she ever mention a casual relationship?"

"Not that I remember. But who wants to talk about boys with the local preacher?"

"You said *Sonia* didn't have any trouble. What about Jenny?"

Reverend Jansen nodded. "Jenny was... a different story. She was raised by a single mother, Barbara, out at the Little Bear trailer park. That's near the edge of town, about a fifteen-minute drive from the reservation. The trailer park is a bit... rough around the edges, compared to the rest of Delapore. The police keep a very close eye on it for a number of reasons. And even among the residents of Little Bear, Barbara Styles was... notorious.

"She passed away from an overdose shortly before Jenny first came to the group, and I believe that was a great motivator for Jenny. She was determined to make a difference, to be what her mother was not. She went to parties now and then, but it was always because Sonia dragged her along."

"Was Sonia at The Forge nightclub on July 1?" *I.e.*, Jenny Styles' last known location.

"The Canada Day party? Yes, she was. She came to me after Jenny's body was discovered. Poor thing was distraught. The two went over together, but Sonia left several hours before Jenny did. She kept saying that she'd killed Jenny, that this wouldn't have happened if she hadn't brought Jenny to The Forge. I did my best to calm her down, but I don't know if I got through to her." He cleared his throat and rubbed a hand over his eyes. "I suppose I won't ever know now."

"Do you mind telling us where you were the night of July 1?" asked Abby. "Or the night of July 19?" AKA, the night Sonia Hall disappeared.

The reverend shrugged. "I was here with my daughter both nights."

"Can your daughter confirm this?"

He sighed. "It's… not that simple, I'm afraid." Without another word, Reverend Jansen stood and beckoned for Simon and Abby to follow him down the hall. The door at the end was partially open, and David Attenborough was speaking softly on the other side.

The fair-haired girl from the photo was lying on the bed, propped up on a wall of pillows so she could sit up and look at the TV on the opposite wall. It was playing a nature documentary with the volume low. The subject appeared to be marine life. When Reverend Jansen came into the room, the girl did not look up. But she didn't seem to respond to David Attenborough either.

"This is Grace."

At the mention of her name, the girl gave a little sigh. She tilted her head to the door, but she didn't make eye contact with any of them. Abby noticed the wheelchair in the far corner of the room and started to get the picture.

The reverend went and sat on the bed. He put a hand under Grace's head and gently turned her to face the TV again. "There was… an accident a few years ago. Grace suffered serious brain damage. She hasn't said a word in five years. When I'm not at the church, I'm here with her."

"Is there anyone else who could take care of her? Your wife or a caregiver?"

Reverend Jansen shook his head. "We do have a caregiver, but she isn't full-time. I can only afford to have her in three days a week. The Anglican Church isn't exactly Bay Street. As for my wife, well… Claudia looked after our girl for over a year after the accident, but the emotional toll… our marriage just couldn't survive. She moved to Calgary three summers ago. Credit where it's due, she has a good life there."

Abby nodded at Grace. "So this is a full-time job."

"Just about. At the end of any given week, I always count myself lucky if I've put in less than 80 hours between my duties at the church and my duties here."

"That must be very hard for you."

The reverend brushed a few loose hairs out of Grace's eyes and stroked her forehead. She cooed a little. It was probably as close as she ever got to a 'thank you.' "It could have been so, so much worse," the reverend said. "Grace was in a coma for nine days after the accident. Claudia and I didn't know if she'd ever wake up. She's my miracle girl." He kissed her on the forehead and whispered, "O death, where is your victory? O death, where is your sting?"

"1 Corinthians," said Simon. "Isn't it?"

Reverend Jansen looked up and smiled. "Well done, Sergeant. Chapter 15, verse 55. Are you a religious man?"

Simon shook his head affably. "Not your religion, I'm afraid. Though I have… dabbled in a few holy texts. 'Behold, I tell you a mystery: we shall not all sleep,' *et cetera*."

"One of my favourite passages. It was my reading the first Sunday service after Grace's accident."

"Is that where the tattoos came from?" Abby asked suddenly. "The ones that Jenny and Sonia wore."

The reverend nodded. "They were Sonia's idea. A sign of respect and a reminder of God's mercy."

Abby looked at the girl on the bed and had to wonder about that last part. Mercy might have been letting her slip away while she was in the coma.

The reverend patted Grace's hand and stood up. "I know how this looks. Two of my group members dead. Me without an alibi. But I didn't hurt Jenny or Sonia. I could never hurt any of my children."

Abby glanced at Reverend Jansen's aura and tried to get a reading. The cold, thorny sensation of black magic swept over her instantly and her stomach did a backflip. She stumbled back against the doorframe and shut her eyes before she could process the reverend's aura. The light above them flickered and the image on the TV stuttered, but Reverend Jansen seemed not to notice.

"Problem, Constable?"

Abby opened her eyes. Reverend Jansen was staring at her, and the cold sensation was still there. She felt sick, and she couldn't concentrate on his aura for more than a second or two. A part of her had to wonder if that was by design.

She forced a smile and straightened up. "I'm fine. This heat just… has me a little light-headed. Not the first time today I've felt like this."

The reverend nodded. "I was the same yesterday. Would you care for a glass of water?"

"I'll be okay. We've probably wasted enough of your time as is." She cast her eyes over to Simon in a look that said *Let's get the hell out of here.* He tilted his head in a subtle nod of understanding.

"Suit yourself," said Reverend Jansen. "I'll show you to the door."

He led them back down the hall. Abby was still feeling queasy, and when they reached the living room, a chill ran up her spine. But she was pretty sure that didn't have anything to do with black magic.

It had everything to do with the two cops standing in the doorway, blocking the light from outside. Reverend Jansen paused when he saw them, and Abby almost bumped into him. "Constable Eckhart! Constable Foley! Is there something I can do for you?"

"Sorry to bother you, Reverend. The door was open. Do you mind if we talk to you for a minute?" Eckhart asked.

"I suppose not. Your colleagues here were just leaving."

Foley cocked his head like a confused dog. "Colleagues?"

Reverend Jansen stepped aside to let Abby and Simon past. "From the city."

Eckhart pursed his lips and met Abby's eye. "Right. *Those* colleagues." She could tell from the look on his face that he didn't want to make a scene in front of the reverend, but she had a feeling her and Simon's cover had just been blown wide open. No doubt Eckhart would be checking their identities as soon as he had a free moment, and then there'd be a half-dozen squad cars waiting at the motel to arrest them all for impersonation.

Simon took Abby's hand and dragged her out of the house as fast as he could while still being subtle. "Yes, well, I think we have everything we need. We'll be in touch if anything comes up, Reverend. Constables, we leave him in your capable hands."

As she squeezed out the door, Abby caught Eckhart giving her the side-eye. The thorny sensation faded as she reached the end of the driveway, but the goosebumps and the sweaty palms remained.

*****

George Hall yawned as he sat down at the kitchen table. "Is this going to take very long, Sergeant…?"

"Arnaud," said Natalie. She tugged at the bracer on her right arm. Why did Simon always have to make the damn things so tight?

Leanne gave the man a reassuring smile and said, "We won't keep you long, Mr. Hall. We just wanted to ask you a few questions about your daughter."

George Hall leaned back in his chair and rubbed a hand over his unshaved jaw. He'd still been in bed when Leanne and Natalie showed up on his front step. "I've said everything I have to say to the local cops. Two or three times, now," he added with a yawn.

"We're just dotting some I's. You know how it is."

"Not really. I own a deli."

"When was the last time you spoke with your daughter?" Natalie asked. She kept fiddling impatiently with the bracer, and Leanne gave her a firm kick under the table to get her to stop.

George Hall looked at the two like they had twice the normal number of heads between them. Natalie gave him a smile that was somewhere between *Don't worry, you can trust me* and *I dare you to call bullshit.* Leanne saw the twinkle of menace in Natalie's smile and gave her another kick. Her eyes pleaded with Natalie to take it easy.

Natalie scowled at Leanne and cooled off. "So when was it you last spoke to Sonia?"

George Hall blinked and looked at the table. "An hour before she disappeared. She'd been taking summer courses this year for one of her degree requirements. She called to say her last class would be running late. Asked if I could pick her up at the bus stop at Cates and Springfield. It's only a ten-minute walk from here, but after what happened to Jenny and that Prudhomme boy… she was terrified to go out at night by herself. I told her of course I'd pick her up, and I arranged to meet her at the bus stop at ten to ten." He rubbed a hand over his eyes and stifled a sob. Tried to turn it into a cough. "I never saw her again," he croaked.

"And can you think of anyone who would have had a reason to hurt her?" Natalie asked.

He sobbed again. "No. I couldn't even believe it. Who could hurt my Sonia? I could see it happening to Jenny Styles or that Prudhomme boy. But not Sonia!"

"What do you mean?" asked Leanne. "You could see it happening to them?"

George Hall sniffed. "Oh God, I shouldn't say that. That sounds horrible. All I mean is… they were troubled. Broken homes. Jenny's mother used drugs. OD'd when Jenny was 17. David Prudhomme's father has been in and out of jail for 20 years, and he's had legal troubles himself. Shoplifting, DUI. What I mean to say is… I could understand if… things went badly for them… but Sonia was good!"

"Mr. Hall, I hope you're not suggesting that Jenny Styles and David Prudhomme deserved what happened to them because of how they were brought up."

George Hall shook his head and ran a hand through his hair. "God, no, I didn't mean it like that! I just meant I didn't know who'd want to hurt my daughter. Diane—my wife—thought it might have something to do with Grace, but I can't see it."

"Who's Grace?"

"Grace Jansen. Reverend Jansen's daughter, over at St. Catherine's Anglican."

"He's the one who runs the youth group that Sonia was a part of?"

George Hall nodded. "Sonia, Jenny, and Grace all knew each other for years. Thick as thieves. But Grace was a rebel. She was hooked on drugs and alcohol since she was 16. Reverend Jansen did everything he could to straighten her out. Nothing worked. She fell so far that the girls eventually cut ties with her completely. One night she tried to drive home after a party at the local club and…" He shrugged sadly. "She wrapped her car around a tree six blocks from her house. Serious head trauma. She's been a vegetable ever since."

"Why would your wife think this has something to do with Sonia's death?"

"She believes the reverend is holding some sort of grudge. Sonia and Jenny were at that party, and they could have stopped Grace from getting behind the wheel. They didn't. My wife thinks Reverend Jansen is bitter because the crash was preventable. If Grace's friends had been more patient with her and had given her a hand when she needed it, she might not be in a wheelchair. For what it's worth, my wife watches too many crime documentaries."

"Where's your wife now?"

"Working. She's an ER nurse in the city. That's why Sonia wants to go into nursing." He rubbed his eyes and held back a sob. "Wanted."

"That must be hard," said Leanne. "Having to work ER after something like this."

"It keeps her mind busy. Keeps her from jumping at shadows. I love Diane, but everything has to be a conspiracy for her. She still won't admit the body in the morgue is really Sonia."

"Really?"

"There was some mix-up or disagreement at the morgue. The coroner's first estimate for time of death was over three weeks before the body was discovered. But Sonia disappeared on the 19th. Fourteen days ago."

*****

The walk back to the motel took Abby and Simon straight through Hudson Park. They stopped on the footbridge for a moment to watch the lazy trickle of the creek.

"What did you sense in that house?" Simon asked, not looking away from the water.

"It's that obvious, is it?"

"Was it black magic?"

"Yeah. Same as I felt when we found that wand fragment. I tried to have a look in Reverend Jansen's aura and I just got slammed."

"How do you feel now?"

She swallowed. "Not great, honestly. Bit better than I was, but…" She trailed off and looked to the creek's shallow bank. A scrap of police tape fluttered from a low tree branch, and wisps of inky blackness rippled across the water. The thorny, clammy fist wrapped around her guts and gave them a good shake. She staggered back from the railing and clutched her stomach. "Jesus!"

"What is it?"

She blinked. The smoke bobbed on the water below them, higher and more erratic than it had been at the Safeway. Fighting a wave of nausea, Abby croaked, "This is where they found Sonia Hall. I'm sure of it." She blinked and looked over the railing again, tracking the smoke to where it was thickest, about six or seven feet off the bank.

She leaned on Simon as she took off her socks and shoes and gave him no explanation or chance to protest when she climbed over the railing and jumped the six feet into the creek.

The water went up to her hips. It was freezing and silty, and the shock of the landing only made her more nauseous. She saw smoke beneath the surface, and the thorny fist shook her guts like a pair of maracas. Something was here, some physical fragment of the Harcourt House or of Sonia Hall. Whatever it was, she had to find it fast, or she was going to throw up everything she'd eaten in the last week.

She waded forward, trying to ignore the squidgy feeling of the mud on the creek bed as it squished between her toes. She looked down into the water and traced the shadows to their source, a smooth black pebble the size of a toonie. The dark magic coming off it looked like an oil gusher, and she could feel her head getting lighter and her stomach more nervous by the second. She plunged her hand into the water, fished out the pebble, and held it up to the sunlight. She could see a black-and-orange wing poking out of a gap in the surface, and she remembered the black gunk from her dream. This was the same stuff, dried and congealed around the husk of a dead cicada.

Abby worked the artifact around between her fingers. She felt a mounting pressure in the back of her head and her nose started to bleed as a vision overcame her. She rocked on the balls of her feet and went weak in the knees, but she tightened her grip on the dead bug.

Boom! Abby felt a small explosion in her head, and suddenly she wasn't in the creek anymore. She was standing on the shore of Okanagan Lake in the middle of the night, underneath a fiery moon that shone through a smoky haze. There was a tingle of electricity in the air around her, and then she heard a loud buzzing some 50 feet above the water.

Looking toward the source of the noise, Abby saw a band of white sparks flitting across the sky. The electric sensation grew stronger, and then an orb of white light exploded in front of the moon, with a force that blew Abby off her feet. The space around the orb seemed to bend and lengthen like in a funhouse mirror, and the buzzing of cicadas filled the air.

Abby felt a tug at her shoulders, and she realized the white orb was pulling her toward it, like a whirlpool in spacetime. She grabbed a tree trunk with both hands and dug her heels into the ground where she stood. After a few moments, the light dimmed and the pulling sensation stopped. She could see a faint human outline within the orb, pushing at a heavy-duty trash bag.

The figure and the orb disappeared, and Abby tracked the trash bag's movement as it plummeted into the lake. It ripped on contact with the water, and a human arm poked out. A noxious black-and-green syrup leaked into the lake, and there were the faint outlines of several twitching, half-drowned cicadas floating in the sludge. Abby retched as the smell hit her, and she dropped the chunk of dried muck she was holding.

"Abby? Abby, I say, Abby, are you okay?"

She blinked away the vision and found herself flat on her back at the edge of the creek. Her shorts and the back of her shirt were soaking, and Simon was kneeling over her, barefoot and likewise drenched from the waist down. She sat up and gave her head a shake. "Simon? What happened?"

"You passed out. Went right down, flat on your back in the middle of the creek." He checked his watch and added, "Almost five minutes ago, I hasten to add."

Abby massaged her forehead with one hand and wiped away her nosebleed with the other. "Ugh. Dammit." She sat with her head between her knees for a few moments until the world stopped spinning, and gradually managed to tell Simon what she had seen.

"And how did this vision come about?" Simon asked. "What was that object you found in the creek?"

Abby looked down and tapped the petrified cicada with her foot. "That. I think I probably had some kind of psychometric response to it."

Simon crouched down and picked up the chunk of dried muck. "I'd say that's a fair assumption..." He worked the thing over in his hand a few times and murmured, "My word..."

"What's up?" Abby crouched beside him.

"If I didn't know better, I'd say this was... ectoplasm!"

"Ectoplasm? Like, ghost goop?"

Simon rolled his eyes. "That's rather a crude analysis, Abigail. Ectoplasm is a substance generated in the Elsewhere, *by* the Elsewhere. You see, all matter in the spirit world is fundamentally unlike anything that exists in the mortal world. When an object from our world enters the spirit realm, it will leave bits of itself behind. And because the bits from the two worlds are so different, they can react quite violently with one another. They lose mass and form, or they clump together and become charged with Elsewhere energy. They decompose and... congeal into a slurry that's not quite native to either realm. Ectoplasm is the by-product of natural, Middangeard-born matter colliding with Elsewhere matter."

"That's what that black goo is, isn't it? It's ectoplasm."

"Almost certainly." He stood and stroked his chin, pacing back and forth along the bank. "You know, I think… I think I might be starting to work this out. Yes, an idea is presenting itself. But I'll need to gather some more evidence to confirm my theory. Come nightfall, we need to get up to the Harcourt House."

"I'm all yours. But can we head back to the motel first? These wet undies are kind of starting to chafe."

Simon looked down at his own wet jeans. "Well, that goes without saying."

The two walked briskly back the way they had come. Just as they reached the main entrance to the park, Abby's Vokarion crystal hummed under her shirt. "Hello, Abby?" It was Leanne.

"What's up, Lee? How did you and Natalie get along?"

"Not too badly," Natalie chimed in. "We just talked to Sonia Hall's dad. We were about to check in on David Prudhomme's aunt."

"You get anything useful from the dad?"

"Possibly," Leanne said. "He mentioned an angle we might want to consider." She repeated what George Hall had said about Grace and Reverend Jansen.

"Wait, this is Matthew Jansen?" Abby asked. "At St. Catherine's Anglican?"

"Yeah. Why?"

"Simon and I already talked to him. I got a really bad vibe off him when we were leaving. And he didn't say anything about Grace being a wild child."

"We'll have to keep an eye on this guy," said Natalie. "We also got the names of the other youth group members. We can shake a few more trees and see what falls out. Abby might get another whammy."

"That's a good plan, but we might need to take it slow. Simon and I had a close call at Reverend Jansen's house. We're heading back to the motel now, so you two do what you can, and then meet us there. We need to regroup before we check out the Harcourt House."

CHAPTER 9

THEY ALWAYS GET THEIR MAN

"PLEASE! WHY are you doing this? My husband didn't do anything!"

As Mona entered the garage of the big blue house on Clayborn Road, she could hear Inspector Pembroke and Superintendent Campbell in the front hall, tag-teaming Shirley Grover with their best Calm Voices. (Relax, ma'am. We're not accusing your husband of anything. We have to explore every possibility. *Et cetera.*)

Bill Grover's wife had been in hysterics all night. The kids, Eric and Jessica, would be sitting together in Eric's room upstairs, Mona guessed. Door shut tight, pretending they couldn't hear their mom's breakdown. As she flicked the lights on with one nitrile-gloved hand, Mona wished she could huddle in there with them. Eric Grover had been one of the first kids in Delapore who had actually extended a friendly hand to Will when Mona and he first moved here, and Bill and Shirley had been the same for Mona herself. How many dinners had she and her son eaten in this house? How many game nights had there been?

"First you won't release his body!" Shirley was screaming. "Now this? Why can't you leave our family alone, Phil? Why can't you leave us alone?"

The garage was big enough for two cars, but half of it had been converted into a home workshop. A rack of heavy-duty carpenter's equipment lined one wall, and the joining wall had been extended out to make room for a drill press, a table saw, a belt sander, and a few other machines that Mona only vaguely recognized from her high school shop classes. The floor was spotless, and a quick check of the cupboard in the corner revealed two brooms, a vacuum cleaner, and two black garbage bags stuffed with what Mona presumed was sawdust. Her dee-you-eye shone on a tarry black footprint at the base of the cupboard and she bent down for a closer look. The smell from it was like a slap in the face, and Mona recalled that she had smelled the same smell when they'd hauled Jenny Styles' body out of that dumpster.

She gave herself a second to recover from the smell, and then she noticed the garbage bags. The knot on one of them was misshapen and there were stretch marks on the plastic, as if it had been pulled open and then re-tied in a hurry. She lifted that bag out of the cupboard, moved to a clear spot on the floor, and undid the knot. Then she stuck the dee-you-eye light between her teeth, shoved her hands into the mound of sawdust and wood shavings, and had a good rummage.

Shirley Grover had stopped cussing out the superintendent. That was something. Now the only sounds from inside the house were a few muffled, croaking sobs and the groan of RCMP leather on the Grovers' hardwood floors. If Mona was honest, she preferred the cussing out. At least that way it was harder for her to think and reflect on this whole mess.

She fished something out and very gently brushed the sawdust off it back into the garbage bag. If the forensics crew had to get in here later, they wouldn't appreciate her dirtying up the nice clean floor.

She turned the thing over in her hands and riffled the pages with her thumb. It was a small journal, not much bigger than the notepad she carried in the pocket of her uniform vest, but much, much older. She opened the book to a random page and, just as her son had done many weeks ago, stared in bemusement at the mad scrawlings on the page.

BUUUUUZZZZZ. Mona looked up. There were insects beating their wings all around her. Insects she couldn't see. Under the workbench, behind the walls, in the sky outside.

In the back of her head, a voice urged her to turn the page. *Do it. Know me, Mona August. Know what I am.*

Mona's hand shook at the corner of the page. She didn't want to, but she flipped it anyway.

BAM! An image flashed at her from within the text, like a Magic Eye poster drawn by a mental patient. It was the Harcourt House, with a midday sun shining behind it. But the House wasn't in Pearson Heights now. It was floating some two hundred feet up in the open sky, with a mound of earth dangling from its foundations like dirt in a backhoe.

BAM! Mona flipped the page again and saw an empty coffin spilling out of a smashed limestone tomb.

BAM! One more turn of the page, and there was Jenny Styles. Spread-eagle and hovering just below a wooden ceiling, screaming her head off as her throat opened like a zipper. Mid-scream, Jenny Styles became David Prudhomme, who became Sonia Hall. *One little, two little, three little Indians*, as Mona Brady's Nana used to say.

She became aware of her right thumb and forefinger, worrying the top corner of the page. The voice in her head got louder. *Yes. Know me. Know what I am. Let me in, Mona. You can get me to him. Just let me in.*

Both hands shook as she turned over the next page. But it wasn't her making the choice anymore. It was the voice in her head. *Keep looking. Keep reading. Know me!*

She wanted to. Yes, yes, she wanted to know! She wanted to turn page after page and know everything! She *needed* to know!

But then, out of the corner of her eye, Mona saw him. The man from the Little Bear trailer park. The man with the axe. He leaned down and whispered, "Don't take the book, Mona. Put it down."

Mona gasped. Her fingers released the page mid-turn, and it fluttered back to its starting position. The man with the axe repeated, "Put the book down. Now." His voice was soft but firm. Tough, without being loud. Mona did as she was told and dropped the book.

And that was it. No more cicadas. The buzzing stopped, the Magic Eye visions stopped, and Mona was alone in the room. The ceiling light died with a *pop*, leaving her in darkness. Mona's hands were shaking and her nose—it took her a few seconds to notice this—was bleeding.

Mona sniffed and stood up. Stuck the penlight between her teeth for illumination. She grabbed the roll of paper towels sitting on the top shelf of the cupboard and wiped her nose with one. That couldn't have just happened. It was impossible. Worse than that, it was unnatural. So, if it was impossible, then it hadn't happened, right? That was the logical answer. She'd been hallucinating, obviously. The daytime temperature had been sitting comfortably above 30 degrees for weeks now, and the smoke from the southern fires was causing all kinds of air-quality issues. Mona was overheated and out of breath, and her brain had played a stupid practical joke on her.

Yeah, and if a frog had wings, it wouldn't bump its ass when it hopped. That was another of Nana Sophie's old gems.

Mona discarded the bloody paper towel in the big green garbage bin on the other side of the garage and then looked at the little book, sitting so innocently on the floor. She couldn't take it to her superiors. No way in Hell. They wouldn't believe what she'd seen. Or worse, they might. What would they see when they opened it? What secrets would be revealed? Would any of them hear the voice telling them to keep reading?

But she couldn't leave it here, either. Shirley and the kids were already reeling after Bill's death. If one of them saw what Mona had just seen... then what? More cicadas? More screaming in the library parking lot? No. She couldn't say a word about this to Campbell, or to Pembroke, or to Shirley Grover. This had to be her cross alone.

Listening for any noise from the house, Mona tore off a length of paper towel and gingerly wrapped up the little book like a pork chop fresh from the butcher. Then, she undid the Velcro straps on her bulletproof vest and reached up underneath to unbutton her uniform shirt.

It was an old joke that the women in the August family had always been built wide and low to the ground. Nana Sophie used to say it was harder to knock 'em down that way. As Mona jammed the book down the front of her waistband and felt the paper towel rasp against her stomach, she thought, *What's one more love handle between friends?* She fixed up her uniform and patted herself down. The bulge was nowhere close to obvious. As long as she didn't have to do any jumping jacks before the end of her shift, she could smuggle the book home, away from the prying eyes of her colleagues. Then she'd burn it, or bury it, or rip out the pages and flush them down the toilet.

Mona Brady was a good cop. She was. *Maintiens le droit,* that was the Force's motto. Maintain the right. Surely, she would maintain more right by ensuring this book never again saw the light of day than she would by bringing it to Campbell. The whole town would probably sleep a lot sounder if they never knew this kind of crap existed.

Just in case, Mona tightened her belt by an extra notch and winced as the book pressed on her bladder. Then she pulled the radio from her vest. "Pruitt? Mona. How are we doing so far?"

"Nothing yet. Rickards and I just swept the living room, and Boyd and McDonald got the kitchen. They're both clean.

Pang and Innes say the upstairs bathroom and bedrooms are clean. Eckhart's doing the downstairs bathroom right now, and Evans and Foley are just starting on the basement."

"Alright. I've got a shoe print out here in the garage. I need a camera and a fingerprinting kit, and I want the garage taped off now. We might be able to get an impression. And bring some flashlights. The ceiling bulbs are dead out here."

"Roger that. You find anything else out there?"

"Negative. Just wine bottles and sawdust."

Mona Brady was a good cop. She *was*.

CHAPTER 10

THE HARCOURT HOUSE

BY ONE o'clock on Sunday morning, Delapore was all but closed for business. Natalie kept the headlights off as the Thunderbird crept through Pearson Heights, and parked the car in a cul-de-sac at the top, near where the gravel path up to the Harcourt House began. Simon led the way, clutching an old leather doctor's bag in his off hand. The bag was filled with everything they needed for a ghost hunt, including three tennis ball tubes full of Simon's proprietary mix of salt, grave dirt, and iron filings.

These tennis ball tubes were the best defence they had against the spirits of the dead. Ghosts often fought hard to reclaim any reminder of life that they could, but the flipside of this was that they abhorred reminders of death. Soil dug from the grounds of a churchyard or cemetery symbolised the open grave; iron reminded a ghost of the nails on their coffin; and salt was a natural desiccant. It took the moisture from a body and left behind only the husk of something that had been.

In Simon's dominant hand was the group's guiding light. Confusingly enough, this was a third hand. The Hand of Glory was the severed, mummified appendage of a hanged criminal, with five dry wicks stuck in under the fingernails, enchanted to give light only to the person or persons who had lit the match. The four weren't expecting to be seen, but just in case they were, they'd all taken up the enchanted leather bracers and Skeleton Cards that let them pass for officers of the law.

As the group reached the high fence around the property, Simon passed the satchel to Natalie and rummaged around in the front of his shirt, revealing the Vokarion crystal that hung around his neck. "Right," he whispered, "before we go in, I think we should do a radio check. We don't know what might be waiting for us inside."

Everyone adjusted the crystals around their own necks, then closed their eyes and concentrated. After a moment's silence, Simon's crystal began to glow and pulsate with energy as it repeated the words he was thinking: "Check one, check two... Everyone online?"

"Yes," said Natalie's crystal.

"Good to go," answered Leanne.

Simon opened one eye and looked at Abby impatiently. She still had her eyes closed and her face was screwed up in concentration. "Abby?" he said.

Abby's crystal was silent for a moment. Then it began to glow as the first verse of Idle Eyes' "Tokyo Rose" filled the night.

"Oh, for heaven's sake..." Simon snapped his fingers in front of Abby's face and frowned. "Abby!"

Abby opened her eyes and grinned sheepishly. "Sorry. I've had that song stuck in my head all week."

Simon gave her a weary look and said, "Right, we're all linked up then. Let's hop to it!"

There was a gate on the south side of the fence, installed in case the town ever worked up the nerve to start demolition. Two weather-beaten chains looped through the gate and the fencing beside it, and the whole thing was secured with a large padlock older than Will Brady. Simon inspected the padlock and held the Hand close to it. "Hmm. Curious..."

"What's curious?" Abby whispered.

"This lock's been disturbed recently. Look at these scratches by the keyhole." He traced the Hand of Glory down, illuminating a small scrap of dark fabric caught on the bottom of the chain link. There were a few spots of dried blood and dusty half-footprints dotting the ground in front of the lock as well.

"These prints haven't been here long," said Natalie. She had brushed Simon and the girls back far enough that they wouldn't disturb the scene any more, and was now on her knees to get a closer look. "Hard to tell, but my guess would be two, three days. Definitely the prints of a grown man, too."

"The killer?" Leanne gulped.

"Could be. We have to be careful in there."

Simon nodded and raised the Hand of Glory. He put his free hand over the old chains and whispered softly.

"Open, o lock
For the Dead Man's knock!
Thou bolt, thou bar, and band,
Now move, now swerve,
For muscle and nerve.
The spell of the Dead Man's hand!"

The chains rattled for a few seconds and then went still again. Then the lock opened and fell to the ground with a *thunk*. The chains uncoiled and snaked to the ground, and the gate opened with a creak.

Moving as one, the four slowly crept around to the front porch and crossed the threshold into the Harcourt House. When they were all inside, Simon turned and pointed the Hand of Glory back at the open door. He muttered a few magic words, and it creaked shut.

No sooner had the door bumped against its frame than Leanne shivered and blew on her hands. "Brrrr. Is it just me, or did it just get a *lot* colder in here?"

Abby crossed her arms tightly and stamped her feet on the wooden floor. "It's n-n-not just y-you," she said. "It's like a m-m-meat locker in h-here."

Simon smiled a wide, toothy smile and raised the Hand of Glory to eye level. "Brilliant. This is *just* what we need!"

"H-how is th-this b-b-brilliant?" Leanne asked.

"Look at the flame!" Simon thrust the Hand of Glory toward Leanne and gestured at the flames. They were dancing as if in a high wind, though there was none in the House. "The energies in this place are shifting. Something's awake."

They crossed into the den and Simon planted the Hand of Glory on the mantel above the fireplace. He dumped his satchel out on the floor, grabbed a piece of chalk from the pile of stuff, and started issuing instructions to the other three. He passed around the tennis ball tubes and outlined a chalk circle on the floor around the couch.

This done, Leanne shook out a line of salt and grave dirt over the chalk. Natalie and Abby poured out more of the same in the doorways, along the window sill, and in front of the crumbling chimney, while Simon turned one of the armchairs to face the room at large and drew another circle around it. For a few moments after, he hustled around the room in a low crouch, chanting to himself and rapping on the floor. His eyes and fingertips crackled with blue electricity as he infused his circles with defensive magic. Natalie rolled her eyes a little, and then went searching in the satchel for some more practical defensive measures: a long machete in a battered leather sheath, and an antique Webley revolver in a custom shoulder holster. She strapped the machete to her leg, loaded the Webley from a box of cartridges in the satchel, and then passed the gun to Abby.

Simon completed the last of his spells and hopped back up. "Right, nothing's going to be getting in *here* without my say-so." He dusted off his hands and adjusted his waistcoat in a *look-at-me-aren't-I-so-terribly-clever* kind of way.

"And we're sure all of this is kosher, yeah?" Leanne asked. "If we summon up anything, it's not going to come through the barriers and turn us inside out?"

"We just have to be careful not to break any of the lines, and the ghosts won't be able to touch us," Simon said. "Trust me, Leanne, it's all perfectly safe."

"Yeah, you said that last time, too, and Abby nearly got her mind ripped to pieces by a shadow demon."

Simon harrumphed. "Your boundless optimism never fails to inspire, Ms. Waller."

Leanne stuck her tongue out at him, but they were both smiling while she did.

Abby chuckled. "Okay, children, let's quit screwing around. We have a job to do."

"Indeed we do," Simon nodded. He retrieved a dented blue thermos from the satchel and handed it to Abby. She sat down in the encircled chair and unscrewed the top of the flask. The liquid that she poured into the little cup was thick and green like pea soup, and smelled like a spice rack downwind of a landfill. Simon's own homebrewed meditation aid.

"*Slàinte mhath*," Abby said, raising the cup. Then, she knocked back the green concoction in a single gulp and closed her eyes. The potion did its work quick, and she went still as a statue. If not for the slow but steady heave of her bosom, she might have been dead. But while her body was slack, her mind was working twice as hard as it entered the Bridge.

The Bridge was a deep, magical trance achievable only through singular mental focus. When in the Bridge, a Gospel could detach their mind from their physical body and temporarily project their consciousness into the Elsewhere, which was the common name for the spirit world. In the Elsewhere, the Gospel could call forth and communicate with the spirits of the dead, reach out and enter the minds of other living beings, or even offer their own body as a vessel to a spirit being. Theoretically, Abby could have Bridged from anywhere in Delapore and attempted to contact one of the Harcourts, but she stood the best chance of getting through to one of them if she went where their spiritual energy was strongest.

Simon threw himself onto the couch, which expelled a large cloud of dust around him that made him cough. "Blimey, I should think this place would certainly be terrifying for an asthmatic." Then he looked at Natalie and Leanne and patted the cushion beside him. "Well, come on, you two. Don't want to be outside the circle when the ghosts show up."

As Leanne and Natalie sat next to Simon, Abby's Vokarion crystal began to glow against her chest, as her spirit-self announced its entry to the Elsewhere in the traditional way. "My name is Abigail Margaret Henderson, of the line of the Gospels. My father was Donald Richard Henderson, himself the son of Philip Henderson. From these names have I learnt the wisdom of my ancestors. From these names do I draw strength. I offer these names now to that noble witness, the ancient Countenance of the High Celestial!"

Simon checked his pocket watch. "We should see some activity any minute now."

The telepathic link to Abby's mind continued: "I seek the counsel of one who cannot lie at rest, a soul taken from the mortal life before their natural time. I would speak with one of the name of Harcourt. Josiah, Isaac, Hector, Olivia. Spirits, I you name. In the name of the Holy Witness, the Earth-maker and the Glory-giver, I implore you to reveal yourselves, that one in the future might gain wisdom from the past."

There was silence. Abby sat slumped in the armchair, mindless, while Simon and the others watched her intently. After a moment, Simon cleared his throat. "There, er, there should be something happening shortly." Another two minutes passed. "Any minute now," he insisted. Five minutes later, he was impatiently winding his watch when a noise caught his attention.

Boom.

Leanne jumped on the couch and looked around the room. "What was that?"

"It came from upstairs," Natalie said. "Whatever it is, it sounds big."

Boom.

Simon clapped his hands, bouncing on the edge of his seat. "Ah, this is what we've been waiting for!"

BOOM.

Natalie looked up at the ceiling. "Is it just me, or does it sound like it's getting closer?"

Leanne looked to the floor and gulped. "Uh… guys?"

Simon and Natalie followed Leanne's direction and looked to the floor, where Simon's discarded supplies were hopping around like dust bunnies in an earthquake. On the mantelpiece, the Hand of Glory began to wobble and the blue flames leapt higher.

BOOOOOOM! The entire den shook, making ragdolls of the three of them. As they scrambled to disentangle themselves from one another, Simon looked up and gasped. "Crikey!"

"What is it? What?" Leanne asked as she turned to look in the same direction. Her next thought died on her lips, as little more than a frightened moan of air rushed out of her lungs. She crawled across the couch and crossed herself frantically, putting as much distance between herself and the horrid sight as she could.

In the doorway to the front hall, just on the other side of a line made of salt and iron shavings, a large figure in a shabby green cloak stood watching the trio on the couch. Its stooping shoulders rose and fell as it snorted hot, angry breaths at the intruders, and its pink tail twitched.

"What the hell is that thing?" Natalie said.

"I presume that is Master William's 'Rat King,'" said Simon.

The Rat King opened his mouth and screeched. Simon went rigid and dug his nails into the tattered fabric backing of the couch. "Stay calm, everyone. Just stay within the circle."

The Rat King took a step forward, and sparks of blue lightning crackled in the doorway. He bounced back like a crow striking a window and snarled at the untouchable intruders.

"Yes, you're learning the rules, aren't you, big man?" Simon murmured as the Rat King paced in the entrance hall. "These are no ordinary ghost hunters, are they? But then, I rather think you're no ordinary ghost."

The Rat King slammed his fist on the invisible wall and screeched through a wave of sparks. He nudged the line of salt with his toe, got a nasty zap, and growled in frustration. Then he looked down at the floor and the proverbial lightbulb went off. Suddenly, he jumped on the spot and shook the den when he landed. He did the same thing again. And again. On the fourth jump, the floorboards surrendered with a loud *crack*, spraying salt and iron everywhere. Then the Rat King bared his yellow teeth and lurched into the den. Simon looked in the beast's blazing red eyes, then to the large sack in his dominant hand, and moaned, "Oh, sod."

The Rat King howled and battered the floor with his claws. The wood cleaved like thin ice on the first day of spring, all the way down the middle of the room and through the circles Simon had made on the floor.

"Everybody: MOVE!" Simon hollered.

The Rat King lunged. Natalie met him halfway and dug her machete into one of his thick legs, coating the blade in ectoplasm. She caught his swiping claw with both hands and ducked under his legs, heaved him over her shoulders, and tried to pin him.

"One of you, wake Abby! The other, help me with this thing!" She knocked the Rat King onto his front and drove a knee in between his shoulders. He kept clawing at her with one hand while she held the other fast. She might as well have been wrestling a Buick.

Leanne picked up the broken spinning wheel and smashed it over the Rat King's head. She opened a wide gash above the monster's right eye, and the wound sprayed black and sticky ectoplasm onto her glasses.

Meanwhile, Simon crouched beside Abby's chair and smacked her on the cheek to rouse her. "Come on, Henderson! Come on, come on, rise and shine!"

Nothing. Behind him, Leanne had her glasses off and was trying to wipe away the ectoplasm. Natalie hollered at her to get her head in the game. The Rat King hissed and writhed.

Simon clapped his hands beside Abby's ear and shouted at her to wake up. "*Metodes miht*, Abigail, this is no time for sleeping on the job!"

The Rat King rolled onto his back and crushed Natalie underneath him. He stood, grabbed her around the middle with one scabby hand, and threw her sidelong into the wall between the den and the living room.

Leanne got her glasses back on just in time to see Natalie crash through the wall. She dodged under his swiping claws and punched the Rat King right in his furry family jewels. All that did was make him angry, and he smacked Leanne away like a fly on a hot dog. Her feet left the ground and she tumbled headfirst into the living room wall, less than five feet from the Natalie-shaped hole.

The Rat King advanced on Simon and Abby. It was time to unleash the nuclear option, so Simon squared up his shoulders and groaned. He was going to pay for this later. "Right, forgive me for this, Abby." Then he wound up and slapped her hard across the face.

As soon as he made contact, Abby opened her eyes and kicked him in the stomach. Then she stood and slapped him right back. "What the *CHRIST* was that?" she snapped.

Simon doubled over, rubbed his cheek, and jerked a thumb over his shoulder. "That! That's what!" he croaked.

"Oh, shit!" Abby yelped. She grabbed Simon's hand, and the pair of them dove between the Rat King's legs as he clawed at the chair. "What the fuck did you guys *do*?" she demanded as she yanked the Webley out of its holster.

"Us?" Simon spluttered. "You were the one in the Bridge! This ugly brute didn't show up until you began the summons!"

"I sure as shit didn't summon this thing! I think I would remember something like that!" Abby gripped the revolver with both hands and shot the Rat King twice in his broad chest. The creature screeched, but fought through the pain and kept advancing. His wounds leaked still more ectoplasm on the floor and he dropped his burlap sack in the puddle, flaunting his deadly claws. Simon stepped forward with fire in his eyes and the first syllables of a magic spell on his tongue, but the Rat King jumped to the ceiling and scampered out of the way.

Before either of them could blink, the Rat King dropped on top of them. Eleven hundred pounds of teeth, claws, and fur filled their fields of vision, and the only sound was the mad rodent's shriek, punctuated by the low hum of cicadas' wings.

Then, everything went dark.

CHAPTER 11

AT THE MANSION OF MADNESS

"OOOOOH, GODS, my *head*." Simon tried to sit up. His torso was like a lead weight dragging him down, and it didn't help that he was trying to pull himself up on two arms made of spaghetti. There were aches in muscles he didn't know he had, and his skull felt like there was a little man in there playing croquet with a backhoe and cast-iron wrecking balls. "That," he declared, "is positively the *last* time I go to the mead hall with you, Unferth."

No answer. Simon blinked and gave his head a shake. "Unferth?" Then he smacked his forehead. No. No, of course not. He was well past all that now. Those days were dead. This was the work of that anthropomorphic meat grinder called the Rat King.

He finally managed to sit up. It looked like he was in the kitchen of the Harcourt House, but something was off. Every flat surface and fixture was cold to the touch, and they glowed with a silvery haze that made them look out-of-focus. The walls buckled and flexed in time with a deep *basso profundo* hiss of air. The angles in the corners of the room didn't add up like they should, and he got dizzy just looking at them.

He stood, gave himself a shake, and began to think aloud. "Right. I am standing in the kitchen of an earthly house that is *not really* the kitchen of an earthly house. Cold air, illogical geometry, surroundings out of focus... suggests room is a spiritual construct of some kind, built by the ghosts to keep me sated. Or perhaps... occupied? To lull me into a false sense of security, perhaps? But then... where are the ghosts?"

There came a purring, sultry reply from behind him. "Ask and ye shall receive, Ætheriċ..."

Simon faltered at the sound of his birth name. At the sound of *that* voice speaking his birth name. No. It couldn't be her. She had died with the rest of her clan. With the rest of the race, for *heofon*'s sake.

Defying all reason and logic, the voice spoke again. Simon felt warm breath on the back of his neck and a set of long, slender fingers caressing his spine.

"What's the matter, Ætheriċ?" the voice cooed in a musical Welsh accent. A sensuous, erotic tingle crept down Simon's spine, as a pair of warm, round lips kissed the back of his neck. "Don't you recognize me? Don't you recognize your own Elinora?"

Simon turned and glared at the woman behind him, his eyes cold and stinging with tears. "Of course, I recognize 'my own Elinora.'"

Elinora stood as tall as Simon, her back straight and her noble chin held high. Her forest-green gown trailed to the floor, the gold-trimmed neckline plunging low to reveal a silver medallion dangling over the pronounced curve of her bosom. The medallion was inscribed with ancient and powerful runes, much like the nearly identical medallion Simon wore around his own neck under his shirt at all times. Her nose was upturned and freckled and her long red hair, which flowed down to the small of her back, was set with a wreath of ferns and wildflowers. She was exactly as Simon remembered her, but for one detail. Elinora's eyes had been blue like sapphires, and they had sparkled with intelligence and wisdom.

Not so these eyes. They were an awful, pallid red, like something from those Hammer Horror films Abby liked. And in the pupils, a spark of wickedness danced.

'Elinora' smiled and took a step forward. "What is the matter, my love? Are you displeased with me?" She licked her lips and blew him a kiss. "What can sweet Nora do to allay her liege-lord's suffering?"

Simon recoiled as 'Elinora' reached out to him. "Stop! Stop this grotesque charade at once! You are not Elinora, and you never will be!"

"Are you… so sure?" the Not-Quite-Elinora purred. Before Simon could answer, she glided forward, wrapped her arms around him, and kissed him.

Simon tried to pull away, but the spirit held him tight, and her grip only strengthened as he tried to deny her. His lips parted and he felt a slimy worm charge into his mouth, groping between his teeth and caressing the inside of his cheek. He fought back cold, furious tears as a ghastly voice from above whispered, *"She is lost to you, Vanguard. Lost in the sands of time. This is known to us both. Does it not make you sick?"*

Nora started to rot in Simon's arms. Her hair grew as dry as a scarecrow's straw and fell in tangled clumps on the floor. One of her teeth loosened, slid along her tongue, and landed in Simon's mouth. He gagged and pulled away from the thing that was not his lover, coughing and spitting on the floor. From the corner of his eye, he could see Nora's grey skin peeling off, revealing the fat and muscle underneath.

She gave Simon a pained look and asked, "Am I not beautiful to you, my love?" Then she collapsed in on herself, just a pile of bones and putrid offal. While her voice echoed around the kitchen, a swarm of cicadas rose from the corpse and launched themselves at Simon. Their intent was to leave only a pile of scraps. Something that would match Elinora.

*****

Natalie opened her eyes, pulled herself up to her knees, and took in her immediate surroundings—old furniture, shelves of broken knickknacks, and a large gravity furnace with pipes sticking out of it like octopus tentacles. She was in the Harcourts' cellar.

She grabbed hold of an old wardrobe with no doors and pulled herself up, giving her Vokarion crystal a tap as she did so. "This is Natalie, calling Simon, Abby, or Leanne. Simon, Abby, Leanne. Are any of you there?" The only response she got was a loud buzzing noise. Natalie tapped her crystal and said, "Hello? Hello, anyone? Can you hear me?"

The buzzing stopped. On the other side of the cellar, a drumbeat took its place, fast and lively. Male voices cheered and laughed, and Natalie felt a warmth on the back of her neck. Odd. She couldn't remember the last time she'd felt warmth anywhere.

The male voices began a quick call-and-response as the drums picked up speed. For a second, Natalie forgot where she was, and let the music take her back to another century. She reveled in a language she'd not heard or spoken for more than 200 years, and was surprised to realize that she still remembered all the words of the old song.

Then the drums stopped. Dogs began to bark in the distance, gunshots rang in the air, and the back of Natalie's neck was cold again. Sharp pain arced across her back in a zig-zagging pattern, and she fell back to her knees. A voice behind her whispered, "*Comment appeles-tu, cherie?*"

Natalie said nothing. She just curled her lip in disgust.

She felt another lance of pain cut across her back. Again, the voice in the dark asked, "*Comment appeles-tu?*" It wasn't a request this time. Still, Natalie said nothing.

Two more lashes. Her tank top ripped against her back, and she felt hot blood binding the fabric to her skin. "*Dîtes-moi ton nom!*" hollered the voice. "*Dîtes-moi maintenant, chienne bête!*"

She felt the lash again, and this time the pain made her cry out. She got to her feet, spun around and reached for her machete, remembering too late that she'd left it in the Rat King.

She heard the dogs barking again, heard the overseers trying to keep them on their leashes. The foreman called for order, and a gun went off.

Natalie doubled back as pain exploded in her chest. The powder burned hot between her breasts as the lead ball chewed her up from the inside. A red spot blossomed on her shirt and she staggered back, tripped on a protrusion in the floor, and fell on her ass.

It wasn't hard wood she landed on. It was snow. Dry, airy flakes the size of dimes stuck to her pants as she hauled herself up, and a cold, biting wind whirled around her head, blowing more snow into her face along with those strands of hair she hadn't tied back. Natalie spat hair out of her mouth and scrubbed the snow out of her eyes with her hands. Visibility had dropped to almost nothing, but she didn't think she was in the Harcourt House anymore.

As Natalie looked around, trying to get a bearing, she heard a deep, bellowing whinny behind her, and the sound of gas escaping from a pipe. She turned toward the noise as it repeated, and this time she saw two jets of orange flame escaping from twin black holes in the snowy white void. A third whinny, and the black holes came toward her at terrifying speed. They were the nostrils of a monstrous pale stallion in full gallop. Even though the snow came up to Natalie's ankles, the creature's thundering hooves barely left a mark, and little bursts of fire erupted from its nostrils with every snort and huff of breath.

Natalie turned and ran before the stallion was more than halfway into view. The snow made it hard to see anything, but there had been no mistaking the sterling silver bit in the creature's mouth or the diamond-encrusted pommel rising from the saddle on its back. The horse whinnied again and was answered by the hollow note of a hunting horn. Natalie picked up the pace and stuck her arms out for balance so she wouldn't fall in the snow. She heard the crunch of the horse's massive hooves pounding flat the frozen drifts, but she never looked back. She didn't dare. She didn't want to see the thing that was riding that horse, that was blowing that horn. Not again.

As a little girl growing up in bondage on the plantations of Saint-Domingue, Natalie had always been taught that death would be a great homecoming. When she died, she would be reborn in *lan guinée*, the place where her ancestors had been stolen from by the white devils. There, she would live in freedom for all time, side-by-side with the *lwa* and the ones she had lost. But when she had died for the first time, she hadn't woken up in *Guinée*. She had woken up here. She had seen that pale horse, with its gaunt, dark-eyed rider swathed all in black, and she had run. And just as the rider had stretched out his hand, had tangled his long pale fingers in her hair, and had hoisted her off her feet, she had woken up. Just before she had been swung onto that jet-black saddle, her body had fought its way out of the grave, and her soul had been dragged back to the living world.

At first, Natalie had hated what she was turned into when she crawled out of the ground. Some days, she still did. But she was smart enough to know how to make the best of a bad situation. She could push herself farther and fight harder than some creatures three times her size, or she could break an opponent's will by just refusing to go down. Every time she picked a fight with the Rat Kings of the world, she did so secure in the knowledge that the magic animating her would heal any mortal injuries she sustained. But part of her was always terrified that the magic might not last, that one day she'd pick a fight she couldn't heal from and have to face the Rider again.

If she had anything to say about it, 'one day' wouldn't be today. She threw herself to the ground, listened to the sound of the hooves getting closer and closer, and then rolled to one side.

Two seconds later, and the horse would have flattened her head like a pancake. Natalie rolled into the biting wind and snow, picked herself up, and sprinted off perpendicular to the horse's track. She could hear the beast off in the distance, whinnying and snorting fire as the Rider tugged on the reins and tried to change course. Natalie ducked her head low so the snow wouldn't get in her eyes, and ran blindly in the opposite direction of the Rider.

The wind suddenly broke, and the last of the snowflakes drifted lazily to the ground. Natalie's boots creaked on the hardwood, and she froze. She was back in the cellar. She turned and made for the stairs, but there were no stairs. There was no door either, and no window at ground level. The old wood and concrete made a box around her, sealed tight on all four sides.

"NATALIE ARNAUD," hissed a voice in her ear. It was hollow and cold, with a scratch in it like someone was scraping a tree branch over thick ice. *"THE WHEEL OF YOUR YEARS HAS TURNED. WINTER COMES AGAIN…"*

The great octopoid furnace rattled and roared, and a blast of arctic air nearly blew Natalie off her feet. The pale horse whinnied somewhere in the distance, and the freezing wind arced around Natalie's body, lifted her off the ground, and set her spinning like a top in midair.

She landed roughly, facing the great furnace. She could see where a section of the concrete had been chipped away and the earth beneath dug into an open grave, with a weather-worn slab of granite at its head.

NATALIE ARNAUD

BORN 1749

DIED ~~1782~~

(2020)

Natalie felt a hand on her shoulder. Simon wiped away a tear, closed his red eyes, and pushed her solemnly toward the grave. Abby and Leanne took up positions graveside, dressed in black and holding bouquets.

"No," Natalie said. "I need more time, dammit. I need more time!" She dug in her heels and pushed back with all her might, but the thing wearing Simon's face held firm and pushed back even harder.

As she got closer and closer to the grave, Natalie could hear the buzzing of a thousand cicadas. There was a swarm of them inside the grave, crawling all over the dirt walls and each other, beating their wings in unison.

Simon gave Natalie a pat on the shoulder and said, "Farewell, Natalie. You were a very dear friend." Then he pushed her into the grave.

*****

As best Leanne could tell, she was in the Harcourts' master bedroom. She'd lost her glasses, but she could still make out the fuzzy outline of the four-poster bed and a dresser with a mirror on top. Two doors—one of them a closet, presumably, the other the main entrance. A nightstand with an oil lamp atop it, and a warped lump of metal that she took for an overturned chamber pot. The floor on which she crawled was cold as death, and the sticky gobs of ectoplasm stuck out like hideous botflies against the faded blue bedsheets and the floor.

She found her glasses at the foot of the bed, tangled up in trailing scraps of bedding. The lenses were smudged and sticky with ectoplasm, so Leanne tore a strip off the duvet and gave them a wipe down. It wasn't a perfect fix, but it would do for now.

Leanne stood and walked toward the door, giving her Vokarion crystal a tap. She had to find her way back to the others. But before she could make the call, two gunshots split the air like firecrackers. They were followed a second later by a shout of, "LEEEE!" and the shriek of a hungry Rat King. Only after the third gunshot did Leanne realize the noise wasn't in her head or on the Vokarion crystal. It was coming from downstairs.

"Lee, where the hell are you?"

Leanne yanked the door open and hurried into the dim corridor. "Abby! Abby, where are you?"

"Second floor!" came Abby's reply. "Hurry! I can't hold this thing off much longer!"

Another monstrous roar travelled up the stairs, and Leanne followed the noise down to the second floor. Heavy footsteps thundered in the corridor below, followed by a sound like someone dropping a couch from a great height. "Oh, shit!" Abby hollered. "Oh, shit, oh, SHI—" Her voice trailed off, half an octave higher than normal. And then, silence.

Leanne paused on the stairs, digging her nails into the rotting banister. "A-Abby?" she called. "Abby, are you there?"

Abby fell with a slam, right where the staircase met the second-floor hallway. Her shirt was ripped to pieces and stained with a muddy off-red mix of blood and ectoplasm. A wide slash across her face had torn away most of her lips and half the skin on her nose. One eye was squinted shut, and blood leaked down her eyelid like heavy tears. With her good eye, Abby looked up the stairs at Leanne, and reached for her with a trembling hand. Half the skin above her wrist was missing, exposing an ugly lump of fatty tissue and bones that bent the wrong way.

Through the hole in Abby's cheek, Leanne could see her partner's teeth clicking together as she tried to speak. "Lee... help me... please..."

Leanne crouched and took Abby by the wrist, where the skin ended. She wrapped both hands around Abby's forearm and pulled. "Come on, Abby, stay with me! We're going to get you out of here! It's going to be okay!"

A scabby, grey-furred hand leapt out from around the corner and clamped down on Abby's scalp. With a shriek, the Rat King sank his claws into Abby's head and yanked her back out of sight. Abby's blood-slicked wrist popped out of Leanne's grasp. Leanne fell the rest of the way down the stairs and landed chin-first.

She stood and pressed a hand to the wide cut on her chin. There was no trace of Abby or the Rat King anywhere, and not so much as a single drop of blood on the stairs behind her. Her own hands were clean as a whistle and her nails were perfect. Not cracked and chipped like she'd just been scratching the hell out of the banister.

Had she imagined it all? No, her imagination wasn't nearly that creative. It must be this damn House. It was playing tricks on her.

Behind her, there was a soft *thump*. A wet, thready voice croaked, "'Foreverways.' That's what you said, Leanne. You said you'd be there foreverways."

Leanne spun around. The gory vision of Abby stood on the corner landing, one hand pressed to her stomach, the other hanging uselessly at her side. The Rat King had gone to town on her torso. A deep, pulsing red gash cut straight across her belly, and ragged strips of chew-up flesh hung loose above her right hip. Abby limped down the stairs, her chest rattling when she breathed. "Where were you, Lee? Where…"

Abby lost her grip and fell down the last few steps before landing at Leanne's feet. Abby's head smacked loudly on the floorboards and her chest heaved once as a dull sigh of breath crept out her mouth. Her dead eyes, like two polished marbles, looked at the ceiling without seeing it.

"No. No, no, no, that's not her," Leanne stammered. "That's not her that's not her that *can't* be her!"

A hideous voice trickled down from the ceiling. *"Are you so sure? Can you say with confidence your lover will not end her days like this?"* This must have been the so-called 'Master' that Abby and Will had heard in their dream.

"Do you know for certain that you and she will live happily together?" the Master inquired. *"Or will she leave you in the heat of battle? Carried off by a stronger opponent, like so many soldiers in so many pointless wars since man first sharpened one rock against another?"*

"Shut up!" Leanne snapped. "You don't know what you're talking about! Just shut up!"

A doorknob rattled at the end of the hall. *"She has a hero's complex,"* the Master observed. *"Kelly Munro. William Brady. You, Leanne. Your Abigail fights for those who cannot fight themselves. It is not a fight she can win forever."*

The doorknob continued to rattle, and something slammed into the wood on the other side. A plume of black smoke leaked out underneath the door, and Leanne could see the glow of a red fire in the crack at the bottom.

Another Abby crashed through the door and landed in a disjointed heap just in front of Leanne. Just in front of the other version of her: the corpse that had lost a fight with the Rat King.

The still-breathing version of Abby stood and wiped a streak of blood from her lower lip, never acknowledging Leanne's presence. In her dominant hand, she held Natalie's machete. Leanne had a good idea what was coming. She shouted for the Master to "stop it! Stop it right now!"

John Leland emerged from the raging fire in the other room, both hands gripping the handle of his razor-like cane sword. He leaped toward Abby with bloodlust reflected in his red eyes, and she rushed forward to meet him.

The machete clattered to the floor, and Leanne saw Abby flat on her back, with Leland standing above her. He planted his foot squarely on her neck and slowly, slowly increased the pressure. Leanne fell to her knees. "STOP IT!" she screamed. "STOP THIS, PLEASE!"

"Very well, Leanne Waller," the Master said with a chuckle. *"But remember, those were your words."*

Leland looked right at Leanne and stamped on Abby's neck like he was crushing a bug.

Leanne closed her eyes as Abby's neck snapped. "Why?" she sobbed. "W-why are you doing this? Is this *fun* for you? Is this a *game*?"

"This is an object lesson," the Master replied sharply. *"Next time you seek to enter a man's home, wait for an invitation."*

By the time the cicadas came buzzing up the stairs, Leanne was too exhausted to scream.

CHAPTER 12

HOMEWRECKERS

THE LIBRARY on the first floor of the Harcourt House was the only room not thick with dust. In fact, if Abby didn't know better, she'd say it looked almost lived-in. The high bookshelves along the walls were newly varnished, and the books on them were well cared for. Abby ran one hand along the nearest shelf and it came away clean.

She couldn't raise her friends on the Vokarion relay, which spooked her more than a little. Abby knew from past experience that only a powerful psychic force—more powerful than her—could block a Vokarion's telepathic signal. It probably wouldn't end well for the little psychic fish that went swimming around blindly in a bigger psychic fish's pond. So, she had decided it would be best to stay where she was, learn what she could, and form a plan.

"Somebody's been here," Abby said to the room at large. "Someone's been picking up in this room very recently…" She crossed from one end of the shelf to the other, her fingers going *bump-bump-bump* along the leather and canvas spines of the books before her. She stopped as her hand passed over a gap in between two of the books, just large enough for a single slim volume to fit. She looked at the books to the left and right of the missing one, and pulled one from the shelf for a closer look.

A journal. It was handwritten in some bizarre form of code that cycled around in loops and zig-zags, falling down the margins of the page and coming back in on itself. Lines of text were crammed together so tightly that no white space showed through. Text ran up and down, left to right and right to left, diagonally down the page and up again, and in V-formation in the margins. Abby flipped through several pages, trying to find some meaning in the text, and when it didn't come, she put the book back where it was, and tried the one on the other side.

If it was possible, the next one was even worse. Some of the pages didn't even have words on them, just diagrams and crude sketches of random arcana. A wand with a handle carved like a snake. A cross-section of a human brain with a dozen eyeballs dotting its surface. A tall, thin mesh cage with a large iron spike atop it, like an old Prussian *pickelhaube*.

As she kept reading, Abby tasted blood on her lips and felt her skull shiver. Drops of red splashed onto the curling pages and smeared the old ink.

Somewhere behind her, Simon called out. "Stop this grotesque charade at once!"

Abby spun around and dropped the little book. "What? Simon? Are you there?"

Simon's voice was replaced by Natalie's. "I need more time, dammit!"

More drips from her nose, and then Leanne was screaming in Abby's ear. "Why are you doing this? Is this fun for you?"

Abby jumped like a frightened deer, and her dominant hand went toward the holster at her shoulder. "Whoever or whatever you are, I know you're out there! I know what you're trying to do!" She walked briskly to the door of the library as a cacophony of her friends' screaming rattled her teeth. "These cheap scare tactics aren't going to work, you hear me? Not on me, they're not!"

She drew the Webley as she opened the door, blinking against the pronounced blackness of the corridor. But no matter how hard Abby blinked, her eyes simply would not adjust. Another of the House's cheap scare tactics, surely.

As she fumbled forward in the dark, Abby smelled the ectoplasm on the floor before she saw it. Or before she stepped in it. As her shoes squelched around in the black mess, an air bubble shifted and popped under her nose, releasing a smell that made her want to vomit.

Her gun arm quivered, and Abby took a deep breath in through her mouth. "If you're trying to put me off balance," she hollered, "it's not going to work!"

The hallway tilted, and Abby lurched to one side. The hallway tilted the other way, and so did she. The whole House shook, and Abby went face-first into the black ectoplasm.

Above her, the Master laughed. *"'Put you off balance.' My, my, what an amusing turn of phrase."*

Abby looked up, spitting out a clot of the foul goo. "Oh, har-dee-har-har! 'Off balance'! That's really cute! Why don't you quit dicking around and show yourself, Laughing Boy?"

Eight feet in front of her, the ectoplasm bubbled, and a scabby grey hand poked out of the floor. *"Very well. On your own head be it, Abigail Henderson,"* chirped the Master.

As the Rat King pulled himself up, Abby tried to stand. But the ectoplasm stuck tight to every part of her and held her tight.

"This is how I die, isn't it?" she grumbled to herself. "Glued tits-first to the floor of a haunted house, with a one-ton rat monster bearing down on me. Wouldn't have been my first guess," she added with a sigh.

The Rat King stalked toward her, his long pink tongue dangling from his open mouth. He bent low, readying himself for the kill, and Abby's breath stopped in her throat.

THOK! A long-handled axe whistled through the air above her, and the blade buried itself deep in the Rat King's skull. A bright white light shone from the wound, and a fountain of ectoplasm spewed forth like lava. Screeching and shrieking in pain, the Rat King pulled out the axe, slapped a hand over his wound, and retreated into the dark.

Abby felt two hands scooping into her armpits and pulling her to her feet. "Thanks," she said without thinking. "He probably would have made hamburger out of m —" The last word died on her lips as she turned to face her rescuer: the bloodstained ghost of Hector Harcourt.

*****

Leanne swatted at the cicadas buzzing around her head and wiped bug guts off her glasses. "SIMON!" she hollered. "NATALIE! ABBY! Anybody, *please!*"

In the distance, a voice cried out, *"Eagan heofena!"* and a great orb of white light cut through the swarm. Cicadas fell dead by the dozens and Leanne ran toward the voice. She could see Simon's thin silhouette, ejecting the light from the palm of his hand.

"Oh, thank God! Simon, Simon, over here!" She stumbled toward him, but he didn't look at her. His eyes were fixed on another figure, hidden by the darkness.

"Whatever manner of creature you are," he said to the second figure, "if you are not already dead, then by the High Celestial I will make you so! *Fyres blæst!*"

Leanne shrieked and fell on her bum as Simon lobbed a fireball at the second figure. The figure roared and somersaulted under the shot, then leaped up and tackled Simon to the ground. In the light of Simon's spell, Leanne could now see that the second figure was —

"Natalie?" she yelled. "Natalie, what the hell are you doing?"

*****

Natalie shoved her knee into her assailant's chest and wrapped her arms around his throat. She smiled as the Pale Rider struggled for breath beneath her weight, his hands clawing desperately at hers. "I'm not going with you," she vowed. "I'm not done fighting. Not by a long shot!"

*****

Simon's vision was going black. Nora was on top of him, her knee in his chest and her hands around his throat.

NO! No, it's not Nora! said the little voice in his head.

Whatever the hell it was, it was squeezing the life out of him. He put his hands on his opponent's shoulders and yelled, *"Bānhūs ber on lyfte!"*

Nora shot eight feet straight into the air and Simon stood. While she levitated in place, red sparks danced in the palms of his hands. "This grotesque masquerade ends now. I promise you that."

*****

The Pale Rider grabbed Natalie's shoulders and threw her into the air. She hovered halfway between the floor and ceiling and watched as a bright ball of blue fire blossomed in his hands. *"You shouldn't have done that, Natalie,"* he hissed in his cold voice. The fire grew to the size of a basketball, and the Pale Rider took a step back. He wound up to make his shot.

*****

"STOP!" Leanne picked herself up and ran toward Simon, throwing herself between him and Natalie. "Stop, Simon, stop it! What the hell are you doing?"

Simon quickly dropped his hands and the fire went out. "Leanne? What the hell are *you* doing? I could have barbecued you!"

"Well, it's not like I had a choice! You were about to torch Natalie!"

Simon blinked. "What are you talking about?"

Leanne pointed behind her. "Hello? Who do you think that is there?"

"Well, that's… that's…" Simon swayed and put his head in his hands, giving it a good shake. "No… it's not…"

"Simon, I'm really sorry about this, but…" Leanne stepped forward and slapped him.

"OW!" Simon rubbed his cheek and looked down at her. "*Metodes miht*, you and Abigail both: what is it with you and the slapping?"

"Simon, look behind me again. Tell me, who do you see back there?"

Simon looked. "Bloody hell, you're right!" He quickly reversed the spell and Natalie's feet touched the ground once more. "Natalie, I am so sorry! I could have sworn you were—"

Natalie blinked and rubbed her forehead. "Don't sweat it. You didn't look like you either."

"Don't you see, guys?" Leanne said. "This House is making us crazy! We're doing exactly what it wants us to!"

Simon nodded. "You're right, Leanne. Whatever's haunting this place has us at a disadvantage. We need to find Abby and get the hell out of here."

*****

Abby and her ghostly rescuer beat a retreat through the ectoplasm-soaked corridor. He pulled her toward the stairs and hissed, "You must leave this place, do you understand? It is not safe in the night! That is when his power is greatest!"

"This doesn't make sense!" Abby gasped. "You killed your whole family! Why do you want to help me?"

"Despite what you may have heard," said Hector, "I am not the monster here."

"Then who is?"

There was a roar and the ground shook beneath them. A geyser of ectoplasm erupted at the top of the stairs, and the Rat King emerged with Hector's axe in his fist. The Master hollered: *"What do you think you are doing, boy?"*

Hector extended a hand to the ceiling, and a new axe formed from the very aether around him. "This one is not yours to take, do you hear? None of these people are! You must stop this madness at once!"

"You dare to give me orders? Here? This place is mine, you arrogant child!"

The Rat King lumbered toward them, and Hector swung at his neck. "The Master is preparing his next assault!" he yelled at Abby. "You must leave before he gathers his full strength!"

"This *isn't* full strength?"

"*Go*, you foolish girl! Take your friends and do not return!" He chopped at the Rat King's leg, but the beast skittered around behind him and swung his own axe.

Hector took his axe in both hands and blocked the blow. Then he planted his feet and tried to force the Rat King back. The Rat King grabbed at Hector with his other hand, but Hector ducked back and sunk his blade into the Rat King's wrist. The monster screeched, raised its own weapon again, and Hector chopped into his belly. Ectoplasm poured out of the Rat King like a waterfall, and he doubled over as white light burst from under his skin. He gave one last indignant shriek and sank back into the floor.

"Close your eyes!" Hector commanded. "Now!"

Abby did as she was told. Hector screamed, and she felt the warming glow of a light so intense that she could almost see it behind her eyelids. There was a low, musical hum, and she peeked one eye open. For an instant, she saw a more vibrant and spectacular display of colours than she'd ever thought possible. First the light turned red. Then green. Then orange, gold, purple, blue, rose, magenta! The music rose, and somewhere on the other side of the rainbow, she saw three fuzzy blobs of varying heights.

"What on earth is that?" asked one of the blobs, in a voice not unlike Simon's.

"Whatever it is, it scared those bugs away," said the second blob in Natalie's voice.

The third blob, by process of elimination, could only have been Leanne. "Guys, look! I think I see Abby up there!"

They all called to her, and she crawled to the bottom of the stairs. Hector was gone, and she could feel the ectoplasm drying under her hands and feet.

She reached out a hand while her friends kept calling her name. "Guys! Guys, I'm here!"

Leanne's hand grabbed Abby's and pulled her forward into a tunnel of sound, fury, and light. The sensation overwhelmed her, and she blacked out.

*****

Ba-boom. Ba-boom. Ba-boom.

Abby opened her eyes. Then she shut them again and groaned. The morning light coming in the front window made her head throb and cooked her eyeballs in their sockets. Every time her heart beat, a tiny explosive detonated in her brain.

Wait a second. Morning… light…?

Despite the pain, Abby opened her eyes again. Forced herself to sit up. Poked at her head with one hand and found a lump the size of a boiled egg behind her right ear.

As her eyes adjusted to the light and the room stopped dancing, Abby pulled herself off the couch and ran to the front window of the Harcourt House. It was early dawn, and from where she stood Abby could see the rising sun above Okanagan Lake, cutting through a break in the smoke.

"No…" she whispered to herself. "That's… that's not right… we weren't…"

A footstep groaned on the hardwood behind her and a hand rested on her shoulder. Abby grabbed it, spun, and twisted the hand behind its owner's shoulder.

"Ow, bloody hell! Wait just a minute, it's me!" Simon shouted.

Abby let go of him and backed away. "Simon? Is that really you?" She scanned his aura while he stood and rubbed his arm.

"Of course, it's me! The one and—" Simon looked out the window at the rising sun. His mouth hung open and he shook his head. "No. No, no, no, no, that's—that's not possible—that—we can't—we were never—" He opened his pocket watch to check the time, then pressed his nose against the window. "But that—*how*?"

Another groan on the floor. Natalie and Leanne emerged from the den, each propping themselves against the other. "Simon?" said Leanne. "Abby? What the hell's going on?"

Natalie looked out the window. "Wait a minute. What time is it?"

Simon paced the room anxiously. "It's dawn. It's dawn and that doesn't make any sense! How can it be dawn?"

"We can focus on that later, Simon!" said Abby. "Bigger question right now: where the hell is all our stuff?"

She pointed to the empty mantel, where the Hand of Glory was not sitting, then to the floor, where Simon's satchel clearly wasn't.

Simon stopped pacing. "Oh, damn! I paid an arm and a leg for that Hand!"

"That doesn't make sense!" said Leanne. "Who would steal a mummified hand? Who would even know what it was?"

"How would they get in here, get it, and get out without us noticing?" Natalie asked.

Simon smacked his forehead and shut his eyes. "I'm missing something. There is an answer to this right in front of my nose and I'm too thick to see it. What am I missing? What—am—I—missing?"

Abby raised her hands. "Guys, let's just all take a deep breath, okay? This place has been playing mind games with us since we got here. It might still be, for all we know. For now, why don't we go back to the motel, sleep for a couple hours and reboot the system? We can—"

Leanne cut her off. "Shush! Do you guys... do you hear something?"

They all held their breath and listened for a moment. The sound of a million pairs of insects' wings echoed throughout the corridors of the Harcourt House. They thundered in time with a peal of sinister, mocking laughter, getting closer every second.

As the noise reached its apex, Abby gulped and said very firmly, "Everybody: *run*."

The others didn't need to be told twice. As the swarm came pouring out of the fireplace, the four bolted toward the door, swatting away as many of the things as they could. Simon pointed a hand at the door and shouted, *"Bēamas berstaþ!"* A bolt of green energy flew from his hand and the door exploded outward into a million wooden fragments. The gang dashed out of the House and over the fence at top speed and tumbled down the hill, still screaming and swatting at insects. They reached the bottom in a knotty pile of sweaty, terrified limbs.

Abby pulled herself out from the jumbled mass of her friends and gingerly rubbed the bump on her head. "Well, it could be worse," she admitted. "At least we're all alive. Or... undead," she added with a quick glance at Natalie. Natalie gave a soft chuckle at that, which for her was as good as a belly laugh. The four untangled themselves, and as Abby was brushing twigs and burrs off the back of Leanne's shirt, they heard the *whoop whoop* of a police siren.

"Oh, now what?" Natalie groaned.

The squad car had boxed in Natalie's Thunderbird behind the red SUV. Its roof lights flashed blue and red on the faces of Constable Eckhart and Corporal Rickards. Clear plastic evidence bags sat on the car's hood, containing all of Simon's gear, including his prized Hand of Glory.

Rickards shook his head and failed to suppress a smile that betrayed how very pleased with himself he was. "Looks like we've got some troublemakers in town."

*I looked upon the scene before me — upon the mere
house, and the simple landscape features of the
domain — upon the bleak walls — upon the vacant
eye-like windows — upon a few rank sedges — and
upon a few white trunks of decayed trees — with an
utter depression of soul which I can compare to no
earthly sensation more properly than to the after-
dream of the reveller upon opium — the bitter lapse
into an every-day sinking, a sickening of the
heart — an unredeemed dreariness of thought which
no goading of the imagination could goad into
aught of the sublime. What was it — I paused to
think — what was it that so unnerved me in the
contemplation of the House of Usher?*

*

"The Fall of the House of Usher"
Edgar Allan Poe

BOOK TWO:

WELCOME TO THE FAMILY

CHAPTER 13

A THOUSAND CUTS

"ABBY?"

"Yeah, Lee?"

"If you write this story up for your blog, do you think you could skip the part where we spent half a day in a jail cell?"

"Yeah, I don't think the internet needs to know about that."

As she said this, Abby lay on a metal cot chained to the wall, staring up at the ceiling and counting the imperfections in the white plaster. Leanne and Natalie sat on the floor on either side of her, and Simon was in the next cell over. The bracers and Skeleton Cards had proved to be bugger all use to them in the heat of the moment. As Simon had warned, the illusions completely shut down with too much sudden movement, and apparently "Sudden Movement" was the Rat King's middle name.

"What time is it?" Leanne sighed. "My butt's going numb from all this sitting."

"I'll be damned if it's still morning," Natalie said. "We have to have been here five, six hours."

Abby lifted her head and looked at the back of Simon's. "Simon, do you think you could magic this door open or something? We've got work to do!"

Simon didn't respond. Worried, Abby got off the cot and went over to him, squeezing her forearm between the bars so she could rest her hand on his shoulder. "Simon? Are you okay?"

"Nora…" he mumbled. "Bloody… Nora… how could it possibly know…?"

"How did what know?" Abby asked. "Who's Nora?"

"I'm not entirely sure," Natalie admitted. "I've only heard him say the name a few times, mostly when he thought I wasn't listening. I think she was Vanguard, like him. I think they were close."

"You think he saw her ghost in there?" said Leanne.

Simon shook his head, though he didn't turn to look at them. "I'm not certain they were ghosts, Leanne."

The other three all looked at him with surprise and concern.

"Well… what were they then?" Leanne asked.

"Psychic manifestations, I expect," Simon said flatly. "I can't explain how, but I think whatever's lurking in the Harcourt House reached into my mind to find my worst nightmares and then created hyper-realistic illusions of them in order to torture me."

"Us," Abby said.

"Pardon?" For a brief moment, Abby caught Simon flicking his eyes back toward her. It wasn't much, but it was a start.

"Torture *us*," Abby asserted. "When we were up there, you all saw the things that scared you the most, at the same time as the person beside you was seeing something totally different. The same thing happened to me in my dream with Will. I saw Leland, and Will saw his dad."

Simon's chin rose a little. "You never mentioned that."

"Well, I'm mentioning it now. This might sound crazy, guys, but I don't think we were really in the Harcourt House last night. At least, not the Harcourt House on that hill."

Natalie shook her head. "Run that by me again?"

"Look, wherever we were, something was just… *wrong*. There's this sensation I get when I'm dreaming or when I'm in the Bridge, that I don't get when I'm awake. It's like energy in the spirit realm moves through me in a whole different way. I didn't think about it last night, but I had that sensation the whole time we were in the House. What if we opened a door to the spirit world when we first got there and then something pulled us through it? Something that could read our minds and make us think what it wanted us to think, see what it wanted us to see?"

Simon grinned and finally looked at the others. Abby could see the colour return to his cheeks as he stood and began to pace. There was a puzzle that needed solving, and oh mama Simon Lockhart was *on it*. Whatever his troubles in the House had been, they were forgotten as The Mystery hove into view.

"I think you're absolutely right, Abigail! I had my suspicions when you found that petrified ectoplasm in the creek, but the Rat King confirmed it. Remember, when we attacked him, he bled ectoplasm. The only way he could do that is if he himself was an Elsewhere construct: created in the spirit world by whatever's haunting the House, and then thrown at us in this reality to take us out!"

"And time in the Elsewhere doesn't move at the same rate as it does on Earth, does it?" Abby responded. "It doesn't make any sense that Jenny Styles and Sonia Hall could be dead for longer than they were missing, unless they were killed in the spirit world! The killer could pull them in like we were pulled in, do the deed, and spit them back out over the course of two or three days here. But it could be weeks in there!"

Simon nodded. "And when they came back out, they'd be covered in ectoplasm."

Abby smiled. "Do you want to say it, or should I?"

Simon reached through the bars and high-fived her. "Top of the class, Henderson!"

"So, we got teleported to the spirit world," Leanne said. "I can buy that, but how did we get back? I don't think the...

presence would have let us go willingly after it put in all that work."

"We can thank Hector Harcourt for that," said Abby.

"Hang on," said Simon. "As in 'took an axe and gave his father forty whacks' Hector Harcourt?"

"I know. I didn't believe it myself at first. But I saw him last night, in the Elsewhere-House. He saved me from the Rat King. And he spoke to the presence. Called it 'the Master.' It sounded like there was no love lost between them."

Leanne blinked. "The Master… like Bill Grover said, remember? 'The Master is Good. The Master is Wise…'"

"'The Master is Kind,'" Natalie finished.

Abby tapped a finger against her chin. "Those letters Leanne found at the library said the Harcourt servants didn't die how they were supposed to have died. What if Hector didn't kill them? What if the Master did, and Hector took the fall? Hell, what if the Master took control of Hector and *made* him kill his family? And let's say, for the sake of argument, there's a magician running around town. A small-timer, maybe, never amounted to much, but interested in dark magic. What if the magician falls in with the Master, learns the secrets of True Magic from him, starts killing people? With the Master's help, the killer can bend space and time in the Elsewhere and commit unsolvable murders. Yes?"

"It all sounds plausible," Simon said, "but to what end? What's in it for the Master? If he has the kind of power we saw, why trouble himself with a few piddling homicides in the mortal world?" He rested his head against the bars and growled in frustration. "There's too many variables here. I wish I could have a look at one of the bodies. Then I might be able to figure out what sort of spell the killer is using on the victims."

"You think that would help?" Abby said.

"There are many different ways to kill a person using magic," Simon answered. "But different spells have different effects, sometimes on both the killer and the killed. A loss of life for one party can mean increased power for the other in a variety of ways. Knowing what spell was used would clear up a lot of the whys."

"Well, why don't we take a look?" Natalie asked.

Leanne rapped her knuckles against the bars, then pointed to the camera in the corner of the room. "Uh, couple of reasons. And considering the trouble we're already in, I think breaking out of here and into a morgue isn't going to help our case much."

Natalie smirked. "Damn, you're right. If only we had somebody with us who could project their mind out of their body and phase through different sections of reality." She looked at Abby and smiled.

Abby got a deer-in-the-headlights look in her eyes. "Wait, are you asking me what I think you're asking me?"

Natalie grabbed Abby's wrist and raised it to the sky. "Show of hands, who here has the power of astral projection?"

Abby snatched her hand away. "But I haven't done that since I was a teenager! Even when I did, I never got more than six feet from my body!"

Natalie shrugged. "Well, if we're going to make a proper Gospel out of you, you need to get back into practice. No time like the present, I say. Walk out of your body, nip into the morgue, and tell us what we're dealing with here."

"I don't know. Simon, couldn't you just open a portal to the morgue or something and walk through for two minutes?"

"That would draw too much attention. The magical energy I'd need to do that would interfere with the wiring in the security systems around here. I might end up killing the cameras or blowing the locks, and then they'd send someone down here pretty sharpish to check on us. And if there were anyone in the morgue when I popped in, I'd have to answer some rather difficult questions. Leanne's right: we're in enough trouble with the local plod as it is, and we do not need them taking a closer look at us. I think astral projection might be the best bet here."

"Well, I'll give it a try. If I'm not awake in fifteen minutes, give me a boot." Abby laid down on the floor beside the bars, so Simon could reach through and lay a hand on her forehead.

"This would be easier if I had my watch," he said, "but needs must."

Abby closed her eyes and took a deep breath. "Just do your best."

Simon closed his eyes as well and whispered to her in the language of the Vanguard, beginning an incantation that would ease her into a trance and make it easier for her mind to untether itself.

"Ic me on þisse gyrde beluce   and on godes helde bebeode
Wið þane sara stice,   wið þane sara slege…"

Abby opened her eyes and lifted her hand. It was pale, vaguely translucent, and fuzzy at the edges. But it was, in every other way, identical to the flesh hand resting on her stomach. Her soul sat up, and her corporeal body stayed where it was. She stood and stretched, invisible and intangible to her friends. Natalie gingerly picked up Abby's body and laid it on the cot so she'd be more comfortable. "Back in a few minutes," she said. "I hope." Her body opened its mouth and repeated the words in a flat, hypnotized voice.

She walked toward the bars of the cell and felt a tug around her midsection. Her feet slipped on the floor and she fell headfirst through the bars. She tried to pull herself forward, but she had nothing to grab hold of, and the invisible rope around her waist had her tight.

This should have been easier, she told herself. Astral projection was little more than the first step in The Bridge, when her mind would unhook itself from her body and ascend to a higher plane of existence. But she wasn't trying to ascend to a higher plane right now. She just wanted to go a little way down the hall. That wasn't what she was used to, and that cognitive dissonance was keeping her from totally detaching her mind.

She closed her spiritual eyes and took a deep spiritual breath. She told her cognitive dissonance to shut the hell up and willed herself to move forward. The invisible rope tugged at her for a moment, but then it slipped free and her spirit-self melted through the bars.

Cold. Cold like she'd never felt before, all up and down her body. Abby's whole spirit shivered as she phased through the solid metal, and her vision spun as the last of her personal gravity disappeared. She felt the energy of the spirit world tingling on the back of her neck and along her forearms. The Elsewhere was calling to her and her brain was trying to answer, trying to force her into a Bridge. She concentrated on the concrete cell block around her, even while she floated belly-up toward the ceiling. Trying to keep herself on Earth was like swimming against a fast current through a freezing cold river, but she fixed her gaze on one spot and kept her breathing steady.

As Abby passed through the ceiling and emerged in the cops' bullpen, she felt the same rush of cold and tried to flip herself around. Swimming against the current would be easier if she were facedown, at least. She threw all her nonexistent weight to one side and slowly managed to tip herself over. She did a breaststroke through the empty air and managed to work her way forward through the bullpen. As she looked for any signage that might point the way to the morgue, Constable Foley suddenly walked right through her from behind. She shivered like someone had just injected ice water right into her bloodstream, and Foley sucked in a breath.

"Yikes. Does anyone else feel a draft in here?"

*****

The cop shop was in a large L-shaped building complex near Delapore's town centre. The main bullpen was in the bottom corner of the L, in Delapore's original Old Justice Building, which had been designed by Josiah Harcourt in 1919. The cops had the ground floor of the three-storey structure, while the offices of the Crown Counsel and local judge were on the second and third floors. Since early July, however, these upper levels had been commandeered by Inspector Margot Pembroke and her Major Crime team. The vertical bar of the L was a concrete addition from the early '70s that housed the communications room, family room, changing rooms, and evidence lock-up, and the horizontal bar was home to the local morgue and medical examiner's office. The three sections of the L connected by a series of internal doors and gravel walkways through a surprisingly well-tended garden.

Abby float-swam through the northwest corner of the Old Justice Building along one of the gravel paths and made a beeline for the wall of the morgue. She entered the room just a few feet from the first of three long, low operating tables where the pathologist did his job. Mercifully, the table and the morgue were empty.

Abby went to the other wall, examining the names on each of the built-in freezer drawers. She felt the tickle of breath on her neck as Simon whispered in her body's ear, and her unconscious mind relayed the information to the subconscious her floating through the morgue.

"Abby? Can you hear me? What do you see?"

His voice came out distant and hollow, and when she opened her mouth to respond, her own voice came out the same way. "I'm in the morgue now. Just looking for one of our girls…"

She paused as she passed one freezer. She looked at it, sucked in a ghost-breath, and felt suddenly cold. The familiar thorny sensation of dark magic returned, and when she blinked, she saw black smoke leaking from the crack in the freezer door. The name on the door was "HALL, S."

"Abby? Are you still there?"

"Yeah, I… I've found Sonia. Just… threw me for a second, is all. I'm fine now, I'm fine," she insisted, and put a hand on the freezer.

Her fingers vanished into the metal. She put her other hand on the freezer door and pushed it through as well. Then she shimmied her whole body through into the freezer, and floated inches above Sonia Hall's corpse.

It was too dark to see more than the vaguest outline, but Abby felt cold dread crawling all over her. Her arms and the back of her neck tingled in the presence of dark magic, and she surmised that the hairs on her physical body were standing on edge. She put a hand to the sheet and muttered, "It is a far, far grosser thing I do…"

Black magic oozed out of the corpse and Abby's pulse quickened. An electric jolt ran up her arm and she felt the *ba-boom, ba-boom, ba-boom* of her brain exploding in her head. She closed her eyes and grimaced, holding back a scream behind clenched teeth. A vision flashed in her mind as a series of still images. Four red wax candles. A wand. A bathtub. An empty coffin.

She saw a skull with glowing red eyes, its jaw hanging open as it whispered, *"Cutting… cutting… cutting… feeding… feeding… blood… blood… cut… cut…"* While the skull whispered, layers of muscle and fat crept over the bone and a face began to take shape.

The skull disappeared, to be replaced by a large red sigil that pulsed in time with the beat of her heart. It was the same symbol she had seen in her dream, the first time she met Will.

The vision ended. Abby yanked her hand away from Sonia Hall's corpse and gasped, "Ffffuck!" When she blinked, the image of the dream-sigil was burned into her retinas.

A hand grabbed her wrist, and Abby gasped again. The translucent ghost of Sonia Hall sat up in the freezer, screaming, and the frantic heaving of her naked chest strained the stitches in her Y-shaped autopsy scar.

As Sonia rose, the aura of dark energy coming off her hung heavy around Abby's head, sticking to her like a bad smell and making her dizzy. Sonia looked straight past Abby, screaming herself hoarse and tightening her grip on Abby's wrist.

Abby guessed Sonia had been beautiful in life, but the ugliness of death was upon her now. Her hair was tangled and knotted over her stricken face, which was nearly as white as the sheet that covered her physical body. Her long eyelashes were crusty with dried tears, and her lips were cracked and dry.

The wounds were the worst part. Nearly every inch of visible skin was covered in long cuts and gouges of varying width and depth. There were faint spider webs of pale green around the deepest cuts, which looked almost like pockets of neon gas beneath the skin. All the cuts were surgical in their precision, some of them running deep into arteries and veins while others were mere nicks on Sonia's skin. A sizable hole in her throat stretched from one ear to the other, and the skin around the wound flapped and fluttered as the girl kept screaming.

"Sorry about this," Abby murmured. Then she slapped Sonia hard.

Sonia stopped screaming and panted for a moment. Then she looked at Abby and gulped. "W-what happened to me? Where am I?"

"Well…" Abby said. "You're kind of, uh… dead…"

Sonia put her head in her hands and closed her eyes. "No," she whimpered. "No, no, no, no, no…"

"To be specific, dead and… a ghost," Abby admitted.

Sonia covered her eyes and sobbed. "He did it! He really did it!"

"Who did it?" Abby asked. "The Master?"

"Don't!" Sonia sobbed. "Don't say that name! He… oh God, he…"

Abby took Sonia's hands in hers and spoke softly. "Sonia, Sonia, I need you to listen to me. Who is the Master? What does he want?"

Sonia shook her head and rocked on her slab. "Can't. Can't say. He'll hear. He'll hear, he'll hear, he'll hear!"

"Sonia, it's okay! You can talk to me!"

"No!" Sonia shouted. "Go away! Go AWAY!"

Sonia broke free of Abby's grip and pushed her off. Abby flew backward out of the freezer unit, across the morgue, and through the wall. She heard the rush of wind as she picked up speed, zooming through the Old Justice Building like a bullet.

BOOM! She landed back in her body with such force that she lurched off the cot and hit the floor.

"Oh my God!" Leanne exclaimed. "Are you okay?" She helped Abby to sit up and kissed her forehead.

Abby gave her very solid, very sore head a shake. "Ooow. God*dammit.* Stronger than she looks, that one."

"What happened?" Natalie asked. "Did you see anything?"

Abby winced and poked at the sore spot on her head. "Oh boy, did I ever…"

But she clammed up as the thick metal door opened at the end of the hall, and Mona Brady entered with the detention guard at her heels. Mona glowered at Abby and barked, "Open it."

The detention guard did what he was told and pulled Abby out of the cell. Mona pointed at her and said to the detention guard, "I want this woman in an interview room in five minutes."

"Hey!" Abby spluttered. "What gives?"

Mona ignored her. "Five minutes, Ridley."

*****

It took just under four minutes to get Abby into the interview room. Secretly, she was a little disappointed that it didn't look more like all the cop dramas she used to watch with her dad. The walls were painted a fresh coat of white, there was no faulty light bulb hanging from a chain on the ceiling, and the chair they'd sat her in had actual padding. Padding, for God's sake. At least they still had the requisite two-way mirror on the far wall. It probably didn't see much use these days thanks to the security camera in the corner, but some clichés just couldn't be denied.

Mona Brady came in and shut the door behind her. She sat across from Abby and dropped a manila folder on the table. "You and your friends had a busy day yesterday."

"I don't know what you mean," Abby said blankly.

Mona opened the folder. "Then I'll run down the list for you. Trespassing at night, causing a disturbance, mischief, possession of a restricted firearm... And Constable Eckhart told me about that stunt you pulled at the reverend's house, so we can add impersonating a peace officer to the list. Or did you honestly think we were so stupid that we wouldn't check your identities?"

Abby dropped her head on the table and groaned.

Mona pointed to a photo of the Hand of Glory. "This is the one that really gets me: interfering with human remains."

Abby mumbled into the tabletop. "Is it too late to ask for a lawyer?" At least she'd had the good sense to leave her phone at the motel last night. If the cops had searched that and found her email chain with Will, her goose would have been absolutely cooked.

"I hope you have a very good explanation for all this, Miss Henderson."

Abby sat up and met Mona's gaze. "Sergeant, you would not believe me if I told you."

"Do you realize what kind of trouble you're in? The firearm charge alone could get you ten years in prison. Inspector Pembroke wants you all charged with obstruction of justice. I'm not even sure how to categorize half the contraband we found in your friend's car, but believe me when I say that you people are in very deep crap."

"You think I don't know that? A man tried to ventilate me with a screwdriver the other day!"

"And that was a very frightening experience for all of us, but it does not let you off the hook for any of this."

Mona's face didn't change, but dread and disgust broke out all over her aura. She was thinking about Bill Grover's last moments, Abby knew, and trying not to shudder as she remembered the cicadas swarming out of his dead mouth. And there was something else in the back of her mind, something that Abby couldn't quite reach. A memory that Mona was suppressing, or a feeling she was refusing to express. Abby had the briefest impression of bloodstained Hector Harcourt sitting in a police cruiser.

"You want to know the truth?" she asked.

"Try me," said Mona.

"We heard about the Harcourt House. And we heard about the murders. We thought there might be a connection, so we came to town to have a look."

Mona sighed and rolled her eyes to the ceiling. "Ghost chasers. Jesus, Mary, and Joseph…"

"We went up to the House last night to see what's up there. As it happens, something very big is up there."

Mona pinched the bridge of her nose. "Let me guess: you came armed in case the bogeymen of the Harcourt House tried to pick a fight with you."

Abby shrugged. "It sort of got the drop on us and booted us out of the House. That's when we ran into Rickards and Eckhart."

"Did you get a look at this… thing in the Harcourt House?" Mona asked dryly.

"Big. Furry. Lots of teeth. And I'm pretty sure it can shapeshift. We got separated and each of us saw something different. My working theory right now is that it read our minds and became things we were afraid of."

Mona frowned. Abby crossed her arms and shrugged again. "Go ahead: call me crazy if you like. Believe me, you would not be the first. But if I'm crazy, then that means you are too."

"How so?"

Abby leaned across the table. "You were at the library. You saw what happened to Bill Grover, same as I did. You know that wasn't normal. And that's not the only thing you've seen, is it?"

Mona shook her head. "I'm not playing this game."

"Tell me I'm wrong. A man covered in bloodstains, holding an axe. Does that sound familiar?"

Mona straightened up like she'd gotten an electric shock. Her eyes darted up to the camera for a second before she snapped, "I don't know what you're talking about."

"Yes, you do. You've seen Hector Harcourt. Your eyes weren't playing tricks on you, Sergeant. It wasn't the heat or the smoke getting to you. He is out there. I've seen him too."

"Hector Harcourt and his family have been dead for nearly a century."

"And they're clearly not letting that get them down. Or did you always think the stories about the Harcourt House were a practical joke?"

Mona leaned forward. Abby could see the tension in her shoulders and the little quivering of her hands. "I'm going to say this clearly so you understand: there is nothing, and there has never been anything, paranormal in the Harcourt House."

"Simon always said there were people like you. Normal people, not born with any kind of magic in them, who had keener perception than the rest. Not a fraction as keen as the Gospels, obviously, but keen enough that they could brush up against the uncanny once or twice in their life."

"You're babbling. I don't even know why I'm listening to this."

"You can't deny it forever. These things are out there. You've seen them and you're trying to ignore them, but what you don't get is they don't *want* to be ignored. They don't like it one bit. It took me a long time to learn that for myself."

Mona shook her head vigorously, but Abby could tell she'd struck a nerve. The sergeant was like the proverbial Egyptian river: she was deep in de Nile.

"You're crazy," Mona hissed. "There's no such thing as ghosts. Or magic."

Abby nodded. "You're goddamn right I'm crazy. So who do I talk to around here about an insanity plea?"

*****

Mona sent Abby back to the holding cells without an insanity plea and took Leanne into the interview room. Over the next two hours, Simon and Natalie got the same treatment. When every one of them had been interviewed, they were left to their own devices in the cells. It was just before sunset when the detention guard came back downstairs, followed by a beefy, tired-looking man with the single crown and pip of a superintendent on his epaulettes. The beefy man grunted at the detention guard to open both cells and told the four they were free to go.

"What? Just like that?" Abby said. "Aren't you going to charge us with anything?"

Superintendent Campbell grumbled and scratched his unshaven face. "Oh, we definitely are. Don't worry your pretty head about that. But I don't need some goddamn ghostbusters clogging up my nice clean holding cells, so you four have just made bail. Lucky you." He smiled and spoke more slowly, as if to a very stupid child. "First, you're gonna come up to my office, and we'll sort out some paperwork. After that, I strongly advise you to get your car, get your stuff from your motel, and get the fuck outta Delapore."

"Are you seriously trying to run us out of town? This isn't a Jim Thompson novel!"

The superintendent loomed over her and narrowed his eyes. "What this is, is me being nice. You've got clean records, all of you, so I've persuaded the Crown to try you on summary charges. That means you pony up some cash and walk out of here, you go to the courthouse when the court tells you, and the judge gives you a smack on the head and tells you to behave. If you want to stick around and keep playing Harry Potter, that's fine by me, but if you cross the line again, the charges get more serious, and then I will personally see to it the Crown fucks you all sideways. My advice? Take the win where you can get it and scram."

The hairs twitched on the back of Abby's neck as she caught a whiff of *eau de black magic*. The superintendent's eyes were red and dilated, as Bill Grover's had been in his last moments, and she could see the little cicadas darting around in his pupils. She fought down the rising nausea and squared her shoulders, trying to pretend she didn't notice. "Well, how can we say 'no' to an offer like that?"

Campbell nodded. "Now you're getting it."

*****

It was a long walk back to the motel. The Thunderbird had been towed when the four were arrested that morning, and the impound lot was already closed for the day. After a late dinner of 24-hour Chinese takeout, Abby explained what she had seen in the morgue. The longer she spoke, the quieter

Simon got, and his hands twitched on the table like he wanted to hit something.

"My God," Leanne whispered, "that sounds terrible. Poor Sonia…"

Simon dug in the pockets of his waistcoat and extracted a small pencil. He then handed this and a spare napkin to Abby. "Abigail, I want you to draw for me, as near as you can recreate it, the sigil you saw in your vision."

"Simon, I just told you what it looked—"

He held up a hand. "Please," he hissed. "For my own elucidation. I want to be completely sure on this."

Abby shrugged and drew the symbol she had seen. When she showed it to Simon, he sighed and hung his head. "*Metodes miht.*"

"What's the matter?" Leanne asked.

He crumpled up the napkin and shut his eyes. "I didn't want to believe it. I really, *really* didn't want to consider that this kind of evil could still exist in the world."

"What kind of evil?" said Abby.

"I tell myself that humanity's worth saving. I tell myself that everyone on this planet has a spark of goodness in their heart, and that it's my duty to protect that goodness from the things that would try to hurt it. But every now and then, I begin to doubt. Every now and then, one of you stupid, hairless monkeys goes and does something like *this*!" The napkin burst into flames in his hand and he hurled it into a trash can beside the bed.

Abby ran to stamp the fire out. "Jesus, what's gotten into you?"

"*Seo morþdæd þūsenda dolga.*"

"The which?" said Natalie.

Simon let his head fall back. "In Modern English, 'The Death of a Thousand Cuts.' That's what that symbol means, and that's what killed Ms. Styles and the others."

"I guess you've seen this before," said Leanne.

"Yes, but I haven't seen it for a *very* long time. Perhaps… I didn't *want* to see it. Perhaps I wanted to fool myself into thinking that this sort of thing didn't happen anymore."

"It's that bad, huh?" Abby asked.

"The Death of a Thousand Cuts is one of the cruellest curses in existence. It's a targeted attack on every facet of a person's mind and body, designed to elicit the most potent sensations of fear and pain that a living being can possibly experience. The caster begins by paralyzing the victim in order to make them supplicant, and to terrify them beyond all reason. Then the torture begins. Each cut hurts more than the last, and by the end the victim is absolutely *begging* for death. The throat is always the last to be opened, both as a mercy to the victim—finally ending the torture—and to release the lifeblood for the benefit of the killer."

Leanne crossed herself, her face very white. "Mary, Mother of God! How could human beings do that to each other? That's just… *vile.*"

Simon nodded in bitter agreement. "Perfectly said, Leanne. There was a time when the use of the Thousand Cuts on another living being was considered nothing short of a war crime."

Abby swallowed. "I hate to ask, Simon, but what were you saying about lifeblood?"

"Legend says that by drinking the lifeblood of another living being, one can absorb their emotional and spiritual power. Fear and pain are powerful emotions with a tremendous capacity for fuelling black magic. And that's what makes the Thousand Cuts so heinous: it's no mere torture. It's a means of wringing as much raw energy out of a person as possible, and using that power to advance one's own goals."

"So *that's* what our killer is after," Abby concluded. "Torture people, kill them, drink their blood, and become a super-powerful magician."

"*Warlock*," Simon spat, as if it was the ugliest epithet he could think of. "Somebody this far gone into the dark magicks can only be described as a *warlock*."

"Okay, become a super-powerful warlock," Abby amended.

"The only thing I'm having trouble with is the amount of blood taken. If our killer is using the blood himself, one harvest every couple of months should be plenty. But draining three people in a month would cause a massive overdose. Spontaneous bodily combustion, or worse."

"What if he's drinking for two?" Abby asked. "Remember what we learned about Reverend Jansen? What if he's storing some of that Thousand Cuts blood so he can use it to heal his daughter?"

"That's a bit of a long shot. If you want to heal someone with magic, there are plenty of less destructive ways to do it. Baldwin's Ninth Charm, the Mystery of the Sundered Frame, the Physician's Miracle... And those are just the most mainstream spells."

"Humour me. Is it or is it not theoretically possible?"

"Theoretically, I suppose it is. The power released by a Thousand Cuts rite is substantial, and that power could be applied for healing purposes. With three victims, there'd be enough blood for both of them."

"Maybe it's that simple. Maybe Reverend Jansen wants to fix Grace up, and the Master made contact and convinced him this was a faster way to do it."

"I'd still need to see some physical proof."

"Then we'll go find some first thing tomorrow. We need to make up for lost time, and I'm in a tree-shaking mood."

CHAPTER 14

CHALLENGE OF THE OKANAGAN

MONA BRADY stifled a yawn as she walked Bill Grover's autopsy report up to the superintendent's office. 9:00PM, and they were all burning the candle at both ends. God, but she hoped that Will was having a better time than she was.

She'd started the day attending Bill's autopsy, then she'd had to interview that Henderson girl and her freaky friends while Rickards and Foley talked to everyone who owned a Ford van matching Jim Cardinal's description. And she *still* had a late patrol with Pruitt to look forward to. She thought of the son she'd barely seen for two days, and the soft, unmade bed she hadn't slept in for two nights. Then she thought of the little package she'd hidden underneath the bed. *Know me, Mona August. Know what I am…*

Bill's autopsy had left her with more than the usual queasy feeling. Nearly as soon as Doc Hummel got the body out of refrigeration, the breaker to the morgue had blown. All the lights and the doc's computer went dead, and there was a five-minute delay before the power was restored.

Then Dr. Hummel made his first incision and a chill crept into the morgue. Bill Grover's internal temperature was nearly four degrees below the ambient temperature of the refrigerated drawer he'd been lying in for the last 43 hours.

Dr. Hummel had checked and re-checked the numbers on three different thermometers before he believed it.

And of course, the less said about those goddamn cicadas the better.

She stopped short just as she reached the superintendent's office door. Two voices on the other side were speaking in heated whispers and hisses, obviously making an effort not to scream at each other. Mona wasn't surprised. Superintendent Campbell and Inspector Pembroke hadn't had an argument in almost two days, so they were well overdue.

"...we having this discussion?" growled the superintendent. "I did you a favour, Margot. We've got plenty of shit to deal with as is!"

"That's not your decision to make, Phil! I told you I wanted those four brought up on obstruction charges! They could have completely screwed up my inquiry! You had no right to let them walk out of here."

"You want to talk about rights? This is *my* precinct, Margot. You and your team are here to help find the twisted fucker that's cutting people's throats, and *that's it*. I still have the final word on normal operations. Far as I can tell, those ghostbusting fruits aren't the ones we're looking for, so what we do with them is my decision!"

"They interfered with *my* investigation! They ran roughshod over that Harcourt place! I have witness testimony that says a van matching Jim Cardinal's description was seen at that house *twice* in the last month. I had planned to send my officers to check the property today, but those lunatics smashed it to pieces! God knows how much evidence they destroyed!"

"Larry Vogel already backed my play. If you think you know more than the Crown Counsel, then you're free to tell him that yourself. But I don't know that he'll be feeling very charitable after you stole his office from him."

"You are unbelievable, Philip!"

"And you're getting real close to insubordinate, *Inspector*. Look, it's done. Those idiots have their court date, they're not going back in the House, and we can focus on what's important again. Now, fuck off and find me a serial killer. That's what you're here for, isn't it?"

Mona stepped aside as the office door slammed against the wall and Inspector Pembroke stormed through the bullpen. Mona watched the inspector go, and then knocked on the doorframe. Superintendent Campbell looked up and beckoned her in.

When she got near his desk, the smell of booze hit her immediately. The superintendent's eyes were red and bloodshot, his uniform was rumpled, and he had a healthy crop of stubble coming in on his many chins. And she suspected, though she couldn't be sure, that that was the cap off a bottle of Fireball Whisky hiding at the bottom of the superintendent's pencil mug.

Trying her best to ignore this, she handed the report to Campbell and said, "Autopsy report on Bill Grover. There's not much new."

Campbell opened the folder and gave the report a cursory glance, then threw it aside. He rubbed his forehead and sighed deeply. "We get DNA back on those blood samples yet?"

"The blood tested as O+. That's Jenny Styles' blood type. It's also Bill Grover's. We won't have a full DNA test before the end of next week at least."

"Jesus. Alright, I'll make a couple calls, see if I can't light a fire under their asses. I want those test results first thing. Any progress with this ring angle?"

"Yes and no. According to the church's files, over two dozen current and former members of the St. Catherine's congregation wear the ring, excluding our victims. Three of those members are our own officers. Jim Cardinal says it was a man he saw at The Gaslights, but even eliminating all the female parishioners, we're still looking at fifteen people. Four of them are currently out of town, and we're working through interviews with the rest. So far, every one has a solid alibi for the night David Prudhomme disappeared. Pruitt spoke to the staff who were on duty at The Gaslights that night. None of them saw anyone who matched Cardinal's description. However, two witnesses did corroborate his statement about the yellow van. We also re-checked the security footage from The Forge for the night of July 1. Cameras at both entrances and every corner of the parking lot. At about 10:30PM, one of the cameras shows a mid-2000s Ford Econoline van pulling into the lot. Nobody gets out on camera, and the van stays parked there until just before midnight."

Campbell's head was still, but his bloodshot eyes rolled toward Mona in their sockets. In his pouchy, pale face, the effect was quite unnerving. Like two red widow spiders in a snowdrift, she thought. "Jenny Styles was last seen alive about 11:45."

"Exactly, sir. I suspect it is the same van in both cases. It could be Bill Grover's van in the footage, but there's no clear view of the plates."

"You still like Reverend Jansen for the killings."

"He has connections to at least two of the victims, he has a van the same make and age as Bill Grover's, and he has no alibi for any of the three nights our victims disappeared. Plus, he wears a St. Catherine's ring. Bill Grover did not."

"But Bill had Sonia Hall's phone in his van," Campbell replied. "What's your answer to that?"

"Sonia Hall was the Grover kids' regular babysitter. I saw her at the house myself a couple times. Shirley Grover says that Bill regularly drove Sonia home after she would sit the kids. He did so at least once in the week before she disappeared. I'll admit the evidence we found in Bill Grover's van is a more solid physical lead, but it's not rock-solid. I just want to make completely sure we're not barking up the wrong tree."

"Alright, run with this ball and see what happens. But keep it *quiet*. If you're wrong, the church community will tear us a new one." Leaning back in his chair, Phil Campbell folded his hands over his ample gut and turned to look out the window. Straight at the big old melanoma sitting above Pearson Heights. One of his hands began to tremble and he smacked his lips nervously.

"Superintendent, is everything OK?" Mona asked.

Campbell shook his head, still looking at the Harcourt House. "Nothing's OK, Sergeant. Nothing's OK at all."

"Sir?"

"There's something wrong with this town, Mona. Something wrong… at the heart, you know?" He turned to her and tapped his chest with a finger. "Delapore's got a sickness, right in here. Pembroke doesn't get it. None of 'em do. This ain't their town."

"I'm… I'm afraid I don't understand you, Superintendent."

Campbell gestured to the framed photos on the office wall. "That's my father up there, Mona. And that's his dad, and his dad's dad. Time was, all three of them sat in this very office. I ever tell you that?"

"No, sir."

"When I was a kid, Grandpa used to tell me stories about some of the old cases he worked when this town was all dirt road. Most of 'em were hayseed bullshit, but… There have been killings in Delapore before, Mona. A nasty string of them in the late '20s. Grandpa told me about them just before he died. Nine people cut up and sucked dry of their blood between '25 and '27. Nobody was ever charged, but Grandpa Campbell said that whatever did it, it wasn't human. When he first told me the story, I thought it was the Alzheimer's talking. But he knew what he was saying. I think he was… *confessing*. His whole squad was too scared to do shit about it, and he had to make his peace. They didn't like what that case meant for Delapore, so they looked the other way, and they leaned on the press to keep quiet."

"Sir, why are you telling me this?"

Campbell pointed a sausagey finger at Mona. "Because I need you to understand what I'm saying," he rumbled. "Because this town *is* sick. And its sickness didn't come from this world. I'm telling you this because this killer's MO, everything about this case that doesn't add up, it's all stuff that my grandpa said *he* ran into working that case in the '20s." He lowered his hand and stared at her with those weary, red-widow eyes. "I know what you're thinking, Sergeant. I can see it in your face. You don't believe me. You don't believe this town is *wrong*. But I'm telling you, with God the Father and Sweet Sonny Jesus as my witnesses, Delapore has a *curse* on it. And it's got something..." He looked out the window and pointed. "It's got something to do with *that house.*"

"Sir, with all respect, what you're saying is absurd. Honestly, you sound like my son."

Campbell nodded. "Yeah, your son believes, doesn't he? He believes in the Harcourt House. Let me tell you, Mona Brady: that boy is smarter than you give him credit for. And the next time he tells you the Harcourt House is bad news, *you fucking well listen.*"

*****

Abby didn't sleep well that night. The heat was unbearable even with a fan on and the window open. She couldn't shake the thought of the Thousand Cuts murders, and her dreams kept circling back to an image of that grinning red-eyed skull chanting, *"Blood. Blood. Blood. Cutting. Cutting. Life. Blood. Life..."* She saw Jenny, Sonia, and David trying to scream as the blood poured from their bodies onto the chalk sigil, and she saw Hector Harcourt chopping his family to bits with a wild look in his eyes. She woke up, and fell back asleep, and then woke up again about five times in the night. The last time she woke up, the clock on the nightstand said 3:30AM, and the weather app on her phone said it was 24° C. She went into the bathroom, had a pee, then shucked off her pyjamas and turned the shower on cold.

It was too quiet when she got out of the shower, and Abby realized after a moment that the fan had turned off. She wrapped herself in a towel and cracked opened the door. "Lee?" she whispered. "Lee, are you awake?"

The bathroom light died with a *pop* and Abby felt a thorny wave of black magic roll over her. She threw the door open all the way and shouted, "LEE!"

Leanne sat bolt upright on her side of the bed and turned on her reading light. The man standing over her wore a dark turtleneck and balaclava and held a wand in his gloved hands. When the light came on, he shielded his eyes and growled, *"Morere!"* Leanne shrieked and rolled over to Abby's side of the bed as a bolt of black lightning shredded the mattress. As the warlock readjusted his aim, Leanne kicked him in the stomach and knocked him back against the wall. Then she grabbed her glasses off the nightstand and bolted toward Abby.

The reading light died, and the warlock's next shot blasted a hole in the closet door. Abby saw his red eyes shining in the dark, so she picked up a glass from the bathroom counter and threw it right at them. Red Eyes swore as the glass broke on his head, and Abby pulled Leanne into the bathroom. The two braced themselves against the door but Red Eyes blasted the doorknob into the back wall and kicked down what was left. Without breaking stride, he slammed Leanne headfirst into the mirror and aimed his wand at Abby for the killing blow.

Throwing caution and modesty to the wind, she took off her towel and brandished it like a whip, knocking Red Eyes off-balance. His next curse went wild and blasted the mirror into a thousand dime-sized shards. Abby screamed as glass raked across her shoulders, her breasts, and her forearms, and Red Eyes pressed the advantage. He kicked her in the chest and threw her into the corner of the shower, jamming his forearm against her throat so she couldn't call for help.

Leanne staggered over and turned the shower on as hot as it would go. Red Eyes screamed as the water scalded him through his turtleneck, and then Abby kneed him in the balls. He crumpled at her feet and grunted, *"Sum quasi aquam..."* Suddenly, his whole body seemed to melt into a puddle and slide down the drain.

"Eagan heofena!" The motel room lit up as Simon and Natalie rushed in. Twin orbs of light floated in his hands, and he swept these around the room as he scanned for the threat. "Where is he?" he demanded of Abby. "Where did he go?"

Abby looked out the window and felt the black magic coming from that direction. Two points of red light appeared in the darkness and she hollered, "GET DOWN!"

The black lightning obliterated the window and tore a strip out of the wallpaper. Simon returned fire from his spot on the floor, but Red Eyes had already melted away.

Abby felt the tingle of black magic on the back of her neck, and she was on her feet a second before Red Eyes sprang out of the closet shouting, *"Gravitas!"* A ball of orange lightning struck the huddled pile of Simon, Leanne, and Natalie, and they all sank heavily to the floor like they'd been magnetized. As Red Eyes turned his attention on her, Abby turned and ran out into the motel parking lot as naked as the day she was born. She heard Red Eyes chase after her, so she screamed at the top of her lungs, "HELP! POLICE! RAPE!"

A few lights went on in the motel. Red Eyes kept coming, so Abby kept screaming. She risked a look back just as Red Eyes loosed another spell. *"Carnis lapidis!"* Blue lightning hit her in the small of the back and every muscle in her body seized up. Red Eyes came up behind her and pressed his wand up under her chin.

Natalie's heavy footsteps pounded rapidly across the parking lot, and Red Eyes moved to face her. She ducked under his first spell, jinked to dodge the second, but the third sliced across her forearm. She bit back a scream of pain, wrapped one massive hand around Red Eyes' throat, and hoisted him off the ground. He kicked in the air as she strangled the life out of him, and Abby found herself able to move again. About two seconds before Natalie broke his neck, Red Eyes gasped and stuttered, *"S-sum quasi aquam!"* His body melted right out of Natalie's hand and soaked into the tarmac.

"Thanks," Abby whispered. Natalie nodded and gave her a one-armed hug, wincing as she flexed her injured arm. Then they walked back to Abby and Leanne's room.

After he had pulled all the glass from Abby and Leanne's wounds, cleaned, and dressed them to the best of his ability, Simon's final prognosis was, "You're lucky."

"Lucky?" Abby snapped. "Simon, you just pulled what's left of the mirror out of my tits! How the hell does that qualify as lucky?"

"I didn't pull any of it out of your arteries, for one thing."

"Okay, fair point. Can I please put on a bra now?"

He gave her the all-clear to get dressed. As she did so, she looked at the wreckage of the motel room. This was now the second time in a year she'd been stark naked and bleeding in front of Simon and Natalie, and it was tough to look them in the eye when she was in that state. "This thing's escalating too fast," she grumbled. "The Master couldn't drive us over the edge in his Funhouse of Horrors, so he sent his pet warlock to finish the job. Guy probably would have made us disappear like David Prudhomme if he had the chance. Hell, I'm willing to bet that's the whole reason the cops let us go."

"What do you mean?" asked Leanne.

Abby sat down on the bed. "I got whammied with black magic when we were talking to that Superintendent Campbell. And his eyes just… didn't look right. It was like there was something else inside him. I saw the same thing in Bill Grover's eyes when he came at me. I don't know if he was possessed or what, but something was up."

Simon nodded. "And you think 'something' convinced Superintendent Campbell to get us off on lighter charges."

"Yup. If they'd kept us in custody and slapped us with felony charges, and then something happened to us, it'd be a total clusterfuck. There'd have to be an investigation, and I doubt the Master needs that kind of attention right now. But if we were let go, and we were told to get the hell out of town, suddenly it's not their problem if we come to harm and the bad guys don't have to answer any awkward questions."

Natalie grunted in agreement. "You could be onto something. I was going to ask: did anybody notice how the warlock was holding his wand?"

"Not really," Leanne admitted. "Why?"

"He was using a CAR stance at first. That's Center Axis Relock. It's a way of holding a gun in a closeup fight. And then when we were in the parking lot, he fell into a Weaver stance. That's better for long-range accuracy. It takes training to know how to do that stuff, and the warlock did it without thinking. If Campbell was touched by magic, then the warlock could be someone close to him."

"He might be a cop himself," said Leanne.

Natalie nodded and tapped her nose.

"We need to start being more careful," Leanne said. "We've drawn way too much attention to ourselves since we got here, and now we're paying for it. Maybe we should lay low for few days and let things calm down. It'll give us a chance to recharge our brains."

"That's the best idea I've heard in ages," Abby said. "I'm starting to forget what a good night's sleep feels like."

Simon looked out the shattered window as a police siren went *whoop whoop* in the parking lot, and Mona and Pruitt got out of their cruiser. "Speaking of too much attention..." he muttered.

When Abby gave her statement, she was brutally honest about her attacker's bright red eyes, and for the second time in less than 24 hours, Mona wound up believing Abby slightly more than she wanted to admit. She made calls to the rest of the squad, and by 4:00, cops were sweeping the motel and the eight blocks around it, knocking on every door in that radius. A handful of people had heard the screaming, and a couple guests at the motel had seen the naked young woman bleeding all over the parking lot, but they didn't know a thing about a madman with red eyes. When she asked to review the security footage, Mona discovered that all three of the motel's cameras had shorted out. The last thing they picked up was a few cicadas crawling on the lenses at 3:26AM.

Abby and Leanne's room was cordoned off for the forensics team, and the two were upgraded to a slightly nicer room on the second floor. The motel staff were tripping over themselves trying to apologize for the incident, but Abby just wanted to forget the whole thing. Somebody had tried to kill her while she slept, and if Natalie was right, he could be out in that parking lot right now, wearing a badge.

It was nearly four more hours before the investigation wrapped up. By that time, Abby had completely given up on the thought of getting any sleep, and she was leaning on the balcony with her morning cup of tea, watching the police lights flash on the tarmac. Mona Brady came up the stairs and said, "There's no sign of the man who attacked you, but we'll leave an officer here in case he comes back. Stay where you are for now. If you have to go out, check in with the officer when you leave and when you return."

"That's not the advice your superintendent gave us."

"My superintendent's not here right now. Two homicides is a lot for a town like this, and I don't want to wake up tomorrow and find out that number's climbing." She stifled a yawn and rubbed her eyes. "Excuse me."

"You want some coffee?" Abby asked. "My partner just got a fresh pot going."

"No, thanks. As soon as we're done here, I get to clock out. I'm having a shower and getting straight into bed."

Abby turned and looked Mona in the eye. "Look, I'm sorry about all the trouble we've made so far. We just wanted to get some answers to the mysteries in this town, but we crossed a line to get there."

"Apology accepted. Just don't let it happen again." Mona paused and looked over the balcony. Then she checked to make sure nobody was having a sneaky peek through their blinds. "The man who attacked you: you said he had red eyes?"

Abby nodded. "Like Christmas lights from Hell. They were almost glowing."

Mona lowered her voice and leaned in. "You know I think all this magic stuff is a bunch of crap."

"I do."

"But suppose for a second… that a part of me believed you."

"Hypothetically speaking."

"Exactly. If, hypothetically, I *did* accept your story, I would tell you to talk to Jim Cardinal and ask him about the night of the 12th."

"But you're *not* telling me that. Because you think magic is a bunch of crap."

"Exactly." And she walked away without another word.

CHAPTER 15

I TELL YOU A MYSTERY

FOR MOST of the next week, Delapore was mercifully quiet. Abby didn't have another rude awakening until Friday morning, when her real life called to check up on her. Simon had gone off early to meet his mystery contact, while Abby and Leanne enjoyed a late breakfast in their room. They were just finishing washing up when Abby's cellphone started buzzing. Before she could say hello, the caller demanded,

"Why am I taking calls from the RCMP?"

Abby gulped. "S-sorry, what?"

On the other end of the line, Adam Sakurai let out a breath. Abby heard a creak and imagined the big man leaning back in the too-small chair in his too-small manager's office at MacReady's Social House, the Vancouver restaurant where she'd been employed as a hostess for the last two years.

"Last weekend," said Adam, "I got a call from a Sergeant Mona Brady, of the Delapore RCMP. She was asking me a lot of questions about you and how long you'd been working for me. She didn't say why she was calling, which had me a little concerned. I tried calling you, but you never answered."

"You tried to call me? When?"

"Sunday afternoon. And Monday morning. And Tuesday. Didn't you get my messages?"

Abby shut her eyes and swore inwardly. Ever since Red Eyes had attacked, both her phone and Leanne's had been struggling to hold a consistent signal. The energy released by his magic had damaged the SIM cards, and they'd had to make a trip into the city on Thursday to buy replacements.

"Look, Abby," Adam said gently, "if you're in some kind of legal trouble, then that's not my business. You wouldn't be the first person in the service industry to have... made some mistakes. But you need to understand that as long as you're a member of the MacReady's team, what you do reflects on the MacReady's brand."

"God, Adam, *please* don't give me the corporate lecture right now! I've had an awful week."

"Abby, I'm trying to help you here. Don't forget, I have people I have to answer to myself, and ever since the remodel last fall, they've been keeping a close eye on you."

Abby winced. The very lengthy, very costly remodeling of the restaurant had been partly her fault, after all. One of the Deacon's hench-demons had ransacked MacReady's trying to get to her, and enough of the incident had been caught on video to make some people very suspicious.

"I'm sorry. You're right," she relented. "You're definitely the least of several evils that I'm dealing with right now. I admit that things got a little out of hand, and I did something stupid that I really shouldn't have. Believe me, it's not a mistake I plan to make again."

"Good. I'll see you when you get back to town. And Abby?"

"Yeah?"

"Any more 'mistakes,' and we're going to have to have a serious talk about your future as part of the MacReady's team. Understand me?"

"Yeah. I guess. Bye." She hung up, threw herself facedown on the bed, and spat a few stifled curses into the pillow. "Goddammit, that's all I need," she moaned as she rolled onto her back. Then she looked over at Leanne and asked, "If I lose my job because I'm too busy fighting magical bad guys, do you think I can come work at the Shoppe?"

Leanne shook her head. "I'm still paying off my own repair bills, Abby. Frankly, it doesn't even make financial sense for me to be in Delapore right now. I should have been working this whole time."

Abby propped herself up on her elbows. "Are things honestly that bad right now?"

Leanne didn't say anything, but Abby could see the answer in her eyes. The Olde Curiosity Shoppe, the used bookstore where Leanne worked, had been another victim of the Deacon's cult last year. After the death of the Shoppe's demon-possessed owner, Leanne had taken out a loan from her parents and had bought the place herself, both to keep herself employed and to preserve the memory of the place where she and Abby had first met. But the Shoppe, like MacReady's, had required extensive repairs after the demons ransacked it, and Leanne had spent her first year as a small business owner operating on a razor-thin margin. It was the one conversation she always tried to avoid having with Abby.

"Lee, if you need to go home and run the Shoppe, then go home and run the Shoppe," Abby said seriously. "I don't want you to go bankrupt because of my dumbass crusade. It's only a few days."

Leanne set her jaw and shook her head. "No. No, I said I was going to be here foreverways, and I meant it. There are people in this town who need help, and none of us are leaving until they get it. Besides, if I left now and something happened to you..." She laid down on the bed beside Abby and squeezed Abby's hand to her chest. "You have no idea what I saw in the Harcourt House," she whispered. She closed her eyes and suppressed a crack in her voice. "I couldn't forgive myself if I wasn't beside you and... and something happened."

Abby kissed Leanne's hand and wriggled closer to her. "You're too good for me," she whispered. "I don't deserve you."

Leanne smiled and kissed her. "Right on both counts."

The door flew open and Simon breezed through the room with several thick manila folders under one arm. On seeing Abby and Leanne on the bed, he quickly covered his eyes with his other hand and turned his back on them. "Not interrupting anything, am I? Only I have some work for you two."

Abby gave an exasperated sigh. "What do you have?"

Still without looking, Simon threw the manila folders onto the bed. "Well, after your little *tête-à-tête* with Sergeant Brady the other day, I asked my contact to find out what he could about one Jim (or Jimmy) Cardinal, who was the last person to see David Prudhomme alive. Our own Sergeant Brady and Corporal Rickards interviewed him the day we arrived. According to Mr. Cardinal's witness statement, he and David were at their local on July 12th when they ran into a man with red eyes."

Leanne got up from the bed and looked at one of the folders. "And David Prudhomme disappeared that night, didn't he?"

Simon finally turned around, obviously relieved to discover that he hadn't caught the girls *in flagrante delicto*. "Indeed he did. Unfortunately, Mr. Cardinal didn't see the red-eyed gentleman's face, but he claims the man was wearing a St. Catherine's ring. The police have been interviewing everyone they can who wears that ring, and my contact—being an industrious little so-and-so—has pulled the transcripts of those interviews. We are going to have a look through and see if anything jumps out."

Abby grabbed a folder and started flipping through, her earlier troubles forgotten. "Holy crap, that's a real result! How the hell did your guy manage this?"

"A magician never reveals his secrets, Abigail. Now, while we're doing this, I've got Natalie scoping out the local hardware market. Our warlock's already had to make at least one replacement wand, and for violent offensive magic like this, it's common sense to craft a few spares, so I'd like to know if anyone in town has been buying Pacific yew wood. I expect she'll be on the phone for a while."

"Do either of you even know how to *use* a telephone?"

He huffed. "The principle *is* simple enough to understand, thanks very much. However, with magic as strong as ours, not blowing a breaker can be a bit of an issue."

Leanne's cell phone buzzed on the nightstand. "Speaking of which…" she said, and went to answer it. It was a short call, and she ended it with a smile on her face.

"Good news?" Abby asked.

"Could be. I've been thinking a lot about Arnold Tremblay and what he found about the Harcourts' servants."

"How they didn't die the way they were supposed to have died."

"Right. I did some more digging online yesterday, and you know what I found? Arnold Tremblay's granddaughter is still alive and she lives here in town. I got in touch with her yesterday to see if I could pick her brain about the Harcourt murders. That was her phoning back."

"And she's willing to talk?"

"Extremely," Leanne said. "She lives in Pearson Heights, and she told me I can come over any time today."

Simon nodded his approval. "Round of applause for you, Leanne. Go chase down those servants. Abby and I can manage without you."

*****

Leanne left them to it and went to go bug Natalie for a ride. Arnold Tremblay's granddaughter lived in one of the grey-

and-brown identikit houses at the bottom of Pearson Heights, but her front garden was thick with the liveliest, most vibrant rosebushes Leanne had ever seen. It was almost like the woman was trying to apologize for the sterility of the neighbourhood, but when Leanne's nose started to twitch as she rang the doorbell, she decided that she would have preferred an apology for own allergies.

After a few moments, Leanne's doorbell orchestrations were answered by an air raid siren of a voice. The door opened with a flourish, and Arnold Tremblay's granddaughter came onto the front step. She was nearly as tall and wide as the doorway itself, with glasses as thick as Leanne's own and a screwed-up bird's nest of hair dyed bright red. Her glittering gold bangles, rings, and earrings could probably blind a person in direct sunlight, if her perfume didn't get there first. The artificial scent of roses made Leanne's eyes water and her throat dry up, and she coughed out a weak, "Dolores Browne?"

The gigantic woman seized Leanne's hand and shook it amiably, though not gently. "Call me Dot, for gosh sake! Everyone does! Leanne, isn't it?"

Leanne nodded. All the moisture in her mouth had retreated up to her eyes, and she just managed to ask for a glass of water before her throat closed.

Dot Browne nodded and pulled Leanne into the house. "Of course! Of course! It's a scorcher out there!"

She sat Leanne down in the living room, got her a glass of water from the kitchen, and then took a seat on the other side of the coffee table. The furniture was frilly and lacy, and probably not the kind of thing Dot Browne would have picked out herself. Leanne's parents would have called it old maid furniture, and while Dot was admittedly well north of 60, her dye job suggested a woman who was terrified of any number above 50. Leanne guessed that this was an inherited style from Dot's parents.

She took two Claritin tablets from the blister pack in her purse, swallowed them and half the glass of water, and then thanked Dot for agreeing to meet with her. "I imagine you probably get a ton of calls from people like me."

In her air-raid-siren voice, Dot laughed and said, "You'd think so, wouldn't you? Behold: the last living connection to the man who broke the biggest news story in this town's history! But you'd be wrong. I think a lot of folks around here would just prefer if I kept my yap shut."

"Why do you say that?"

Dot smiled and spread her arms wide. "Look at me, hon. I'm a kook. The whole town thinks so, I think so, and I'll bet folding money you think so. And as luck would have it, I'm also the only person around here who'll give you the straight poop on the Harcourts. Everyone else likes to pretend there's no house at the top of that hill at all. Sure, the podcasters and the bloggers out in the aether will talk big about 'the Harcourt Horror,' and the *heinous crime* and all the *mysterious occurrences*, but they don't care. They just want their clicks, and what gets more clicks than blood and guts and things that go bump in the night?"

"But the local kids sneak into the House all the time, don't they? If nobody cares, why is there a fence around the place?"

Dot scoffed. "Kids are idiots! Most of them think the Harcourt House is a joke or a theme park ride! Sure, they go in, but most of them never see a thing. And then they stop caring. And the ones who do see something, well, they don't like what they see. So they'll deny they saw anything, and then they'll try to pretend the House was never there. Most of the folks who keep the story going have never been anywhere near the Harcourt House. They wouldn't know Hector Harcourt if he was standing right in front of them. And that's what separates kooks like us from the rest of 'em."

Leanne stifled a laugh. Was this what Abby was going to be like in 40 years? "What makes you think I'm a kook?"

"For starters, you're here talking to me. You've done more research than most, and you're already looking farther ahead than the rest. When folks see a living ghost story like the Harcourt House, in my experience they either write it off, or they don't see anything *but* ghosts."

"They don't see human beings," Leanne said. "They don't see the servants."

"Bingo. Aside from my granddad, I haven't ever met one living soul who's cared to ask what happened to Joseph and Celia.That's what everyone forgets. Before there was a ghost story, there was a human tragedy, and it didn't start with Hector Harcourt. People died up on that hill, but nobody gives a hoot about them. My granddad was still a young buck when it all happened, and he fought tooth and nail for the servants until he drew his last breath. Something about their deaths in particular never sat right with him, and he couldn't bring himself to think that Hector was the monster the town wanted him to be. My granddad knew Hector Harcourt from way back, and what happened on the hill… well, that wasn't the man that Granddad knew. But he was alone in the fight. Even my grandma wasn't completely on his side."

"But you were?"

She shrugged. "Sometimes it skips a generation. Being a kook. After Granddad died, my parents didn't want much to do with the 'Harcourt conspiracy.' That's why they left all his papers with the library. More or less." She gave Leanne an exaggerated wink, almost baiting her into asking for more. So Leanne did.

"I went through all the boxes my parents had," said Dot. "A week before they drove 'em over to the library. I saved a few of Granddad's juiciest files for myself."

"Do you mind if I…?"

"Aw, hell! I didn't invite you over for a game of pinochle! Files are in my office, this way."

Dot Browne stood and led Leanne upstairs to a small home office opposite her own bedroom. An IKEA computer desk in one corner formed an 'L' with a large roll-top writing desk against the far wall. Ring binders and manila folders of old laminated paperwork had been scattered across the latter surface, and two large cardboard boxes were stuffed into the tight space beneath the former. "I laid some things out when I knew you were coming over," Dot said. She hurried Leanne into a chair in front of the old writing desk. "I had a system going, but then I started wandering down memory lane and it all kind of turned into one big pile. Sorry about that."

"No problem," Leanne said, more than a little impressed. "I think this is going to give me a lot to go on." She looked over her shoulder and pointed at the computer desk. "Do you mind if I use your scanner? Just in case I find anything good."

Dot went and turned on the computer and the copier hooked up to it. "Be my guest. The old girl's a bit finicky sometimes, so if she gives you any grief, just give her a smack like this and tell her to suck an egg. Always works for me."

"I'll keep that in mind. Thanks."

"Shout if you need me. I won't be far." Dot Browne turned and left Leanne alone in the office, whistling a Sinatra tune as she went.

*****

After 90 minutes spent elbow-deep in thick manila folders, Simon and Abby still hadn't found a thing. Natalie checked in to see how they were getting on, and admitted that she wasn't having much better luck. "I talked to eight different hardware stores in the area and five lumber wholesalers. It's a pretty short list of people who placed orders for Pacific yew in the last year, and the only local on that list is Bill Grover. Couple of the guys I talked to said he liked yew for kitchen furnishings. I don't know how much of a lead that is, though.

Bill had open accounts at a few places going back six or seven years."

"Do we know if Bill Grover wore a St. Catherine's ring?" asked Simon.

Abby shrugged. "I didn't see one when he attacked me."

"I asked if anyone remembered selling to a guy with a ring," Natalie said. "None of them did."

"Great," Abby muttered. "Dead end. Well, as long as you're here, you want to help us with this?"

Natalie got stuck in, but it took another twenty minutes of reading before any of them found anything good. It was Abby who spotted it, in the interview transcript of one Lucas Scott. She nudged the others to get their attention and asked, "Did you see this?"

Simon read over the transcript and nodded. "That sounds like motive to me."

"It really does. When the warlock attacked me here, I remember thinking that he looked pretty athletic. Not like a weightlifter or anything, but maybe a jogger or a cyclist. And he was definitely a few inches taller than me. Reverend Jansen fits that profile."

"He does seem to be in rather good nick for his age. Of course, we can't forget what Natalie said about the warlock's shooting stance. The notes in here say that Corporal Rickards and Constables Pang and Pruitt all wear the St. Catherine's ring."

"Pruitt's way too short. And when I talked to her the other day, I didn't see a speck of magic in her aura. But Rickards and Pang… maybe." She started looking through the folders again. "All their interviews have got to be in here. It won't hurt to double-check a few things, but I think this could be a real lead."

Abby's phone buzzed on the nightstand. It was Leanne.

"Hey," Abby said. "How are you getting on?"

"Not bad. Listen, I left my iPad in the room. Can you grab it? I found something that you guys need to see."

Abby put Leanne on speakerphone and went to grab the iPad from where it was plugged into the wall. The device buzzed with an email alert and Abby opened the first attachment.

"Did you get it?" Leanne asked.

"Yeah. I got it. What exactly am I looking at?"

"These are some of the pictures that Dot Browne had in her house. I really had to dig to find some of them. That first image you see is a family portrait of the Harcourts. I thought it might help us to put faces to all the names, but it's not the real meat and potatoes."

The photo had been taken on the front porch of the House. Josiah Harcourt was a straight-backed, serious-looking man with a neatly-trimmed beard and lightly-coloured hair. He stood with his arm around Olivia, flanked by his two sons. Hector and Isaac looked like mirror images of each other, with the same roguish good looks and thin, Clark Gable moustaches. In fact, without all the gore running down his front, Abby wasn't totally sure which one was Hector.

"On your right," said Leanne. "It's kind of hard to see in the photo, but Isaac's wearing a ring on his left hand. Hector isn't."

"Gotcha. But this isn't why you called, is it?"

"You're right. Check the last two images."

Abby did. "Whoa. Is that…?"

"Yeah. The way Dot told the story, when the milkman found the bodies on November 4, he ran screaming to the nearest house and made two phone calls, one to the police and one to the paper. Arnold Tremblay took the call at the newspaper and got to the Harcourt House before the cops did. He took some pictures that morning, but the police confiscated his camera as soon as they arrived. It took him four years and a crazy amount of bribes just to get the negatives back, but he didn't even develop them until 1939."

"Six years after the police barbecued all their files."

"Exactly."

The black-and-white image on the screen showed two human bodies sprawled on the floor of the Harcourt living room. These were apparently the servants, bloodied and mangled by Hector's axe. A large cargo hook lay on the floor at one edge of the frame, along with a short, frayed length of rope. The image right after that was of a crude chain-and-pulley system dangling from the ceiling. It looked like someone had tried to rip it out of the rafters and given up halfway through.

"They *were* on the ceiling..." Abby whispered.

"And look at the floor underneath the servants."

Abby went back to the previous photo and enlarged it. It was hard to make out under the bloodstains, but she thought she could see the border of a chalk circle running under the bodies. A couple demonic glyphs were just visible around the border, and behind one of the servants' heads, part of a sigil she knew too well. "Holy shit..."

"Yeah. Either I need new glasses, or that's a Thousand Cuts symbol on the floor."

*****

STATEMENT TRANSCRIPT

```
Subject: Lucas Cameron SCOTT    DOB: 1996/11/11
Address: 1603 Nichols Dr, Delapore, BC
Date of Interview: 2020-08-03
Officers: Sgt. Mona BRADY
```

BRADY: Do you prefer Lucas or Luke?

SCOTT: Either one's fine. I was Lucas when I was in school. Friends generally call me Luke.

BRADY: What were you doing on July 12, Luke?

SCOTT: Straight into it, huh? I worked until 5:00, then I went home and got dinner going. Wednesday's my *D&D* night.

BRADY: *D&D*. That's a fantasy game, right?

SCOTT: Yeah. Tabletop game. You get a bunch of people in a room and run through a fantasy adventure. I'm DM'ing right now. That means I'm running the current game, so I put together a big pot of chili for five. My regular group came by around 6:30 and we just went for it until… man, 10:30 or 11:00 I think.

BRADY: And what happened after the game was over?

SCOTT: My girlfriend's part of the group, so she hung around after the rest of them fucked off. We watched some stuff on YouTube, played a little *Borderlands*, went to bed. That was probably a little after one.

BRADY: How well did you know David Prudhomme, Luke?

SCOTT: Not that well. He was my mechanic, but it wasn't like I was exchanging Christmas cards with the guy. Always got the feeling he was… kind of shifty.

BRADY: What do you mean by that?

SCOTT: Look, I'm just saying it's not a coincidence that he bought it the same way those church girls did.

BRADY: What makes you say that?

SCOTT: The whole thing circles back to Grace Jansen, doesn't it? I mean, David and Jenny and Sonia, they're the reason she's in a wheelchair.

BRADY: Are they?

SCOTT: You probably don't know. It happened a few years before you got here, but that was always the rumour.

BRADY: What rumour do you mean, Luke?

SCOTT: That party at The Forge, the night Grace crashed her car. Papers said she was four times over the limit when it happened. She never should have gotten behind the wheel. But she did. And you wanna know why?
BRADY: Enlighten me.
SCOTT: She was running from David Prudhomme. He cornered her in the ladies' room and shoved his hand up her dress. Jenny and Sonia watched it happen, and they didn't do a goddamn thing to stop it.

CHAPTER 16

GRAVEYARD SHIFT

GURINDER DHILLON took a pull on her bottle and smiled up at her gentleman escort. At the beginning of the month, her mom had dragged her to a Punjabi cultural night at the rec centre, and the only good thing Gurinder could say about it was that she had finally scored a date with Mandeep Sihota. He'd been captain of the lacrosse team in the year above her at high school, president of the student body, class valedictorian, voted Most Likely to Succeed, all that good stuff. Oh, this'd be one hell of a feather in her cap, alright.

A crack in the sidewalk upset Gurinder, and she stumbled into Mandeep. Half a mouthful of cider dribbled down the front of her blouse, and more went up her nose as she struggled not to laugh. She threw her arms around him for support and giggled, "Sorry!"

Mandeep snorted and gave her a squeeze. "You're drunk!" He swigged his own bottle and swallowed a burp.

"Am not!"

"Am too!" He put his bottle to her lips and made her drink. She pulled away, snorting and laughing.

"Stop! Stop! It's going up my nose!"

Mandeep put a finger to his lips and leaned in close. "Shhhhhh! You'll wake people up!"

Gurinder stole a kiss and grinned. "What people? Who's gonna hear us?" It was nearly three o'clock on Friday morning and the street was as dark as dark could get. Ahead of them, the road forked to the left and led down to St. Catherine's Anglican. The fiery moonlight had turned the white walls orange and the green gabled roof a muddy shade of brown, and the high spikes atop the cemetery fence looked like the spines of a sleeping dragon. Gurinder pointed into the churchyard and sniggered, "You worried they're gonna call the cops on us?"

Mandeep laughed and kissed her. "You're drunk."

Gurinder finished her cider and dropped the bottle on the sidewalk. "If I'm drunk, you're drunk. You started before I did."

Mandeep considered this. "I'll drink to that." He raised his bottle in a toast and finished it in one pull. Then he pulled her toward him for a kiss, lost his footing on the sidewalk, and fell on his ass.

Gurinder doubled over laughing and smacked him on the leg. "I told you you were drunk!"

"No, *I* told *you*," Mandeep corrected.

"Oh, yeah. You did." She plopped down beside him and stretched her legs out in front of her. "God, my feet are killing me. Now I remember why I don't wear heels."

"So take 'em off."

"No way! They make my legs look *amazing*."

"Man, you are drunk."

"Takes one to know one."

They sat for a few moments enjoying the sensation as the booze pumped through their systems. Then, Mandeep looked behind him. "Wait, did you hear that?"

Gurinder looked back at the cemetery and laughed in Mandeep's face. "You think there's zombies in there or something?"

"It's not funny! I'm telling you I heard something!"

"Who the hell would be way out there at this hour?"

"I don't know, maybe the sick fucker who's torturing people to death?"

Then Gurinder heard it too. Distant footsteps somewhere at the edge of the cemetery, followed by a few chanted words in some language she didn't recognize, and then the sound of breaking rocks.

"Shit!" she hissed. She tried to stand but couldn't balance herself in her four-inch heels. "Shit, shit, shit! You're right!"

The chanting stopped. Then the footsteps started again, and this time they were coming toward Mandeep and Gurinder.

Mandeep had no trouble finding his balance. He grabbed Gurinder's hand and pulled her down the street. "Let's get the fuck out of here!"

She stumbled in heels again and pulled him back. "Let me get my shoes off!"

The footsteps were getting closer. Another sound, like the wings of a fantastic swarm of insects, rose in the distance. "We don't have fucking time for this!" Mandeep snapped. He turned and pulled her away from the church just as she got the first shoe off. The gate into the cemetery creaked open, and now Gurinder was swearing at him as she hopped and stumbled and tried to remove the other shoe.

From the edge of the cemetery, there was a shout of, "*Secō mortī!*" Gurinder looked back and saw a figure with vibrant red eyes coming through the gate. She tripped on the sidewalk again and felt the wind rush over her head as dark energy missed her by inches. It hit Mandeep dead-on, and he jammed his hands over the bleeding gash in his throat.

Gurinder screamed and pressed one hand against Mandeep's to stem the flow. Her other hand rooted around in her purse for her cell phone as the red-eyed killer moved toward her and adjusted his stance.

Mandeep coughed and spat blood onto the pavement. He took Gurinder's hand off his neck and whispered with his dying breath, "Go." Suddenly sober, Gurinder climbed over Mandeep's body and sprinted into the night, screaming for help as loudly as she knew how.

*****

The blue-and-red lights of the squad cars bounced off the forensic team's puffy white coveralls. On the outside of the police tape, Mona Brady sipped her Coca-Cola and swallowed a yawn. Not even five in the morning yet. She could see Inspector Pembroke leaning on the roof of a cruiser, tearing Superintendent Campbell's voicemail a new one. Mona had already left three messages for her CO and hadn't heard back, so she wasn't sure what Pembroke was hoping to accomplish. What was it they said about the definition of insanity?

Pembroke gave up with a sigh and stalked back toward the perimeter. At the same time, Constable Foley turned and approached from the nearer of the two ambulances, where Gurinder Dhillon was crying her eyes out and holding onto the trauma blanket like it was going to fly away. Her dress and her hands were thick with Mandeep Sihota's dried blood, and Reverend Jansen was sitting beside her with a protective arm around her shoulders. The three officers congregated at the edge of the scene and Pembroke asked for an update.

"The reverend doesn't know anything," said Foley. "He was in bed when it happened, and he slept straight through the attack. Never heard the girl screaming for help, and he only woke up when we got here."

"Convenient," Mona grunted.

"I'd call it pretty inconvenient for him. Once again, Matthew Jansen is the Man Without an Alibi."

"How in God's name did he sleep through this?" asked Inspector Pembroke. "It was right outside his front door."

"Insomnia, the way he tells it. He took a sleeping pill at around one to help him down. It must have really knocked him for a loop."

"And if a frog had wings…" Mona muttered. "How's the girl?"

"How do you think?" said Foley. "When the reverend didn't wake up, she ran eight blocks screaming her lungs out. Woke up half the neighbourhood, but she just wouldn't stop. She's still a mess. All she could tell me was she saw one attacker, he came from the cemetery, and he struck from a distance of at least eight feet."

"With what? We still haven't found a weapon. And nobody's that good with a throwing knife."

"I don't know. I've seen people on YouTube do things with ninja stars that would blow your mind."

Mona gave him a dry look. "If you want to put out a BOLO on the Ninja Turtles, you go right ahead, Foley."

"I would have said Samurai Jack. Different strokes."

Pembroke snapped her fingers to get them back on track. "Save the banter for after this guy's in custody, you two. Do we have a description of the killer?"

Foley shook his head. "She says he was dressed in black from head to toe. But his eyes were the brightest red she's ever seen."

Mona frowned. Score another one for Abby Henderson and her magical conspiracy. She thought about the book she'd found in Bill Grover's garage, still sitting under her bed. She kept meaning to chuck it in the fireplace, but something was holding her back. Mona told herself it was this case. She'd barely been at home the last few days, and when she had been home, she'd been trying to catch up on some much-needed sleep or spending quality time with her son. There'd just been no time to get rid of the damn book. That was what she told herself, but she wasn't sure how much she bought it.

Pembroke snapped her fingers again to bring Mona back to reality. "Sergeant? I said, are you listening to me?"

"Hmm? Sorry, ma'am, I think I dozed off for a second. Didn't get much sleep."

"Then grab a cup of coffee and kindly join us on planet Earth. I want your squad doing door-to-door interviews. One of the neighbours must have seen or heard something. I see cameras at two corners of the churchyard. I want that footage yesterday. And Constable Foley?"

"Boss?"

"You're going to drive to Superintendent Campbell's house and drag him out of bed. This is an all-hands situation."

"Boss."

As Foley jogged toward his cruiser, one of the forensic techs squeezed through the creaky cemetery gate and waved. "Sergeant Brady! Inspector Pembroke! You'll both want to see this!"

Mona and Pembroke got themselves kitted out in the standard coveralls, booties, and face mask, and ducked under the police tape. Two forensic techs led them nearly to the back of the cemetery, where the oldest graves were, and ushered them into a limestone mausoleum whose entranceway had nearly been reclaimed by creeping ivy. The floor was littered with broken ends of vines and trampled leaves where the perp had forced his way in, and Mona and Pembroke walked on their tiptoes so as not to further upset the delicate mess.

A camera flash lit up the dark mausoleum, and Mona's blood ran cold. Five long, low slabs of limestone lay side by side, all unmarked except for a cross carved on the near end above an inscription: *O Death, where is thy sting?* One of the tombs had been smashed open at the end, and the coffin inside pulled halfway out onto the floor. It was open and empty, just like the book had shown her.

CHAPTER 17

DEAR DIARY

WHEN ABBY answered the knock on her and Leanne's door that afternoon, Mona Brady was the last person she was expecting to see. "What am I supposed to have done this time, Sergeant?"

Without waiting for an invitation, Mona came into the room, shut the door behind her, went to the window, and closed the blinds. "Shut up for a second, Henderson, just… just shut up. I—I need to think. Actually, no, don't shut up. You and I need to lay some ground rules, okay? Before I say anything, I'm not here. I was *never* here. Do you understand? I could lose my job if anyone finds out about this, so we need to be on the same page. I. Am not. Here."

Abby knew better than to argue. Mona was pacing up and down the room, tugging at her vest and her shirt, and looking over her shoulder like she expected someone to come through the door any minute and bust her. "Okay. Okay. You're not here. Now what's this all about?"

Mona untucked her shirt and reached down her pants to remove a small bundle tightly wrapped in paper towels. "You need to see this." She threw the parcel onto the bed, fixed her uniform, and stepped back as Abby unravelled the paper towel.

"Blood..." the book said suddenly. *"Blood... blood... feed... feed... cut... cut. Feed. Blood. Blood. Cut. Feed..."*

Abby froze. Mona looked up with terror in her eyes and gulped, "You heard that too?"

"Cutting and cutting and cutting and cutting," hissed the little book. *"Cutting and cutting and feeding. Feeding. Blood. Life. The blood is the life..."*

"Yeah," Abby said. "I heard it."

The sound of a toilet flushing and a sink running suddenly caught Mona's attention. As the bathroom door opened and Leanne emerged, Mona spun on her heels and reached for her gun. Abby caught her before she could draw it and eased her hand away from the holster. "Whoa, whoa, slow down, Sergeant! Jesus Christ, just take a breath!"

Mona's hands were shaking as she sat on them, as far away from the book as she could get. "Sorry, sorry. It's been a really long day already. The man with red eyes has been busy."

"Oh, shit. When?" Abby asked.

"Last night. You didn't hear it from me, but a body turned up right outside the church. A fresh one. One person saw it happen, and she said the killer had red eyes."

"Now do you believe me about the Harcourt House?"

"I don't know what the hell I believe. That's why I'm here. That's why you need to see that book."

"Where did it come from?" Leanne asked. "How did you get it?"

"After Bill Grover died, we traced a possible lead back to his house. I found... *that* in the garage. When I picked it up, I... I saw things. I got scared, and I smuggled it home. No way was I going to take it to my super. I was going to destroy it before... before there was another Bill Grover. But I just... never got around to it. It was like some kind of mental block. I still don't know if I buy this magic stuff you're spouting, Henderson, but I thought you should see this for yourself."

While Leanne got Mona a glass of water, Abby had a closer look at the book, suddenly remembering the gap in the shelves of the Harcourt family library. She'd bet a month's pay this thing had come from the same place. It had that familiar aura of raw, violent power, which came at her now in waves and made her stomach quiver. A deep sense of hunger and emptiness rode on the back of those waves of power, cutting right into Abby's very soul, and she suddenly knew exactly what Simon was talking about when he described the addicting effects of dark magic.

She asked Leanne for a pencil. Remembering the wand fragment and the petrified ectoplasm, Abby felt instinctively that it would be a bad idea to touch something as powerful — as evil — as this book with her bare hands, and she turned the pages with the pencil one by one. Every one was covered in the same messy code she'd seen the other night.

"I think you did the right thing bringing this here, Sergeant. Thank you."

Mona drained her glass of water in one more swig and stood up. "I should go. I told my superiors I had to run a personal errand. I'll leave this with you, if it's all the same. God help me, but I think you're the only person who's actually ahead of the eight-ball on this." Without a word of thanks, she pushed the glass into Leanne's hands, peeked through the blinds, and briskly slipped out the door.

"What do you think it is?" Leanne asked, coming to stand beside Abby.

"I'm not completely sure. Could be a journal. Could be a spell book. But it's definitely important."

As she said this, Abby's eyes returned to the book. Curiosity got the better of her and she continued flipping through it, stopping on a page that showed several sketches of an insect, seen from different angles. The legend below the largest sketch was written in Latin and English: *MAGICICADA SEPTENDICEM* – PHARAOH CICADA.

Below this, there was a note written in the same encrypted text as the rest of the book. The handwriting was straighter and blockier here, as if this page had been added later by a different author.

Abby shook her head. "Why cicadas?" she mumbled to herself.

"Sorry?"

Abby looked up. "I'm just thinking out loud." She pointed at the largest cicada sketch and said, "I'm pretty sure this is the same type of bug the Harcourt House keeps throwing at us."

"But periodic cicadas aren't even native to this part of the country," said Leanne. "And the swarms we've seen are all kinds of screwed up."

"Exactly. Something's rotten in the state of Denmark."

Abby wrapped the book up again as the Master whispered to her in muffled tones. She felt a familiar thorny sensation in her gut and sat back on the floor.

Leanne knelt beside her and laid the back of her hand against Abby's forehead. "Are you okay? You look really pale."

Abby was only vaguely aware that Leanne was speaking. The noise was too muffled by the thrum of cicadas' wings. Black smoke leaked from between the pages of the book and a sudden strong blast of arctic wind blew it open to a random page. Cicadas spilled onto the bedspread by the dozens and Abby shielded her eyes before they took flight around her head. When she looked again, Bill Grover was standing on the bed before her, all shimmering and translucent, with a screwdriver in one hand and a red stain down the side of his neck and chest.

Abby stood and squared her shoulders. She locked eyes with the dead man and swallowed. "Mr. Grover. Fancy seeing you here."

Bill Grover's voice was hollow like the rest of him, and he talked at Abby rather than to her. "I'm sorry…" he mumbled. "I'm sorry. I didn't know."

"Sorry for what, Bill? For what you did to me?"

"I'm sorry for all of it," said Bill Grover. "I didn't know… I couldn't know…"

Abby approached Bill slowly and raised one hand. She waved it before his eyes, but he made no sign of noticing her. "He came inside…" Bill said. "He came in and I didn't know. He left and I didn't remember…"

Abby reached for Bill's hand and grabbed a fistful of cold vapour. "Bill! Bill, listen to me! Where did the Master come in? What are you trying to say?"

Bill fell back a step and pressed his hand to his head. "Me… Inside me… my head! He was inside and I didn't know! I didn't know what he was and I didn't know when he was in!" Doubling over, Bill smacked himself with both hands. "Stupid, stupid, stupid! I didn't know and I couldn't remember!"

"Do you mean he used you as a vessel, Bill?"

Bill looked at Abby and snapped his fingers. "Vessel! Vessel is the word! I filled up with him, but I never knew! I never knew, until I did! And when I knew, and he was with me, and I was with him, I didn't want it! I didn't want it, and I fled! But we weren't where we were. Where we should have been." He looked vacantly into the distance and pointed over Abby's shoulder. "We were out there. We were somewhere else, and I didn't know, but I *did* know, and I didn't want it, and I ran! I ran and I got… lost…"

"You got lost," Abby repeated. "But then you found your way back, right? You came out of the fog, and you tried to warn everyone about the Master. Isn't that what happened?" She held up the book. "Was this yours?"

Bill nodded. "His plans… all his plans… in his books… stole the evidence… hid it so he wouldn't find… Had to warn them… but it went wrong… you were there… saw your magic… panicked…"

"That's why you attacked me, isn't it? You thought I was in cahoots with the Master. He was the only magic you ever knew, and you assumed all magic was like that."

Bill shook his head and bit back a sob. "Stupid… stupid and panicked… I didn't think…"

"It's okay, Bill. It wasn't your fault. You said you were trying to warn people, right? About what?"

"All of it… He's looking for… he's found…" He shook his head again and smacked himself, trying to clear the fog. "Three things. Three. He's found two! Two! The third… later. He'll come again. He'll come for the third, and he'll come again."

"What three things, Bill? What is the Master looking for?"

The image of Bill Grover flickered and started to fade. His voice grew still more distant. He closed his eyes and shook his head, baring his teeth in concentration. "I don't… I can't… it's fading! The memory is… is fading! The blood… the b… blood first, then… no, it's gone!"

Light shimmered through Bill Grover's image like a refracting lens. The edges went fuzzy and mist rose off his frame. He, too, was fading.

"Bill! Before you go, just tell me one thing! Who is the Master? You've been so helpful, just please tell me one more thing! Who is he?"

"He is the Master," Bill said. "He is Good. He is Wise. He is Kind."

"I know, I know all that, but who is he really? You must know!"

"Not who you thought he was. Ask not 'who is the Master?' Ask '*why* is he the Master?'"

And then Bill Grover faded to nothing but a few wisps of smoke, curling around Abby's outstretched fingers. She looked to her left, where Leanne was watching her with a curious expression. "Uh, how much of that was out loud?"

"Did you really see Bill Grover?" Leanne asked, wide-eyed. "What did he say?"

"Something very useful," Abby replied. "Get Simon and Natalie up here. We need to put our heads together, and then I'm going to need some space to Bridge. I want to ask Hector Harcourt a few questions about his dad."

CHAPTER 18

SÉANCE

WHEN THEY were all together, Abby told Simon and Natalie about the provenance of the book and explained what it had shown her. When she had finished speaking, she could hear Simon's teeth grinding behind pursed lips and saw his hand twitch like he was ready to throw another fireball.

"That poor man…" Leanne whispered. "That poor *family*."

"This madness has to stop," Simon growled. "Abby, Bill Grover told you the Master is looking for three things. Did he say what they were?"

"The blood first. That's all I got out of him. But supposedly, the Master's already found the second, and he'll come again for the third."

"Three things… could he be talking about ingredients for a spell?" asked Leanne.

Simon nodded. "Almost certainly. Western ritual magic is usually tripartite in some way. Three ingredients in a spell or potion, three magical artefacts, three incantations—"

Abby snapped her fingers. "Three witches! You know, 'thrice to thine and thrice to mine'?"

Simon nodded. "'And thrice again to make up nine.' Top of the class, Henderson. We assumed the Thousand Cuts murders were for someone's personal benefit, but let's suppose instead that they were sacrifices to fulfill the first requirement of a three-part ritual. This is very complex magic, so somebody will have to have taken extensive notes on the procedure. I'd bet my life that the other two components of the spell are listed in this handy little notebook. I'll start working on the Master's code straightaway. Leanne, Natalie, I hope you can assist me with that?"

"We'll do our best," Leanne said.

"While you're busy with that, I'm going to try and Bridge with Hector Harcourt again," said Abby. "Bill Grover told me I should ask *why* the Master is 'the Master,' instead of asking *who* is the Master. I think he was talking literally."

Simon smacked the table. "Josiah Harcourt! The patriarch. The Master of the House."

"Bingo. We know Hector had been out of town for a while before November of '27. We know somebody was messing with the Thousand Cuts back then, and the Harcourt servants got on the wrong side of it. We also know the servants were already dead when Hector chopped them up. Hector's not the monster at the end of this book, but he knows who is. My money's on Josiah."

*****

While Simon prepared a kettle of his meditation brew, Abby closed the blinds, turned off all the lights, then lay down on the bed. When the steaming, soupy potion was ready, Simon decanted some of it into a mug for her, whispered, "Good luck," and left her alone in the room.

As Abby swallowed the concoction and closed her eyes, her muscles numbed and began to tingle, while her mind kicked into overdrive like she'd just had a double shot of espresso. It unhooked itself from the heavy, fleshy shell around it and ascended like a rocket, blasting through the metaphysical barrier between Middangeard, the natural world, and the Elsewhere.

Upon opening her eyes, Abby found herself lying in a soft four-poster bed in a stately bedchamber fit for a queen. The walls and ceiling were all a rich, pure white, with gleaming pillars of gold running up the walls at regular intervals. The bed sheets were as soft as clouds, and so warm and cozy that Abby felt like she could lie in this bed for the rest of her natural life and never get bored of it. But she had a job to do here, so instead she climbed out of the bed, stretched, and cleared her throat.

"My name is Abigail Margaret Henderson, of the line of the Gospels," she announced to the spirits. "My father was Donald Richard Henderson, himself the son of Philip Henderson. From these names have I learnt the wisdom of my ancestors. From these names do I draw strength. I offer these names now to that noble witness, the ancient Countenance of the High Celestial!" Mist swirled at her feet and danced around the bed. Abby paused, waiting for the Rat King to jump out and gobble her up, but he didn't show. So far, so good. "I seek the counsel of one who cannot lie at rest, a soul taken from the mortal life before their natural time. I would speak with Hector Jeremiah Harcourt!"

Thunder boomed outside her bedchamber. Speaking the full, true name of any spirit being was a powerful act in itself. For some creatures, their name was the quickest way to summon or banish them. For others—like the old gods that the demons and the faeries still revered—speaking their names improperly could invoke their wrath, or even bring lethal curses on the speaker. When the thunder passed, Abby continued. "Spirit, I thee name! In the name of the Holy Witness, the Earth-maker and the Glory-giver, I implore you to reveal yourself, that one in the future might gain wisdom from the past."

Slowly, the mist started to thicken and solidify into the form of a teenage girl. She was dressed in a lacy white nightgown and had messy red hair that curled around her shoulders. Abby recognized her as the girl from the second-floor window of the House: Olivia Harcourt.

Olivia's skin was white and bloodless, save for two dark rings around her eyes. A large, red gash in the side of her head went deep into the centre of her brain, and another similar wound had opened her belly. Smears of blood pasted her hair and her nightgown to her skin. These were the wounds left by Hector Harcourt's axe, but they were not the only ones. Her left ear was missing, its absence marked by a bloody hole in the side of the girl's head; her right arm ended in a stump just above her elbow; and there was a gaping hole in her chest where her heart should have been

"Olivia Harcourt? My name is Abby. Abby Henderson. I... I'm looking for your brother. I need to ask him some questions about what happened on that night in 1927."

The ghost let out an anguished sob and shook her head. "It wasn't his fault! It wasn't! He was protecting us!"

"What do you mean?" Abby asked.

"Hector!" the ghost said apologetically. "Hector only did what he had to! Otherwise he wouldn't have stopped!"

"Who wouldn't have stopped? Do you mean Josiah?"

Olivia nodded, then put her hands to her mouth and started to cry. "Father was... he was like an animal! He... Hector had to stop him!"

Abby took a step forward and reached out to the terrified spirit, but Olivia shrank away.

"Olivia," Abby said calmly, "Olivia, listen to me. I need to speak with Hector. Do you know where he is?"

"I am here," said a weary voice behind her. "I have always been here."

Abby turned. The bloodied phantom of Hector Harcourt dragged his axe on the ground as he approached, and Abby shivered when he phased right through her without a word. She turned to see Hector sitting on the ground with his sister in a tight hug, rocking her like he would a baby.

"It's alright, Olivia," Hector whispered, "it's alright. This woman is no threat to us." He kissed his sister on the forehead, then looked up at Abby and said, "Time and again, I have told you to stay away from this gruesome business. Yet here you stand. Why?"

"I just want to help, Hector. I want to fix what's been broken in this town and bring some bad people to justice."

"You spoke a powerful incantation to summon me. Are you a Gospel, Abigail Margaret Henderson?"

"Yeah, I am. And you can just call me Abby. How do you know about the Gospels, Hector?"

"Everyone on this side of the veil knows of the Gospels. It has been said lately that a Gospel slew the Deacon and destroyed the cult of the Following. Their downfall caused tremors throughout the Elsewhere."

Abby tried not to blush. "If you know about me, then you know why I'm here. I need you to tell me about the Master and about the night you died."

"If that is your wish, then I will tell you. But I warn you, Abby Henderson, when you know the full truth, you may wish you had stayed ignorant."

"I'm willing to take that risk."

*****

Back on Earth, Simon and the others had already been at the Master's code for nearly an hour and hadn't yet been able to translate one letter. It didn't help that the book appeared to be written in a mix of languages of varying ages, and all those languages had been copied second-hand from other sources by someone who only half-understood any of them.

"Damn," Simon muttered. He crumpled up the sheet of paper in front of him and tossed it across the room. It landed in a growing pile of similarly discarded sheets that was nowhere near the wastebasket. "Damn, damn, damn, damn!"

"My sentiments exactly," Leanne said, shaking a cramp out of her writing hand. "All these dead languages are giving me a headache. I don't know how you keep all this stuff straight in that big Vanguard brain."

"It's not the languages that are the problem," Simon said. "In fact, I'm fairly certain I've got that part worked out." He tapped an open page with his pencil. "These six lines here, they're written in High West Elvish script, filtered through what I currently believe is some form of Vigenère cipher. The problem is, I don't speak High West Elvish."

"Wouldn't it be in one of your books?" Leanne asked.

"No. You see, the Elves—like many races among the Fair Folk—are highly protective of their language and customs. They almost never share their cultural knowledge with outsiders, and because theirs is a primarily oral tradition, written records of the language are remarkably scarce. What few sources do survive today are poor copies of manuscripts that were lost during the Renaissance. If the Master copied these letters from an earlier text, I doubt he'd have had any clue what they were."

"So what you're saying is, we can't translate the code until we find one of the Fair Folk," said Leanne.

"More specifically, a Fair Folk scholar. The High West dialect is the language of the educated upper classes, so we'd need to find a faerie with a thorough classical education. And we do *not* want to be in hock to the faeries, so ideally it would be a Fair Folk scholar who already owes me a favour or three."

"That's a pretty tall order. Especially on such short notice."

"Well, short notice isn't actually much of a problem. If any Earth-born creature speaks a faerie's true name three times, they can immediately summon said faerie to their own current location."

"Like a 'Beetlejuice, Beetlejuice, Beetlejuice' kind of thing?"

"Precisely. And as luck would have it, I have learned the true names of a small handful of faeries in the course of my 1500 years." Suddenly, he cleared his throat and drummed his fingers on the table rather sheepishly. "It, uh, it so happens, in fact, that one of my Fair Folk acquaintances has, er, recently found himself in my debt…"

Natalie made a fist and squeezed her pencil until it snapped. "Wait a minute… this wouldn't be the *mystery informant* you've been so cagey about, would it?"

Simon looked at the floor like he was a teenager who'd just been caught with a nudie magazine. "Well, as it happens…"

Natalie gritted her teeth. "Simon," she threatened, "you better not be going where I think you're going with this."

"I'm sorry, Natalie, but I'm afraid I very much am." He rose from his chair, cupped both hands to his mouth, and called up to the ceiling: "Robyn ab Godfelwe!"

Natalie put her head in her hands and groaned, "Goddammit, Simon."

"Robyn ab Godfelwe!" Simon repeated.

Leanne leaned over to Natalie and whispered. "I don't get it. Who's Robyn ab Godfelwe?"

Natalie shook her head and snarled. "Robyn ab Godfelwe. In English: Robin, son of Goodfellow. R.G. Think about it, Leanne."

Leanne thought about it. Then she shot a dirty look at Simon and snapped, "You didn't!"

Simon shrugged apologetically. "Robyn ab Godfelwe! Thrice named and bound to my service, I summon thee!"

From the aether, there came a sulky voice that told Simon to, "Buzz off!"

"Relax, it's me!" Simon shouted.

"I know it's you!" said the sulky voice. "Why do you think I'm telling you to buzz off?"

"That's not the arrangement!"

"Screw you!"

"Robyn ab Godfelwe! Robyn ab Godfelwe! Robyn ab Godfelwe!" Simon repeated. "Thrice named and bound to my service, I bloody well summon thee!"

The sulky voice groaned, and then there came the sound of snapping fingers. The air in the room shifted with an audible *crack*, and suddenly a grubby-looking man with a backpack appeared directly in front of Simon. It was the same bearded, woolly-hatted hitchhiker that Natalie had driven past on the day they arrived in town. "What do you want now?" the hitchhiker grumbled.

"For you to drop the glamour, for a start. It really doesn't become you, Whittaker."

The hitchhiker's scowl deepened. "Not becoming me is the whole point, jackass." Then he snapped his fingers. The illusion of the hitchhiker disappeared, and the creature beneath revealed his true self: he was a hair under five feet tall, with bright yellow skin, a hooked nose, black hair slicked back, and a three-piece pinstripe suit.

The imp known as R.G. Whittaker huffed out a breath and said, "Make it quick."

CHAPTER 19

FACTS CONCERNING THE LATE HECTOR HARCOURT AND HIS FAMILY

NATALIE GROUND her teeth and her eye twitched a little. As Whittaker lit a cigarette, she brushed past Simon, grabbed the imp by his lapels, then slammed him into the wall.

Whittaker coughed and spluttered, "OW! Jesus, Nat, what's your problem!"

Natalie tightened her grip and pressed him harder against the wall. "Don't call me 'Nat,' you little creep!"

"Okay, okay, we're establishing boundaries. That's good, first step in any healthy relationship."

Simon put a hand on Natalie's arm. "Natalie, Natalie, it's alright! Really! He's not going to be any trouble! He's already been working for me this long, hasn't he?"

Whittaker nodded frantically. "Yeah! Yeah! What he said! No trouble at all. Scout's honour!"

Natalie looked from Whittaker to Simon and back again. Then she stepped back and let go. "Okay, but I'm watching you."

Natalie and the others had good reason not to trust Whittaker. Imps were a race of faerie with a particular talent for teleportation and crafting illusions that felt real to the touch (or in Natalie's words, feeding people bullshit and then running away before they caught on). And Whittaker was as bad as they came. When the Deacon and his cult had been chasing Abby last year, Whittaker had tried to profit by bargaining with Abby for the life of her best friend, who had got caught in the crossfire. When the demons attacked the meeting place, Whittaker had high-tailed it and left the others to fend for themselves.

"What are you doing here, Whittaker?" Leanne asked, with an expression like he was some foul mess that she had been forced to scrape off her shoe. She pointed between Simon and the imp and added, "How long has *this* been going on?"

"A couple of months," Simon admitted. "Ever since the debacle with the Following, our Whittaker has suffered something of a reversal of fortunes. I've been helping him get back on his feet." He grinned and gave Whittaker a friendly clap on the shoulder.

Whittaker scowled and shook Simon off. "Yeah, you're a real Mother Teresa, aren't you? But he's right about the reversed fortunes. After the Following torched my club last year, my business went completely tits-up, and there's more than a handful of folks who think it was my fault for getting involved in the first place. Ever since Christmas, I've been hopping around the province trying to duck disgruntled ex-employees, legitimate business rivals, and the occasional bounty hunter."

"Bounty hunters?" Leanne asked.

"Remember the cloud that my club was sitting on?" said Whittaker. "I leased that from the Court-Among-the-Oak, so technically it's Fair Folk soil. And *apparently*, imprisoning and torturing a demon on Fair Folk soil is a capital crime where I come from. So now I'm a wanted man, and the bounty on my head could buy half of California. And we're talking the *good* half."

Natalie raised an eyebrow and looked at Simon. "And I suppose you have been making sure that no one collects that bounty."

Simon smiled. Whittaker, like all faeries, lived by a code of fair trade: equal pay for equal favours. If one wanted to secure any service or kindness from a faerie, one had to be prepared to give them something in return. "Let's just say that Whittaker and I have entered into an exchange. I keep the bounty hunters off his trail, and in return he supplies me with free information and does the occasional odd job. But if he breaks my trust in any way, I will name him thrice and summon him into a room full of bounty hunters. There's only a handful of living beings in this world who still know Whittaker's true name, and it is my good fortune that I am one of them."

Natalie thought for a moment and then nodded. "Okay. But this better not bite us in the ass."

Whittaker straightened his tie and puffed on his cigarette. "Alright, let's try this again. What the hell do you want, Ætheric?"

Simon laid his handkerchief over the journal and showed it to Whittaker. "We need a translation. There are some passages in here written in High West Elvish."

Whittaker blinked and took a second to put the pieces together. "Oh, fuck. Did you get this from the Harcourt House?"

"In a roundabout sort of way."

"No. Nope. Nuh-uh. That is where I'm drawing the line. This whole Harcourt thing is getting way too hot. Didn't you hear what happened at the church this morning?"

Simon winced. "Yes, we're aware of what happened at the church. But this is why we need your help, Whittaker. There may be something in this book that can help us stop these killings, and you're the only person around who can read High West Elvish."

"Well, too bad, 'cause I am seriously allergic to getting my throat cut by lunatics with red eyes! Look, the whole reason I called you when Jenny Styles got killed is because I figured you and your flying circus could handle this thing! I don't need any of this horseshit coming down on *my* head!"

Simon smiled. He cleared his throat, lifted his head, and called out, "Auberon ab Nethe!"

Whittaker jumped and fell back against the wall for support. "Don't you fucking dare!"

Simon waggled the journal. "If you help us with this, I won't have to. Auberon ab Nethe!"

Whittaker cringed. "Jesus, seriously, man! You're walking a fine line between crazy and suicidal right now! You say that name again, and the Thousand Cuts is going to look like a bad rash!"

Simon smiled. "Whittaker, the King-Among-the-Oak is prepared to pay a handsome sum for your head on the point of his sword. If I summon him directly, I'm sure he will be exceedingly grateful that I have saved him the money, and I rather think that he will relish the opportunity to put you in your place himself."

"You don't have the balls! You summon him, and he's just as likely to kill you for inconveniencing him!"

"In that case, would you prefer I bring the King-Among-the-Holly to Delapore instead? I'm sure he'd have some very choice words for you."

"Ætheric, I swear to God…"

"I assure you, Whittaker, you are in no position to be making threats. Now, will you help us, or must I summon Lord Au—"

"Okay, okay, Jesus! Just… don't fucking say it. Look, I'll translate your goddamn book if it shuts you up, but you and me are going to have to renegotiate the deal."

"And so we shall. *After* you provide us the translation we need."

As they shook hands to make it official, Whittaker grumbled that he may have been better off taking his chances with Oak.

*****

In the Elsewhere, the ghost of Hector Harcourt extended his free hand to Abby and said, "Come. Let us walk, and you will see what I have seen."

His hand wasn't as solid as it had been when he'd grabbed her in the Harcourt House; it was more like trying to hold fog on a cold winter morning. As they walked, a thick grey mist rose up around them and molded itself into an environment Abby recognized. Bursts of colour suddenly bled through the fog as the high hilltop above Pearson Heights came to life and Hector brought Abby to the front porch of the Harcourt House, as crisp and bright as it had been when he was alive. At the front door, Hector dropped Abby's hand and gave a slight bow, accompanied by a gentlemanly, "After you."

Abby reached out and grabbed the doorknob, but it shimmered and dissolved in her hand, sending another chill through her. As soon as she drew back, the doorknob reformed. Taking a deep breath, Abby closed her eyes and braced herself for the chill. Then she walked right through the closed door.

As she emerged in the front hall, she gasped and started jogging on the spot to try and warm up. Without speaking, Hector passed through the wall beside her and escorted her into the living room. The Harcourt family were all there, going about their business like nothing was out of the ordinary. Josiah was sitting on the couch smoking a pipe, watching as Isaac and Olivia played chess in front of the fire. None of them looked up when Abby or Hector came into the room, but Abby didn't expect them to. These people weren't ghosts like Hector; they were merely his memories given form.

"It started with my great-uncle," Hector said suddenly. "Ephraim Harcourt. Ephraim was... a queer sort of fellow. Independently wealthy, but totally reclusive, and given to a paranoid and wrathful disposition. I only met him on a handful of occasions myself, and all of those in my early youth, but he always struck me as a very intimidating and somewhat deranged man."

The living room and the apparitions of the Harcourt family faded into smoke. Now a new player took centre stage: a man with a lean, hawkish face, a slightly hunched back, and messy red hair and a goatee.

"Because he took no pleasure in the world at large," Hector said, "Uncle Ephraim spent many years pursuing more scholarly ventures. He learned about ancient cultures by studying their literature from the safety of his estate in Ipswich. One of Ephraim's great passions was collecting antiquities from around the globe. Macedon, Persia, Indochina, Northern Europe... all the great epochs of history."

Ephraim Harcourt's image changed. His lips pulled back in a wide, hysterical smile, revealing many crooked yellow teeth, his eyebrows knit together even as the orbs beneath began to twitch and burn red with ambition, and a large, black-covered book of magic appeared in his hands.

"Besides history, another of Ephraim's fascinations was the occult," Hector said. "He diligently researched the ways of witchcraft and magic from the wizards of Ancient Egypt until the American witch trials in the age of Puritanism. His goal was to become a master of magic himself. He had a set of talismans and charms he had crafted himself in order to aid this pursuit, as well as various books and scrolls of occultist knowledge that he had acquired. Ephraim died a bachelor in 1925, and all of his worldly possessions passed to my father. So did my uncle's mania and his more… perverse appetites."

Ephraim Harcourt disappeared and the smoke around Abby and Hector became the library of the Harcourt House.

Josiah sat in a chair in the middle of the room, surrounded by several open grimoires and unfurled scrolls of ancient parchment. The pages were covered in ink marks and scribbles in the margins, where Ephraim had crossed things out or made notes and annotations. As Abby watched him, Josiah's eyes darted from page to page, scanning his uncle's research and transcribing it in code into a small leather-bound notebook.

The door to the library opened and a young Indigenous woman entered the room with a tea trolley. Abby recognized her from Arnold Tremblay's photos as Celia Alexander. The woman kept her eyes locked on the tea set as she walked, like she was afraid that it would shatter if she made too much noise. She brought the trolley to a stop behind Josiah's chair and whispered, "Tea, Mr. Harcourt."

"What?" Josiah barked sharply. "Speak up, child!"

Celia flinched. "Tea," she repeated a little louder.

Josiah dropped the notebook on the table and looked back at the tea trolley with a scowl, as if tea was the most inconvenient thing in the world. Then he looked up at Celia, who flinched again and hid her eyes behind her hand. "P-please, sir," the girl stammered, "you asked for tea at three o'clock."

Josiah's face relaxed into an easy smile. "So I did," he admitted. "Thank you, Celia." As Celia poured the tea, Josiah stood and circled around behind her. He sniffed deeply and whispered, "The scones smell lovely today." He positioned himself so that her thigh was nestled between his legs, and his long fingers reached up to rub her shoulders. "You will make a fine cook, yet."

Celia tensed her shoulders and diligently poured the tea, but her hand trembled and a few drops splashed on her sleeve.

Josiah tsked and reached past Celia to pick up a napkin. "Ah, careless. Careless, Celia!" As Celia put down the teapot,

Josiah held her wrist with one hand and dabbed her sleeve with the other. "There, that's better. And what do you say now?"

Celia closed her eyes and breathed heavily.

Josiah squeezed Celia's wrist hard and dug in his nails. "What do you say, Celia?" He put down the napkin and twisted her wrist the wrong way until Celia let out a yelp.

"Th-thank you, Mr. Harcourt! Thank you!"

Josiah stepped back and nodded. "You're very welcome."

Celia blinked and sniffed as she dropped a single sugar cube into the teacup. Then she turned and handed him the cup, still not meeting his eyes. "W-will that be all, sir?"

"Not quite." There was a small cheese knife on the trolley, which Josiah picked up and handed to Celia. "I believe you know what I want."

Celia looked at the knife and shook her head, holding back tears.

Josiah simply nodded again and extended the knife to her. She took it with much hesitation and rolled up her sleeve. Her forearm was covered in narrow horizontal scars. The tears rolled freely down her cheeks as she took the knife and gritted her teeth. Josiah grinned and licked his lips. Then Celia cut herself.

Josiah took Celia's wrist and held it over his teacup until her blood mixed with his lapsang souchong. She pressed a napkin over the wound and choked back a sob. Josiah stirred his tea with a little shiver of delight and whispered, "Thank you, Celia. That will be all."

Celia fixed her sleeve and bowed. "Thank you, sir." She turned and walked briskly to the door. She had nearly made her escape when Josiah raised a finger in the air.

"Oh, Celia?"

The girl stopped, her shoulders tightening as she turned back around. "Y-yes, sir?"

"Are you happy here?"

Celia paused, watching Josiah's eyes. After a moment, she nodded and murmured, "Yes, Mr. Harcourt."

Josiah raised an eyebrow. "Yes?"

Celia looked away for a second and wiped her eyes with the back of her good hand. "Yes, I am very happy here, sir."

"Then why don't you smile?"

"I-I'm sorry, sir?"

Josiah sipped his tea and grinned. "I want you to show me how happy you are, Celia. I want you to smile."

Celia curled in on herself for a moment and shivered. Then she looked back at Josiah and smiled back at him. "I am very happy here, Mr. Harcourt. And I am grateful to you for giving me a home. You have always treated me well."

"Indeed I have. You are dismissed, Celia."

Celia bowed one last time and fled from the room weeping.

Josiah and the library dissolved into smoke, and Abby now saw the distraught Celia hurrying through the halls of the Harcourt House. She ran straight into the arms of a decidedly alive Hector and told him everything, crying into his shoulder as she did.

The scene froze and the blood-stained, dead Hector stepped forward. "As he immersed himself more and more in Ephraim's teachings, my father became a tyrant. When he was in town, he presented himself as the great philanthropist and man of the people, but in private, he was a beast. He beat our servants. He harassed and belittled my sister. He cajoled and lied to my brother, to turn him against me. Our household became his slaves, and he insisted that we call him 'Master.' He spent days on end shut up in the library, conduction heinous experiments. I would often hear him through the door, talking in a language I did not understand. And he would be answered by voices I did not recognize, as if he was conferring with devils out of Hell.

"I began to have nightmares about him. I saw him with eyes red as blood, consorting with beasts beyond imagining. I believe he was attempting to invade my mind and take control of me when I would not bow to him willingly. That is part of the reason I left home when I did."

"And what happened when you came back? That's what I need to know about."

Hector nodded. "Yes, you are quite right. I have stalled for long enough, I think."

The smoke rippled, and Abby and Hector were in the living room once again. It was dark outside, and Celia and the other servant, a broad-shouldered Indigenous man, hung upside down from a chain on the ceiling. Their hands, dangling toward the floor, were bound with thick ropes. Their faces were frozen in expressions of terror and they were covered in the telltale wounds of the Thousand Cuts.

Josiah stood by the fireplace, looking up at his captives. His beard and hair were longer and greyer and his face was wan and skeletal. His eyes were the bright, blazing red that Abby had seen in her dreams. One hand was wrapped around a thin wand, and the other held the journal that Sergeant Brady had found. The chalk circle on the floor was unobscured, and Abby could now clearly see the Thousand Cuts sigil in the middle, as well as the full sequence of demonic glyphs running along the edge. Isaac and Olivia Harcourt stood at the back of the room in matching white robes, each one of them holding a burning red candle.

"I left home not long after my father began to study the black arts," Hector said. "I could not stand what he had become, and I told him so. I begged my siblings to stand up to him and come away with me, but they would not. Father had indoctrinated Isaac too well, and Olivia was terrified of his wrath. Perhaps I gave up on them too easily. Perhaps if I had fought harder, I..." His voice began to crack, and he looked away from the apparitions. "Perhaps I could have broken my father's grip. Perhaps I could have saved them. Before it was too late."

Abby reached out and held Hector's hand. He squeezed it in gratitude, and for a second his ghostly flesh began to feel warm and alive.

Before them, Josiah Harcourt read aloud from his grimoire in an ancient tongue. Olivia was on the brink of crying, but Isaac drew her in and squeezed her shoulders. The gesture was probably supposed to be reassuring, but it came off looking like Isaac wanted to throw his sister to the floor and kick her to death. It didn't help that his crooked smile was about an inch too wide and never seemed to meet his eyes.

Josiah looked up at the servants and raised his wand for the grand finale. Olivia screamed and turned away as the blood came down like a waterfall, making a crimson pool on the floor that expanded to the very edge of the chalk circle and then stopped.

Josiah knelt at the outer edge of the circle and bowed his head. "Lords of Niðerdæl," he said in a steady, reverent voice, "I offer to you a sacrifice. Let the blood of these creatures, which I have spilt in your name, prove to you my fealty. I ask only for an audience with one of your kind and pray that you accept my terms."

Olivia stepped forward, the dam bursting and her tears coming thick and fast. "Father, please stop! This is madness!" Isaac grabbed her by the shoulder, pulled her back roughly, and clamped a hand over her mouth to stifle her cries.

Josiah nodded at his other son approvingly, and the flash of red in his eyes was matched by an identical flash in Isaac's. Abby didn't feel the need to go in for a closer look, but she was pretty confident she could find the insects darting around in Isaac's pupils if she tried. Indoctrinated, brainwashed, same difference.

"Thank you, Isaac. Olivia, dear, be quiet while I am working."

Olivia was a sobbing wreck now, but she did not speak out again. Isaac ran his hands through his sister's hair and whispered, "He knows what he's doing, Livvy. It will be alright. Really, it will be. The Master is Good. The Master is Wise."

Olivia nodded and cried into her brother's chest. "The Master is Kind."

Josiah made a gesture with his wand, and together the Harcourts moved to form a triangle. Isaac and Olivia kneeled and held their candles out over the circle, the wicks toward the centre. Josiah conjured a flame at the end of his wand and did the same. Then he raised his other hand like he was conducting a family singalong. "All together, now."

Josiah closed his eyes and said, "Come forth, beasts of the Lower Realm, you great lords of Niðerdæl. Come forth and reveal yourselves to me, who seeks your wisdom and knowledge of greater things." He growled through the harsh syllables of several demonic names, and Isaac and the girls repeated the invocation.

A drop of wax fell from one of the candles and landed in the pool of blood. Suddenly, there was a deafening roar and a creature rose up from somewhere below the circle. It was a massive beast with porous green skin, membranous wings on its back, four long arms that ended in razor-sharp claws, and the furry head of a monstrous jackal. Another creature appeared beside it, this one with bulbous, orange eyes all over its body and a mouth full of pulsing tentacles. More demons appeared in the circle, crawling and squirming over top of each other like bees in a hive, until there were thirteen in all. One of the creatures opened its mouth and spoke in a surprisingly soft, even baritone. "Say thy business, mortal. Wherefore hast thou summoned us to this plane?"

"Good my lords," Josiah whispered, bowing his head, "I have studied your ways for many months now. I have given myself to your crafts, I have read the Word of the Eldest One, and I know much of your magicks. I have heard of the gifts you can bestow on mortal men. I seek a boon from you, my lords."

The demon gave a curious little hiss. "Indeed? What is thy wish, man?"

Josiah met the demon's eye and pursed his lips. "I have received… a terminal diagnosis." He tapped the wand to his forehead and hissed, "A cancer. Here. I have tried to strengthen myself with the blood of the living, but it is a temporary fix. I know that he is coming for me. The Pale Rider. But my work is not yet done. I desire *life*. Life everlasting and never fleeting. I know it is within your power, lords. The Eldest One's years were already beyond counting when Rome was sacked. You know the secrets of immortality, and I implore you to share those secrets now."

The demon laughed deep in its throat. "Life eternal? To preserve thee forever beyond the Harvester's reach… that would take such strength as has not been known in many centuries. What canst thou offer us in return?"

Josiah smiled. "There is a town in the valley below this house. Even now, the people sleep soundly in their beds. If you examine my wards, my lords, you will see that they encircle this house. Until I give the word and dissolve them, I have you trapped in this place. And I will dissolve them if you give me what I desire. Then you shall have your pick of vessels to possess and souls to consume."

The demons turned inward for a brief huddle, and then their emissary laughed again. "The bargain is well-made, man! We accept the terms! I think there shall be some good sport in this!"

Josiah extended his hand into the circle, and Abby held her breath. She knew that a handshake with a demon was as good as a signature on the dotted line.

There were mutters and shouts outside the House, and then the front door burst open. Hector stormed into the living room, axe in hand, and pointed at Josiah. "There he is!" And then Abby saw that Hector wasn't alone.

Nine hard-faced men in police uniforms marched in after him, with revolvers, shotguns, and axes at the ready, as if they were about to bust up a Chicago speakeasy. The man at the head of the procession was bulky and red-faced with a bristly silver moustache, and Abby guessed that this was Superintendent J.A.B. Campbell. He hollered Josiah's name and leveled a shotgun at the Harcourt patriarch's head, but the rest of the cops faltered when they saw the monstrous creature that was about to take Josiah's hand.

The demon snarled. Josiah lowered his hand and turned to look at Hector, not even registering the other men. Surprise showed on his face, but it quickly gave way to bitter hate. "So. Is the prodigal son returned at last?"

Hector fell in line with Superintendent Campbell. "Didn't I tell you? Martin Simpson. Caroline King. It was all him. Gentlemen, you are looking at the Delapore Ripper."

The cops recomposed themselves and inched forward, training their weapons on Josiah and the demons. Josiah paid them no mind and turned away from the circle. "Hector, what is this?"

"Celia phoned me three nights ago. She told me all of it. I've been hearing rumours. They say that a wild animal has been attacking people in town. But it's been you. You killed nine people since I left!" He looked up at the bodies of the servants. "Celia told me the victims were cut up. Drained of blood. And now I find her and Joseph."

"You don't know what you're saying, boy."

The elder Superintendent Campbell stepped forward. "There's no use denying it, Harcourt! We saw you through the window! You butchered those two like hogs. And for what? To please these... these *things*? What kind of Hell have you brought to Delapore?"

"How *dare* you, John Campbell?" snapped Josiah. "I *am* Delapore! The office you work in, the church you worship in, even the hotel where my son gambles and whores away his best years! None of those would be here if not for me!" He raised his wand and took a step forward. "I have made Delapore what it is. I have given my heart and my soul to this town, and it is time for this town to pay me back."

"You'd kill Delapore to save your own life?" roared one of the officers. "We're your neighbours, Josiah! Your friends!"

"Then you should be glad to have this opportunity. I am a dying man, gentlemen, and this is my last request. After all I've done for Delapore, can you say I deserve any less? I'll give you all one chance. Leave this place. Forget what you've seen. And Hector: *never* darken my doorstep again!"

The squad gave no ground. Campbell made a motion with the barrel of his gun, and his officers moved to take Josiah down. Suddenly, Isaac forced his candle into Olivia's hands and drew a long, curved dagger from within his robes. He lunged, Olivia screamed, and a gun went off.

The dagger clattered to the ground and Isaac fell at Josiah's feet, clutching his chest and taking in short gasps of air. As the blood pooled between Isaac's fingers, Josiah screamed and took his son in his arms.

"O... O Death..." Isaac stammered, "where... where is thy..."

His hand went slack. Josiah squeezed it desperately, smearing blood on Isaac's signet ring. "Isaac... Isaac!" He looked at Hector with wild fury in his eyes and raised his wand. "You... you brought them here." The tip of the wand sparked with black lightning and Josiah lunged, clawing like a wild animal with his free hand. "You did this! You killed my boy! God damn you!"

The cops pushed forward again, jostling Hector in the confusion. He swung the axe defensively and it thudded into Josiah's neck. Olivia shrieked and dropped both candles into the circle of blood on the floor. As the flames went out with a *hiss*, the first of Josiah's wards fell. The servants' blood began to expand beyond the edge of the magic circle, and the demons roared and laughed. Josiah collapsed beside Isaac and pointed an accusing finger at Hector. "Your fault… killed us… all… damn you… no son of mine…"

The demons exploded from the circle and ran riot. The officers fired blindly in a vain attempt to ward off the creatures and Campbell ordered the retreat. Two of the demons jumped into Olivia's body and twisted her skeleton around like a pretzel. Her ribcage tore open from the inside and another of the monsters plucked out her beating heart for an appetizer, then had her arm for a main course. Josiah and Isaac jerked and spasmed as the demons filled up their empty bodies and stood them up. They swayed and made halting, awkward movements like faulty animatronics, pumping blood from their various wounds as they lurched toward Hector.

Taking the axe in both hands, the prodigal son screamed in horror and swung for the fences. He sheared off his brother's leg at the knee. He struck Josiah's head from his shoulders. He spilled his sister's intestines across the floor. The corpses crumpled and fell as Hector cleaved through their flesh, and eventually he started to laugh. But the demons laughed too. Their magic closed the family's wounds as fast as Hector's axe could open them, and soon the creatures were upon him.

When the cops had fled, one officer had dropped his own axe in his terror. Hector reached for it now and crossed it over his own axe. "Keep me, O Jehovah, from the hands of the wicked!" he bellowed. "Preserve me from the violent man!"

The axe handles glowed white with the power of Hector's faith and the demons howled in pain. Black smoke billowed from the crumpling bodies of the Harcourts and the pool of blood frothed as the demons returned to their own realm. Hector kept praying until the house went quiet, and when the bubbles had stopped, he took a long look at himself and began to scream.

The cops emerged from their hidey-holes and crept back into the House. Hector's screams had reduced to a few broken moans and he was trying to wipe his hands clean on a bare patch of floor.

"What in God's name was that?" whispered one of the men. "What were those… creatures?"

Superintendent Campbell kneeled in front of Hector and waved a hand before his eyes, but got no response.

"What do we do?" demanded another. "What do we say? That there's a… a witch in Delapore?"

"We can't say that!" stammered a third. "They'll think we've gone mad! Josiah was… good God, he was the best of us! He couldn't be… *this*!"

The superintendent snapped his fingers in front of Hector's face. Still no response. He looked up at the ceiling for a moment and pursed his lips. Then he stood and turned to his officers. "Gentlemen, you all know Delapore. You know this is a good town. We do not have murders in Delapore. We do not have witches. We are a God-fearing community here. And Hector Harcourt left that all behind, didn't he? Josiah turned him away after Hector's… indiscretion. And it seems Hector's anger finally got the better of him, didn't it?"

The men looked at each other, unsure. For a moment, none of them could meet their CO's eyes. They couldn't accept what he was asking of them.

The first man to step forward had a platinum-blond moustache and the same ruddy complexion. Abby guessed this would be J.A.B.'s son or nephew. "Hector got off the last train and came straight up here," he said. "Nobody saw him or talked to him. Even we didn't know he was back in town. Right?"

The superintendent nodded. "Good lad, Jack. Anyone want to hazard a guess at what happened next?"

Another officer slowly raised his hand. "He couldn't live with himself. Not for a second."

"Very insightful, Constable Styles." Superintendent Campbell turned and bashed the butt of his shotgun into Hector's forehead. Then he fixed his peaked cap and started barking orders. "Get those servants off the ceiling. Get me a length of that rope and a strong branch. Somebody grab that axe and make sure the servants look the same as the rest." He pointed at Jack. "Give me your revolver, boy."

"Sir?"

"These damn fools shot the place to bits when we retreated. Hector must have had a revolver with him when he came up the hill, or else there'll be questions. Don't worry, you'll get it back."

The young man nodded and gave the superintendent his gun. Superintendent Campbell held it by two fingers and looked out over the rest of the squad. "Listen to me, all of you! Hector did this by himself. That's as far as the story goes. If you think you saw anything… unusual, then I am sorry to tell you that you were badly mistaken. Tomorrow morning, the milkman will come. And the postie. They'll call us. From there, I'll handle everything. I can fix it so that as far as Delapore knows, none of us were ever here. But we have to be united in this. Not just tonight and tomorrow, but forever. Until you go to your graves, not one man among you will say a word about this to *anyone*. Understand me?"

Someone raised his hand. "What about the others? All those people that Josiah killed?"

"Did Josiah kill them? Or was it an animal, somewhere out in the hills? We don't have murders in Delapore, Constable Hall."

The men nodded and eyed each other with suspicion. Woe be to him who spilled the secret.

The scene faded into mist again, and Abby turned to the dead Hector standing beside her. "Jesus…" she whispered. "You were just as much a victim as any of them."

Hector shook his head sadly. "I do not blame those men for what they did."

"How can you not?" Abby spluttered. "You saved the whole town and those… those *pigs* let you hang for it! They covered up almost a dozen homicides! Why? Because it wasn't *convenient* for them! None of them deserved to wear those badges!"

"What is past is past, Abby Henderson. It was so much easier for Delapore to think the wayward heir of Harcourt had gone mad than it would have been for them to confront the ghastly truth. The town blamed me for what happened, and through no fault of my own I was damned to this state of unrest. Delapore fears me as a monster. The Spirit of the Harcourt House. How ironic. I cannot even enter the House."

"Yes, you can. I saw you in there."

"You saw me here. In a corner of the spirit world that my father molded to look like the House. But I cannot enter the physical structure. My father forbids it, and his will is stronger than mine. His spirit has dominated the House for so long that I fear he has become one with its very foundations. But the House is old and rotting with every passing day. As it decays, my father's influence in your world weakens, and when the House is no more, my father will be less than a shadow even to the most perceptive Gospel. In the past, my father would try to delay the rot by projecting his mind into other bodies. But he can only possess mortals for a short time, and the House always calls him back. It is not enough."

"That's what he needs the blood for. To keep himself from fading."

Hector nodded. "Salt is anathema to the spirits of the dead. It is dry and still and unliving. But warm blood fascinates, because it signifies vitality. It is the water of life. My father seeks a permanent reversal of his current state, and his blood harvests may give him the power to achieve it. I do not have the strength to stop it, but I believe you do, Abby Henderson. You must confront my father and his apprentice, and you must *destroy* the Harcourt House. It has done nothing but poison this town for nearly a century."

Abby nodded. "Don't worry, Hector. I will."

Hector whispered a silent "Thank you," and his image began to fade before Abby's eyes. "All my hope is in you, dear Gospel. All my…"

The last sentence died in midair as Hector disappeared. The silver mist shifted around her, and she was back in the bedchamber where she had started. She walked over to the king-size bed, laid down on the covers, and closed her eyes.

*****

She awoke on the motel bed. According to her watch, it was nearly five in the evening. She pulled herself upright and tried to reorient herself to the physical world. Her mouth was dry, her stomach was pleading for food, and she badly needed a piss.

After a detour to the bathroom, Abby walked out into the smoky August air and trudged down to Simon and Natalie's room. She opened the door and stopped dead when she saw the selfish yellow-skinned face at the table. Whittaker was on his fourth cigarette, studying the code in Josiah's journal. When he heard her enter, he looked up and blew smoke out through his nostrils. "Heya, chickadee. I like the hair."

"What the hell is he doing here?" Abby hissed.

Simon stepped between Abby and Whittaker. "Easy, Abigail, easy! He's helping us out." He quickly explained the High West Elvish problem to her, but failed to add that he had agreed to pay for Whittaker's room at the motel in exchange for the imp's help with the translation.

"Yeah, my family weren't good for much," said Whittaker, "but they got me some of the finest tutors in the Capitol. Time was, I could translate from High West in my sleep. Actually, I think I just about got this code figured out." Pointing at Leanne, he said, "Hey, Glasses, hand me another sheet of paper, will you?"

Leanne frowned. "Humans tend to say 'please,' Whittaker." But she handed him his paper. For nearly ten minutes after, Abby caught the others up on what Hector had shown her while Whittaker scribbled away.

At last, he put down his pencil, stubbed his cigarette out on the table, and gulped. "Oooooh boy."

"What's 'oh boy'?" Simon asked.

Whittaker took a breath. "Well. Good news is, I think I cracked this part of the code. Bad news is, if I'm reading this right, then Josiah's just getting started."

CHAPTER 20

OLD RED EYES IS BACK

SIMON TOOK a breath. "Walk us through this, Whittaker. What do you have?"

Whittaker put Josiah's journal in the middle of the table, together with his solution to the code. The journal was open to the page of cicada sketches, and Whittaker pointed at the note near the bottom. "I started with this page just to give myself a crib to work from. That wasn't too hard."

Leanne read what Whittaker had written. "'*Ex creātūrae minimae, arcānum maximum Dei.*' From the smallest creature, God's greatest secret." Simon looked at her in amazement, and she shrugged and said, "Catholic school. Latin was kind of their thing."

Whittaker rolled his eyes. "Yeah, yeah, round of applause and a gold star for ya, Glasses. Anyway, once I got that cribbed, I was able to work out the High West passage pretty easy." He flipped to the next page. "You know how you guys said Josiah was looking for three ingredients for his spell? I think these lines here are the shopping list." He cleared his throat and read the translation aloud:

"Bones of the slain,
Uncovered at night.
Blood forsaken,
Stolen by might.

*Breath of the innocent,
Morning's first light."*

Simon leaned back in his chair and whispered, *"Metodes miht."*

"Oh yeah," Whittaker said with a nod.

"I don't get it," said Natalie. "What's the problem?"

"The Rite of Ka'thonn," said Simon. "It's a resurrection spell. Very old, very black necromancy. The bones of the slain are Josiah Harcourt's mortal remains. Forsaken blood is from the Thousand Cuts victims."

"And what's 'morning first light'?" said Abby.

"It refers to an old Vanguard folk belief that if a family's first son were born at dawn on a clear day, the boy would grow up to be a great warrior and leader of men. And 'the breath' is the breath of life that the High Celestial gave us all at the moment of our creation."

"Taken all together," Whittaker said, "it's a metaphor. For the soul of a living child. Josiah Harcourt wants to rip the life force out of some kid and use it as fuel to bring himself back to life."

"Back to his full fighting strength, even," Simon added. "The Rite of Ka'thonn converts the spiritual energy of the child into new flesh for the decedent, free of any wound or corruption. And that means no more brain tumour."

Abby suddenly flashed back to the first dream she'd shared with Will, and recalled Josiah Harcourt's red-eyed skeleton sitting in a bathtub of blood. He had said then that he would have all the power in the world very soon, and that Will was going to help him. "Oh God," she whispered, "three guesses who Josiah has pegged as his 'breath.'"

"It would explain why so many roads seem to lead back to our Master Brady," said Simon. "Bloody hell, I should have seen it before! Mandeep Sihota was killed right outside the cemetery. I'll bet you anything he was in the wrong place when the warlock was robbing Josiah's grave! And God's greatest secret out of the smallest creature? It's talking about the secret of conquering death! Cicadas have been revered as symbols of resurrection and new life for thousands of years. I can't believe I missed it."

"Don't beat yourself up, Simon," said Abby. "It's not easy to think too clearly when there's a gajillion of the things right in your face. At least now we know why all of this is happening, so we can start being proactive. We can stop this Rite of Ka'thonn before Josiah and his apprentice take it any further."

"Yes, you're right, Abby, you're right. If Josiah's spirit has indeed bonded with the House like Hector said, then that's what we need to focus on right now. It'll take some heavy-duty pyrotechnics to bring that place down. But we'll also need to apply them very carefully. The last thing the Okanagan needs right now is another uncontrolled fire. I could conjure the flames with enough preparation, but controlling them would be entirely another story."

"I can handle the pyro," said Natalie. "I know a thing or two about controlled demolition."

"You do?" Abby said.

Natalie smiled at Simon. "You never told them about Berlin '43?"

"Hasn't come up, I'm afraid."

"What's Berlin '43?" asked Leanne.

Natalie's smile got bigger. "Four dozen Nazi vampires with a biological weapon. Me with a homemade flamethrower. That was one hell of a Christmas."

Abby did her best to hide how badass she thought that sounded. "How long would it take you to put that all together?"

"A good few hours, assuming I can find everything I need in this backwater."

"Okay, we'll leave that to you. We also need to figure out for certain who the warlock is. I've been whammied twice so far, when I was talking to Reverend Jansen and Superintendent Campbell. They're tied to black magic and we need to figure out how, so I say we search their homes and look for clues. Simon and I can handle that. He knows magic when he sees it, and I know it when I get whammied."

"Should we put a watch on Will Brady?" asked Leanne.

"Good point. The warlock's killed again, so he'll either be laying very low, or he'll be in a hurry. He might come looking for the 'breath' before too long. Leanne and Whittaker, you two can be on surveillance duty just in case."

The imp frowned. "What's in it for me if I have to babysit?"

"I kind of like Simon's idea about peace of mind. Simon, what was the name of that faerie king you mentioned? Auberon ab something?"

Whittaker flinched like he'd been slapped. "Okay, okay, I'm on board! I didn't realize it was that time of the month, Bossy Pants."

Abby quietly flipped him the bird. "Simon, do you have anything in your bag of tricks that could turn us invisible or something? I don't want anyone to raise an alarm if we're going warlock-hunting."

"I could try to recalibrate the enchantments on the bracers. They wouldn't exactly make us invisible, but we'd be much harder to spot. I'd need a few hours to rework the magic, of course."

"Take your time. I haven't had a proper meal since breakfast, and I am just *dying* over here."

*****

It was a little before midnight when Abby and Simon returned to Reverend Jansen's house. Simon and Whittaker had spent nearly two hours together reworking the glamours that the bracers projected, so that they would now make the wearer functionally invisible in all but the most direct light.

Unseen by the church's security cameras, Simon and Abby tiptoed onto Reverend Jansen's property, down a gravel path that led into the backyard. Simon unlocked the back door with a whispered spell, and he and Abby slipped into the house.

Simon closed his eyes, and the Vokarion crystal under his shirt started to glow as Abby heard his thoughts in her head. *From now on, let's communicate only through the telepathic channels. It'll keep the noise to a minimum.*

Abby gave him a thumbs-up and they split off in opposite directions. As she searched her half of the house, she checked in with the others over the Vokarion relay.

Any updates, guys?

Natalie responded first. *I'm putting some incendiaries together now. I pulled what I could from Simon's stores, but I had to substitute a few ingredients, so they might be messier than usual. It's been a while since I did this.*

We'll make do. When you get all that sorted, why don't you meet up with Leanne and Whittaker? Just in case things get hairy.

Roger that.

Great. Speaking of Leanne, how are you and Whittaker getting on?

Leanne's voice echoed in Abby's head. *All quiet so far. I've got a decent view of Will's bedroom from where I am. The lights are on and he's still awake. Hasn't left his room since we got here. His sitter's watching TV in the living room. Rest of the street's pretty quiet.*

Okay. Keep us posted.

Abby signed off as she reached Grace Jansen's room. The door opened with a low creak, and she froze in her tracks. The bedsheets rustled and Grace coughed and moaned.

A light snapped on in the room two doors down and Reverend Jansen said, "Grace? Grace, is something wrong?" Abby quickly pressed herself flat against the wall and held her breath. Reverend Jansen came out of his bedroom in a light t-shirt and boxer shorts and walked right past her into his daughter's bedroom. "Now, now, Gracie, it's okay. It's all okay. Dad's here now."

Abby peeked around the doorframe. Grace was sat up in bed as much as was physically possible for her. Her eyes were half-closed, and she rocked from one side to the other as Reverend Jansen patted her shoulders and calmed her down. "It's alright, Grace. It's me. It's your father."

Grace slowly stopped rocking and acknowledged her father's presence with something like a drowsy nod. As the girl closed her eyes again, Abby focused on her aura. It was as thin as fishing line, and so dull it was almost imperceptible. Grace was about as empty a shell as she could be.

Reverend Jansen sat on Grace's bed and held her hand. "I… I don't imagine you can hear me, Grace. I don't imagine you've ever heard me since, well… But I don't expect you to. I love you, Grace. I will always love you. I'm sorry if I ever hurt you. I'm sorry I couldn't be there when you needed me."

A bead of drool descended from Grace's bottom lip. Reverend Jansen wiped it away with his finger. "And I'll tell you the same thing tomorrow night. Just like I did last night, and the night before that."

Abby looked away and hung her head. *Simon?* she thought. *You there?*

Yes, Simon answered. *Is everything alright down that way? I thought I heard voices.*

It's just the reverend. He didn't see me. Look, Simon, I think we have to go. Reverend Jansen's not our man.

You're sure.

Yeah, I am. I don't feel a trace of magic here. Not like I did last time. The Jansens are just broken people. There's no way they're drawing power from the Thousand Cuts.

I think you're right. I haven't found anything incriminating myself. I'll meet you at the back door and we can move on to Superintendent Campbell.

Abby held her position until she was sure Reverend Jansen was back in his bed. Then she crept back the way she had come. When she passed by the kitchen, she heard the squeak of a sneaker on tile. The hairs prickled on the back of her neck as she remembered she was standing on carpet. She sensed the black magic coming from the kitchen and peeked in.

There was Red Eyes, illuminated by the moonlight coming through an open window. Abby clenched her jaw and pressed herself against the wall as he stepped out into the hallway and turned toward the bedrooms. He looked at the wall where Abby was, and she carefully activated her crystal. *Simon. He's here.*

Red Eyes leaned forward and cocked his head to one side, his nose six inches from hers. He extended his free hand to the wall just below her left arm.

Who's here? said Simon, as Abby shimmied along the wall out of Red Eyes's reach.

The warlock! she answered. *The warlock is here and I'm looking right at him!*

Red Eyes looked left and right, then shrugged. Whatever he thought he'd seen there, he must have imagined it.

Thumpa-thumpa-thumpa-thump. Abby could hear the beat of her heart in her ears. It was picking up steam as she held her breath, but she refused to exhale until her foe was out of earshot. She felt a jolt of energy running through her bracer as the illusion started to waver.

Listen to me, Abby, listen. You have to stay calm, Simon commanded. *Stay calm, or the illusion won't hold. I need you to breathe, alright? You're building up too much adrenaline. Just breathe.*

Abby stretched her shirt up over her nose and slowly exhaled. Her heartrate began to slow, and the bracer stopped tingling. The illusion was solid again.

Good. That's good, said Simon. *Just keep breathing. Where are you? I'm coming to you.*

I'm outside the kitchen. Red Eyes was on his way down the hall now.

Roger that. If I can get close enough, I might be able to incapacitate him. Can't promise I won't wake up the reverend, though.

Whatever you have to do, man! What the hell is he doing here, anyway?

I don't know, but we can't let him leave!

Red Eyes reached the reverend's door and Abby gave a sigh of relief. Red Eyes raised his wand, turned in her direction, and shouted, *"Lūx!"*

An orb of dazzling white light bloomed from the wand and struck Abby in the chest, illuminating the room like a fireworks display and shattering the glamour around her. She was fully visible as she slammed on the ground, and Red Eyes stepped toward her. "You thought you could hide from me, Gospel?"

The light went on in Reverend Jansen's room, and he burst into the hall in shock. "What in God's name is happ—"

Red Eyes turned his wand on the reverend. *"Carnis lapidis!"* The reverend froze where he stood, stiff as a statue. Red Eyes leaned toward him, put a hand on his shoulder, and whispered, "O Death, where is thy sting?" Then he turned back to Abby and snarled, "I don't know what the hell you're doing here, Henderson, but you have interfered for the last time! This is between me and Jansen!" He pointed his wand at her, and the black smoke at the tip raced up his arm.

"Āhefe mūr!" As Red Eyes unleashed a curse at Abby, a wall of blue sparks rose from the floor to the ceiling between them. The dark spell dissipated against the barrier, and Simon pulled Abby to her feet.

"Good timing," she said with a weak smile.

"The magician-prince," purred Josiah Harcourt's apprentice. "Ætheriċ, son of Wulfrecg, son of gold-giver Hroðmund. The Master warned me you might be a problem."

Simon pressed his nose against the wall of energy. "I am your worst bloody nightmare is what I am, sunshine. If Josiah knows so much about me, then he will know that I've forgotten more about magic than he ever learned in his pathetic life."

Red Eyes chuckled. "A bold claim, Vanguard. Do you have the skill to support it?" He pointed his wand at the floor beneath him, and the carpet rippled like water. Red Eyes sank into it, rose up behind Simon and Abby, and fired another spell.

Simon pulled Abby out of its path and shouted, *"Mægnes sweor!"* A rush of invisible power struck Red Eyes hard and sent him flying into the coffee table. "Get to safety!" Simon hollered. "I'll handle this!" Red Eyes stood and launched another spell.

Abby crawled into the kitchen as Simon ducked and returned a spell of his own. As showers of red, gold, black, and blue sparks danced in the other room, Abby's heart thumped louder and louder. Suddenly, she screamed as the *thumpa-thumpa-thump* of her heart became the *ba-boom, ba-boom* of an explosion in her brain. A vision was coming, and a searing needle of pain stabbed Abby in the head.

She blinked, and suddenly she was outside the Brady house. There was a bulky figure on the doorstep, clad all in black and holding a bolt-action rifle. The man threw all his ample weight at the door, and like the wall of Jericho, the whole thing came tumblin' down.

The big man stomped into the house and turned his attention toward a thin, pale woman with lots of frizzy auburn hair. Mrs. Tenenbaum shrieked and reached for the phone on the coffee table, but the big man heaved the rifle to his shoulder and shot her between the ribs. As he stepped over her and went into the living room, Abby's mind zoomed upstairs, where Will was crawling underneath his Spider-Man bed.

Abby snapped back to reality, and the noise of the duel rose over the ringing in her ears. She peeked around the kitchen door and called for Simon.

"What?" he called back. Red Eyes had transformed the pieces of the coffee table into a cluster of deadly coral snakes, which were now hissing and leaping at Simon.

"Will Brady's in trouble!"

Simon levitated three of the coral snakes and threw them at Red Eyes, then asked Abby if she was sure.

"I had a vision! There's someone at his house, and he's got a gun! Will's sitter is hurt bad!"

The many coral snakes were now one big coral snake the size of a Saint Bernard. Simon produced a blade of energy between his hands and sliced the creature's head off in two strokes. "Bloody hell, like we don't have enough problems!"

Then their Vokarion crystals started to glow, and Leanne was shouting at them to "get your butts in gear, now!" She screamed as a single gunshot echoed over the psychic relay, and the line went dead.

In the confusion, Red Eyes turned and hurled himself through the front window of the house. "Dammit!" Simon snapped. "Alright, you go help Leanne and Whittaker. I'll take care of this one." He pointed at Abby and shouted, *"Duru onhlīde on lyfte!"* There was a flash and a roar as a large blue-green wormhole opened in front of Abby. She gave Simon a thumbs-up and leaped into the portal just before it closed. Then Simon ran toward the broken window. "This. Ends. *Tonight!*"

CHAPTER 21

MAINTIENS LE DROIT

AFTER THE murder of Mandeep Sihota, it was all hands on deck for the Delapore RCMP. At the start of that night's patrol, Inspector Pembroke had paired every available local officer with a member of the Major Crime team to ensure that there were as many boots on the ground as possible. Mona Brady had drawn the short straw and was partnered with Pembroke herself. So far tonight, the two of them had broken up a brawl at The Gaslights Pub, settled a domestic out at the Little Bear Trailer Park, and chased some rowdy teens off the playground at Delapore Elementary. One of them had spilled half a beer on Mona's uniform pants, and now the whole patrol car smelled like Molson Canadian.

"Did you get everything sorted out with your boy today?" Inspector Pembroke asked.

Mona blinked. In order to give herself enough time to get that book to the Henderson girl, she'd told her superiors there was some trouble at home that she needed to attend to. She hoped Pembroke wasn't about to press her for details of what mischief Will had supposedly been up to that required her attention. When she'd looked in on him before retrieving the book, he'd been playing on his Nintendo Switch. "Um, yes. Yes, ma'am, I talked to his sitter and I'll be talking to him first chance I get."

"I hope you don't go too hard on him. It can be rough for kids, having a cop as a parent. A lot of them act out at that age. I know my girls were rotten to the core."

Mona blinked again. She knew the inspector wore a wedding band, but she never heard her talk about her domestic situation. As a matter of fact, Pembroke had hardly said two words to Mona that weren't direct orders in the entire time that she and her team had been in Delapore. This was getting weird. "You have kids, ma'am?"

"Stepkids. Two of 'em, from the wife's first marriage. The youngest graduated high school this year, but they were Will's age once. It is Will, isn't it?"

"It is."

"What is it, Mona? A year now that you've been in Delapore?"

Mona blinked a third time. This morning she'd been 'Sergeant Brady.' Now she was 'Mona'? What was going on? "Uh, not quite, ma'am. End of August, that'll be a year."

"So you've got the lay of the land a bit, but you're not really a local, are you?"

"I suppose not."

"I'm trying to get a read on this town, Mona. I've been trying for weeks. But I keep coming up short. I want to ask you, one outsider to another, is there a way in to Delapore?"

"I'm not sure I follow you, ma'am."

"Oh, I think you do. I saw the tape. From when you interviewed the Henderson girl."

"Did you? What did you think of her?"

"What she was saying was insane. But she definitely believes it. I get the feeling that more than a few people in this town do. A lot of the kids, for sure, but even some folks who should know better."

"Is this about the Harcourt House? Ma'am, you can't tell me you believe—"

"I never said that. But you have to admit, this case has taken some strange turns. I'm seeing things in Delapore that I've never seen in thirty years of police work. And it does make me think. So I'll ask you again: you have the lay of the land, but you don't have the same biases Phil Campbell has. What do you think is happening in this town?"

Mona opened her mouth. She wanted to throw her head back and laugh, to congratulate Inspector Pembroke on a joke well made. But to do that would be to leave too many dangling threads. The man with the axe. The killer with the red eyes. The book that spoke.

Cutting and cutting and feeding and cutting...

Mona reached for an answer, but nobody threw one to her. She became acutely aware of Pembroke's eyes on her and she started to squirm in the driver's seat as the silence stretched to uncomfortable lengths.

Mercifully, the squawk of the car's radio broke the tension at last. "All units please respond; we have a 10-73 at 8615 Springer Avenue."

10-73 was the RCMP code for an alarm, and 8615 Springer was Rev. Matthew Jansen's home address. It was also six blocks away from Mona and Pembroke's current location. The inspector grabbed the radio handset to answer the call, but someone else got there first.

"Dispatch, this is Constable Innes. McDonald and I are in the area right now. We'll have a look."

Suddenly, green light flashed in the sky to the car's two o'clock. Red Eyes sprinted into the road and Mona slammed on the brakes. He turned to face her as the car skidded to a halt, and then he melted into the tarmac. Pembroke braced herself against the dashboard and gasped, "What the *hell* was that?"

His eyes... Mona thought to herself. *Jesus, his eyes! Like Christmas lights from Hell...*

The ringing of her cell phone pulled her away from that thought. She answered and heard Will crying on the other end of the line. "M-mom?" he whispered. "Please, you ha—you have to come home, Mom. I-I think th-there's somebody inside."

"What?" Mona quickly put Will on speakerphone and cranked the car into reverse. "Will, I'm with Inspector Pembroke right now. Tell us everything!"

"I he—I heard the door slam. I heard a g-gunshot. I-I think Mrs. Tenenbaum might be hurt!"

By way of response, Mona switched on the siren and did a sharp U-turn in the direction of home. Pembroke radioed dispatch to let them know the situation, and Mona tried to keep her son talking. "Listen to me, William! We're coming to you, and we're bringing backup! Find a safe place to hide, don't make a sound, and don't move until I get there! Do you understand?"

"I do!" Will said. "I do! Please hurry, Mom. I'm really scared."

"Don't worry, baby. Don't worry. Mom's coming."

*****

Simon heard police sirens as he crashed through the trees onto the road. He saw a cruiser to his left, going hell for leather away from him. Then he looked to the other side of the street and saw Red Eyes about to round the next corner. Simon shouted, *"Bind þone bānsele!"* and green lightning burst from his hand.

Red Eyes spun on his heel and swept his wand in a wide arc. *"Redī!"* Simon had to duck under his own spell and heard it strike a tree, petrifying the leaves that had been swaying in the summer breeze.

The warlock leapt a garden fence and disappeared into a backyard. Simon raised both hands with a cry of, *"Bēamas berstaþ!"* and a patch of fencing exploded. Red Eyes ducked the flying splinters and swore as a light went on in the house and a dog started barking. The warlock tripped over scattered toys of the dog and human variety and pointed his wand over his shoulder.

"Secō carnem!"

Simon ran straight toward the spell and shouted, *"Hyd īsenu!"* Red Eyes's spell bounced harmlessly off his skin, dissipating in a flash of blue sparks.

The back door opened and a very angry German Shepherd tore through the yard, barking its head off and snapping at the intruders. Behind the dog came a muscular man in pyjamas and a dressing gown, brandishing a well-used pitching wedge and yelling, "Get 'em, Caesar, get 'em!"

Just before he jumped over the fence into the next yard, Red Eyes aimed his wand at the dog and shouted, *"Frangō ossum!"*

There was a loud crack and the dog yelped painfully. Simon glanced back briefly and saw the animal lying on the ground in a heap, its right foreleg badly broken.

Red Eyes cleared the fence in one jump and Simon followed suit. As he landed, he raised two fists to the sky and roared, *"Āhefe eorþan!"* A massive disc of grass and soil jumped out of the lawn. *"Gār eorþan!"* Simon opened his hands, and the disc became a spear of earth that struck Red Eyes in the back. He fell into a bird bath, and Simon didn't give him a chance to recover. Taking a pitcher's stance, he wound up and hurled a ball of fire at Red Eyes's head. *"Fyres blæst!"*

"Ēdō aquam!" The wand went off like a fire hose. Steam filled the yard and before Simon could fight through it, Red Eyes had vanished.

"Secō carnem, secō et cruciō, secō mortī!" The warlock came from the roof, jumping at Simon wand-first and blitzing the yard with black lightning.

"Āċyr fēondræs!" Simon folded his arms over his chest and a dome of protective energy rose around him. The force of the

curse knocked him off his feet, but the sharp edges tore through everything except him. Windows shattered, branches snapped off of trees, chunks of the birdbath went flying into the next yard, and Red Eyes screamed.

Two cuts went deep into his side, staining his clothes and the grass at his feet. As the first police sirens approached, Red Eyes put pressure on the wounds, whispered a spell, and melted into the lawn.

*****

Thunder rolled and a bright flash of light signalled the opening of a wormhole. Abby stumbled out of it onto the Bradys' front lawn and found Leanne and Whittaker huddled outside the front door, holding their positions until backup arrived.

Abby scurried over to join them in the porch light. "Dammit. Dammit, dammit, dammit. It's a two-pronged attack. How didn't I see this coming?" The rifle fired and a section of the doorframe exploded two feet from Abby's face. She shrieked and covered her head.

"What's the plan here?" Leanne asked. Another gunshot answered her, and she yelped as the bullet struck the ground near her feet.

Abby crawled over to the front window and peeked into the living room. Mrs. Tenenbaum was lying beside the coffee table with a large red stain growing on her blouse. Her attacker stood in the doorway with his rifle trained on the front entrance. His mouth moved under his balaclava, and Josiah Harcourt's muffled voice came out. "I know you're out there, Gospel! The boy is mine! Come and face me if you say otherwise!"

Abby looked at Whittaker and whispered, "Can you teleport us into the house?"

"Are you nuts?" hissed the imp. "Where that Froot Loop is?"

"Whittaker! You're being a team player, remember?"

"Okay, okay, fine! Glasses, grab my hand. Normal, you grab her."

The three formed a human chain, and Whittaker snapped his fingers. Abby's ears popped, and suddenly she and the others were standing in the house, behind the masked intruder. He turned in surprise as Abby and the others dogpiled on top of him. He hit the ground with a thud, and his gun went off in his hands. The shot went wild and shattered a china figurine above the mantel in the living room.

The intruder shook off Abby and the others and retreated into the living room so he could reload. Tires screeched on the kerb outside and a heavy pair of boots went *thoom thoom thoom* on the lawn. Then Natalie hurled herself through the front window. She caught the gunman in a flying tackle, and the two of them crashed through the wall between the living room and the front hall. Natalie grabbed the rifle's barrel and bent it like a pretzel, so the gunman broke her nose with the butt of the gun.

Leanne knelt over Mrs. Tenenbaum and rolled up her sleeves. "Somebody, find me a first aid kit!"

A single rifle round had entered Mrs. Tenenbaum's abdomen on the right side, just below her floating rib. She was still breathing, but she was fading quickly. As Abby ran off to find a first aid kit, the gunman pulled a Smith & Wesson from the back of his waistband and fired, obliterating the banister behind Abby's head. Leanne turned to Whittaker and told him to remove his jacket. She needed to put pressure on the wound.

Whittaker shook his head. "Okay, nope! Drawing the line! This suit is from Savile Row! I can't just—"

"WHITTAKER! Shut up and do as you're told!"

Whittaker flinched and took off his jacket. He flinched again as Leanne pressed the jacket into Mrs. Tenenbaum's wound and pressed her knee into the jacket. Mrs. Tenenbaum grimaced at the pressure, and one eye fluttered open. "Who… who are…?" she gasped.

"Shh, shh, don't try to speak," Leanne whispered, "you've been badly hurt." She raised her head and yelled, "ABBY! How are we coming with that first aid kit?"

"I'm looking!"

Sirens whined as Mona's patrol car skidded to a stop behind the Thunderbird. She was out the door and running while Pembroke was still on the radio. "Dispatch, this is Inspector Pembroke! 10-33 at 714 Jackson Road! Multiple shots fired, repeat, multiple shots fired! I need all available units at my location ASAP!"

Natalie took the pistol and hammered the grip in the gunman's face. He got one meaty hand around her throat and squeezed, so she rolled onto her back and kicked him off. That should have finished any normal opponent, but Josiah Harcourt's ghostly influence seemed to have tripled the gunman's strength and durability. As the gunman got up, so did she, with another low tackle that knocked him through the door onto the front lawn. They grappled as they rolled on the grass, and the gunman's balaclava came off. Beneath it, Phil Campbell was foaming at his ruddy mouth, and Natalie could see the tiny cicadas darting around in his pupils.

*****

Abby climbed the stairs and called out, "WILL?" She'd found the first aid kit, and Leanne was doing all she could for Mrs. Tenenbaum now. "Will, are you up here? It's Abby! Abby Normal!"

Will ran out of his bedroom and right into Abby's arms. He buried his face in her stomach to hide that he was crying and whispered a thousand thanks into her shirt. She gave him a pat and said, "It's okay, Will. I made you a promise. And Abby Normal doesn't go back on her promises."

Will sobbed and wiped his eyes on her t-shirt. "Where's my mom, Abby? I just want to see my mom."

"Well, then let's go see her. I heard a siren downstairs."

*****

Mona and Pembroke stopped dead as Natalie tore off the superintendent's balaclava. None of this made any sense, but this wasn't the time for questions. It was time to *maintenir le droit*. Both officers drew their Tasers and Mona shouted, "FREEZE!"

The superintendent froze for a second—then he drove his knee into Natalie's chest and threw her off. He stood and took several slow, lumbering steps toward Mona.

Pembroke fired her Taser. The wires crackled as electric current pummeled the superintendent's heart, but he didn't even feel the shot. He knocked her down with a right hook and swung his boot into her stomach. Then he turned on Mona. She backed up and fired her Taser, but Campbell still didn't stop. Mona threw down the Taser, but before she could unholster her gun, Campbell grabbed her wrist and punched her in the side.

Mona hit the ground with a gasp. Campbell landed on top of her and wrung her neck. His face was flushed and slick with sweat, and white foam dripped from his mouth into Mona's eyes. She reached for her gun, but Natalie grabbed Campbell by the shoulders and pulled him back.

Mona staggered to her feet and gasped for breath. Natalie got the superintendent in a headlock and snarled, "Yield, Josiah. It's over."

Josiah Harcourt laughed and whispered, "No, my dear. Not yet." The superintendent opened his mouth and vomited a cloud of cicadas into the air. Josiah made his escape, and Campbell dropped to the ground. He crawled toward Mona and grabbed her ankle, coughing and gasping for breath. His eyes were back to normal, but his face was still way too red.

"Heart..." he gasped. "Jesus... heart... help..." Mona kneeled and flipped Campbell onto his back. He grabbed her arm and looked at her. "Listen!" he gurgled. "Mona... listen... he got in... Master... saw... I saw... your boy... he's..." His grip loosened, his eyelids fluttered, and air rushed out of his lungs. Mona ripped open his black turtleneck and checked his pulse. It was going like a hummingbird, so she started on chest compressions and tilted back the superintendent's head.

"You!" she barked at Natalie. "First aid kit in the trunk! Get it! Then call an ambulance!"

BANG! Simon staggered out of a portal on Campbell's other side and got the gist in a second. He raised his hand and whispered, *"Heofonfyr,"* and lightning crackled in his palm. He slammed his hand down on Campbell's chest and the superintendent jerked on the ground. Simon repeated the spell. Once more. Twice more. On the third shock, Campbell's eyes snapped open and he took a great, gasping breath. Simon and Mona rolled Campbell into the recovery position as he sucked in two more lungfuls, coughed, and then threw up on the lawn. Mona held him so he wouldn't keel over in his own sick, and her finger found his pulse again. Back to normal.

"What did you do?" she gasped to Simon. "What the hell is going on here?"

"I wish I could tell you there's a logical explanation," said Natalie, "but I'm not that good of a liar."

Simon pulled Inspector Pembroke to her feet and made sure she was okay. Then he put his hands on his knees and exhaled heavily. "Everyone still alive?"

Natalie stood and looked to the house. "I think so. I hope so."

"Thank the Celestial for that."

"What about you? Are you okay?"

"The warlock threw one hell of a Cutting Curse at me before he disappeared. I feel like someone hit me in the chest with a sledgehammer. I'll be fine."

"Yeah, we'll let the paramedics decide that."

"I'm *fine*, Natalie. Really! Glass of water and a good night's sleep is what I need."

"Don't give me that martyr shit, Simon Lockhart. Last time someone attacked you with a Cutting Curse, you were laid up for three weeks after. When the ambulance gets here, you're getting a check-up."

Whittaker stepped out of the house with the home phone in his hand. "It's already on its way. Your sitter's got a pulse, Sergeant, but she ain't going to be happy when she wakes up."

"What about my son? Is William okay?"

"You tell me." Whittaker stepped aside as Abby led Will out the front door. Mother and son ran at each other and collided in a long, warm hug.

"Oh my God, Will! I'm so glad you're safe! What happened? Are you hurt?"

Will buried himself deeper in his mother's embrace and wiped his eyes and nose on his sleeve. "I'm okay, Mom. I'm okay now."

"What happened here?"

"I don't know exactly. Somebody came in the door and I heard a shot. I hid like you said. I thought I was gonna die! But then I didn't, 'cause Abby and her friends came like they said they would! They fought the burglar and they saved Mrs. Tenenbaum!"

Mona paused and looked up at Abby. "Like they said they would? Do you know this woman, Will?"

Will gulped and looked at Abby, letting out a sheepish, "Oops."

Mona stood and glared suspiciously at Abby. Abby backed off a step and made a few hemming and hawing noises as she tried to dig herself out of the sinkhole that had suddenly appeared beneath her feet.

"Okay, Henderson, let's try this one more time. Tell me everything."

CHAPTER 22

...AND NOTHING BUT THE TRUTH

"JESUS, I thought you were insane before," Mona said at last. "You can't expect me to believe this nonsense? Ghosts? Other dimensions? Necromancy?"

Abby spread her arms and gestured to the general chaos around them: the ambulances that Mrs. Tenenbaum and Superintendent Campbell were being packed into; the paramedics tending to Simon and Inspector Pembroke; the cops taking statements from Leanne, Whittaker, and Will; and the neighbours demanding to know what the hell kind of police department their taxes were paying for, if this kind of shit was becoming the new normal day after day. "Look around you, Sergeant. Look at all of this and tell me it's a regular day at the office for you."

Mona closed her eyes and shook her head. "You're right. God help me, but you're right. I've been kidding myself since Jenny Styles died. This town *is* haunted. Everything you were telling me, everything the superintendent said, it's all true." She opened her eyes and looked at Abby with a face like a woman drowning on dry land. "But it *can't* be true, do you understand that? I don't want this to be the answer!"

Abby nodded. "I get it. If this is the sanest explanation, then that means you have to throw out everything you think you know about how the world works. The answer just raises more questions, and you're afraid that you don't have it in you to dig all the way down. Something like this makes you realize you mean even less in the grand scheme than you ever thought possible."

Mona considered this for a moment. "That's... yeah. I think that's it exactly."

"It ought to be. Because I feel exactly the same way every single day when I first wake up. The trick is remembering the things in your own life that *do* make sense, and that you *can* hang onto. Because as long as you've got some of that, you know you've got something to rely on." As she said this, Abby looked past Mona and nodded toward Will.

Mona looked at her son and tried to smile. "Good advice. Thanks."

They walked together toward the cluster of squad cars and cops. Mona stuck her hands in her pockets and said, "Why did Josiah Harcourt come here? What does he want?"

"He's after your son. That Rite of Ka'thonn I mentioned? It needs a child's soul to work."

"But why Will? There are hundreds of kids in this town! Why is he special?"

"Beats me. Maybe Josiah's still pissed that Will got away from the House the first time. He's pretty protective of that place, and I don't think he's one to let go of a grudge."

"Jesus... I should have listened to him. He's been warning me about the House for weeks! If I'd listened to him, if I'd listened to you, this wouldn't have happened. I put my son in danger because I was too freaking stubborn."

"No. Listen to me, Sergeant: this was not your fault. Josiah was going to come after Will one way or the other. Even if you'd had Will in protective custody since Day One, Josiah would have found a way past. You never could have predicted all this. Hell, we didn't know it was coming until you brought us that book. One more time: this was not your fault."

Mona fiddled with her hair again. "Is that something else you do every morning? Tell yourself that and hope that you'll believe it one day?"

"Yes," Abby admitted.

"God… is this seriously normal for you? How does someone your age even fall into a life like this?"

Abby shrugged. "I mean, I have an English degree. What else was I going to do with my life?"

Mona stared for a moment, and then she burst out laughing. Jesus, she needed to laugh right now. She couldn't think of a time when laughing had ever felt so good.

Abby cleared her throat. "Mona — can I call you Mona?"

Mona stopped laughing and exhaled. "Why not? I think you've earned it at this point."

"You told me you 'saw things' when you picked up Josiah's book. Do you mind me asking what you saw?"

"I'm… honestly, I'm not sure what it was. I saw the victims, right as they died. I saw… an empty coffin in a wrecked tomb. And I saw Hector Harcourt. He told me to put the book down. I'd seen him once before by that point, sitting in my squad car. He was covered in blood and holding an axe. But you already knew that part, didn't you?"

Abby shrugged. "As my gran once said, 'I'm sort of magic that way.'"

"You really are, aren't you?"

"So, Hector told you to put the book down. He actually spoke to you?"

"Yeah. Is that important?"

"It could be. From what I've read, apparitions don't usually speak except to practiced mediums. Just the fact that you've seen him more than once is unusual."

"I didn't even know it was him at first. The first time, in the squad car, I thought it was my ex come back to haunt me!"

"Will's dad?"

"Yeah. That's crazy, isn't it? A monthlong killing spree, a ghost sitting in my cruiser, and there I was thinking about Nick! How the hell do you make that leap?"

"Good frickin' question," Abby muttered. While she chewed on that for a moment, Mona went to get the attention of Constable Pang, who was currently talking to Will and Leanne.

"Pang! Can I borrow my son from you?"

Pang nodded and stepped back. "Yes, ma'am. I think I have what I need." Abby and Mona welcomed their respective loved ones with open arms.

Abby kissed Leanne and laid her cheek against her partner's hair. "Long night, huh?"

"One for the record books," Leanne confirmed. "At least we're alive."

Abby smiled and kissed Leanne's forehead. "Yeah. At least."

Mona was on her knees, giving her son the hug of a lifetime. "I'm so sorry, William. I should have listened to you sooner. I should have accepted that something was really wrong here."

Will nuzzled his face in the crook of his mom's arm. "It's okay, Mom. You were just trying to do your job."

"No more secrets from now on, okay? If you have a bad feeling about something, you can tell me. I promise I will listen."

Will smiled. "That's all I ever wanted. For you to believe me."

Inspector Pembroke escaped the paramedics and marched toward the group, sporting a tight frown and an ice pack over one eye. Mona saw her approach and murmured, "Uh-oh. Jesus is coming."

"Look busy," Abby finished.

Mona gave her son one last squeeze and then stood at attention as Pembroke drew near. The inspector gave Abby the once-over and grumbled, "Okay. Somebody had better start talking now."

Abby gave her the short version. Pembroke's frown grew deeper as she listened, but by the end she just sighed, nodded, and said, "That actually makes a lot of sense."

Abby blinked. "It does?"

"It does?" echoed Mona.

"I just watched a man jump out of a hole in thin air and create lightning with his hands," Pembroke said drily. "I like to consider myself a rational person, but I'm not completely obtuse. So tell me, Miss Henderson: you and your friends have clearly done your research here. Do you have any theories who this so-called 'warlock' might be?"

"I suspected Reverend Jansen at first," said Abby. "But I was wrong. Although I'm certain the warlock still has some connection to the reverend and Grace. When he showed up at Jansen's house tonight, he talked like there was personal beef there. Looked the reverend right in the eye and said, 'O Death, where is thy sting?' The reverend said the same thing the day I met him."

Mona frowned. "1 Corinthians again. Just like the tattoos. And all of a sudden, we're back at the church group. I assume you didn't check Jim Cardinal's story?"

Abby winked. "You told me not to, so we did not. For what it's worth, I think one of the people you interviewed might be lying."

"Who?"

Abby leaned in close and dropped her voice. "I didn't say so the other day, because I didn't know who was listening, but when the warlock attacked me at the motel, he moved like a cop. I know some of the local officers did the St. Catherine's thing, and a couple of them are about the same build as the warlock."

Pembroke held up a hand. "Back up. Back up. Are you saying this person is one of Campbell's squad?"

"He might be."

Pembroke snapped her fingers and bellowed for Constable Pang. "Get me a head count," she told him. "I want to know who's on duty tonight, when they clocked in, when they talked to dispatch, and where they are now. Anybody who's off-duty, I want their whereabouts confirmed as soon as possible. If anyone doesn't have at least one corroborating witness, I want to speak to them first thing tomorrow."

"Ma'am?" Pang looked totally lost.

"Just do it, Constable. Now."

Pang nodded and went to radio dispatch. As Pembroke opened her mouth to give another order, the handset crackled on Mona's vest. "...lo? ...geant Bra... you... opy?"

Mona grabbed the radio. "Innes? Innes, is that you? This is Sergeant Brady. Do you copy?"

"...e's... don't... copy? ... you copy?"

"Say again, Innes, say again! You're breaking up."

Innes's voice finally came through clearly. "Sergeant? Thank God. We need bodies over at the reverend's house right now!"

"What's the matter? Is Jansen okay?"

"He's gone! The whole place is empty."

"What? Start from the beginning, Innes. What's going on?"

"McDonald and I were en route to his house. Then Pembroke called in the 10-33. We were about to radio in and then... I don't know, there was this white light in the road. I saw this cloud of bugs fly into it. I couldn't brake in time and... we went in too. We came out eight blocks away from where we started. The car died half a block from the church, and the reverend's van was just gone."

"When was this? Why didn't you radio in when you got there?"

"What do you think I'm doing, Sergeant? We've only been here a couple minutes!"

"Innes, you last radioed in more than half an hour ago. Are you telling me it took you that long to get to the reverend's house?"

There was a pause. "Half an hour? Are you sure?"

"Yes."

"But… no, that's not right. The clock on the dash said it was five minutes. Sarge… where the hell were we?"

Mona sighed and stifled a yawn. "Damned if I know. Just hold your position, Innes. We'll send someone out to meet you. We need to regroup and then we need to find the reverend and Grace Jansen."

"Roger."

Mona signed off and rubbed her eyes. "When it rains…" she grumbled. Pembroke had already stormed off to shout orders at the rest of the assembled officers. Two members of her own team took off in the direction of Reverend Jansen's house and a line of officers started herding the neighbours back to their own houses. "God, this is going to be a circus."

"Is there anything we can help with?" asked Abby.

Mona shook her head. "Just go back to your motel for now. Try to get some sleep. We need to get this mess sorted out. If the situation changes, I'll call you."

"Are you sure?"

"Trust me. Someone has to be awake and alert tomorrow. You've done plenty already, Henderson, but it's not your job to keep this town safe."

Abby looked down at Will. "Sure feels like it."

*Watch ye therefore: for ye know not when the
master of the house cometh,
at even, or at midnight, or at the cockcrowing, or
in the morning:
Lest coming suddenly he find you sleeping.
And what I say unto you I say unto all, Watch.*
*

Mark 13:35-37

BOOK THREE:

CORINTHIANS

CHAPTER 23

SINNER MAN

THE ENGINE in Matthew Jansen's old van growled like a bear on the defensive. He was pushing the Ford as hard as it could go, putting the shocks through Hell itself as he took the main road out of Delapore. The high beams sheared away most of the surrounding darkness, but Jansen kept one eye on the shadows along the shoulder.

He knew that the cops couldn't help him now. Nobody could. This was Satan's own magic at work. Reverend Jansen had seen it as plain as day, in the red eyes of his attacker. Those had been the eyes of the Deceiver, wearing a borrowed face. And in that instant Matthew Jansen had known his fate was out of the hands of mortal men. When the the dust had settled, he had taken Grace to the sanctuary at St. Catherine's, where the devil could not follow.

And the devil hadn't followed, had he? Oh no, he'd gone ahead. No sooner had Reverend Jansen unlocked the church's front door than he'd seen the devil's red eyes glowing in the dark, like a ghoulish jungle predator. The devil had screamed at him about the last trumpet, about the corruptible putting on the incorruptible, and Reverend Jansen had fled.

His home breached. His sanctuary profaned. His verse mocked. What choice was there but to flee? As the van's headlights lit up the grizzly bear carving at the town line,

Reverend Jansen exhaled. He just had to get out of town. Out of town and onto Highway 97. Onto Highway 97 and down to the border. If he kept driving at this speed with minimal stops, Reverend Jansen figured he could be halfway through Washington state by noon. Put some distance between himself and the devil.

KA-CRACK! A white light exploded on the road ahead of him, and Reverend Jansen slammed on the brakes as a swarm of cicadas threw themselves the front of the van. The windshield wipers cleared away some of the bugs and smeared others across the glass. Through a translucent film of smashed insects, Reverend Jansen could see the red-eyed devil stepping into the road. He braked hard and cranked the steering wheel. The van swerved off the road, bumped through the ditch, and smashed into the grizzly bear sign.

The hood flew up and obliterated the windshield. The steering column shot forward and struck Jansen dead center, cracking two ribs and bruising his spleen. A large chunk of wood from the sign stabbed him in the shoulder, and two fingers broke when they bounced off the dashboard. The horn blared ceaselessly. Reverend Jansen tasted blood and felt the steering wheel creak against his chest as he breathed.

The red-eyed devil stalked toward the van, favouring one side and holding a hand to a bleeding wound on his side. Reverend Jansen tried to unbuckle his seatbelt, but it was stuck firm. He jiggled the door handle, and the door didn't budge. As the devil drew nearer, the radio squawked and crackled, and then a song started to play through the static. Johnny Cash, "The Man Comes Around."

The large panel door opened behind the reverend, and the devil jumped up into the back of the van. "Are… are you going to kill me?" the reverend gasped weakly.

Grace moaned as the devil pressed his wand to her neck. "Not yet," the devil rasped. His breathing was heavy and pained. "Not until everything's set."

CHAPTER 24

WAYWARD SON

ABBY TRIED to get a good night's sleep. She honestly did. But something still didn't sit right with her. Some piece of the Harcourt puzzle had slipped between the couch cushions of her mind and was now slumming it with old pieces of gum and sticky pennies. Josiah had been stewing up in the House for most of a century, so why was he only *now* flexing his muscles? Why hadn't he attempted the Rite of Ka'thonn before? Surely there must have been generations of dumb fools he could have goaded into doing his dirty work. And what did it have to do with Will? Why had she dreamed about him, and why had he dreamed about Josiah? It didn't. Make. Sense!

Her head had hit the pillow less than ten minutes after she and her friends had returned to the motel. She'd retreated into her dreams in the hope that her unconscious mind would have more insight into the Harcourt dilemma, but even here, deep in the recesses of her own brain, the answers just wouldn't come.

She thumped her head against the imagined chalkboard she'd been working at and gave a little groan of frustration. Then she picked up the eraser and wiped the board clean. She clenched her other fist until the chalk snapped in two, swore, and threw the two halves off into the distance of the blank white dreamscape. When she couldn't find another piece of chalk on the ledge, she swore a little louder.

"Are you looking for this?" said a voice behind her.

Abby turned. Some distance behind her in the void, someone had set up a little round table with a lovely patterned cloth draped over it. A sterling silver candelabrum was perched in the center of the table, and two very tall people in Victorian-era formal wear sat in the two high-backed chairs around the table, taking tea. On the right was a man with a pair of pince-nez spectacles perched on his nose, and on the left was a woman holding a parasol. When either of them spoke, it was with a clipped, posh English accent straight out of *The King's Speech*. While the woman stirred sugar into her tea, the man held aloft a new stick of chalk and smiled helpfully. Abby marched over and snatched up the chalk with a frown. "Didn't anyone tell you it's rude to enter people's dreams unannounced?"

The woman looked around and smirked. "Well, it doesn't appear as if you're using the space for much," she trilled.

"Come, come, Sister Dearest," the man said with a chuckle. "An uncluttered mind is the sign of a focused mind. Let us not chide the poor girl for her singular devotion."

Abby rolled her eyes. "God save us..." She had encountered this strange duo twice before. She wasn't exactly sure who or what they were—beyond the fact that they constantly referred to each other as Brother Dearest and Sister Dearest—but they knew more about her than she was comfortable with, and they seemed to enjoy speaking to her in riddles and making her life as difficult as possible. "What are you two doing here?"

"Would you care for some tea?" Sister Dearest asked, ducking the question entirely. "Or we have some cucumber sandwiches here which are simply delightful."

Brother Dearest wagged a finger at her. "Ah, I do believe you are trying to stall us, Sister Dearest," he said in a tone that was half admonishing and half amused. He then turned to

Abby and smiled. "I do apologize for her. My sister does love her little squabbles."

"Will one of you *please* answer the question? Why do you keep popping up like this?"

"But that would be telling!" Sister Dearest said, a bit sharply, as she plucked a cucumber sandwich from a silver platter and took a bite of it. "Mmm. Divine!"

Brother Dearest stood and led Abby back to the chalkboard. "Consider us a sounding board, my dear. We are independent operators, neutral third parties."

"We are a second opinion!" Sister Dearest offered from the table.

"Quite so, quite so. Now, you were wondering where your friend Brady intersects with this Harcourt business, hmm?"

"Yes," Abby replied. "I know how all of this lines up, except for him. It's driving me nuts."

"How ever can you tell?" Sister Dearest quipped.

"Perhaps you are approaching this problem from the wrong angle," Brother Dearest proposed. "Please, allow me." He took the chalk and started drawing on the board. "The boy has seen the true nature of the Harcourt House, has he not?"

"Yeah…"

Without any noise at all, Sister Dearest suddenly appeared at Abby's other side. "But there was something he feared even more than the devils in that house."

"His dad…" Abby whispered.

Brother Dearest nodded. "Indeed, indeed. Fathers and sons, sons and fathers. This is what the equation reduces to on its most basic level." He dropped the chalk and stepped away from the board, allowing Abby to see what he had been drawing.

It was a sketch of the Harcourts' living room, on the night of November 3. The image moved like an A-ha music video and Josiah screamed at the gathered cops about how he *was* Delapore. "The office you work in, the church you worship in, even the hotel where my son gambles and whores away his best years! None of those would be here if not for me!"

Before Abby could speak, Sister Dearest turned the chalkboard over. In only two or three strokes of the chalk, she had produced a sketch of Mona Brady, standing on her front lawn only a few short hours ago. Sister Dearest set down the chalk and the sketch spoke: "I didn't even know it was him at first. The first time, in the squad car, I thought it was my ex come back to haunt me! A monthlong killing spree, a ghost sitting in my cruiser, and there I was thinking about Nick! How the hell do you make that leap?"

"Josiah Harcourt, Hector Harcourt," Sister Dearest said simply. "Nick Brady, William Brady."

"Fathers and sons. Sons and fathers," replied Brother Dearest. He turned the chalkboard over again, erased the sketch of the living room, and started drawing again. "But consider: can not a son also *be* a father? Or a father, a son?" He set the chalk down again and stepped back.

Two sketches, side-by-side. One head-and-shoulders shot of gaunt, roguish Hector Harcourt, and one of sour-faced, bleary-eyed Nick Brady. Booze and bad living had really done a number on Nick, but if you subtracted twenty pounds from his face, then the resemblance was clear as day.

"No…" Abby whispered. "No way. I mean, it—it *can't* be that easy… Can it?" She looked to both sides, but Brother Dearest and Sister Dearest were gone. When Abby looked behind her, their table, teapot, and cucumber sandwiches were likewise absent. She was, once more, alone with her thoughts. But now those thoughts made a hell of a lot more sense.

As she looked back at the chalkboard, and at the nearly-identical faces drawn there, a smile crept onto her own face. "Elementary," she whispered. "Simply elementary, Watson."

CHAPTER 25

HEIR APPARENT

"ELEMENTARY…" ABBY mumbled between snores. "Absolutely… elementary…"

From the dining table, a garbled voice asked, "What's elementary?"

Abby opened her eyes. Leanne had Dot Browne's files scattered around the table in front of her, and she was chewing nervously on a pen as her eyes flicked from the papers to her iPad to her laptop. Abby checked the clock beside her—6:15AM—and then noticed that Leanne's side of the bed was cold. "How long have you been up?"

Leanne spat out the pen and twiddled it between the fingers of one hand while her other hand darted over the laptop's keys. "Not sure. I think I got up an hour after we got back from the Bradys' house. Maybe an hour and fifteen? Even when I was in bed I wasn't really sleeping. I was just so… wired. Too much adrenaline."

"So what's all this?"

"I needed a distraction. Something to keep my mind off last night. And I was lying in bed, and I was thinking something about this whole case just stinks. There's no logical reason why Josiah should have spent so long in the House, just sitting around with his thumb up his you-know-where. Why hasn't he made trouble before?"

Abby threw back the sheets and crawled to the end of the bed, suddenly feeling a lot more awake. "I was just thinking the same thing! I couldn't get the problem out of my brain when I was asleep, and then it just hit me like a bolt of lightning!"

Leanne hadn't heard any of this. "Something has to have changed recently to get Josiah angry," she was saying. "And it's obviously something to do with Will Brady specifically. There are too many connections between the two of them, but there's one connection we're not seeing."

"I know this is going to sound nuts, but you need to indulge me for a sec," replied Abby. She, too, was only hearing her own voice now.

"And I went back as far as I could through the records, and I ran the math, and there's only one answer I can see."

"What if Hector Harcourt had a kid?" they said in unison. There was a moment of stillness before the two looked at each other and smiled.

"Great minds, huh?" said Abby.

"Way to steal my thunder, Henderson."

"Hey, don't blame me if my psychic dreams are faster than your research! What do you have?"

Leanne turned the iPad toward Abby. The screen showed a grainy, black-and-white photograph of a pretty, bespectacled young woman with Will's sharp nose. "Agatha Blaine," she said.

"And who's she when she's at home?"

"She's the reason Hector Harcourt left town. She was a local schoolteacher in the Harcourts' time. About six months after Ephraim Harcourt died, she and Hector were caught in bed together in the honeymoon suite at some swanky hotel in Kelowna." She turned back to the table and rummaged through the scattered papers until she found two photocopies of old articles from *The Delapore Sunday Times* and Kelowna's *Daily Courier*, telling of an unnamed wealthy heir caught in a compromising position. "But here's the kicker," she added.

"Blaine was only her name after she was married. Have a look at this." She scrolled to another image on the iPad and passed it to Abby. It was an enhanced scan of a marriage notice from the *Sunday Times* dated March 14, 1921, announcing the union of George William Blaine, son of Herbert and Margaret, and Agatha Elizabeth Brady, daughter of John and Winifred.

"I triple-checked. It's the same family," said Leanne. "Two months after she's caught in bed with Hector, Agatha's husband files for divorce. Six months after that, her brother and sister-in-law are delivered of a healthy, rosy-cheeked baby boy. I'll bet you anything in the world that was Hector's kid. George Blaine filed for divorce because he *knew* it was Hector's kid, and when the child was born, his mother gave him up to be raised by his aunt and uncle."

"That must be it," Abby said. "Before Josiah died, he disowned Hector. He blamed him for everything. And to know that the son who betrayed him left behind a legacy, that must make him crazy! We need to let the others know what you've found. And I need to call Mona."

Abby reached for her phone and dialled in the number that Mona had given her last night. But before she could hit "CALL," the phone started buzzing in her hand. The same number was calling her. "Mona," she answered. "I was just about to phone you. What's going on?"

"We found the reverend's van. It looks like your department."

*****

Inspector Pembroke passed two photographs across the desk to Abby. After a second cardiac episode late in the night, Phil Campbell was unconscious and on a ventilator at Kelowna General Hospital. As the ranking officer in town, Pembroke had commandeered the big office for her own use, and she'd pegged Mona as her number two. Looking at beak-nosed, grey-haired Margot Pembroke behind the desk, with

Mona standing like a statue behind her, Abby couldn't help but think of Burns and Smithers from *The Simpsons*.

She shook off the mental image and studied the first photo carefully. It was a wide shot of the reverend's wrecked van, taken from the other side of the road just before sunrise. She passed the photo around to the others, and then looked at the second.

An interior shot of the van, centred on Grace Jansen's wheelchair. The girl sat slumped, with one glassy eye toward the camera and a smock of blood running down her front. The HD camera had even picked up the green tinge on the gash in her throat.

"Looks like we had it wrong this whole time," said Mona. "This was never about Grace Jansen at all."

"Then what the hell was it about?" Abby wondered.

"We were hoping you could answer that," said Pembroke. "What's your take on this?"

"Josiah's finishing what he started last night," Abby said. "If the reverend isn't dead already, Josiah will have him squirreled away in some dark corner of the spirit world. We know he's got the blood and the bones, so he'll be after the breath very soon. Our priority now is to protect Will."

"That won't be a problem. Will's in the family room right now with Rickards and Pruitt."

"Are you sure that's wise?" Natalie asked. "Rickards and Pruitt both wear a St. Catherine's ring."

Mona and Pembroke shared a look. "We both saw the guy last night," said the inspector. "Constable Pruitt is way too short. And according to the duty logs, Rickards' shift ended ten minutes after the 10-33 came in. He was on desk duty that night, and the security cameras in the parking lot have him leaving this building right around the time we arrived at the sergeant's house."

"But it couldn't be Pang, could it?" asked Leanne. "He was at Mona's house, and Abby didn't get whammied. Did you?"

Abby shook her head. "Nope. But Pang's the only other person on the force who wears a St. Catherine's ring. So if it's not him, who the hell is it?"

Mona smiled. "We might have caught a break there." She looked at Simon and said, "I don't know what the hell you and that red-eyed lunatic got up to last night, but he must be hurting now. Forensics found blood in the yard where you fought, and in the back of the reverend's van."

Abby nearly hit the ceiling. "Then we've got him! Don't we? I mean, can't you do some CSI voodoo with the DNA?"

"Assuming the lab isn't backed up. And assuming we've got a clean sample. The blood in the van might be Grace's, and the stuff in the yard was sitting in the open air for several hours. This isn't TV, Henderson."

Simon raised his hand and then winced at the effort. Obviously, he was still hurting from getting knocked down the previous night. "We might not have to leave this up to your lab, actually."

"What do you mean?"

"If you've a clean sample of the killer's blood, I can run a tracking spell off it. It will isolate the unique magical signature in his DNA and trace that signature right to the warlock's front door."

Abby's eyes widened. "You can do that? Jesus, Simon, why didn't you lead with that?"

"Well, it's not a guaranteed victory. The spell can't help us if the warlock has already escaped into the Elsewhere. It could only track him while he's on Earth."

"Are you sure you should be doing any serious magic?" Leanne asked. "The warlock really banged you up last night."

Simon waved her away and winced again. "I'm fine. I only got the first shockwave of the curse. Light bruising and a couple aches. Besides, I just need to get the spell set up. It's Abby who'll do the actual tracking."

Mona and Pembroke shared another look, then the inspector folded her hands on the desk and asked, "How long would this... 'tracking spell' take to work?"

"I could have it set up in an hour," Simon answered. "The spell itself would only need fifteen or twenty minutes."

"Versus a week for a standard DNA test," said Mona.

Pembroke leaned back in her chair and gave an exhausted sigh. It was a gesture that would have made Phil Campbell proud. "A few days ago, I wanted to charge you people for interfering with an investigation. Now you're asking to tamper with evidence, and I am this close to making myself an accessory."

"It's your investigation," said Simon. "It's your call."

"This definitely isn't in the rulebook. But straightforward policing hasn't done much for us so far, so maybe it's time to throw out the rulebook. Okay. You can try your tracking spell."

Simon clapped his hands and then stifled a pained groan. "Right, shouldn't have done that... Now, I'll need an empty room, a map of Delapore, one clean coffee mug, a fresh candle, and a willing Gospel." At this last item, he put a hand on Abby's shoulder and winked. She gave him a thumbs-up in response.

"I'll have someone get you what you need," Pembroke said. "And I'll check in with our forensic techs, try and get my hands on that sample."

"Excellent. I'll need a few extra hands for this, so the rest of you are with me for the time being."

"You guys go ahead," said Abby. "I need to have a private word with Mona."

Simon nodded. "Righto. I'll let you know when we need you." He and the others left the office and shut the door behind them.

Pembroke got up from behind the desk and offered the chair to Mona. "I'm going to go motivate the troops. Let me know when you're done." She too left the office, and Mona took the offered seat. Abby sat on the other side of the desk and folded her arms.

"What's up?" Mona asked warily.

"I figured out why Josiah is after your son." She told Mona about her latest dream and about Agatha Blaine, née Brady. She asked if Mona had any old pictures of Nick on her phone, and when Mona reluctantly showed her one, Abby pulled up a scanned photo of Hector Harcourt on her own phone.

Mona saw the resemblance even faster than Abby had. "I keep thinking this thing can't get any worse. Every morning is just a new kick in the head."

"That's how this life generally goes."

Mona was silent for a moment. "Just to be clear, you got this from a dream?"

"Leanne came to the same result in her research. My dreams tend not to be wrong about stuff like this."

Mona put one hand to her forehead and drummed the other on the desk. "Jesus Christ. I transferred to Delapore to get away from Nick Brady. Now you're telling me I have to deal with his psycho ancestors?"

"I'm sorry, Mona. I really am, but these are the facts."

"Nothing I do," Mona growled, "*nothing* is enough to get me away from that asshole! Do you know what the screwed-up thing is? I never even wanted to take his name when we got married! In my tribe, out on the island, August is a good name. It's a name with history, and it's *my* name. I wanted it to be my son's name. And when I told Nick that, when we first got engaged, he picked up the TV remote and he threw it at my head." She pointed to a spot just above her right eyebrow and added, "If you look close, you can still see the scar." She sank back in Campbell's chair and uttered a low, drawn-out groan. "So I took his goddamn name. And now it's a year since they buried him, and it's still his name that I pin to my shirt every morning. I can't get away from the man. No matter what I do."

"I know the feeling," said Abby. "Guys like that always need you to know that they have power and you don't. They never tell you the rules, so you never know when you cross a line until it's too late. And after you do cross their line, they make you hurt so bad that you never want to do it again. Believe me, I've been there too." She lifted one side of her shirt up high enough to reveal a spider's web of twisting pink scars that snaked up her left side.

"Oh my God…" whispered Mona. "Who—"

Abby lowered her shirt. "His name was John Leland. He was a Grade A piece of shit, even before he was a vessel for an insane demon. He stalked me from before I could walk, and he threatened my family as a way of controlling me when I grew up."

"That's how you fell into this lifestyle," Mona surmised. "This Leland character forced you into it."

"Pretty much. Leland died badly, just like Nick, but there's still some days I can hardly look in the mirror for fear I'll see him looking back."

They stared at each other for a moment. Then Mona smiled and chuckled at the sheer uncomfortable weight of the silence. "Man, oh man, we're a sorry pair, aren't we?"

Abby chuckled back. "What, you mean you don't normally blow off steam by reminiscing about abuse?"

Mona got up from the desk. "I'm going to have to talk to Pembroke about this. You should check if your friends need you."

"Actually, do you mind if I go talk to Will first? I want to make sure he's okay."

"Go ahead. It might do him good to talk to you right now. The family room's on the other side of the building. Across the bullpen and down the hall. Two lefts and a right. Just past the washrooms."

Abby stood and left the office. "Thanks."

*****

The family room made a passing attempt to be more cheerful than the rest of the station. The walls were painted a warm, soothing blue, the carpeted floor was spotless, and there was a large, comfy couch at one end of the room facing a flat-screen TV, which itself was hooked up to a couple different sixth- and seventh-generation video game consoles. A few shelves of donated toys lined one wall, but Will Brady had elected to entertain himself with his own Bionicles, brought from the wreckage of his house after the attack. Rickards stood by the door, while Pruitt was at the table watching Will play, and starting to get more invested than she cared to admit.

Rickards let Abby into the room and gave her the once-over. He was obviously still a little wary after the donnybrook at the Harcourt House. "The sergeant said you'd be by, Henderson. So, what's all this I hear about you being some kind of psychic?"

"It's a long story. Mostly, I'm just a concerned citizen."

"Well, I wish you would have kept your concern to yourself. You wouldn't believe how much paperwork I had to do after Sunday."

"I've heard that song a couple times now. Believe me, I'm sorry things got so out of hand."

"You know, there's a reason so many people in small towns don't like city folk. You have to watch your step in a place like this."

Abby stepped back and gazed into Rickards' aura. Nothing. She got the feeling he didn't like her much, but he definitely wasn't a magic-user. "Don't worry. I'll keep my nose clean from now on. Everything OK here?"

"All quiet so far."

"You mind if I speak to the kid?"

Rickards nodded. Abby asked if she could have the room. Rickards told her no, but he called Pruitt to the door so that she wouldn't be breathing down their necks. Abby gave the officers a nod of thanks and went to sit across from the boy.

She rapped her knuckles on the table to get his attention and tried for a smile. "Hey."

He looked up at her, unsmiling. "Hey."

"How are you doing?"

"I'm… I don't know. I was really scared last night. I think my mom's really scared today. Do you know that was her boss that attacked Mrs. Tenenbaum?"

Abby nodded. "I do. You remember the day we met, when you were talking about how the House made Mr. Grover sick? How it got in his head? Well, your mom and I think it did the same thing to Superintendent Campbell."

"All because of me," Will snarled. "The House wants me all for itself and it's hurting people to get to me!" He took a breath and wiped his eyes and nose with his hand. "I know what's going on. This is the room they put kids in to calm them down when something bad happens. Or when they think something bad's going to happen. I spent a lot of time in rooms like this when Papa used to…"

"Bam?"

"Yeah. I'm right, aren't I? The House does want me. Please don't lie to me, Abby."

Abby sighed. "Yeah. It does. Does the name Josiah Harcourt mean anything to you, Will?"

"You and Mom were talking about him last night, weren't you? Is he the one haunting the House?"

"Yeah. He's the Big Bad pulling all the strings here. And he's got his eye on you for… something nasty."

"My mom was right. I never should have gone up there."

"We're going to put a stop to this, Will. My friend Simon, he's working a lead right now. If we're lucky, we could end this thing before dinnertime."

"You really think so?"

Abby reached out and held the boy's hands. "Hey. Did I or did I not make you a promise?"

"Yeah, you did." One corner of Will's mouth had a go at smiling. "Thanks, Abby."

Abby gave the kid a gentle noogie. Then she looked at all the plastic, brightly-coloured action figures between them. "You like Bionicles, Will?"

"Do you?"

Abby grinned. "Bionicle was my jam when I was a kid. I think I still have a box or two of these little guys sitting in my dad's basement."

Will smiled. "My cousin Walt gave me most of these. I think you'd like Walt. He's almost a grown-up, but he's not lame about it. He doesn't try to be too serious."

"Who's your favourite character?"

Will immediately snatched up one figure with black armour and large, three-fingered claws at the ends of his plastic arms. "I like Onua. He's smart and patient, but he's strong enough that he can really mess you up if you try and hurt his friends."

"Plus, he controls the Earth element," Abby pointed out. "Who doesn't want to start an earthquake right under a bad guy's feet?"

"Yeah, that too."

Abby picked up a green figure who held a large axe in one hand. "I always liked Lewa. He doesn't let life get him down, he can take the air out of any bad guy with a joke, and he's always ready to help anyone who needs help. Even if he doesn't know them."

"I think you'd make a pretty good Toa-hero, Abby."

"So would you." She looked around the table. "Why aren't there any water Toa here?"

"The blue ones?" Will shook his head. "Walt never had any blue Bionicles, 'cause he said the blue ones are the girl ones, and the girl ones are lame."

Abby frowned. "Hey! I'm a girl one! You're mom's a girl one! Since when are the girl ones so lame?"

"I never said Walt was right about everything."

Abby leaned in. "Hey, I've got some time until Simon has everything set up. You mind if I stick around and play Bionicles with you for a bit?"

Will nodded. "I'd like that. You can be Lewa if you want."

From beside the door, Constable Pruitt cleared her throat. "Can, uh… can I play too?"

CHAPTER 26

THE WARLOCK'S APPRENTICE

AFTER 45 minutes with the plastic Toa heroes and their equally-colourful enemies, Leanne dropped by the family room to collect Abby. Simon had readied the tracking spell, Leanne said, and all he needed now was the aid of his lovely assistant.

Abby smirked and rose from the table. "If he ever calls me that to my face, I'm going to knock his teeth out." Looking back at Will, she said, "I'll see you in a bit. Don't have too much fun without me. Same goes for you, Pruitt."

"We won't," said Will. Constable Pruitt gave Abby a thumbs-up and fiddled with a gear on one of the figures' backs, making its arms swing from side to side.

Leanne led Abby to the interview room. A stone-faced constable with a buzzcut and no neck stood watch at the door, and Simon hopped around the table laying out the implements he'd requested. The mug and candle stood at opposite corners, and two small wooden bowls were laid out on top of a large map of the town. Simon directed Abby to sit down, then gave a thumbs-up to Constable No-Neck and told him to shut the door. No-Neck didn't thumbs-up him back, but he did shut the door. Abby guessed the guy was probably trying to calculate how much he'd have to be getting paid before he asked any hard questions about the screwball in the waistcoat.

"So, how does this work?" she asked Simon.

Simon paced stiffly around the room as he spoke, pointing to the various tools of the trade. "First, you'll need to drink from the bowl on your left. That's my meditation potion, as you need to be in a trance for this to work. I've diluted it so you won't go into a Bridge, but it will calm your mind enough for the purposes of the spell.

"When you're in the trance, you need to light this candle." He plonked a book of matches down on the table. "You'll notice I've scored a line across it just here: let the candle burn down to that line. When it has, you will take the second bowl—" Abby looked and saw that the second bowl contained a few bloodstained scraps of the killer's shirt. "—and you will tip its contents into this mug. The solution in the mug will dissolve these items, so keep everything at arm's length. Finally, when the solution in the mug begins to turn blue, take the mug and empty it over the candle."

"That's it?"

"That's it. When the solution in the mug meets the flame, it will cause a reaction that will—Celestial willing—reveal the warlock's location."

"If you say so."

"If at any point you need help, or if things start to go pear-shaped, just yell. Constable Evans there will be standing guard the whole time. Natalie's keeping watch in the next room, and Leanne, Whittaker, and myself are on crystals. We'll be in the family room with Master Brady." Simon went over to the two-way mirror and rapped it with his knuckles. "Alright there, Natalie?"

The mirror rattled as Natalie knocked on it from the other side.

"Okay," said Abby. "I'll get to it, then."

"Good luck," said Leanne. Then she and Simon left the room and shut the door behind them.

Abby looked at herself in the mirror and gave a thumbs-up to Natalie on the other side. Then she picked up the first bowl and drained it in one swallow. She stifled a belch as her Gospel senses awakened, said, "Excuse me," to the room at large, and lit the candle.

*****

Jimmy Cardinal brought his pickup truck to a stop as he reached the town line. The road past the grizzly bear sign was blocked by two police cruisers parked nose-to-nose in front of the wreckage of a large van. As Constable Pang approached his window, Cardinal put the truck in park.

"What's going on here?" Cardinal asked. "I gotta get through!"

Constable Pang shook his head. "No traffic through here. This is a crime scene."

"Crime scene? Jesus, they find another fuckin' body already?"

"I can't discuss the particulars of an ongoing investigation," Pang said, in his best Cop Voice.

"Well, I gotta get through! I got an appointment in the city!"

Pang shook his head again. "Nobody gets through, Mr. Cardinal. Those were our orders. If you need to get out of town, you can turn back and take the First Western Road onto the highway."

Jimmy Cardinal scowled. "That'll put twenty minutes on my trip, and you know it! Come on, I'm already runnin' late!"

"I'm sorry, Mr. Cardinal. Orders are orders."

"Don't give me that 'orders' stuff, Danny. I knew you when you was still playin' Little League over at the rec centre! You really can't cut me some slack here?"

Pang shrugged. "Sorry, Assistant Coach Cardinal. My hands are tied."

Constable Foley approached from the other side and looked in the passenger's window of the truck. "Is there a problem here?"

"Nah. I was just leavin,'" Jimmy Cardinal replied sullenly. Pang and Foley stepped back to give him room to make a U-turn and drive back the way he'd come. Another police cruiser passed Jimmy Cardinal on the road and stopped just short of the roadblock. Constables Eckhart and Boyd climbed out and waved to the younger men.

"Good news, boys," said Boyd. "Relief's here."

"You finished with the scene on 5th?" asked Pang.

Eckhart nodded. "Forensics wrapped up about half an hour ago and we got everything secure. We'll take over here and you two can grab a coffee."

"Did forensics find anything good?" asked Foley.

"Man, did they ever. The perp took one hell of a beating after he ran from the Jansens' place last night. Bled all over the scene. They get a clean sample, and we'll have this guy by the balls."

"Muh-ther-*fucker*!" exclaimed Constable Pang. He slapped Foley hard on the shoulder and gave him a shake. "That's the best news we've had in weeks!"

Foley nodded slowly. The jolt from Pang had awakened a stinging pain in his side and made him hyper-aware of the itch from the gauze and surgical tape. "Yeah. The best fucking news." Then, he drew his sidearm and shot Eckhart once in the head.

As Eckhart fell, Boyd and Pang went for their guns and grabbed at Foley. He jumped away like a gazelle escaping a cheetah and shot them both down. Brakes squealed nearby, and Foley turned to see the skid marks as Jimmy Cardinal's truck twisted across the centerline, still well in earshot. Cardinal's eyes met Foley's through the cracked back window of the truck for a moment, and then Cardinal gunned the motor. Foley fell into the Weaver stance and unloaded the rest of his clip at the truck.

The back left tire exploded and Jimmy Cardinal's truck rolled into the ditch. The horn went off when Cardinal's forehead cracked against it, and Foley took his time walking toward the scene of the crash. He hopped down into the gutter, ignoring the mud and litter, and knocked on the truck's roof. He leaned in to face Jimmy Cardinal with a smile. "Have we been drinking today, sir?"

Cardinal wheezed and blinked deliriously. The back of his shirt was saturated with blood where he'd been shot and one arm was dislocated from the crash. "You—you killed them…" he moaned. "It was you at The Gaslights that night… Oh Jesus, you… killed all of them… Davey… those girls…"

"The wheels of justice grind slow, but they grind fine."

"Justice?" spluttered Jimmy Cardinal. "The fuck kind of justice is there killing people like that? The fuck did they do to you?"

"They murdered us. They *forgot* us. They carried a legacy of corruption and lies together through the century. They got off easy, as far as I'm concerned."

Jimmy Cardinal coughed and spat blood onto his dashboard. "Fffffuck you!" he snarled. "Fuck you, you fucking piece of shit! You don't deserve to wear that goddamn badge!"

Foley calmly reloaded his weapon from a spare clip in his vest. "That's where you're wrong, Mr. Cardinal. I'm the only person in this fucking town who does." He pressed his gun to Jimmy Cardinal's temple and fired once.

Jimmy Cardinal's head hit the steering wheel—permanently, this time—and Foley holstered his gun. He felt another jolt as the dark energy within him awoke, and his more monstrous urges started whispering in his head. *Cutting and cutting and cutting and feeding. Feeding. Feeding. Blood. Blood. Blood for the Master. The Master. The Master is Good. The Master is Wise…*

"The Master is Kind," he said out loud. He reached into a pocket of his uniform vest and extracted a gold signet ring, stained with flecks of its owner's blood. Those stains had never faded since that chilly November night nearly a century ago, and the ring had never lost its polish. When Foley slipped the ring onto his left pinky, it was like a switch was thrown in his brain. A key turned in a lock. A door opened. The monster leaped out of the closet.

Jimmy Cardinal had been half-right. Linus Foley had been at The Gaslights on the night David Prudhomme disappeared. But he hadn't killed David or the girls. True, his hand held the wand and his mouth spoke the words, but the mind that memorized those black rites? That willed the True Magic to act in that way on those bodies? That was another story.

As power surged through Linus's body and his eyes turned an angry red, he felt the monster inside him seize control of his focus, darkening his thoughts and re-tuning his synapses to the task. His muscles went a little numb as he slipped into the back of his own mind, and his gauze stopped itching quite so bad.

KA-CRACK! An explosion of electric white light blinded him for a moment, and a rush of cold wind stung his face. He took a breath, let his eyes adjust, and stepped into the wormhole that had just opened in front of him. The shimmering, silvery ghost of Josiah Harcourt met him on the other side, in the blank void of the Elsewhere. "It is time to finish what we started."

"Time to finish off the bitch Henderson," he replied. "She and her friends will be all over this by now."

Josiah nodded. "Indeed. After your injury, they will doubtless be mounting a tracking spell. Perhaps at this moment." He reached behind his back and drew a thin shaft of yew wood from his back pocket. "Do try to be careful this time. We are running low on spare wands at the House."

He bowed his head and took the wand. "I won't fail, Master. I promise."

"I know you won't. I have faith in you, my boy. I always had faith in you." Josiah raised his other hand and another wormhole opened beside him. "Now go. Show them what we are truly capable of."

Linus Foley smiled, pushed through the wormhole, and emerged on the front steps of Delapore's Old Justice Building.

*****

As the candle burned down to the line, the flame flickered and then jumped to twice its original height, turning a bright pale green at its base. Abby picked up the second bowl and poured it into the mug, and the solution in the mug hissed and bubbled as soon as the warlock's belongings hit the surface. Shielding her eyes with her hand, she scooted her chair back to a safe distance as the stuff in the mug spat and spluttered like bacon grease in a too-hot pan.

Blue smoke rose from the mug as the reaction slowed, and at the same time the candle's green flame softened to an aquamarine hue. Abby checked the mug. Satisfied that the solution was blue as Simon had promised, she picked it up and poured it out over the candle.

WHOOMF! A dazzling multicoloured fireball erupted when the solution met the flame. Abby dropped the bowl and nearly fell out of her chair in surprise. As the flame died back down to its normal level, she called up Simon on her Vokarion crystal. "Hey, Simon? Do me a favour and warn me the next time you want to heat-blast my eyebrows off, will you?"

Simon cleared his throat sheepishly. "Ah, yes. I was wondering if there was something I'd forgotten to mention. Yes, the reaction can be a little… violent sometimes."

"No crap. Now what do I do?"

"Do you see a sort of golden light rising from the candle?"

Abby blinked a couple times. She'd been momentarily blinded by the fireball, but now she could indeed see a few scattered dots of golden light around the tip of the flame. They looked almost solid, like beads of mercury, and as Abby watched they drew together and swirled in the air for a few seconds before landing on the map, where they pressed together into one golden blot. Abby leaned in for a better look and gulped. "Oh crap."

"What? What's wrong?"

Abby stared at the map. The L-shape of the Old and New Justice Buildings was barely discernible beneath the golden blot. Her skin tingled and she felt that thorny sensation in her stomach as a shadow darkened the crack under the door. Then she turned to face the two-way mirror and shouted, "Natalie! Get in h—"

The door exploded out of its frame and flattened the table, and the broken body of Constable Evans flew across the interview room on a wave of black lightning. Abby leaped out of her chair and hit the floor as Evans's skull cracked the two-way mirror. Her eyes took a second to adjust to the dark flash of the curse, and then she saw the figure in the doorway. Saw the second presence inside his body, crowding his aura.

She shook her head. The presence's eyes glowed as red as his hair. As red as his Clark Gable moustache. And his roguish face was stretched in a mad grin, showing off lots of crowded yellow teeth. "Hector?" she groaned. "No…"

As she tried to pick herself up, Foley stormed into the room, grabbed a fistful of her hair, and slammed her head into the concrete floor. The two-way mirror shattered as Natalie threw herself at Foley, but he sidestepped the tackle and swept his wand at her midsection. *"Secō corpus!"*

Natalie screamed as the curse opened a deep gash across her belly. She landed awkwardly on her hip and threw a hand over the wound, snarling as her intestines threatened to spill out of her. A bloody foam gathered at the corners of her mouth and primeval rage flashed in her eyes. Foley lifted his wand again, but Natalie swept his legs out from under him and grabbed at him with one hand. She caught his dominant wrist and pulled him in close enough to head-butt him, then wrapped her legs around his neck and squeezed. With one hand still on her wound and the other on Foley's wand arm, she pulled him in using only her abdominal muscles and gnashed her teeth like she wanted to bite his nose off. Foley reached across his body with the other hand, unholstered his gun, and jammed it under her chin. His scream matched hers as he emptied the clip into her head, and then he tore away from her and whipped the barrel at Abby, just as she was coming to. Abby scrambled out of his reach and concentrated on her Vokarion crystal, screaming a psychic warning at the others. *Guys! Get the fuck in here! It's Constable Foley! He's the warlo* —

Foley dropped the empty gun and grabbed Abby's head with his other hand. Then he slammed her face-first into the floor again and primed himself for a killing spell.

There was a hiss and a crack as Whittaker teleported into the interview room and threw himself onto Foley's back. He rode Foley like a kid playing horsey and chirped, "Heya, chief. I don't think we've been properly introduced yet. Name's Whittaker."

Still in a daze, Abby met Whittaker's eyes and took a second as her throbbing brain did the math. Then she reached out and grabbed Foley's ankle with one hand, and Whittaker snapped his fingers again. There was another loud crack as he, Foley, and Abby teleported out of the interview room.

*****

Abby's ears popped as the bullpen of the station appeared around them. Foley bucked Whittaker off and threw him halfway across the bullpen with inhuman strength, sending the imp to an inglorious crash-landing on someone's desk. As Whittaker rolled to the floor, Abby let go of Foley's ankle and scrambled across the bullpen. There was a flash of light in the corner of her and she ducked as a curse blew over her head, ripping apart another desk in a wave of green sparks. She didn't see the next curse until it had blown a six-inch crater in the floor right at her feet.

Two strong hands caught Abby as she fell and pulled her behind a pillar. Mona Brady put one finger to her lips, drew her sidearm, and pointed to Abby's right and left. Four officers, two on each side, were taking cover behind a line of desks, their guns at the ready.

"Where's your friend?" Mona whispered. "Natalie?"

"Interview room. Foley took her down. She'll get back up, eventually."

"Get clear as soon as possible. Get to the family room and get Will to safety."

"What about you guys? You can't beat Foley's magic!"

"No. But we can keep him busy." Mona stepped into Foley's line of sight, raised her weapon, and yelled at him to stand down. Two officers rose from behind the desks, while the others crept around to the sides to take up flanking positions. Foley dropped into a defensive stance, and six more officers poured into the bullpen from the door behind him—the major crimes squad, led by Margot Pembroke herself.

"It's over, Foley!" Mona barked. "We know about the Rite of Ka'thonn. Put your hands up and we can end this quietly."

Foley raised his wand and pointed it at Mona. "You can't be serious. How do you see this playing out, Sarge? Pang, Eckhart, Boyd, and Evans are dead already. That zombie bitch's head is spread across half the interview room. You can't stop me any more than they could. Any of you."

Mona took one step forward. Abby had to hand it to the sergeant: she didn't give Foley an inch. "Linus, you have betrayed every value we swore to uphold as peace officers. If you think for a second that I'm going to let you walk out of here, that I am not going to do my sworn duty and take you down for that, then you are the single stupidest person I have ever met."

Foley smiled. "Okay. But just remember, when this is all over, I gave you a warning." He dropped to his knees, shouted, *"Edo aquam!"* and melted into the floor. The major crimes squad surged forward, and Foley came up behind them and fired a spell right through one officer. *"Morere!"* Black lightning arced across the bullpen and Mona ducked back toward cover.

Two officers screamed as Foley swept his wand at them. One man's head fell from his shoulders and the other clutched his throat as blood poured out between his fingers. Inspector Pembroke ordered her men to fall back and opened fire. Foley jumped away and brought his wand to his chest. Pembroke's shots slammed into a wall of invisible power six inches in front of him, and the constable returned fire with another curse.

Corporal Rickards and another officer sprang up from their flanking positions and fired. Foley twisted his wand to summon shields in that direction, and Pembroke's men fell back to safety. Blue sparks flew and a sound like a hammer on a metal pipe filled the room as the cops pumped more and more bullets into Foley's energy shield, and Abby saw her chance. She peeked out from behind the pillar, sucked in a deep breath, and then sprinted for her life.

Foley heard the squeak of Abby's sneakers on the floor and snapped his head toward her. In that moment, Pembroke dropped out of cover and fired at his head, but he melted back into the floor before the bullet found its mark.

Abby heard the shot too and hit the floor on instinct. The bullet whizzed over her head and she felt a thin trickle of blood along her scalp, creeping down toward the back of her neck. When she touched it, the narrow cut felt hot, and she tried not to throw up when she realized just how close she'd come to being an RCMP incident report. Ignoring the hot pain along her scalp, Abby picked herself up and kept running. Foley rose from the floor a couple metres ahead of her and lifted his wand, so Abby dropped low and tried for a power slide across the floor. She aimed for the space between Foley's legs, and ended up knocking him off his feet. The cops moved in to take him, but Abby kept running.

Foley pointed his wand at the ceiling and cried, *"Flagrō!"* A cone of fire burst from his wand and melted a hole in the ceiling. Fire bells clanged and the shock of the blast knocked the squad off their feet. Abby rounded the corner into the corridor and pressed herself against the near wall as the sprinklers came on overhead. Foley stood and shouted, *"Flagrō semper caelum!"*

A wave of fire swept from one end of the bullpen to the other and met the rainstorm from the sprinklers head-on. Officers screamed and sprinted for cover as the opposing forces met, and an unlucky few got scalded by the steam. Abby took a peek and saw cloudy figures running around the bullpen, but visibility was somewhere between slim and none. So she kept moving forward. Her shoes squeaked and slid on the floor and the torrent from the sprinklers soaked right through her clothes without effort, and she could hear Foley's pounding footsteps behind her. It sounded like he had more of a grip on the wet floor, but he was also breathing hard, fighting to replace the energy he'd burned up during his wand-work.

As Abby rounded the first corner, she heard Foley yell, *"Flagrō!"* She shrieked and jumped forward as a wave of heat rushed past her back, accompanied by a sound like a ruptured gas pipe. Looking behind her, she saw blackened, burned plaster falling from the wall and picked up the pace.

Abby reached for her Vokarion crystal and directed a telepathic message at Simon. *You guys have to get Will somewhere safe! I'm heading for the family room, but Foley is right on my ass! I don't know if—*

Her concentration broke when Foley screamed, *"Glaciō!"* The tile floor froze beneath her feet and Abby went into a slide. She spun as she lost her balance, so she could see Foley smiling when he yelled, *"Carnis lapidis!"*

Abby's muscles seized up and she hit the ground with a heavy *thud*. Her mind was still moving at a normal pace, and she screamed over the live Vokarion network: *Simon! Get your ass out here, for God's sake!*

Simon came around the corner at the other end of the corridor, and Foley stopped where he was. With a grimace of pain, Simon brushed a soggy lock of hair out of his eyes and nodded to his opponent. "Constable."

Foley returned the nod with an odd look of respect. "Vanguard."

As fast as blinking, Simon dropped his centre of gravity and took a combat stance. He shouted, *"Mægnes sweor!"* and the water rippled as invisible force raced down the corridor toward Foley.

"Scūtum!" Foley conjured a wall of blue energy before him, which caught Simon's spell head-on. The unstoppable force pushed the immovable object further down the hall and Foley went with it, sliding back on his heels as he tried to maintain the spell.

Simon planted a hand on the wall and yelled, *"Brece seles stānas!"* A spiderweb of cracks spread out from where his hand was and raced down the hall in Foley's direction. Simon slapped the wall twice and a large section of it exploded right behind Foley. The constable dropped his spell as chunks of concrete and plaster bombarded him on the left side, driving him into the opposite wall.

"Grippe fēond!" Simon reached toward Foley with both hands and closed his fists. Foley jerked away from the wall like a puppet on a string and slammed into the other wall. Then he flew up to the ceiling and smashed face-first into the floor, carried by the movement of Simon's hands.

Bloodied and battered, Foley tried to pick himself up. His shoulders trembled as Simon raised a hand to the ceiling and looked at the sprinklers, still spitting water in all their faces. Simon clenched his teeth and hissed, *"Hēst gārseċġes."* The pipes groaned up in the ceiling, the sprinkler heads rattled, and water started dripping through the old plaster. Simon met Foley's eyes and whispered, *"Ādrenċ fēond."*

The sprinkler heads exploded from their moorings and Simon marched through the cascading waterfall with his head held high. The water followed the twisting, arcing movement of his arms and curled around his body in thick plumes. Then, he pointed at Foley and the water slammed into the rogue constable as one bone-crushing wave.

Abby's muscles started to twitch. Foley's spell was wearing off, and it was with considerable effort that she managed to roll herself onto one side and look at Foley and Simon. The constable was on his knees, his eyes wide with fright and his hands grasping at his throat as a sphere of rushing water compressed around his head. He opened his mouth in a noiseless scream and bubbles broke on the surface of the water.

Simon kept his eyes on Foley and spoke in a cold voice. "'It is the law in those northern lands that if any man twists the True Magic to cause the death of another, who has never wronged him before, that man has sinned before the High Celestial. And it is the duty of any who has witnessed or possesses knowledge of the sin to avenge the innocent dead, and to exact justice.' This is the will of the Vanguard, and I will see it done. Linus Foley, I name thee *wærloga*: oathbreaker, deceiver, murderer, and I confer upon thee a sentence of death."

Foley's eyelids fluttered and his body started to sway as his strength left him. Simon remained rooted to the spot, numb to the struggle of the dying man in front of him. One of Foley's hands dropped to his side, and he grabbed at something on his belt. Then he pointed it at Simon's chest and pulled the trigger.

Simon arched his back and dropped his hands when Foley hit him with the Taser. The sphere burst and Simon collapsed to the floor, leaving Foley coughing and spitting out water. "I don't have time for this," he croaked. He threw down the spent Taser next to the still-twitching Simon, pointed his wand at the floor, and snapped, *"Sum quasi aquam!"* It was only seconds after he had melted away that Abby heard the screams coming from the family room. Three gunshots rang out, and Will Brady's voice carried down the hall.

"Help! Help me, please! Mom! Abby!"

"No…" Abby groaned. "No…" Her muscles were still too stiff to move with any kind of speed, but she got her hands under her and pushed herself up to a sitting position. The precinct rumbled as something like a bomb went off in the family room, and then the sound of cicadas drowned out Will's pleas.

"No…" Abby scooted over to the wall and pulled herself up. She was about halfway to her feet when three angry cops rounded the corner: Mona, Rickards, and Pembroke.

"Henderson! Where is he?" Mona demanded.

Abby struggled to get the words out. "Family… room… he jinxed me bad… Simon's tased…"

Mona nodded and pointed to Simon. "Rickards," she said.

"On it." Rickards hauled Simon to his feet and supported him on his shoulder. Mona took hold of Abby in the same way and led the charge to the family room.

They found the door blocked by a swarm of angry cicadas, and Mona passed Abby to Inspector Pembroke. She herself forced her way through the swarm and called for her son. "Will! Will, where are you?"

"MOM?" came a shout from beyond the swarm. "Mom, are you there? Please! Please, I don't want to go!"

The swarm parted just enough for Mona to see her son crouched under the table. Leanne and Constable Pruitt stood between the boy and Foley, fighting to keep their balance as the widening wormhole in the back of the room threatened to draw them all in.

Pruitt's gun shook in her hands and blood tracked down one leg of her uniform trousers from a wound above her kidney. The Cutting Curse had gone right through her bulletproof vest and left part of it dangling awkwardly toward the ground. She fired on Foley again, but he caught the bullet on one of his shield spells and sliced her leg open with another curse. Then he shouted something toward the wormhole and more cicadas flew into the family room, homing in on Pruitt's wounds and chowing down. She collapsed with a scream and Foley turned his attention to Leanne.

But Leanne Waller was nobody's fool. And the bear spray in her purse was definitely no fashion accessory. As soon as Foley's wand came up, so did the black-and-red aerosol canister in her hands. She turned her head away, held her breath, and gave Foley a full blast. He reeled back with his face tucked into the crook of his arm and swore at her through clenched teeth. Black lightning raced up the tip of his wand and the first syllable of a death curse passed his lips, so Leanne beaned him with the empty canister. Then she picked up one of the chairs and beaned him with that. As Foley rolled on the floor, Leanne grabbed Pruitt's dropped gun and aimed at Foley's head. "Stay down!" she yelled. "Just stay down, you twisted little—"

Foley spat blood on the carpet, focused his swollen, tear-filled eyes on her, and giggled. "Please. You don't know one end of that thing from the other." He raised his wand and hissed, "*Compellō.*" Dark red sparks danced around the barrel of the gun and made it twitch in Leanne's hand. Her arm shook, and she grabbed her wrist with her other hand to keep it still, but the gun kept fighting against her grip like it was alive. "But I do…" Foley flicked his wand, and the gun jerked toward Leanne's head. She tried to force the weapon away as it traced a line through her hair, but Foley's willpower was stronger than hers. He made her stick the gun against her temple and compelled her finger to dance on the trigger.

Mona broke through the last layer of bugs and fired. Foley quickly dropped the compulsion spell and caught the bullet on his energy shield. His next spell sliced the table in two, leaving Will exposed, and then the cicadas descended. From out of the swarm of buzzing, wriggling bodies emerged the apparition of Josiah Harcourt. He seized the boy by the waist, hoisted him bodily over one shoulder, and broke for the wormhole. Mona gave chase, and Josiah summoned a wave of insects to intercept her. They knocked her down with the force of a speeding car as Foley jumped into the worm hole. Then Josiah snapped his fingers and another blinding explosion ripped through the family room, scattering the insects and knocking everyone senseless.

"No…" Mona whispered as she came to. "Please…"

Black ectoplasm stained the walls and the furniture, and the TV, toys, and game consoles were smashed to pieces. Will's Bionicles were in a heap around the body of Constable Pruitt, who lay pale and motionless on her side. Pembroke and Rickards started triage on their fallen colleague, and Abby ran to Leanne's side. Leanne realized to her horror that she was still holding Pruitt's gun, and she threw it across the floor out of reach. "Oh Jesus!" she stammered, as the full weight of Foley's actions sank in. "He—he almost—he could have—"

Abby hugged her tight and whispered, "He could have. But he didn't."

Leanne swallowed. "No. He didn't, did he? He didn't." That calmed her down, but she didn't let go of Abby.

Inspector Pembroke gasped. She and Rickards had cleared Pruitt's clothes away from her wound so they could have a look, and neither of them liked what they saw. "Christ, we need an ambulance here," said Rickards. "I'll make the call, Inspector. You stay with Pruitt. And somebody has to grab the first aid kit from the bullpen."

Leanne's knees wobbled as she stood, but she was able to compose herself after one look at Pruitt. "I'll do that," she whispered. She and Rickards left the family room together, leaning on each other a little as they went.

It was then that Abby noticed Mona. The sergeant was holding one of Will's Bionicles, turning the gear on the figure's back and making its arms swing lazily in their sockets. She looked like she was two seconds from crying.

"I just checked on him two hours ago. He wanted me to stay. To just… sit with him for five minutes. Just five minutes. I… I was just too busy." Mona blinked and put a hand to her mouth. "I couldn't even… I couldn't give him five minutes…"

Abby sat down beside her. "Hey. We're going to get him back. We know where they've taken him. Right back to where all this shit started. Once we get Pruitt stable, we walk up to the Harcourt House, we rescue Will, and then we kick their necromancing asses."

Suddenly, the floor beneath them gave a little shiver. Abby looked down. "What the hell?"

A violent tremor rocked the building. Abby put one hand out to steady herself and suddenly felt a wave of dark magic coursing through the earth beneath her. It surged up her arm and into her brain, making her head explode with crippling agony.

As Abby screamed and fell back to the floor, Whittaker stumbled down the hall and braced himself in the doorway. "Everybody, come on! You're not gonna fucking believe this!" Simon helped Abby up and roused her back to reality, and then he and she followed the others through the precinct to the front entrance. Rickards, Leanne, and the other surviving officers had gathered outside the doors and were all staring out to the western hills of Pearson Heights. Car alarms blared on the stretch of road outside the building, accompanied by the full lights and sirens of the police cruisers in the parking lot. Street lights sparked and people were starting to emerge from the other buildings on the street.

"What the hell is going on out here?" Abby hissed through gritted teeth.

The sound that answered her echoed right across the valley, like a mountain collapsing into a river. At the top of Pearson Heights, the earth split, and then the Harcourt House—the whole goddamn enchilada—lifted into the air. The dirt and stone around the House's foundations went with it, leaving a crater the size of a baseball diamond above Pearson Heights.

The chain-link fence teetered over and fell into the yawning pit as the earth beneath it gave way.

The House rose two hundred feet up. Rocks and clumps of sod fell from the foundation beneath it, and the wind carried some into people's yards, others onto parked cars, and a couple into the middle of the road. The bystanders started screaming, and a few of the cops went out to herd them back into their homes and businesses. As the House slowed in its ascent, lightning sparked in the sky around the roof, and a wormhole burst open in the sky. Abby and Mona jumped as the precinct's glass doors shattered, along with most every window in Delapore. The Harcourt House receded into the wormhole, and Mona screamed her son's name. She was drowned out by another terrifying explosion as the wormhole closed. When everyone's sight returned after the attendant flash, the Harcourt House was gone.

"NO!" Mona cried. "No! No! No! WILLIAM!" She staggered aimlessly into the middle of the street and dropped to her knees, weeping. She was still holding Will's Bionicle figure. "William… please… please come back…"

CHAPTER 27

A DOOR IN THE RAIN

WILL BRADY just wanted to go home.

He'd been crying. The ceiling creaked as somebody moved around above him, and he sniffed and wiped his eyes dry with the back of his hand. If Papa was up there… if he caught a whiff of any faggy behaviour… Will didn't want to think about that.

They'd carried him through the Harcourt House and down to the cellar. There, the ghost of Josiah Harcourt had said some magic words, and then a cold metal chain had appeared out of nowhere and a manacle on the end had clamped itself around Will's leg, its other end wrapping around a pipe sticking out of the large furnace. Only after they had left did Will notice the other figure: a man dressed all in black, curled up on the floor on the opposite side of the room. He was either sleeping or ignoring Will intentionally, and Will hadn't seen his face since Josiah and Foley had left him down here.

Will didn't know how long he'd been in this cellar. It was long enough for him to have thrown up twice—once after they'd chained him up and again when the House had started to shake and tilt like a roller coaster—but beyond that, he had no clue. The second time Will had thrown up, Foley had come downstairs and apologized for "the rough take-off" (whatever that meant). Then he'd given Will a Kit-Kat and a small plastic bottle of ginger ale. Where Foley had gotten them, Will couldn't say. But he had a feeling that the food meant Foley planned to be here a while.

Will hugged his knees to his chest and cried into them, and the man in black began to stir. Will peeked at him over the tops of his knees and blinked away tears. The man sat up, groaned, winced and stared at Will. "Dear God," he whispered, "he didn't... a child... for the love of God, a child..."

Will tried to place the man. He'd seen him before, in town. Squinting through the darkness, Will sniffed and croaked, "Reverend Jansen?"

The man blinked and shuffled forward along the floor. Will heard the rattle of a chain like his and saw that the reverend was also trapped here. He kept one hand tight to his chest, and Will noticed that two of the fingers were swollen and bruised to the colour of old grapes. "Yes," said the man. "You're... you're Mona Brady's boy, aren't you? William, isn't it?"

Will nodded and sniffled. "W-what's going to happen to us?"

"I don't know, son. I really don't know." He shuffled forward again and reached out his good hand. It didn't quite reach Will's knee. "But I promise you, whatever they're planning up there, I will not let them hurt you."

Will nodded and said nothing. He recognized the tone in Reverend Jansen's voice: it was the tone grown-ups always used when they were telling obvious lies to make kids comfortable. The reverend was probably more scared than he was.

The cellar door opened and the room suddenly got a lot colder. "Behold!" bellowed the Master. "I tell you a mystery!"

Will shrank back against the wall as Josiah Harcourt's silvery ghost descended the stairs with a gaunt, toothy grin. "We shall not all sleep," the grinning face boomed, "but we shall all be changed! In a moment, in the twinkling of an eye, at the last trump. For the trumpet shall sound, and the dead shall be raised incorruptible, and we shall be changed. For this corruptible must put on incorruption, and this mortal must put on immortality. But when this corruptible shall have put on incorruption, and this mortal shall have put on immortality, then shall come to pass the saying that is written, Death is swallowed up in victory. O death, where is thy victory? O death, where is thy sting?" He reached the bottom of the stairs and looked at Will as if he was noticing him for the first time. "One of my favourite passages. And it won't be long till the trumpet sounds, my boy." Will made a little squeak and Josiah stalked toward him like a jungle cat eyeing a wounded gazelle. "Oh, I'm sure you must have a thousand questions right now. 'Why me? What could this tired old man want with William Brady?' Have you not worked it out yet? Has *she* not told you? Your friend Abigail is terribly clever. She must have figured it out by now." He crouched before Will, and his red eyes drilled right through the boy.

"You know me, William. Deep in your heart, you know what I am." Josiah's face changed, becoming saggier and more haggard. His hairline receded, and when next he spoke, the stink of Crown Royal and Craven A's lingered on his breath. "The blood. The life. The blood *is* the life."

Will shook his head. He breathed hard and blinked so fast that the tears couldn't creep past his eyes. *Men don't cry, boy. Real men don't ever cry.*

"One night," Josiah sighed. "That was it. One night of passionate abandon, and my Hector left behind a shame we could never erase. His sin clung to our family like dog shit on the heel of a shoe. His bitch came to me afterward, when she was starting to show, and I paid her a king's ransom to take her sprog as far away from this town as she could. Hector confronted me when he found out, but my concerns were much greater by then. We fought. He ran. Good riddance to him, I thought. But then! Then you walked through my front door. I recognised you in a moment, boy. The last whiff of Hector's *stink*." Will cringed as Josiah put a cold hand on his knee. "Were it up to me, I would have struck you dead the moment you first walked through my door. But I need you, William. I need a body of my own. I cannot hold a human host for very long, and I cannot leave this place behind without one. But the House is rotting, and I with it." He gave Will a light smack on the cheek and hissed, "Shall my son's bastards thrive while I die and am forgotten? No. That is unacceptable." Will shuddered and shut his eyes, but Josiah pressed his thumb against one of the boy's eyelids and lifted until Will couldn't help but look. "For I Jehovah thy God am a jealous God, visiting the iniquity of the fathers upon the children, upon the third and upon the fourth generation of them that hate me."

*****

Corporal Rickards put away his cell phone. "It's going to be twenty minutes before we can get an ambulance. At least."

They were all gathered in the bullpen again. All the desks had been shifted against the wall and the floor was lined with mattresses and blankets from the holding cells. A makeshift triage for the dead and the wounded. Of the twelve officers who had been in the Old Justice Building when Foley attacked, four were dead, three had non-life-threatening injuries, and one—Constable Sydney Pruitt—was in critical condition. Rickards, Pembroke, and Leanne had patched up her wounds as best they could, but without proper medical attention, she probably wouldn't make it. Rickards looked down at her and said, "I'd take her to the hospital myself, but—"

Mona Brady entered the bullpen. She'd just been out to the parking lot to check the cruisers. With a shake of her head, she reported that none of the cars would start. "Whatever that… portal thing was that screwed up the power, it must have fried the cars' batteries as well."

"Magic and electricity," Abby said. "You throw around enough magical energy for long enough, you can kill just about anything electronic. With the amount of power it took to transport the Harcourt House like that, I'm surprised the whole town isn't in a blackout."

"I didn't see a single light in the building working when I went to wash my hands," Rickards said in agreement. "Computers are dead, phones are dead, even the radio in the breakroom has crapped out." About ten seconds after he'd said that, his cell phone clicked and whined in his pocket. He took it out just as the screen glitched and went black. "Dammit." He threw the phone onto his desk with Abby's, Leanne's, and Mona's. All of them had died in the last fifteen minutes.

One of the officers sat between two mattresses, looking at the mangled corpses of his colleagues. "Magic," he said with a little giggle. "It—it was magic. There's… there's… the House was… flying. And it was magic. Is that… is it… magic? Killed those kids?"

Pembroke went to sit beside the man and tried to comfort him. He sniffed, giggled, and scrubbed tears out of his eyes with the heel of his hand. "Magic…" he stammered, "is real."

Abby stood and kicked a trashcan halfway across the bullpen. "Goddammit! I promised him!" The officer on the floor flinched and rocked from side to side. Abby ignored him and laughed bitterly. "I promised Will we'd beat Josiah. And now we're sitting in a fucking graveyard. Pruitt might die if we can't get her to a hospital. And if Reverend Jansen isn't dead already, he will be before too long! Motherfucker…"

"Henderson," Mona said softly.

"I was so close! When I got whammied at the reverend's house, it happened right when Eckhart and Foley showed up! I should have seen it then. I should have seen so much…"

"Abby," Mona said in the same tone.

Abby looked at her.

"What were you saying to me last night?" Mona asked. "It's not your fault. I had the case on my desk for weeks and I didn't see it. Foley wasn't even in the running as a suspect. He doesn't wear a St. Catherine's ring."

Abby's brain hit a speed bump. "No. He doesn't. But…" Then she remembered Foley in the interview room, with the red-haired, red-eyed presence crowding his aura. The second spirit. "Fathers and sons," she whispered. "Sons and fathers."

"What?"

"He's not Linus Foley. He's Isaac Harcourt!"

Whittaker blinked. "How hard did you get hit, chickadee?"

"Linus Foley was never a member of Reverend Jansen's group, and he's never worn a church ring. But when he attacked me in the interview room, I definitely saw a signet ring on his left hand. Jim Cardinal assumed it was a church ring that the perp was wearing at The Gaslights, but everybody in the group had an alibi. And when Foley kidnapped the reverend, he threw Grace aside like she meant nothing. This whole thing has nothing to do with the church! It never has! This all goes back to November 3, 1927. AKA, the night Hector Harcourt did *not* kill his family. AAKA, the night the cops broke down Josiah Harcourt's front door, broke up the black magic ritual that would have been his ticket to immortality, and shot his other son in front of him! There was a Styles, a Campbell, and a Hall in the squad that night, and I'll bet you anything there was a Prudhomme as well. Maybe even a Grover and a Jansen. This whole thing is another shot at immortality for Josiah, so why shouldn't it also be payback at the men who spoiled that immortality?"

"And you think Isaac's ghost is the apprentice?" asked Leanne.

"When Foley attacked me, I saw another presence in his aura. Not a possessing force, but an inhabiting one. I think they're sharing a body, like Leland shared with the Deacon. I thought that force was Hector, but it was Hector's *twin*. Isaac was loyal to Josiah right till the bitter end. He was wearing a signet ring in that picture you found, and in the vision that Hector showed me in the Bridge. The night the Harcourts died, all their spirits were trapped on this side of the veil. I've seen all of them at one time or another. But I never saw Isaac. His spirit must have become attached to his signet ring, the way Josiah is attached to the House. At some point, Foley put the ring on, and then Isaac was able to jump into his body."

A voice in the doorway grunted, "Makes sense to me." Everyone looked up as Natalie lurched into the bullpen, propping herself up against the wall. The midriff of her shirt had been torn away when Foley gutted her, and she still held one hand over her stomach. She had smears of blood across her mouth and parts of her skull were wriggling, as if they were still trying to put themselves back together the right way. One eye was bulging out a little too far, while the other was sunk too deep in her face. Abby didn't often like to think of Natalie as dead, but it was hard not to now as Natalie groaned and staggered into the bullpen.

Obviously, a few people were thinking the same thing Abby was, because Natalie self-consciously wiped the blood from her mouth and brushed her hair forward to cover the crawling, shifting sections of her head. "Sorry I couldn't be here sooner," she said, as if nothing was the matter. "That last regeneration kicked the shit out of me. So: Constable Foley, yeah? Or do we start calling him Isaac Harcourt now?"

Mona gave a sharp nod. "The bastard had us all fooled. And now he and Josiah have taken my son... I don't know where."

"So what are we going to do to get him back? We've still got the advantage in numbers and we're acting like it's checkmate. Okay, they outsmarted us this time. But we're still plenty smart."

"She's right," Whittaker said. "We just gotta be a different kind of smart. Whether or not he's Foley or Isaac, that freckly bastard thinks like a cop. When he came here, he took out the biggest physical threat around before he did anything else.

His magic couldn't beat Ætheric in a fair fight, so he hit him where he wasn't looking, with modern tech. He didn't come through the front door of the family room because he knew Pruitt would be covering it. The reason you knuckleheads have been spinning your wheels on this case is because you're trying to out-think a smart cop. And in order to get ahead, you've all been thinking like cops. But even the smartest good cop can't beat a smart bad cop. No, to beat a smart cop, you need a smart crook."

"Whittaker, are you volunteering?" Abby asked.

The imp shrugged and gave a wry little smile. "Let's just say I'm being a team player."

As Whittaker explained it, the Otherlands—the native realm of the Fair Folk—existed as a separate dimension on the far side of the Elsewhere. There were several ways to travel through the spirit world, but only a being whose mind was equally attuned to the different energies of Earth and the Elsewhere could open a doorway between them.

"See, Josiah Harcourt, he's been stuck halfway between this world and the next for generations," Whittaker said, "so it's no problem for him to cross back and forth. None of you have walked through the Elsewhere except by accident, so you don't have the kind of connection with it that it takes to open a portal. Probably, that's what Josiah was counting on when he pulled the House in after him. He was fixing it so we couldn't follow after him and save the kid."

"What about me?" Abby asked. "'Attuned to Earth and the Elsewhere' is basically my whole job description."

"Maybe if you had a few years' more training. It takes a crazy amount of energy to open a portal from either side. If you tried it now, you'd probably just give yourself a stroke or a brain aneurysm."

"I could enter a Bridge," said Abby. "Project my mind into the House, find Will, bring him home."

Whittaker shook his head and made a noise like a game show buzzer. "Wrong answer. If you Bridge, you're only throwing your mind into the Elsewhere. You can't open a physical portal to bring the kid back. And if they've set up any kind of anti-spirit defences inside or outside the House, you won't even get a look in. That's even assuming you can find the kid in time. There's a whole lot of different levels to the spirit world, and your spirit-self might not even end up on the same plane as the Harcourt House. You need to open a physical portal and go in body and soul. Otherwise, Will ain't coming home."

Abby looked at him. "I suppose you're going to tell us you're the only one who can open a portal."

Whittaker chuckled. "You ain't just a pretty face, chickadee. Yeah, I can get through to the Elsewhere. Used to do it all the time back in the old days. Spent a solid couple of years smuggling rich Catholics out of England via the spirit world back during the Reformation. Mind you, I wasn't running no charity back then…"

Simon scowled. "This is what you meant by renegotiating the deal, isn't it?"

Whittaker stuck his hands in his pockets and shrugged. "I was happy to keep you in the loop and do an odd job or six before. But getting tossed around by that red-eyed lunatic? That was not part of the deal. I figure I'm due some… hazard pay."

"What do you want?"

Whittaker smiled. "Finally, somebody's asking the important questions. If I help you get the kid back, then this thing between us? It's done. You go your way, I go mine, we never knew each other. I'm not running your errands; you're not picking my brain for answers; hell, I'm not giving you change for a loonie. I'm in the wind, and you can go kick rocks. Got it?"

Simon frowned. "Just like that? You're free and clear?"

"Liberated and transparent. I don't ever want to hear you call my name again, Ætheriċ. Not if I live another 10 000 years."

"You'll still have the bounty on you. And we won't come to your rescue if the Courts find you."

"I've survived this long, haven't I? And I've got favours I can call in if it gets too hot. John Starcross. La Scarlatine. Moony Malone's crew, back east. Trust me, those boys know how to make a fella disappear."

"Suppose I make you a counter-offer: you open a door to the other side, per the terms of our arrangement, or I will speak the name of Auberon ab Nethe three times, and then you will get nothing."

Whittaker managed not to flinch this time. "Yeah, 'cause that's really going to help you find the kid, isn't it? Go ahead, call down the whole Court! They can put my head on a stick, but you're still going to be stuck here when Josiah breezes through with a new lease on life."

"This is the only way to get my son back, isn't it?" asked Mona.

"This is it," said Whittaker. "*If Ætheriċ can do business.*"

Simon sighed finally and extended his hand. "Very well. Upon the safe return of Will Brady and Matthew Jansen to this place, I shall consider our business concluded, with no debts or obligations on either side. Neither shall I use the threat of bounty against you in any way to extract further favours from you."

Whittaker laughed and shook Simon's hand. "Alrighty, kids, we're in business! Time to get your dancing shoes on! First things first, I'm going to need some chalk, a candle, and a rainfall, post-haste."

"I can get you the chalk and the candle," Simon replied, "but the rainfall might be a bit difficult. Especially in this heat."

Whittaker looked at the sprinkler above his head and chuckled. "Will it, though?"

*****

Simon retrieved the candle Abby had left behind in the interview room, and Mona went to the evidence locker to fetch Simon's leather satchel, as well as Abby's Webley and Natalie's machete. When everything was ready, Whittaker took an unused piece of chalk from a box Simon had left in his satchel. Holding the candle in one hand and the chalk in the other, the imp went into the precinct's front entrance hall and took a moment to get his bearings. "I need a clear space to work," he said, with a look at Simon and Natalie. "About… eight feet each way. Somebody's going to have to shift some of this furniture for me."

Natalie scowled like she wanted to punch Whittaker's lights out, but she stomped over to the waiting area and started heaving the chairs, side tables, and water cooler out of the way. Whittaker eyeballed the gap and when he decided there was enough room, he gave her a thumbs-up.

"Now, this works best with a clean floor," said Whittaker. "Do you mind, Ætheric?" He nodded to the floor beneath him. Simon lifted a hand, uttered a spell, and a small gust of wind blew all the dust, dirt, and broken glass into one far corner.

"Seriously, are we just doing housework now?" Natalie snapped. "Do you want us to unplug a blocked sink next?"

"Hey, this is the process!" Whittaker retorted. "You want in to the Elsewhere, you follow my lead! Otherwise, you're welcome to find another faerie willing to drop everything and risk his neck so you can find this kid!"

Nobody spoke. Even Natalie's face softened, though her fists were still tight and her eyes burned with hate for the little imp.

"Yeah," Whittaker said at last. "That's what I thought." Without another word, he turned and pressed the long edge of the chalk to the floor. He counted out his steps to a radius of eight feet, turned on his heels, and walked in a wide circle around the waiting area. When the chalk circle was closed, Whittaker rubbed out the first line he'd drawn and tossed the chalk back to Simon. Then he took the cigarette lighter from his pocket and lit the candle. He whispered a word in his own language and the flame turned purple. The candle wax rippled and bubbled like water on the boil, and Whittaker held the candle out over the chalk circle.

He walked around the circle again, tapping one finger against the side of the candle in a steady rhythm. Every time he did so, a drop of wax fell onto the chalk. He carried on like this for several minutes in nearly total silence, until the whole circle had been covered in blotches of white wax.

Whittaker stepped out of the circle. "Last things last, the rain." He looked over his shoulder at Simon and nodded. It took Simon a second to understand what Whittaker meant, but then he got it and nodded back.

Simon took a step forward, planted his feet firmly, and cried, *"Fyres blæst!"* He threw a blazing ball of fire at the ceiling, and the sprinklers went off again.   Everyone raised their hands to cover their heads from the downpour, except for Whittaker. He put away his lighter and tossed the candle aside, not even flinching as the water ran down the back of his shirt. Whatever magic he was about to do, he approached it with the calm detachment of a man folding his laundry. He spoke a few words in the language of the Fair Folk, and the energy in the room began to change. The downpour from the sprinklers slowed, except within the borders of the wax circle. There, the water flowed as fast as ever, but each individual drop seemed to reduce in size, until the "rain" was little more than a falling sheet of mist that glittered like diamonds. Another few seconds passed, and then the mist parted in the middle like a beaded curtain.

A dark wood was visible on the other side of the misty curtain. It stretched into the distance further than anyone could see, a knot of crooked and gnarled trees in the middle of the police station. A path cut through the middle of the wood, wide enough for three people to walk shoulder-to-shoulder.

Mona's mouth hung open as she brushed past Whittaker and circled around the back of the curtain. Outside the ring of wax and chalk, the police station was unchanged. But the dense thicket of trees was still there. The opening in the mist appeared to follow her eyes, so that the door was open wherever she was standing and nowhere else. "I—I'm not the only one seeing this, right?"

"What the fuck…" breathed Corporal Rickards. "What the fuck…"

"'What the fuck' is right…" whispered Inspector Pembroke. The three cops paced around the circle in opposite directions, shifting their weight and staring in awe as the others appeared and disappeared in turn behind the trees. No matter where they stood, the opening followed their eyes exactly, even while it followed everyone else's.

Whittaker just stuck his hands in his pockets and rolled his eyes to the ceiling. "Fuckin' Muggles," he muttered.

"But where was the kaboom?" Abby asked. "There was supposed to be an earth-shattering kaboom."

Whittaker snorted. "What, you mean like Josiah made? Nah, nah, that's the sure sign of somebody who doesn't have a clue what the fuck he's doing. Opening a door to the Elsewhere is supposed to be a quiet, simple process, like opening a door to anywhere else. What he's been doing is basically kicking a hole in the wall any time he wants to get from Point A to B. Amateur move, believe me. Now look, are we doing this or what?"

Mona snapped out of it and nodded. "Somebody will have to stay back here with the wounded and wait for the ambulance."

"I'll do that," Rickards said in a dazed voice. He was still transfixed by the doorway Whittaker had created. "This is getting way too weird for me."

"I'm staying too," said Pembroke. "We still need some kind of chain of command around here. I need to call in some extra manpower to clean up the mess Foley made."

"Suit yourself," said Whittaker. "Anybody else want to sit this one out? Once we're on the other side, I can't guarantee anyone's safety."

Nobody wanted to sit this one out. Whittaker shrugged, muttered something about how it was their funeral, and walked into the circle. He passed through the rain into the spirit world, and Abby followed behind him. Mona was next. Then Simon picked up his leather satchel and hopped through the door, followed by Leanne and finally Natalie.

CHAPTER 28

THE OTHER SIDE

AS SOON as everyone had crossed through Whittaker's doorway, the image of the police station faded away and the sparkling rain drops fell to the ground. Where the door had been seconds ago, there was now more of the same gnarled, knotty forest. The trees were so thick on either side as to be impassable, and the ground beneath the group's feet was made of large, flat stones. These were cracked and broken in many places, like pieces from a colossal jigsaw puzzle. At the head of the group, Whittaker held up his hands to get everybody's attention. "Look, I'm not going to sugar-coat this, folks. Whatever you think you know about the spirit world, whatever you may have seen in a Bridge—and you know who you are, chickadee—you can go ahead and forget all that right now. When you're in the spirit world body and soul, it's a whole new ball game. You make one wrong move in here, you zig when you need to zag, and you're fucked. You're gone. No do-overs." His eyes flicked to Natalie and he added, "There's even things in here that can put down an undead, so everyone watch—your—ass." He started walking down the long forest path, and the others followed him in a tight huddle.

Nobody had a good sense of time or distance in that place. No sooner had they started walking than it began to feel like they'd always been walking. The forest around them didn't seem to move at all, yet the group would have sworn blind that they crossed a mile with every step they took. At some point during the journey, Leanne nudged her way to the front of the pack and took Abby's hand in both of hers. That, at least, made them both feel a little safer.

Abby looked over at Mona. "How are you holding up?"

Mona's eyes darted around the path and into the trees. "It's…" she began. "This is the most incredible thing I have ever seen. How… How do…?" She met Abby's eyes and shook her head, lost for words.

"Exactly," Abby said. "How do…?"

Mona's eyes returned to the path ahead of her. She spoke absently, without waiting for a response. It was almost like she was speaking more to the forest itself. "My… my nana used to tell me and my brother stories…" she murmured. "About our people, about the ancestors. By the time I was born, she was one of only a handful in our tribe who still spoke Hul'q'umi'num' and who knew the old songs. One story she liked to tell was about her grandfather, a great shaman of our people. When the shaman was a boy, he fell from a high rock and was crippled, so our people called him Sul'kwuléxun.' The white men who came to our island called him August John Broken Shoulders. Nana Sophie said that Sul'kwuléxun' knew a dance that could calm the wild spirits who lived in the woods around his village. The spirits would lure people into the woods and change them into animals that the braves would hunt. They would take children with them into the spirit world and put them to work. But as long as Sul'kwuléxun' was alive, the spirits would never touch anyone who came from his village. They respected him too much. Nana Sophie thought they even feared him a little bit." Mona looked back at the others. Without knowing it, she had wandered several feet ahead of the group. Everyone's eyes were upon her. Even Whittaker was quiet.

"She always said I had no head for stories. My brother did, and she taught him all the ancestral songs before she died. But she said to me, 'You are no storyteller, Mona August. You are no dreamer. You hear the songs, but you won't learn them.' I used to agree with her. I always used to think the stories were just… stories. Fables. But this… this beats everything she ever told me… God, if she could've seen this…"

"She might be able to, for all we know," Abby reasoned. "Just from a… slightly different angle."

Mona nodded. "Yeah. Yeah, she might be." She cleared her throat and turned. "Okay. Let's go find my son."

They walked a while longer, and the trees slowly began to change. Abby noticed cracked, white patches on the trunks, as if they had been stained with bleach. The ground was littered with broken branches, and the snap of wood underfoot made her imagine that she and the others were walking among the bones of the dead. The canopy above their heads was silvery-white and wispy as smoke. Strange bulges and protrusions stretched the leaves at various points, creating the impression of creatures hiding themselves among the treetops.

The canopy suddenly shifted and rustled as something leaped between two trees. A bleached-white branch poked through the leaf cover, and a flash of light on one twig caught Abby's eye. As she examined the branch, her breath stopped dead in her throat and she squeezed Leanne's hand. The glint of light was a reflection off a polished wedding ring. A wedding ring that hung precariously around a thin human finger. What Abby had taken for a branch was a skeletal hand and forearm. And the canopy was not so much made of leaves as…

"Are those… spider webs?" Leanne squeaked.

They were. Some were as gossamer-thin as the spider webs on Earth, and some were as thick as bridge cables. Spider's silk had been spun around, through, and over the topmost branches of every tree, packed as thick as cotton candy. And the bulges in the webbing were the signs of meals past and present.

Leanne shuddered and crossed herself with a whisper of, "Dear God…"

The canopy shook again as something moved above it. Some of the webs parted and the torso of a man fell through the gap. Leanne screamed and pressed herself against Abby. Mona drew her gun and pointed it up at the canopy. The torso dangled limply, but the corpse was still webbed up tightly from the waist. It had been immaculately preserved by whatever magic was in the giant spider webs.

Mona looked at the corpse for a second and blinked. "That's... oh my God, that's David Prudhomme..."

"Well, I guess now we know why you never found the body," Whittaker said.

The canopy rustled again. Branches snapped and cracked as something large and hairy lowered itself to the ground on a strand of silk, blocking the path before them, and Abby felt Leanne shaking in her arms.

The spider that blocked the path was the size of a small pickup truck, with a fat, black-and-brown body, a diamond-shaped head that was ridged like a crab's shell, and slender legs covered in fine salt-and-pepper hair. Two sharp pincers on the front of its head clicked and twitched as a smooth, sibilant voice crept out from somewhere beneath the creature's bulbous eyes. *Mid-landers... in our wood... live Mid-landers... this is a rare treat...*

Whittaker approached the spider and raised his hands in a conciliatory gesture. "Easy there, chief! We're not looking for trouble here. Myself and these Mid-landers have business in the Otherlands. In the court of King Auberon!" The spider flinched and scuttled back a step. Whittaker smiled and nodded. "Yeah, you've heard of him, haven't you? Even way out here..." He reached into the pocket of his waistcoat and pulled out a delicate golden chain with a small charm on the end, shaped like a cluster of three oak leaves. "You see this?" Whittaker waved the charm necklace in his hand. "This marks me as Auberon's courtier and envoy. I have leave to pass through the Spirit Wastes unmolested, and so do my friends here. You touch us, and you'll have a thousand pissed-off faerie knights to answer to. So why don't you just skedaddle and let us get on with our work?"

The spider skittered from one side to another as it did some quick mental arithmetic. Then it paused and narrowed its eight eyes suspiciously. *"Wait… why would a courtier of Oak travel these roads? These are the hunting grounds of the riders of Holly! It is Holly's dispensation that you would need to cross this way…"* The spider took a couple steps toward Whittaker, its pincers twitching menacingly.

Whittaker stuffed the oak charm back in his pocket and bluffed, "Uh… yeah, good point… hang on, I got it here somewhere…"

Hissing laughter rang out in the treetops above, and six more colossal spiders lowered themselves to the ground on strands of webbing, forming a tight circle around the group. Whittaker gulped. "Aw, crap."

Leanne squeezed Abby like a stress ball and stammered, "Whittaker, please tell me you have a plan?"

Whittaker searched frantically in his pockets for something that would appease the hungry, salivating arachnids. "Hang on, hang on, just give me a sec!"

Suddenly, a loud cry went up from the path behind them and the ground shook with the thunder of hooves. The spiders all turned at the noise, and through a gap in the circle Abby could see eight colossal horses charging toward them. "What the hell is that?"

"Oh shit," Whittaker spat. "Oh shit, shit, *shit*!"

"What is it?" asked Mona.

"Dullahan!"

"Dulla-what?"

"Dullahan! Faerie cavalry out of Holly! Quick, everybody, get off the road and shut your eyes!"

The spiders screamed and disappeared into the trees. Everybody else jumped off the road as the hoofbeats grew louder. "Why do we have to shut our eyes?" Mona called out.

"Because if you look right at a Dullahan when he stops riding, you'll drop stone dead!" Whittaker snapped back. "Now shaddap with the stupid questions and shut your damn eyes!"

They shut their eyes. The horses thundered past without slowing and faded into the distance. A couple moments passed, and then Whittaker said, "Okay. I think we're safe."

Everyone opened their eyes. Whittaker stood in the middle of the road, peering into the trees and stifling a laugh. "Dumbasses!" he cackled. "I can't believe they bought that!"

"Who?" asked Abby.

"The spiders, duh! I mean, *wow*, I always knew it wasn't exactly MENSA out here in the Spirit Wastes, but I thought the local ghoulies would be a little smarter than that!"

"Smarter than what? Whittaker, what are you babbling about?"

Whittaker smiled and snapped his fingers. Suddenly, a giant jet-black stallion in full gallop appeared five feet in front of him. Atop the horse was a figure in black riding gear and a long cape, holding a long whip made of human bones in one hand and his own pallid, grinning head in the other.

The horse's hooves beat the ground loudly, but the Dullahan didn't move an inch. Whittaker snapped his fingers again, and the image disappeared. "Dullahan," he snorted. "Give me a break! Nah, I just conjured up a quick illusion. It had to be something that would make those ugly bastards more scared than they were hungry." He noticed the confusion on Mona's face and added, "See, the faerie nation is split into two courts: Oak and Holly. A lot of spirits respect the Court-Among-the-Oak, but there's not one of them who isn't scared shitless of the Court-Among-the-Holly. Now come on. We better move before those bozos realize they've been had."

They walked on for a while longer. Eventually, they came to the foot of a tall hill and Abby got slammed with the mother of all whammies. She stifled a cry of pain and leaned on Leanne as a vision flashed before her.

Constable Foley stood in the living room of the Harcourt House, looming over the claw foot tub from the upstairs bathroom, in which sat the skeleton of Josiah Harcourt. A large red circle on the floor stretched to the very edges of the room so the spell could be contained. Will Brady lay on the floor, bound with thick and rough nylon ropes that had rubbed his wrists raw. Specks of dried vomit made a thin crust on the front of his shirt. Reverend Jansen was hovering near the ceiling above the tub, shirtless and bruised and spread-eagled.

Foley waved his wand in the air and began a long incantation. Hot red blood poured out of the faucet into the tub and Josiah's skull bobbed like a toy boat as Foley circled around and pulled out a fistful of Will's hairs by the roots. The boy screamed and Foley threw the hair into the tub.

The blood in the tub frothed like a witch's cauldron as Foley flicked his wand again and a deep cut opened on the reverend's chest. His blood mixed with Jenny's, David's, and Sonia's, and Josiah's empty eye sockets glowed red. Will gave another muffled scream and rose into the air as a spark of blue light appeared under his shirt, right where his heart was. The light streamed up Josiah's nostrils and the Harcourt patriarch laughed as red muscle tissue sprouted on his old bones.

The vision ended and Abby dropped to her knees, screaming. Leanne grabbed her by the shoulders and tried to shake her back to reality. "What is it? What do you see?"

Abby shook her head to clear it and wiped away a nosebleed with the palm of her hand. "The ritual's starting… we have to go now…" She stumbled and staggered up the hill, still trying to fight clear of the headache and refusing any steadying hand offered to her. Mona started after her and the others followed soon after. Abby was still weak from the vision as she crested the hill, and she fell to her knees again. She felt Mona's hand gripping her shoulder and looked ahead.

The hill dropped off sharply, and a void of black nothingness swirled below. Across a two-hundred-foot gap, the Harcourt House hung suspended in open air, the foundations below it thick with sticky black ectoplasm, and a ring of silvery, smoky ghosts twirling in the sky above the crumbling chimney. Abby caught brief flashes of aura in the smoke, and she recognised, among others, the spirits of Bill Grover, Sonia Hall, and Hector and Olivia Harcourt. These were all the victims of the Harcourt House and the forces within it, stretching back over the last century.

Abby got up and held Mona for support. Behind her, the others came to the top of the hill and looked across. "How do we get over there?" asked Natalie.

"Stand back," Abby said, and they did. She cracked her knuckles, got down on one knee, then shut her eyes and spread her palms flat on the ground, just at the edge of the cliff. On previous visits to the Elsewhere, Abby had discovered that the spirit world would respond to her thoughts if she concentrated hard enough. Sometimes, the landscape could even reshape itself according to an image that she held in her mind. She concentrated for a moment on the image she wanted and told herself, with all her might, that it would be staring her in the face when she opened her eyes.

Four giant wooden poles sprang out of the ground, two at each end of the gap. Long ropes uncoiled from nowhere and grabbed the poles, and wooden planks fell from the sky to span the gap. Abby opened her eyes and stood back up.

The rope bridge was wide enough for two to cross at a time. Abby and Mona went first, followed by Whittaker and Leanne, and finally Simon and Natalie. The bridge creaked and swayed as they inched their way across it, and Abby kept her eyes closed the whole time.

"Are you okay?" Leanne asked from behind her.

Abby's voice was strained. "I didn't realize... the effort... I have to keep thinking about it... keep thinking that it'll hold all of us..." The planks started to groan under her feet and the ropes swayed as if rocked by a wind of self-doubt. "Come on, dammit," she hissed through gritted teeth. "It *will* hold. It *will*." She took shaky steps forward and repeated the mantra even louder. Mona and the others picked up the chant and the planks seemed to become firmer under their feet, bolstered by the vote of confidence in Abby's reality.

The bridge held. As soon as the last two were off, Abby plopped herself down on the tree stump and sucked in several deep, ragged breaths. Mona patted her on the back and said, "You're doing great, Henderson. Here." She handed Abby a tissue and pointed to her own nose. "You're still… dripping."

Abby blinked the spots out of her eyes and saw a drop of red fall from her nose. She sniffed in the back of her throat, tasted copper, and took the proffered tissue. "Thanks," she groaned. "Wait, where did you…?"

Mona took a whole packet of tissues from one pocket of her vest. "I have a ten-year-old son. This isn't my first runny-nose rodeo."

"Fair 'nough."

"Guys. Look at this." That was Leanne, who was by the corner of the House, examining a dark strip of earth that ran under the porch.

"What is it?" Abby croaked.

"I think it's…" She sniffed, dry-heaved, and coughed. "Oh, wow. Yep. Definitely ectoplasm. But there's all kinds of… stuff in it." The strip of earth was finely zebra-striped with chunks of white that looked, at first glance, like carved marble. Leanne borrowed one of the tissues from Mona's pack and extracted one of the white bits from the ectoplasm. "A cicada…" she whispered. Then she looked down, dropped the tissue with a squeak, and hastily backed away. "Jesus! They're all cicadas!"

Simons stepped forward to examine the ectoplasm strip. He picked up one of the cicadas and crushed it between two fingers, where it left behind a powdery white residue. "Salt!" He scooped up a handful of the bugs and crushed them in his palm. "They're all turned to salt!" He stood, followed the dark strip of ectoplasm along the ground, and then turned back to the group. "It looks like it's a ring of ectoplasm. Goes all the way around the House from what I can see. Right to the edges of the foundation"

"It's a moat," Abby said. She sniffed, tossed the tissue aside, and pointed up to the chimney. "To keep the ghosts out of the House. Has to be. Josiah and Isaac get here, Josiah lays down a few layers of ectoplasm, summons the swarm, and then Isaac turns the bugs to salt. This is our chalk circles on an industrial scale."

Simon prodded at the salty cicadas. "I suspect you're right, Abigail. Josiah's not taking any risks. Hector's tried to defy him once already, so Josiah's barred entry to anyone from this side of the veil who might have a score to settle."

"Can we break the circle?" Leanne asked.

Simon plunged a hand down into the salt and winced when he struck something hard. His knuckles were bruised when he drew them out, and he shook his head. "Negative. Only the first few layers are loose. Below that, I think it's just one solid vein of salt and ectoplasm. It would take a hell of a wallop to break that magic circle. I don't know that we have the time to prepare that kind of wallop."

Mona looked at the House. "But we can still get in, right? They haven't blocked the front door? The upstairs windows? The cellar door?"

Simon shook his head. "This is only meant to ward off spirits. I doubt if Josiah would have even considered that we mere mortals had a way into the Elsewhere."

"Right. Then we go in teams of two. Hit them when they're distracted. Two in through the cellar, two upstairs, two through the front. Converge on the living room. Stop the Rite. Save Will."

Whittaker shook his head. "There you go, thinking like a cop again. Josiah's ghost is basically hardwired into this dump, right? He's already looked into these numbskulls' minds the last time they were here, and I guarantee he'll sense them as soon as they're inside. Then he'll throw up as many constructs as he needs and clean house, so to speak. You can't take something like this head-on."

"So what do you propose?" Abby asked.

Whittaker smiled. "Three-card Monte, kid. We just gotta get these idiots looking for the red lady."

CHAPTER 29

THE RITE OF KA'THONN

MONA KICKED the front door open, and she and Abby went in with their guns drawn. When they reached the living room, Foley broke off the incantation and raised his wand. *"Carnis lapidis!"* Abby and Mona froze in their tracks, and Foley pointed his wand to the floor. *"Supplicāte."* Invisible force brought the women to their knees so fast that the Vokarion crystals around their necks bounced up and almost hit them both in the face. At the same moment, the thread of blue light connecting Will and Josiah disappeared, and the boy gasped and whimpered in agony.

"How the hell did you two follow us here?" he demanded.

Abby grunted as she tried to shake her head. "Sorry. That would be telling."

"Fine. Be like that." He aimed his wand at Abby's head. *"Mor —"*

Mona snapped, "How long, Isaac? How long have you been wearing that face?"

The red glow in Foley's eyes intensified and his lips stretched into a crooked smile that was too wide to be human. The teeth that showed were far yellower and more crowded than Mona remembered, and the laugh that escaped from between them was thin and high like Josiah's. "Well done," said a voice that was not Linus Foley's. "I was starting to think you'd never figure it out."

"Does Linus Foley even exist anymore?" asked Abby.

The ghost of Isaac Harcourt stooped a little and shrugged his host's shoulders. They curled inward, making him look smaller and narrower. An old man trapped behind a young boy's face. "Parts of him do," admitted Isaac. "His knowledge and memories are his own, but they have been… useful to me over the years. I defer to him in matters of the day-to-day. But it is my magic that you have been detecting, Miss Henderson. Did either of you ever wonder why Delapore put a fence around our house 15 years ago? Yes, they meant to stop local children from sneaking in, but why did it take them so long?"

"Something happened up here that finally tipped the scales," Abby guessed.

Isaac Harcourt nodded. "Linus Foley was a teenager once. He was dared to do something incredibly stupid. And when he was inside, he wanted a trophy to prove his worth. A memento of this place that he could flash in the school yard." He held up his hand and light gleamed off the gold band around his pinky. "He was only supposed to be in the House for an hour. When he did not return at the appointed time, his friends panicked and left him here. I had never been able to manifest in the physical world before then. Not like my father could. But when Linus put on the ring, I saw my chance. It took me two days to… tame his mind. But eventually, I was able to establish permanent residency in this body and walk out of the House, into a new century. It caused quite a scandal in town. For about a week. But eventually, Delapore did what it always does and went back to quietly ignoring the Harcourt problem."

"So you set yourself up with a new identity. And you left your old man behind to rot, just like Hector did."

If looks could kill, this one would have blown Abby's head off. Isaac shouted a spell, and a force like a bowling ball hit her in the stomach. She doubled over, coughing and gasping for breath. "Don't say his name. Don't you *dare*! My brother abandoned this family when it needed him most! The Master was sick. He turned to Ephraim's research to save his life. He needed his sons at his side and my worthless ingrate of a brother walked away! When he returned, his only thought was to destroy us." He launched another spell that knocked Mona onto her back. "When I wasn't living as Linus Foley, I spent every moment I had trying to get The Master out of this place. It took me over a decade just to translate the language of the Otherlands and learn the Rite of Ka'thonn. Another two years of training before I could perform the Thousand Cuts with any success." He threw another spell. Abby and Mona both felt it like twin kicks in the ribs. "I have been nothing but loyal to my Master for a century." Another spell punched Abby in the gut, and she threw up a little in her mouth.

"Did your little sister teach you how to hit like that?" she rasped. "Because it sure wasn't Daddy."

Mona tried to laugh, then winced and wheezed, "Okay. Hurts too much to laugh. Good note for next time. It's still funny, though."

The voice of Josiah Harcourt burbled out from the tub. "Isaac… is there a problem?"

Isaac gritted Foley's teeth. "No, Master. I have the problem in hand."

"Think, boy! These two could not have made it this far by themselves! They would need old magic to cross the veil! This must be the Vanguard's work!"

Abby groaned. "Give me some credit, old man! Okay, I haven't been at this Gospel thing very long, but I've been working hard on the dimension-crossing! Two hours of practice a day for the last six months! That has to count for something!"

"You lie!" Josiah snapped. "You did not come here of your own will, Abigail Henderson! You don't have the strength!"

"Go ahead: check the rest of the House. You won't find another psychic signature in this place."

The House groaned as a spiderweb of ectoplasm spread from beneath the bathtub, up the back wall, and down through the cracks in the floorboards. Abby and Mona's crystals glowed brightly as Josiah extended his mental energy to every room, like a psychic radar scanning for the brainwaves of his enemies. The radar pinged off Abby's psychic signature, Will's, the reverend's, Mona's, and the combined intellects of Foley and Isaac, but it couldn't go past the ring of salt outside, and Josiah's energy came bouncing back at him.

"Finish the Rite, Isaac. And dispose of these two."

Isaac smiled. "With pleasure."

"Wait!" Abby gasped. "Wait! Don't you want to rant some more about your villainous backstory? It's just starting to get interesting!"

Isaac pointed his wand at her. "No. I'm done talking to you." He cast his next spell straight through her heart, shattering the Vokarion crystal and scorching the floorboards behind her.

Abby blinked and looked down at her chest. No burn marks on her shirt and no wounds on her skin. The spell literally had gone right *through* her. She looked up at Isaac again, gave him a smile and a wink, and then spoke in a voice remarkably similar to Whittaker's. "That's funny. I was just about to say the same to you, chief."

Somewhere, there was the distant sound of snapping fingers, and the illusions of Abby and Mona disappeared. Their crystals dropped to the floor and the purple glow faded as they ceased transmitting the pair's psychic signatures into the House. Isaac reached out to feel the empty air and Josiah howled in anger as he began to understand. "Trickery! Deception! Isaac, find those two and kill them! I know they are close!"

Isaac took one step, and there was another distant finger snap. He saw a hook-nosed yellow face duck behind the tree stump outside, and then he heard hoofbeats behind him.

A bugle blared, hooves clattered, and with a deep-throated whinny, a monstrous black stallion galloped out of the chimney. Its headless rider snapped a whip made of human bone, and the sharpened end punctured one of the floorboards. The cackling illusion flicked its wrist and the floorboards split, breaking Isaac's magic circle. Then the stallion reared, gave another whinny, and stampeded right through the bathtub, scattering porcelain, blood, and bones all across the living room. Josiah screamed, and Will and the reverend both dropped to the ground. Isaac leaped out of the way as the Dullahan galloped past and smashed into the far wall of the House, where it disappeared in a shower of sparks.

*****

Abby — the real, flesh-and-blood Abby — felt her ears pop as Whittaker teleported her, Mona, and Natalie into the cellar. She took a deep breath, gave her brain a second to adjust, then gave the others a thumbs-up when she was steady again. "Okay. Let's party."

Mona nodded and drew her gun. Natalie jumped and grabbed one of the massive pipes extending from the furnace, and Mona and Abby took hold of Whittaker again.

*****

Isaac grabbed his wand, scrambled across the slick of blood, and picked up Josiah's skull. "Master! Master, please, speak to me!"

The red lights flared in Josiah's eye sockets. "Leave me, Isaac! Find the Henderson girl! She and her friends will undo everything!"

Beneath Isaac's feet, the floorboards split as a dark-skinned hand erupted from the cellar, grabbed his ankle, and pulled him to the ground. Natalie erupted from the floor and went for her machete. George Romero presents Grace Jones as She-Hulk. She was looking to dish out some payback, and Isaac bolted like a scared rabbit.

Crack! Whittaker and the others teleported into the room. Mona smashed her gun on the warlock's nose and Abby grabbed Will and the reverend. Then they were gone again. Before Isaac could recover, blue-and-green sparks flashed on the ceiling and Simon and Leanne dropped out of thin air. Simon produced one of Natalie's IEDs from his satchel and threw it at Josiah's scattered bones, and Leanne kicked Isaac in his broken nose.

The bomb's first shockwave turned Josiah's ribcage to powder, and the incendiary charge flash-fried what was left. Simon pumped his fist in the air and whooped, "Berlin! 1943!" Then he hurled a second device at Josiah's skull. The House quaked as cicadas poured out of the chimney and bounced the bomb right back. Simon shoved Leanne and Natalie through a portal and raised his shields as the bomb went high, but Isaac went low with a Cutting Curse.

Ectoplasm oozed out of the floorboards and layered over Josiah's remains, weaving itself into a crude facsimile of muscle, nerve, and vein. The body pulled itself together and stirred on the floor. As a cocoon of ectoplasm enclosed around Josiah's skull, the Harcourt patriarch screamed at his apprentice to: "BRING! ME! ABIGAIL! HENDERSON!"

*****

Leanne and Natalie hit the deck as black lightning danced among a ring of blue-and-green sparks. The Cutting Curse blasted apart Josiah's bookshelves and sent paper flying around the Harcourt library. Pages ignited in midair as the bomb went off and flames leapt through the portal. Simon rode the shockwave and landed badly on the floor, screaming and bleeding all over the place.

"Jesus Christ!" Leanne gasped. "Simon!"

He looked like he'd been run over by a lawnmower. His shirt and waistcoat were red ribbons hanging from his shoulders, and his upper body was a mess of deep, vicious cuts, some of them dangerously close to the bone. As the portal closed, he turned onto his back and hissed, "Stupid me…Tried to jump and shield myself at the same time…" Leanne touched one of his larger wounds and he started screaming again. "Bloody hell! Just leave me to die, you butcher!"

Leanne tore off what clothing remained above Simon's belt and started MacGyvering the strips into bandages. "Shut up, Simon, just shut up. You're going to be okay."

Simon bit his tongue and beat his fist on the floor as Leanne tied part of his shirt sleeve tight around his other arm. *Wulfor cyning!* he swore. "Everything burns!"

"I know! I know! Think how good it's going to feel when we make this place burn back!"

Simon exhaled and his eyelids fluttered. Leanne smacked him on the cheek. "Stay with me, Simon. Stay with me. You're going to be fine!"

Simon winced and opened his eyes. "Are you lying…" he groaned, "just to make me feel better?"

"What do you think?"

Natalie made a pile of Josiah's journals and spell books in the middle of the floor and grabbed the third charge from Simon's bag. She took a short length of homemade fuse from the pocket of her khakis, bit it off, and hooked it to the charge.

"Can you teleport us out of here?" Leanne asked.

Simon shook his head. "I'm… I'm spent…" he hissed. "It hurts… all hurts… sorry…"

"Don't be. You haven't done anything wrong." Natalie took over the first aid and Leanne made a call over the Vokarion network. *Abby? Abby, we've got a problem…*

"BRING! ME! ABIGAIL! HENDERSON!"

Make that two problems.

*****

While Leanne fixed Simon up in the library, Whittaker snapped into the kitchen with Abby, the reverend and the Bradys. Mona and Will both started crying as she undid his bonds, and he gave her the biggest hug he could.

"Oh my God, William! I thought I'd never see you again! Are you hurt?"

"Tired," he croaked. "Really hungry. I didn't think you'd find me…"

She kissed him on the cheek. "I will *always* find you, William. Always. Oh God, my baby boy…"

Whittaker huffed and wiped sweat from his brow. "Okay, this is real touching, folks, but can we get the fuck out of here? We're kind of on a clock!"

Abby looked at him. "Are you okay, Whittaker?"

The imp puffed out his cheeks and shook his head. "I don't normally do so many jumps in one sitting. Especially not with all this extra weight. You might as well be asking me to push a minivan up Mount Everest."

"Just a couple more. Then you can rest."

Reverend Jansen reached for Abby with one clammy hand. He was in bad shape and getting worse by the minute. "Please… somebody tell me… I don't understand what's happening here…"

Abby patted his hand. "It's a very long story, Reverend. We're going to get you out of here and take you to the hospital. Then we'll explain everything."

"Foley…" he gasped. "Constable Foley… he's… not him… he's changed… have to stop him…"

Abby nodded. "We will, Reverend. We'll stop him and Josiah and make sure they can't hurt anyone else."

Reverend Jansen nodded his thanks and then passed out. Abby's crystal started to glow as Leanne's message came in. "Shit! Simon's hurt too. Whittaker, do you think you can get to the library?"

"Just. Between this and all the decoys I still gotta throw up, I've only got one or two jumps left in me. Either I go to the library and get Ætheric, or I get this group outside. I can't do both."

"Let's meet somewhere in the middle. Can you take these guys to the library and then get everyone outside?"

"I can try. I'll have to break for a couple minutes while I send Isaac and Josiah after the red lady. You're going to have to work fast, kid, 'cause the illusion ain't going to last. I can make the decoys a little more stable if I mix my hard light with all the ectoplasm around here, but that's just a Band-Aid fix. I'm already pushed to my limit as is."

"Okay. Do what you can to get everyone clear. The wounded are your priority. Mona, you look after your son. I'll keep Isaac and Josiah busy long enough for you to get out of here, and then I'll finish this."

Whittaker chuckled. "Run away and hide while someone else does the legwork? Finally, you're talking my language."

"BRING! ME! ABIGAIL! HENDERSON!"

Whittaker gulped and grabbed Mona, Will, and the reverend. "Hoo boy. I think they're playing your song, kid. Remember: follow the red lady."

Abby nodded and walked toward the door. Will reached out and grabbed her hand. "Abby! You can't go out there!"

"I have to, Will. Somebody has to set the last charge, and I've got the only free pair of hands. We have to take Josiah down now, because he's not letting you out of here without a fight."

"But—"

"Don't worry. I'll be okay."

"You promise? No joke, Abby Normal promise?"

She winked. "100%."

CHAPTER 30

THE RED LADY

ABBY WENT out into the hall and whistled. "Isaac! Josiah! You red-eyed fucks want a crack at me? I'm right here, assholes!" Something moved at the other end of the corridor, and she hastily fired her Webley into the darkness.

Around the corner in the den, Isaac hissed, *"Sum quasi aquam!"* Abby turned at the noise, and Isaac came up behind her and sliced her head clean off her shoulders.

The severed head landed at his feet and blinked a couple times. It smiled its gappy smile and said, "Fast work, Robespierre."

Isaac looked around as the head and body melted into ectoplasm. Then the cellar door opened and a second Abby stuck her head out. "Hey, what's all the commotion out here?"

A spell blasted the door to pieces, and the second Abby melted away. A third Abby kicked open the front door and hollered, "Do you have a minute to talk about our Lord and Saviour Jesus Chr—"

The third Abby exploded like an ectoplasmic water balloon when the spell hit her. Isaac swept the corridor and screamed, "Where are you, Henderson?"

Two Abbys stepped out of the den. "Well, she's not in there," said the first.

"We checked," said the second. "Twice."

Isaac screamed and blasted them both to pieces.

The principle of Three-card Monte is simple enough on paper. The dealer has three playing cards on a table, and the player (the "mark") has to find one card out of the three after they have been shuffled face down. If the mark can find the "money card," they win a cash prize. If they can't, they walk away with nothing. The queen of hearts is often used as the money card, so the dealer will commonly tell the mark to "follow the red lady." The trick is that the dealer uses sleight-of-hand and misdirection during every shuffle, so the mark is never following the right card. As Isaac stormed through the House chasing the illusions of Abby that Whittaker had produced, and as Josiah's ectoplasm constructs oozed up out of the woodwork to join the search, they never noticed the real Abby crawl out of the pantry and creep down the stairs into the cellar.

*****

It was a red-eyed, ectoplasmic John Leland who came into the dining room and found three Abbys gathered around the table. Just to pour salt in the wound, one of them was dressed as a casino dealer and was shuffling three cards. "Hurr-ay! Hurr-ay! Hurr-ay!" she chirped in a terrible Bronx accent. "Step right up, good suh! Step right up and find the red lady! Everyone's a winnah!"

Leland drew his cane sword and hacked the Abbys to pieces. One of their severed heads smiled at him. "And the gentleman wins a cee-gah!"

At the same moment, a pale creature in hunting leathers kicked open the door of the Dead Room and caught an Abby brushing her teeth. She snapped, "Don't you knock?" and he ripped her head off with one hand.

There was an Abby getting changed in Olivia Harcourt's bedroom. When the construct of Nick Brady found her, she covered herself with a blanket and called him a pervert. There was an Abby on the stairs, who came sliding down the banister and flashed both middle fingers at the construct of Elinora. There was an Abby who dropped out of the chimney wearing a Santa hat and a fake beard, and who wished the Rat King a merry Christmas.

And there was Mona Brady, who spoiled the game by shooting down a construct and shouting at Whittaker from the library. "On your six!" she hollered. "Dammit, Whittaker, keep your head down!"

In the living room, Josiah's skull swiveled on its ectoplasm neck toward the source of the noise. He placed a hand on the floor and redirected all his willpower toward the library. The walls creaked as a second wave of constructs oozed forth. "Hear me, Isaac," he whispered. "This is a mere shell game. Get the boy. I'll find the Gospel bitch."

*****

Mona pumped bullets into the sludgy black horde until her gun went empty. She fell back, reloaded, and snapped, "Any day now, people!"

Leanne helped Simon to his feet and brought him over next to Reverend Jansen. Natalie reached into Simon's bag, grabbed a tennis ball tube full of salt, popped the lid, and swung it at the constructs. Ectoplasm sizzled like bacon in a pan as the salt spilled out, and three of the creatures melted away. The rest of the horde froze, wary of the briny slush in their path, and Mona unloaded another clip. Whittaker yelled at them to move their butts, and they fell back toward the rest of the group.

Cicadas burst from behind one of the bookshelves, knocking everyone off-balance. Nick Brady oozed out of the floor beneath Mona, wrapped one hand around her throat, and started to squeeze. "Hey, babe," he said with a leer, "you look *good*."

A geyser of ectoplasm split the floorboards and coiled into the sky like the proverbial magic beanstalk. Goopy black tendrils made nooses for Leanne, Simon, the reverend, and Whittaker. Four more tendrils grabbed Natalie's arms and legs and retracted into the beanstalk, as if to quarter her like a medieval traitor.

*****

In the cellar, Abby — the real Abby — reached down the back of her pants and shivered as cold metal brushed against her tailbone. The bomb was about four inches in diameter and barely longer than Bill Grover's screwdriver, but stuffed to the gills with lethal danger. It was inert as long as the fuse wasn't connected, and that was hiding safely in Abby's bra. Before they'd even gone into the House, Natalie had given Abby a crash course on how to set everything up. Natalie had warned that the fuses weren't long, and recommended that Abby waited till everyone was clear before she hooked up the bomb.

Abby reached down the front of her shirt and took out the little coil of yellow thread. She really hoped she hadn't sweated on it too much as she set the bomb at the base of the furnace and attached everything as Natalie had instructed. It took a couple tries because her eyes wouldn't focus on the damn thing. Didn't help that the room was going all wobbly, either. She'd been trying to hold it together ever since they'd arrived at the House, but her mind was reeling from all the psychic energy flying around. All bets were off as to whether she'd throw up, pass out, or wet her pants first.

Her hand shook as she clumsily fiddled with the first match. It didn't light on the first strike, and it snapped clean in two on the second. She drew another match and tried again. Blood dribbled out of her nose onto a sticky patch of ectoplasm on the floor. A cicada buzzed around her ear.

Shit! In a brief moment of clarity, Abby dropped the matchbook and drew the Webley. Cicadas barrelled down the stairs toward her and Abby heard her friends screaming in the distance. A golem of bones and ectoplasm appeared in the swarm and reached for her with both hands.

"HENDERSON!"

*****

Mona raised her gun, but Nick took it from her with his free hand and threw it to the floor. "Aw, c'mon, Mo, don't do that. Don't play those games with me."

Isaac shouldered past the constructs standing in the doorway and cleared away the salt with a quick spell. He hooked an arm around Will's neck and dragged him toward the door. The boy cried for his mom, and Nick smiled as the blood vessels burst in Mona's eyes. "Mona Brady," he whispered. "The good cop trying to outrun a bad past. You've spent so long running. Do you even remember what you're running from?" The red shine in Nick's eyes intensified, and his voice became more like Josiah's. "Do you know what you left behind on the island, Mona Brady? Or is it like a dream to you now? A missing piece of the past that you can never quite reach. Perhaps it didn't really happen to you, eh? Perhaps that was somebody else."

Nick screamed and let go of Mona. Reverend Jansen was awake and on his knees, throwing fistfuls of salt from the half-empty tube. As Nick melted into the floor, the reverend turned and threw salt into Isaac's eyes. The warlock backed away, and Reverend Jansen jabbed him with a piece of broken bookshelf. Isaac screamed as the sharp wood entered his curse wound, then pointed his wand at the reverend and screamed, *"Fulmen!"* A bolt of lightning struck the reverend in the chest and Isaac melted into the floor, taking Will with him.

*****

Abby struggled against the cocoon of ectoplasm holding her down on the cellar floor. It felt like a blanket of cinderblocks, forcing all the air out of her lungs. All she could do was watch as the construct of Josiah Harcourt loomed over her and sneered. "I will not lie to you, Miss Henderson. I am impressed. Using my own tricks against me… Keeping me… 'off-balance,' I think you said… Tell me: was it you or the fey who scripted that amusing little fiction? I am almost embarrassed that I did not spot the lie earlier. There is always something they lack, the duplicates. Some *je ne sais quoi* that only the genuine article possesses." He daubed his finger in the blood on the floor, and then flicked it in Abby's face. "Blood will out, as the saying goes. You made a noble effort today, Miss Henderson. But this is my house. This is my *world*. And while I am Master of this place, no one shall get the better of me."

The mist curled around Abby's head and transformed into little effigies of her friends, strangling as they hung from their ectoplasmic nooses.

"You have led your friends to their doom," hissed Josiah. "They will die staring down the ghosts of their pasts. Will Brady will never leave this place." In the misty puppet show, Isaac and Will rose from the landing on the third floor. Isaac pressed his wand between Will's eyes and the boy began to cry. "And you… you will join Hector and the other shades."

He took her head in both hands and his red eyes bored into her with blinding intensity as he threw his strongest psychic attack at her. Pain flared in her head and her nose became a crimson fountain, spilling down into her mouth as she screamed.

"You can't stop what's begun here, Abigail. You may have spoiled the blood of my sacrifices, but I'll just take more. And next time, there will be no heroes to save them."

She pressed her hands flat against the cellar floor and felt around. There was a thin carpet of ectoplasm all around her. Most of it had dried to a hard crust, but some patches were still sticky and malleable. She could feel little pinpricks in the cement where Josiah had sent the ectoplasm coursing through the foundations of the House. And she wondered if the tendrils of ectoplasm that started here were the same ones that ended at the ring of salt outside.

The only reason she'd escaped the last time she'd faced Josiah was because Hector had intervened. Hector had been the key to all of this, right from the start. But if she wanted his help, she had to break the line of salt.

Ectoplasm was a mix of earthly matter and spirit matter. That was what Simon had said. Abby had practice shaping the matter of the spirit world to suit her whims, but how far did that power extend? Could she manipulate ectoplasm in the same way, or was it too diluted?

She wriggled her fingers and stretched them out over a thread of ectoplasm that snaked into a crack on the floor. She forced herself to think through the pain, to concentrate on the feel of the ectoplasm, and to connect her psychic energies to it.

The ectoplasm squirmed beneath her fingers as it picked up the signal. A thread of the stuff creeped up and over her hand, sucking her fingertips down into the crack on the floor. She felt a jolt of electricity up and down her arm, and she forced her mental willpower down into the ground below her.

Vines of ectoplasm stretched all through the foundations of the House, even through the very bedrock, and they started to twitch and wriggle in the ground as Abby extended her psychic will toward them. She felt the familiar buzz of Elsewhere-energy passing through the earth. The further she reached, the stronger the buzz got until it shocked her like ice down the back of her neck, and for a brief second, she stopped hurting.

She imagined the ectoplasmic roots starting to dance in the earth, creating air pockets and shifting the soil. She filled them with her willpower and told them to listen to her. They were Elsewhere matter where it counted, and they would obey her, goddammit. She pictured a Rubik's Cube in a blender and projected those feelings of agitation out into the ectoplasm.

Ectoplasm shifted. Soil and stone shivered in the earth. The cement floor trembled. Just a little tremble at first, but enough to give her hope. She pressed harder, focused more of her own psychic energy on the ectoplasm. China teacups rattled on one of the shelves as the tremors grew stronger. The old wardrobe creaked and the furnace pipes began to clank.

Dust fell from the ceiling and the shelves shook where they stood. The tea set shattered on the ground and the House's old floorboards groaned as Abby made one final push. Every last ounce of her psychic strength flowed into the ectoplasm, making it jump and thrash like a herd of wild stallions. The earth rumbled as she pictured the cataclysmic earthquake that was rocking through the House. The ceiling beams above her head cracked. Ectoplasm sprouted through the concrete and the narrow cellar window broke as a tangle of black gooey vines punched right through it. One of the furnace pipes came free of the ceiling and crushed the wardrobe to kindling. Two shelving units toppled onto their faces with the violence of a thunderstorm.

Abby took a breath and screamed in pain. Ectoplasm burst from the ground and cracked the lowest, most solid layers of the salt line outside. In her mind's eye, Abby saw silver-white fire shooting from the ground as the magical barrier fell. The rush of psychic energy through her body made her ears pop and punched a crater in the floor beneath her. The cocoon of ectoplasm split right down the middle and Josiah clutched at his forehead as the mental attack rebounded. He screamed with a dozen voices as the other constructs in the House dissolved, and a series of splashes and thuds above signalled the collapse of the beanstalk and of Natalie's bonds. Abby took a deep breath and yelled, "MY NAME IS ABIGAIL! MARGARET! HENDERSON! OF THE LINE OF THE GOSPELS!"

Josiah yowled as he tried to shake off the whammy, and Abby hauled herself out of the cocoon. "My father was Donald Richard Henderson, himself the son of Philip Henderson. From these names have I learnt the wisdom of my ancestors. From these names do I draw strength. I offer these names now to that noble witness, the ancient Countenance of the High Celestial!"

She made the call to every spirit she could think of. Bill Grover, Jenny Styles, Mandeep Sihota, Daniel Pang and Ernest Eckhart... She felt little twitches in her brain as every one of them latched onto her psychic signal, like fish on a hook. She called on Hector last of all, and heard his response in her head. *Abby Henderson? How can you be here? What in God's name is happening?*

Long story... slurred her exhausted inner monologue. *Hector, I've broken the salt line. You can come in now... it has to be you that stops him... you and the others...*

Us?

Yes. You and all the ones he's hurt. I've done my best, but he's so strong... this is the spirit world, and it's going to take a spirit to beat a spirit.

But his power is too great. I wouldn't know how to —

Bullshit! There's one of him and dozens of you! Hector, you saved me from the Rat King! You reached out of the Elsewhere to warn me and Mona! You have power in this place, and it's your turn to use it! All of you together... you would burn him.

I... I will try...

Flickering silver lights appeared at the window. The walls groaned and an aftershock rumbled through the cellar as the Harcourt House's many victims came a-knockin.' "What is this?" Josiah hissed. "What have you done? You foolish little bitch, what have you done?"

Abby smiled at Josiah with red-stained teeth. "I just did what I'm good at. I called on the spirits. Do you hear them coming, Josiah? Do you hear them coming for you?"

A shining hand holding an axe phased through the wall, and dozens of ghostly moans echoed around the cellar. Josiah took a step back, trying not to look scared. Abby sniffed and spat blood onto the floor. "Did you say this is *your world*, Josiah? No. Not even close. This reality is so much more than you could ever dream. Even I know that, and I've barely scratched the surface in one tiny corner. I didn't know the Elsewhere existed for most of my life! You've had almost a century in this place, and what can you show for it? You've spent so much time plotting your revenge on Delapore when you could have been exploring all this! You could have been a god! But you're just a vindictive psycho stuck in an empty mausoleum."

Hector took the axe in both hands and led the advance. Josiah raised his hand and cicadas poured out of his sleeve by the thousands, but Hector didn't even blink. The first swing of his axe produced a blinding white light that burned the insects to dust.

The ghosts came through the walls, the ceiling, and the floor. They surrounded Josiah from all sides and pulled him to the ground. "Get away from me!" he screamed. "Get away, all of you! This is my domain, do you understand? I control this place! I am the Master he—"

Hector buried the axe in Josiah's ectoplasm face. White light burst from the wound, and the brittle skull exploded. Then Hector raised the axe again and proceeded to give his father forty whacks.

Abby set the fuse on Natalie's bomb, sniffed away her nosebleed, and stood. Her legs went wobbly, and she felt someone take hold of her before she collapsed. It was the ghost of Constable Eckhart. "You better go while you can," he told her. "Tell the sergeant what Foley did. Tell her he took us by surprise. And tell her… tell her she was a good boss. That son of hers is lucky, having a mom like that."

Abby nodded and ran up the stairs while Josiah screamed for mercy. At the top, John Leland lunged at her and she ducked just before his sword took her eye out. She blew his head off with the Webley and stepped over the body. The Pale Rider lurched down the hall, followed closely by the Rat King. Abby unloaded two shots into each of them, but they kept coming. She backed off a step and looked to the kitchen door. If she was fast, she might be able to make it out the back way.

The library door burst open and Natalie jumped onto the Rat King's back, ramming her machete in between his shoulders like a joystick. She steered the Rat King toward the Pale Rider and the two constructs splattered against the wall. Natalie dropped and shook ectoplasm off her blade. "What the hell happened down there?"

Abby leaned against the wall for support and shook her head. "I'm still putting it together myself. On your right!"

Natalie spun on her heels as two misshapen, half-formed Elinoras came shuffling down the stairs. She kicked off the wall and spun in the air like a jet turbine, cutting the constructs down to nothing.

"What is with these things?" A scrawny, half-skeletal Nick Brady came lurching around the corner from the second-floor corridor.

"You want my guess?" Abby panted. She put her last bullet through the construct's guts, and it splattered on the floor in two pieces. "Josiah's getting torn up downstairs, and he's throwing up these constructs as a last desperate defence mechanism. But he can't concentrate, so they're not stable!"

"HELP ME!" screamed Will Brady. "PLEASE! SOMEONE HELP ME!"

They followed the screams and met the possessed Linus Foley on the stairs up to the third floor. He jammed his wand against Will's temple and yelled, "Stay away, Henderson! Either of you take one step, and the boy dies! Don't forget, the Master wants him gone either way."

Abby snarled and leaned on the wall. "For God's sake, give it up, Isaac! Listen to that screaming! Josiah's dying downstairs. For good, this time. Whatever you think you had going here, it's over. Don't make this worse for yourself."

"The Master will live! There will be a reckoning in Delap—"

The air went *crack*, and Whittaker appeared on the third-floor landing with Mona. As Isaac turned, the imp jumped on his back and rode him like a sled to the bottom of the stairs.

Isaac elbowed Whittaker in the face, and Whittaker dug his fingers into Isaac's wound. Isaac screamed and raised his wand. "You're dead, you little bastard!"

Whittaker grinned and wheezed, "So's your old man, ass-wipe."

And that's when Mona came down the stairs like a charging bull, threw Isaac into the wall, and started hammering her fist into his face. "STAY! AWAY! FROM! MY! SON!" She slammed his head into the wall for punctuation, then drove her knee into his ribs and threw him over her shoulder. When he landed, he went for his wand. She went for her gun.

Two shots. Linus Foley's head snapped back and launched a red spray across the floor, but the spirit of Isaac Harcourt wasn't out of the fight just yet. As Foley's body crumpled, the signet ring on his hand shivered and thrummed with dark energy, and then it shot off Foley's finger like a champagne cork. Mona ducked as the ring ping-ponged off the wall behind her and bounced around the corridor. Natalie reached out to grab it, and it struck her hand with such speed that it broke two of her fingers. Natalie gave a sharp gasp of pain and reached with the other hand, but the ring was already gone. It flew to the end of the hall, spun, and launched itself at Will's face.

The boy cried out and raised his hands defensively, and the ring jumped onto his finger. Suddenly, the cold metal band tightened like a noose and inky waves of dark magic snaked up Will's arm. He screamed and beat his hand against the wall, trying to force the ring off. Isaac Harcourt cackled as the blood vessels burst in Will's eyes, and his irises turned a deep red. "Behold!" the boy cried out, in Isaac's voice, "I tell you a mystery!"

Mona grabbed Will's wrist and tried to pull the ring off him. It didn't budge. Will spat in her face and screamed 1 Corinthians at her, then put his free hand in her chest and shoved her off. He scampered along the floor on all fours, still quoting scripture, and ripped the Smith & Wesson out of Foley's cold, dead hand. Mona looked into her son's blank red eyes as he aimed the gun at her.

A silver apparition floated through the floor and seized both of Will's wrists. Hector Harcourt sternly forced the gun down and said, "*Enough.*"

Isaac screwed Will's face up in a snarl and tried to break free of Hector's grip. But Hector held firm, and twisted Will's wrists until the gun fell from his hands. "It's over, Isaac." His voice was assertive and direct, as if he were telling a child that it was bedtime.

"No! This will never be over!" Isaac snapped. "Not while I have strength! If our father shall not live, then neither shall your bastard! You destroy his legacy, and I will destroy yours!"

"I don't mean to destroy his legacy, Isaac. I mean to save it." He tugged at the ring on Will's finger, and Abby, Natalie, and Mona went to help him. They formed a human chain behind Will and pulled him in the opposite direction. Isaac's voice reverberated around the House, screaming abuse at the living and the dead. The ring sparked with dark energy and held tight to Will. Until it didn't.

Whittaker joined the chain behind Natalie and wrapped one arm around her waist. On the other side, Hector planted his feet and shouted at them all to pull. The ring slipped a hair's breadth down the length of Will's finger, and Hector smiled. "Again!" he hollered, and they all strained against the magic. The ring slipped to Will's second knuckle, and Hector gritted his teeth. "Again!"

The ring slipped free, and Will's eyes cleared of any redness. Hector closed his fist around the ring, and its dark energy burned his hand. His silvery fingertips turned black and he screwed up his face in a tight grimace. He extended his other hand, and the mists of the Elsewhere shaped themselves into an axe. The others took a step back, and Hector threw the ring to the floor.

There was a blinding burst of white light as Hector brought down the axe. Isaac screamed one last time, and then he was silent. Hector winced and examined his burned hand, and a muffled sob came from the back corner.

Will had retreated when the ring came free, with his face buried in his knees and his hands over his ears. Mona kneeled over him and whispered, "Will? Sweetie? Are you okay?"

Will didn't look up, but he did uncover his ears. "Mom?"

"It's me, honey. The bad men won't hurt you again, I promise."

He sniffed. "I-is it r-really you?"

Mona hugged him and laid her head on his. "It's me, sweetie. The one and only."

Will reached out and hugged Mona back, but he still didn't open his eyes. Hector watched the two of them for a moment before looking at Abby. "It's true, then? This boy is... is my heir?"

Abby nodded. "Yeah. It's true."

Hector walked over to Will and kneeled as Mona did. "William?" He reached out an uncertain hand, but quickly drew it back when Will looked at him and flinched. "I'm sorry!" Hector stammered. "I don't mean to—I understand if I frighten you."

Will sniffed and nodded. "Y-you did a bit. But just a bit. I think... I think you saved my life... thank you..."

Hector smiled and nodded. "I could have done nothing less for my family. You have her nose, you know... Aggie's nose..." He reached out and tousled Will's hair. "Goodness. You have my hair. Father always said you can tell a Harcourt man by the hair..." Finally, he looked to Mona, and then back to Will. "But you have your mother's eyes. Such kind eyes. Not so cold as Harcourt eyes. Not as cruel." He stood and laid a hand on Mona's shoulder. "A handsome boy, indeed. Someday to be a fine young man."

Mona smiled up at Hector. "Well, if he's anything like his no-good, black sheep ancestor…" She picked up her son and gave him a kiss on the cheek. "Thank you, Hector."

Hector smiled, bowed his head, and whispered, "Take care of him, Mona."

"I will. As long as he needs me to."

Hector dissolved back into the aether and Mona turned for the stairs. She gave Whittaker a rousing kick on the way, and he groaned and looked over at Abby. "Lemme guess," he slurred, "you let the mark see the red lady." Abby just rolled her eyes, and Whittaker laughed and shook his head. "Rookie mistake, kid! You never, *never* let the mark see the red lady."

"Eat my ass, Whittaker."

He blinked and shook his head again. "No comment."

Abby suppressed a chuckle and went to help him up. "Better not be, you little shit."

Whittaker winced as he stood and held one arm close to his chest. Mona looked at it and said, "Probably a broken wrist."

Whittaker sucked in a breath. "Aw, dammit! That's my snapping hand too. If I can't snap my fingers, I can't teleport! No illusions either."

"Did you get the others clear?" Abby asked.

"Wasn't time. It was get them out, or get the kid." He exhaled and put his good hand on his knee. "Only had one jump left, and that was it. We gotta do this the old-fashioned way."

They went back down to the library. Simon and Leanne were sitting with Reverend Jansen. He'd propped himself up on the pile of books on the floor, and Abby thought back to the sight of Grace Jansen propped up on her bed, not listening to David Attenborough. She knelt by the reverend's side and tried to rouse him. "Reverend Jansen? It's time we were going."

The reverend looked back at her with vacant eyes. "Mm? Constable Henderson… did you… did you find him? The man you were looking for?"

"Yeah. We found him."

"Then... Jenny and Sonia and the others... they'll have justice, yes? And he'll... he'll go to jail..."

"He's going somewhere," Abby allowed.

The reverend nodded and smiled. "Good... that's good..." He ran his finger along the spine of a fallen book. "Look at that..." He showed the dust to Abby and shook his head. "Whoever owns this place... their housekeeping leaves much to be desired..."

"Reverend, we need to get you out of here. You need to go to the hospital. Now."

The reverend shook his head weakly. "Hospital... no... I've never felt better..."

"Well, it's not your call. You're badly injured and you need to see a doctor."

The reverend seemed to come back to his senses, and he shook his head more vigorously. "No. I've... I've got mine. This is... where I should be. They took... took my Grace. Without her, what's there to go back to?" He laid his good hand on Abby's shoulder and gasped, "Take the boy. Take him out of here and see that he's safe. But don't worry about me. I've run my race."

And just like that, Matthew Jansen leaned back against the shelves and died. There wasn't time to say a few words, so Abby closed his eyes for him and folded his hands in his lap. Natalie wrung the ectoplasm out of the fuse, relit it, and shooed everyone out of the room. The charge in the cellar went off a few seconds later, and the whole House rocked.

Abby gulped and looked at Natalie. "Run like hell?"

Natalie nodded. "Run like hell."

They ran like hell. The cellar door belched flames into the hallway, and the rush of heat set off the charge in the library prematurely. The windows on the first floor shattered as they reached the front door, and the beams in the ceiling began to groan. Abby took hold of Leanne for support and closed her eyes to concentrate on the image of the rope bridge again. She felt the Elsewhere reforming around her and Leanne led her across the bridge. Abby dared not open her eyes lest she break her concentration and send them all plummeting to their deaths.

As soon as they reached the far side of the chasm, the roof had started to give way. The noise broke Abby's concentration, and the bridge disappeared with a *pop*. The chimney teetered over and obliterated a section of the roof, which in turn caused a collapse of the southern wall.

The Harcourt House became the Harcourt Bonfire, and Josiah screamed one last time.

Abby turned back for a final look and saw Hector Harcourt leading the dead out the front door. Beside him, Matthew and Grace Jansen linked arms and embraced for a tearful reunion. Dazzling white light shone down on the House from somewhere high above, and Hector gave Abby a wave and a nod of thanks. He and the other ghosts dissolved into twinkling silver fairy lights and ascended toward the light, and to the undiscovered country beyond.

Just like that, it was over. The lights faded from view, and chunks of the earth beneath the House started to crumble into the dark void below. When the base of the chimney slid away, Whittaker gave a sharp whistle. "Hey! *Ándale*, folks! That's going to be us if we don't get gone pronto."

CHAPTER 31

KEEP THE HOME FIRES BURNING

THE LIGHTS were still out in the police station when Whittaker re-opened the portal. It was easier from the other side: all Abby had to do was think about a rainfall, and they were laughing. Natalie came through first with Simon. Mona came next, still carrying Will. Leanne was propping up Abby, and Whittaker was holding his injured arm. It was a lucky break for them all that opening a faerie portal didn't require the use of one's hands.

Mona ordered Abby and Whittaker to sit down, lowered Simon onto one of the empty mattresses from the cells, and gave him the once-over. "Somebody go down to the holding cells. There's another first aid kit down there. Take the bedsheets off one of the cots and find me something hard and straight. I need to make a splint for Whittaker's wrist." Whittaker opened his mouth, but Mona shushed him. "Yeah, I heard it too. 'Hard and straight.' You make one smartass comment, and you can walk to the hospital. Speaking of which, somebody find a working phone and call an ambulance." Abby shifted in her chair and Mona pointed a finger at her. "Don't you move one damn muscle, Henderson. You and Lockhart have both had the living hell beaten out of you." She pointed at Natalie next. "Get some water. Lots of water. I need to clean this wound and I want everyone hydrated and alert."

Natalie and Leanne went to work. Mona collapsed into a chair beside Abby and looked around. "Is it my imagination, or is it dark outside?"

"Probably," Abby groaned wearily. "Time doesn't work the same way in the spirit world. We might have been in there for… an hour, tops. Could've been a day and a half out here."

Mona shook her head. "Jesus. Just when I think I've got this supernatural stuff figured out…"

Somewhere in the dark, a shoe squeaked on the floor. Mona sat up in her chair and laid her hand on the butt of her gun. "Who's out there?" she called.

A dull orange light bobbed around the corner. It was attached to Corporal Rickards, who raised both hands as he came into the bullpen. "Easy! Easy! It's me!"

Mona didn't move. "Is it?"

Rickards raised one hand slightly higher, allowing the kerosene camping lantern he was holding to illuminate his face. "Look in my eyes, Sarge. You see any red?"

Mona relaxed. No red. "Sorry, Rickards. It's been a rough morning."

Rickards blinked. "How long do you think you've been gone, Sarge?"

Mona looked at Abby, who shrugged. "Honestly, I'm not sure."

"It's 2:00AM. You've been away nearly 18 hours."

Now it was Mona's turn to blink. "Bullshit."

"No lie. After that… portal thing closed and the ambulances came for the wounded, Inspector Pembroke put in the call to Kelowna. By noon, we had half the cops in the Okanagan rocking up to our front door, and they scooped up everything that wasn't nailed down."

"When you say everything…"

"I mean everything. Forensic reports, autopsy reports, photos, even the crap these jokers left behind in the evidence lockup. Pembroke and what's left of her crew went back to

Kelowna a little before midnight. I stayed back to make sure you all got home."

Mona slumped forward and put her head in her hands. "Oh God… this is going to be a PR nightmare."

In deference to Will, who was sitting by the mattress and listening to all of this, Rickards chose his next words carefully. "A PR cluster-bleep is what Inspector Pembroke called it. And the wheels are already grinding in the ol' rumour mill. The main road out of town was shut for most of the day, there were cops running all over town until after sunset, and the mayor held an emergency press conference in the afternoon. Nine PM curfew, effective immediately. By the time they piece together everything that's happened here, this is going to be headline stuff provincewide. Maybe nationwide."

Mona slumped even further forward. "Jesus. How the hell do I write a report on this?"

"Pembroke asked the same question before she left. Whatever we tell the big bosses, it's going to have to be airtight."

"It's going to have to be tighter than that," Moan groaned. "If we're lucky, the IIO will only have us under a microscope until Christmas."

"Do I need to be worried about this?" Abby asked.

"I don't know. Maybe. Legally, I have to file a report on what happened in the House. I need to disclose that I discharged my weapon in the line of duty, and the Independent Investigations Office need to investigate if that force was justified. But there also has to be an investigation into everything Foley did for Josiah. They'll want to talk to the people who were harmed by his actions over the last few weeks. After the incident at your motel and everything that happened in the House today, you and your friends definitely count. But when Foley came here, multiple other officers discharged their weapons. So those reports need to be filed as well. There's going to be a spider web of investigations surrounding this case for weeks or possibly months, and it is highly likely that someone way up the food chain is going to want to know what you and your friends were doing in the middle of all this. At that point, you're on your own."

Will shuffled forward and squeezed his mother's knee. "Mom, are you going to lose your job?"

Mona took his hand. "I honestly don't know, William. I shouldn't, if they find I was acting in self-defence. But they could take me off active duty until they straighten all this out. Still, it'll have been worth it to keep you safe."

He smiled. "Hey, if you do get fired, we can spend more time together."

She chuckled and nodded. "Yeah. I suppose we can. That'd be a nice change of pace."

"I love you, Mom."

Mona blinked and wiped her eyes. "I love you too, William. I love you more than anything."

Leanne and Natalie returned a few minutes later with the supplies Mona had requested. Leanne reported that the landline in the holding cells was still functioning, and ambulances would be on the way for Simon and Whittaker as soon as possible. Mona took the first aid kit and a bottle of water, and together she and Rickards set to the task of patching up the wounded. The ambulances showed up about ten minutes later, and it was only after they had departed that Mona noticed her stomach growling.

She rubbed her eyes and stifled a yawn. "Jesus. I just realized: I don't think I actually had breakfast this morning."

"I'm pretty sure I did," Abby said, "but I worked up a major appetite fighting Josiah."

"I guess that sixth sense burns a lot of calories, huh?"

Abby shrugged. "Why do you think I'm so skinny?"

Mona patted her stomach. "I could probably use one of those."

Rickards dragged them both to the couch in the breakroom and told them to sit down. "I'll go and give the vending machine a good kick, see what falls out."

They sat in silence for a moment, relishing the sensation of not moving. Then Mona laid a hand on Abby's shoulder and said, "Thank you. I haven't said that yet. Thank you, Abby."

"Mona, you don't have to—"

"I do. God knows what would have happened to this town if you and your friends hadn't got in the way. I never would have opened my eyes and seen what was really going on. My son probably wouldn't be alive right now."

Abby looked out into the bullpen. Fresh sheets had been laid out on the mattress beside Simon's, and Will had curled up on top of these and fallen asleep. He looked like he needed it as much as any of them. "Yeah..." she said quietly. "That's... that's something."

Mona looked at her. "You're thinking about Reverend Jansen, aren't you?"

"He deserved better than what he got. He gave his entire life to his daughter, and then to be persecuted for something his ancestor did..." She shook her head. "I just wish we could have done more for him."

"That's a lesson that every cop learns the hard way, kid. You just can't save everybody."

"We should be able to. People like me, I mean. People with magic in us. We can do more, we can see farther. We should be able to save more people."

"More isn't the same as all. There's a lot of bad in this world, Abby, and plenty of bad people hurt good people every single day. No amount of magic will change that. You can't be everywhere at once, and you can't protect everyone. But you can protect a few people and keep some of the bad at arm's length, and that makes a hell of a difference. Focus on the people you can protect. Don't dwell on the losses. That's a good way to drive yourself crazy."

"Yeah. It is." Abby slouched forward and rested her elbows on her knees. "You remember what I told you about John Leland? About how he died badly?"

"Yeah."

"Truth is, I was the one who put him down. A demon in his service possessed my best friend, and Leland used that pressure point to attack me. I saved her, and Simon exorcised the demon, but before Leland died, he crippled her. And I just know in my heart that he did it to spite me. I've talked to her about it, and she's told me so many times that it's not my fault, but there's a part of me that always thinks: Kelly Munro is in a wheelchair because of me." She sniffed and covered her eyes with one hand so she could catch the tears. "I've been thinking about that for the last nine months, and I can't convince myself otherwise. I guess that's a bad habit of mine. I just dwell on shit."

"You also don't practice what you preach," Mona said gently. "Take your own advice, Abby, and remember that it's *not your fault*. When somebody puts you through that kind of crap, it is *never* your fault. Look, I'll make you a deal. If I'm not allowed to blame myself for what Nick did to me and mine, you're not allowed to blame yourself for what John Leland did to you and yours. *And* you're not allowed to blame yourself for what people like Isaac and Josiah Harcourt do to the rest of the world." She extended a hand. "Fair?"

Abby dried her eyes and shook Mona's hand. "Fair."

The distant sound of breaking glass made them both jump, but Corporal Rickards returned a moment later and told them to relax. He was laden down with chips, nuts, candy bars, cookies, and every sweet or salty nibble that one could hope to find in a police station vending machine. He dumped his bounty on one of the breakroom's folding tables, and Mona helped herself to a Clif Bar. "Jesus, Rickards. Did you knock over a 7-Eleven while you were out?"

Rickards opened a bag of potato chips and shook his head. "It's a tragedy, Sarge," he deadpanned. "When Foley attacked us, the vending machine got caught in the crossfire. There's glass all over the place and everything's up for grabs." He brushed tiny shards of glass off the front of his uniform and popped a chip into his mouth.

Mona unwrapped her Clif Bar and said, equally deadpan, "Damn shame, Rickards. Damn shame."

Abby took a Clif Bar for herself and raised it in a toast. "Hey. To keeping some of the bad at arm's length."

Mona raised her Clif Bar in response. "To not dwelling on shit."

They touched bars and then dug in.

*****

After three days and three nights in Kelowna General, Simon was released with eighteen stitches and a clean bill of health. Natalie went into the city midmorning to pick him up, but the two of them didn't get back until nearly sunset. A few hours before they returned, Simon got in touch with Abby and Leanne by Vokarion crystal and told them to be at the top of the hill above Pearson Heights by 8:30 sharp. He asked them to relay the same message to Mona, Will, and Corporal Rickards, but wouldn't explain why. Still, Abby said they'd meet him there, and that's what they did.

High blue construction fencing had been erected around the crater that the Harcourt House had left behind. Warning signs had been set up on every side, declaring the area a falling hazard, and a notice board announced that the town would be starting work filling in the pit on the following Monday. Just in case the message still wasn't clear, bright yellow police tape had been woven through the links of the fence. When Mona and Will came to the top of the hill that evening, they caught Abby and Leanne peering through a gap in that same police tape.

"It's so... *empty* up here," said Leanne. "I would have thought all the weirdos would be out trying to get a look at what's left of their local legend. For God's sake, the House was flying! But everybody's just acting like that part didn't happen."

"People love their peace and quiet," Abby said. "Now that the dust is settling, the murders are going to make their rounds in the press, and people are going to cry and moan about what a safe community this used to be, but nobody's going to mention the stuff that happened on the other side of the curtain. Crime stories sell papers, but ghost stories get you a lot of funny looks at the gas station."

"I guess you're right," Leanne admitted. "I mean, they wouldn't talk about what Josiah was doing way back when, so why start now?"

"Linus Foley was such a nice boy. This never would have happened when we were growing up. Delapore is a good town full of good people. *Et cetera.*"

Mona cleared her throat to get their attention. "You've got it to a 't,' Henderson. I've lived in plenty of 'good towns' over the years, and you would honestly be amazed what people are willing to ignore."

"Rough day?" Abby asked.

"I had a meeting with Inspector Pembroke this morning. The first of many disciplinary hearings to come, I'm sure."

"Oof. How did that go?"

"I'm suspended from active duty, pending a full investigation. The IIO is sending a team of investigators out this way as soon as they can. At that point, it's anybody's ball game. But whatever happens, at least it'll happen because I did the right thing."

Abby smiled. "A good cop till the end. The world could use some more of that."

Mona winked. "What the world could use is a few more idealistic young busybodies who don't know when to leave things alone."

They chatted for a few minutes until Rickards arrived, followed closely by Simon and Natalie. The three had run into each other at the bottom of the hill, and Rickards had spent the whole walk up peppering Simon and Natalie with every question he could think of about the magical world. As they crested the hill, Simon not-so-subtly put some distance between himself and Rickards and called over to Abby and Mona. "Well, what are you old women gossiping about, then?" he said with a grin.

Mona stifled a laugh. "You're lucky you're injured right now. Normally I'd knock you down for a comment like that. What's the scuttlebutt at Kelowna General?"

"Good and bad," Simon admitted. "Your superintendent is awake and grumpy. They've scheduled him to have a pacemaker put in at the end of next week, and he's under close observation until then. Mrs. Tenenbaum was in surgery for nine hours, but she's stable now."

"Pruitt?" Mona asked in a small voice.

"ICU. She's in a medically-induced coma. No visitors. I'm afraid that one's up to the High Celestial now."

Mona rubbed her eyes and mouthed a silent profanity.

"So why did you want to meet us here?" Abby asked.

"We have some loose ends to tie up, I'm afraid. There's one last piece of Josiah still clinging to this world." He held up the journal from Bill Grover's garage. It was tightly bound in nearly an inch of plastic wrap, and for once it wasn't saying a damn word. "This little book has caused us all rather a lot of trouble. I thought we should all be here to send it on its way."

Natalie built a fire, and Simon told everyone to form a circle and join hands. Then he carefully unwrapped the book. "Just to be on the safe side, I want to see that Josiah is put to rest properly. If we do this in the old Vanguard way, I guarantee that Delapore shall finally know peace."

He gave them each a handful of small amber beads, which he instructed them to hold in their right hands. "I shall recite Baldwin of Wessex's Charm for a Disturbed Ancestor. I shall do this seven times. At the end of each recital, you will all unjoin your hands and cast one bead into the fire. When all your beads have been discarded, you will take three paces back from the fire and speak these words: 'Now turn aside. Now sleep and be remembered. Your days in this middle-earth have ended and your seat at the mead-bench is open. Raise not your war-irons against another foe, nor don your battle-coat in anger. Consign your best rings, battle-treasures, to the barrow, and seek the glory of the Creator.'"

They followed his instructions to the letter. The flames jumped higher, as if spurred on by the magic, and there was a faint creaking noise as the book's leather binding shrivelled in the blaze. When the Charm had been completed, Natalie broke off from the circle and jogged down to the car. Simon watched her go and said, "Now, in the old days, it was traditional to drink to the memory of the departed and pray for their deliverance into the care of the High Celestial. Of course, that tradition always assumed the departed was someone you *wanted* to remember. In this case, I think it's more appropriate if we drink to forget the unlamented Josiah Harcourt."

Natalie came back up the hill carrying a large plastic cooler, full to the brim with the ice-cold nectar of the gods. There were even some non-alcoholic options for Will. They drank and laughed and forgot their troubles until well after dark. As Mona finished her second beer, she looked over at Will and smiled. Simon had just hit him with the punchline of a joke, and the boy was now snorting and holding a hand over his nose so his apple juice wouldn't come up that way. Abby came up beside her and asked, "How's he doing?"

"Better. He slept in his own bed last night. Or, sleeping bag anyway. Rickards only has the one pull-out. You know Josiah told him the truth. About who he is."

"Yeah. Will mentioned that. Back at the police station. You'd gone to wash up, so he came to me about it. He begged me to convince him that he wasn't going to turn into a monster like Josiah."

"I'm not surprised. For a time before I left Nick, there were days when Will could hardly function because of the anxiety. He *hates* knowing that he came from someone like that. To think that there's a monster like Josiah lurking in the family tree… it's a wonder he's slept at all."

"You want to know something funny? That monster might have saved Will's life."

"How do you mean?"

"I don't think all of Josiah's psychic talent was learned. There must have been a kernel of innate magical ability already there. That's why he was so powerful, and that's why Hector was able to reach out like he did to you and me. Will inherited the same kernel of second sight, and on some deep subconscious level, he had a notion of what Josiah was up to. And that second sight put out a cry for help that was picked up by the strongest psychic transmitter in the province."

"Hmm." Mona looked up at the stars. "Mysterious ways."

"More things in heaven and earth," Abby replied.

Will drained his juice box, crumpled it up, and then tossed it overhead into the fire. He cheered and high-fived Simon as the waxed cardboard burned up, and then he spotted Abby and Mona and waved at them.

Mona waved back, and Abby realized something. In the House, when Hector had finally confronted his brother, he had said that his goal was to save Josiah's legacy, rather than to destroy or spoil it as he had so often been accused of doing. And he had saved it. Because he *was* Josiah's legacy. His living legacy. Everywhere Josiah had gone in his late life and in his death, he had left behind him a trail of bloodied corpses and broken people. His story had been buried and distorted by the police coverup, but Josiah Harcourt's name only truly deserved to be mentioned in the same breath as people like Jack the Ripper, H.H. Holmes, and Robert Pickton. He was a monster with inhuman desires. But Hector had fought to stop that monster. In the end, he had fought with everything he had, even though it cost him the love of his family. He had tried to protect Abby and Mona, and then he had stood with them in the moments when it really counted. And he had broken the long cycle of violence. He had ensured the family line would continue, with children and grandchildren who did not bear the Harcourt name, but were Harcourts nonetheless. Will was also the Harcourt legacy, and his future was so bright and full of hope. If he really wanted to, he could eclipse whatever evil Josiah had done. All he had to do was love his mom, be kind to his classmates, and laugh at his friends' stupid jokes.

For a moment, Abby and Mona drank in silence. Then, out the corner of her eye, Abby saw a flash of uncertainty in Mona's aura. "There's something else on your mind, isn't there?"

Mona nodded. "You're too smart for your own good, Henderson."

"So they tell me. What's up?"

"Maybe Will does have a gift. That's not the craziest theory I've heard this week. But what about me? I saw Hector twice. I heard him speak, and you told me yourself that's not normal. Plus, there was something that Josiah said when we were in the House. He asked me if I remembered what I was running from, or if it was more like a dream."

"If what was like a dream?"

"That's just it. I have no idea. All he said was that I left something behind on the island. And then I had a dream last night that I *was* back on the island, and I think I found that something, but when I woke up, I couldn't remember it. All I know is there was some... power in the room with me. And I was scared of it."

"Are you asking me if you have magic in your past?"

"I don't know. Maybe? If Will inherited something from Josiah, then why couldn't I pick up something from Sul'kwuléxun'? Who's to say my nana's stories were just stories?"

Abby shrugged. "I honestly don't know, Mona. There's a lot that I'm still learning about the magical world myself. But I do know that magic can play with your mind. Sometimes dreams and memories are the same thing. Sometimes you have to go right to the source before you can tell the difference."

Mona nodded. "I've kind of seen enough of Delapore. Maybe I do need a change of scenery. Thanks."

"No problem."

More silence. This time, it was broken by the whistled chorus of Heart's "Magic Man" as Whittaker crested the hill, sporting a livid black eye and a plaster cast on his right arm. Nevertheless, his grin was as smarmy as ever.

"What are you doing here?" Abby asked. "I thought your contract with Simon was dissolved."

"Releasing someone from service is a little more complicated than binding them," said Whittaker. "We got a couple rites and incantations to get through before I'm really clear. It's a whole thing." He grabbed a bottle from the cooler and held it out to Abby. "You want to make yourself useful, chickadee?" He extended his bad arm as far as he could and forced his bottom lip to tremble pitifully. "Have mercy on a poor cripple!"

Abby grabbed the bottle opener that was sitting next to the cooler and took the top off Whittaker's beer for him. "I'm starting to feel like you're milking this."

"Oh, hell yes, I am. But what are you going to do about it?" He took a sip and grinned. "Ah. Mother's milk."

Abby raised an eyebrow. "What kind of fucked-up faerie biology did your mother have?"

"Hey. Don't sass a sasser, kid."

Abby raised her hands. "Easy. I'm not looking for trouble. Actually, I kind of wanted to… thank you." She forced out the last two words like they'd left a bad taste in her mouth and gave a little shudder. "Yuck. Saying that makes me feel dirty."

"If this is supposed to be you showing gratitude, I gotta say I'm not feeling the love so far."

"Look, that was pretty gutsy, using your last jump to knock down Isaac. He could've done some serious damage to you."

The imp's wry little smile disappeared. "My meal ticket was in danger. I did what I had to."

"Did you? Couldn't you have conjured a headless horseman to decapitate Isaac from behind? Or dropped a giant ball of snakes on his head? There must have been a thousand tricks up your well-tailored sleeve, and you went in guns a-blazin.' Didn't you tell me that you never let the mark see the red lady? You showed Isaac the whole deck."

"Don't make this into something it's not, chickadee. I didn't do any of this for you. Or for that kid. I needed something from you people, and I worked an angle until I could get it."

"I know. But you saved a child's life while you were working that angle. We wouldn't have made it to the House without you, Whittaker. We wouldn't have even known the Rite was coming. You really dragged our asses out of the fire here."

"I dragged my own ass out of the fire. You morons just got in my way."

"And we're all better for it."

The imp snorted. "Whatever. Just do me a favour, kid, and don't ask me for any more favours." Then he brushed past her and called out, "Now, where's that Ætheriċ? I need to see a man about a Fair Folk contract!"

Simon took a sip from his bottle and gave the imp a pained smile. "Ah, Whittaker. As if my day couldn't get any worse."

"Save the pleasantries. We gonna do this or what?"

Simon thought it over for a moment and then shook his head. "No. I don't think we are."

Whittaker snarled. "Watch it, Ætheriċ. I might not have the Courts behind me anymore, but I'm still Fair Folk. If you welch on me now, we're gonna have a serious fuckin' problem."

"I promise you, I have no intention of welching, but I'm also not removing that Binding Charm."

"Yes, you are, right here and right now. We made a deal, and it's your turn to pay up."

"Whittaker, do you remember the exact terms of the deal that we made?"

"Our business is *finito* 'upon the safe return of Will Brady —'"

"'And Matthew Jansen.' But Matthew Jansen never made it out."

Whittaker froze. "That's not fair. You know I tried to get him clear."

"You did, and I appreciate the effort, but the terms of our arrangement were your freedom for Will Brady and the reverend. You did not uphold your part of the contract in full, so I am withholding payment."

Whittaker threw his bottle on the ground and jabbed a finger into Simon's chest, right over one of his cuts. "You can't do that! I saved that kid's life! Without me, you jerks would still be sitting here with your thumb up your ass and Josiah would be ripping the town apart! This is extortion! This is highway robbery!"

Simon calmly brushed Whittaker's hand away and stood up to his full height. "Do you know what is 'highway robbery,' Whittaker? Taking someone prisoner when they have never done you any personal injury, then trying to make a profit by holding that person for ransom, and pricing that person's freedom at the cost of a human soul. Specifically, the soul of a young woman who does not yet realize how nefarious your kind can be, and is already trying to make the best of a very bad situation." He leaned in next to Whittaker's ear and added, in a low whisper, "I know about the eulogy."

Whittaker stepped back. "Oh, I get it. This is about the blonde. Varr'rak's puppet."

"Quite. Kelly Munro is dear to many of us, and you crossed a line when you made her your pawn. So I'm not releasing you from your service, and I'm not letting you forget what you did for a very long time. You will continue to serve as my errand boy for the time being, and if you have a problem with that, you're welcome to call on Auberon ab Nethe." He leaned over Whittaker and smiled. "You may be Fair Folk, but I am Vanguard. Once upon a time, it was my job to keep little squirts like you in line."

Whittaker smiled and gave Simon a slow round of applause. "Nicely done. Okay, you got me on this one. I'll admit it. Obviously, on a personal level, I'd love to see you get hit by a truck right now, but professionally? Game recognize game, pal." He snatched the bottle from Simon's hand, reached up, and poured the whole thing out over Simon's head. Then he threw the bottle down next to his own and flipped Simon the bird. "Now sit on this and rotate, jackass. I'll see you in the funny papers." He turned on his heel, flipped them all off, and stomped down the hill.

Abby took a small packet of tissues from her purse and tossed them to Simon. "You know he's going to make you regret that, right?"

Simon brushed a soggy lock of hair out of his eyes and started wiping himself down. "Oh, I'm counting on it. But it's the least he deserves for what he tried to pull with Kelly."

"Amen to that." She cleared her throat and asked, "What, um, what exactly do you know about the... eulogy?"

"I don't blame you for what you did, Abby. That little sneak put you in an impossible position that you weren't prepared for. But you do need to be careful. He has a power over you that could get you into a lot of trouble one day. Dealing with the Fair Folk always comes with costs you can't predict. Sometimes years after the fact."

"But if you're smart enough, that can go both ways, huh?"

"Well..." Simon chuckled and gave a little shrug. "That goes without saying..."

*****

By 9:00AM the next morning, Natalie had the car packed and ready to go for the long drive back to Vancouver. Abby and her friends checked out of their motel, and then met Will and Mona in the parking lot for a few last goodbye hugs.

"I wish you didn't have to go," Will whispered to Abby.

"Me too. But I've used up all my vacation days. Now it's time to get back to real life."

"Some vacation. You didn't even get to go swimming."

"I fought an insane ghost to a standstill in another dimension. I'd call that a vacation well-spent. Besides," she added with a shrug, "I'm a lousy swimmer anyway."

Will giggled. "Promise you'll come back and visit."

"Next time I'm in the area, you'll be the first to know." She got up and nodded to Leanne. Leanne gave her a thumbs-up in return and grabbed something from the trunk of the car.

It was a cylindrical plastic canister with a blue top and a peeling sticker on the front. Abby gave the cylinder to Will and said, "I remembered how you said you didn't have any blue Bionicles, so Leanne and I went into the city the other day and found this little collectibles store that has a lot of second-hand Lego."

"Thanks, Abby. For the record, I think Walt's totally wrong. The girl ones aren't lame at all."

"Glad to hear it. And one more thing before I forget…" She reached into her purse and pulled out a spare Vokarion crystal that she'd found among Simon's things. "This is a psychic communicator. Every one of us has one, so if you ever need anything, or even if you just want to talk, all you need to do is think about what you want to say to us, and we'll hear it. Night or day, rain or shine." She pressed the crystal into Will's hand and said, "Give it a try."

Will closed his eyes and concentrated. The crystal started to glow in his hand, and a few seconds later, Abby's did the same as she got the message. She smiled and gave the boy a soft punch on the shoulder. "Same to you, you little smart-ass."

Will opened his eyes and laughed. "I guess this means you don't have to butt in on my dreams anymore, huh?"

"Hey. *You* butted in on *my* dream."

Will shrugged. "Meh. Six of one."

There was one last round of hugs, and then Natalie started the car. Mona and Will waved goodbye, and Abby, Leanne, and Simon waved back until they lost sight of the Bradys. Then Natalie switched on the radio, and they all settled in for the journey home.

*****

Mona and Will shared a late breakfast at the diner near the motel, and then went home for what they hoped would be a quiet day. Or rather, they went back to the spare basement suite at Ben Rickards's house. They'd been crashing there for the last four days while the cops from Kelowna collected evidence and the contractors plastered over the bullet holes and steam-cleaned Mrs. Tenenbaum's blood out of the carpet. All that was finished now, but it was probably going to be a while before they went back home. But Rickards understood, and he told Mona and Will to take all the time they needed.

He was on duty today—*lucky bastard*, thought Mona—so the Bradys put their feet up in front of the TV, with a bowl of popcorn between them and a Bugs Bunny cartoon on the screen. Somebody said it was duck season, the hunter fired his shotgun, and Will started laughing his head off.

As Daffy re-attached his beak, the doorbell rang again. Mona hadn't even heard it the first time. Will was laughing too hard.

After the third ring, she got up to answer the door. She tried to remember if Rickards had said anything about expecting a package. She figured he wouldn't be coming home himself this early in the day. And if he was, he wouldn't stand outside and ring his own bell.

When she got to the door, Mona braced herself and looked through the peephole. If she saw one trace of red in the caller's eyes, she was going to raise hell.

But she couldn't. The guy on the front step was wearing a pair of dark sunglasses with expensive-looking frames. They matched his black slacks and necktie, which he'd obviously loosened in a frustrated bid to cool off. The guy wasn't wearing a jacket, so Mona could see the sweat stains blossoming under his arms. And the Glock he was wearing in a leather shoulder holster.

The guy leaned in and looked back through the peephole. He was six feet of lean muscle, with dirty blond hair in a high-and-tight military cut. "Mona Brady?" he asked.

"Who wants to know?" she called through the door.

The guy raised his hands affably. "Don't worry, I come in peace."

"Oh yeah? Show me your eyes."

"Pardon?"

"Take off your shades, show me your eyes. Now."

The guy took off his shades and peered through the peephole again. Mona saw no red. "Okay," she said. "Now put down the gun."

The guy drew the Glock from its holster and slowly placed it on the front step. "Okay. I'm unarmed. We're all friends here, Mona."

"Are we? You still haven't told me your name. So how the hell do you know mine, and how did you know I was here? I'm pretty sure you're not IIO."

The guy straightened up and nodded. "You're right. I'm not being fair to you. Sergeant Brady, my name is Jones. I'm with the Canadian Department of Advanced Research and Special Defence."

"Never heard of them," Mona snapped.

"Not many people have," Jones admitted. "We're a small department, and a lot of what we do doesn't make the papers. Look, Sergeant, I'm just here to ask you a few questions. You give me the answers I need, and I'll be out of here in no time."

"Let me get this straight: you show up on my doorstep unannounced, on a Sunday morning, carrying a piece, and you expect me to let you in for a cup of coffee and a friendly chat? I don't think so. How about you buzz off back to the Department of Advanced Research and Whatever It Is before I call my colleagues at the precinct?"

Jones shook his head and reached into his back pocket. "I'm afraid that's not how this works, Sergeant." He produced an ID card in a black leather holder and held it up to the peephole. The heraldic badge beside his photo was not one Mona recognized: a sword and a burning torch crossed in front of a crescent moon, all within a maple leaf sitting above the motto *TRANCHE À TRAVERS L'OBSCURITÉ*.

"This is a matter of national security," said Jones. All the affability was gone now. "Either you open this door, or I'll go get a warrant and make you open it."

"National security?" Mona bit her lip and opened the door. "What am I supposed to have done, exactly?"

Jones put his ID back in his pocket. "It's not what you've done. It's what Abigail Henderson has done."

There is a house in New Orleans
They call it the Rising Sun
And it's been the ruin of many a poor girl
And me, O God, for one
*

"House of the Rising Sun"
Traditional

ABBY NORMAL

WILL RETURN IN

HUNTING PARTY

WITHOUT WHOM

INDEPENDENTLY PUBLISHING one's second book during a global pandemic certainly creates a few unexpected challenges. Several people stepped up in a big way to help me put out the fires that arose during the preparation of the preceding narrative, and to them I offer my sincere gratitude.

Thanks, firstly, to my beta readers, all of whom were willing to jump into a series already in progress: Justin Dew, Alexandra Karjel, Abi Kirubarajan, Miranda Mecha, and Roy Rao. Their insights made a world of difference in helping me polish and refine the manuscript.

Thanks to Shaun Stevens of Flintlock Covers for pinch-hitting and providing me with a stunning cover design when my original artist was indisposed. You'd never know it wasn't the same artist as last time!

And thanks, lastly, to you for making it this far. I hope you had fun and I hope I'll see you again soon.

Samuel Thomas Fraser
June 28, 2021

ABOUT THE AUTHOR

Samuel Thomas Fraser is an actor and author from the rainy mountains of Vancouver, BC, Canada. A lover of literature both medieval and mysterious, Sam is currently pursuing his MA in English at the University of British Columbia Okanagan, with a focus on the relationship between language and magic systems in speculative fiction. His short fiction and poetry has appeared in numerous anthologies and magazines. *The Nowhere House* is his second novel.